KT-495-145

A former job-hopper, **Jessica Lemmon** resides in Ohio with her husband and rescue dog. She holds a degree in graphic design currently gathering dust in an impressive frame. When she's not writing supersexy heroes, she can be found cooking, drawing, drinking coffee (okay, wine) and eating potato chips. She firmly believes God gifts us with talents for a purpose, and with His help, you can create the life you want.

Jessica is a social media junkie who loves to hear from readers. You can learn more at jessicalemmon.com

Jayci Lee writes poignant, sexy and laugh-out-loud romance every free second she can scavenge. She lives in sunny California with her tall, dark and handsome husband, two amazing boys with boundless energy and a fluffy rescue whose cuteness is a major distraction. At times, she cannot accommodate reality because her brain is full of drool-worthy heroes and badass heroines clamouring to come to life.

Because of all the books demanding to be written, Jayci writes full-time now, and is semi-retired from her fifteen-year career as a defense litigator. She loves food, wine and travelling, and, incidentally, so do her characters. Books have always helped her grow, dream and heal, and she hopes her books will do the same for you.

HIS FORBIDDEN KISS

JESSICA LEMMON

TEMPORARY WIFE TEMPTATION

JAYCI LEE

MILLS & BOON

First Published in Great Britain 2020
by Mills & Boon, an imprint of HarperCollinsPublishers,
1 London Bridge Street, London, SE1 9GF

His Forbidden Kiss © 2020 Jessica Lemmon
Temporary Wife Temptation © 2020 Judith J. Yi

ISBN: 978-0-263-27915-3

0220

Printed and bound in Spain
by CPI, Barcelona

HIS FORBIDDEN KISS

JESSICA LEMMON

For Denita. You are so, so missed.

One

Heartbeat pounding in her ears, heels of her designer shoes clacking on the marble flooring, Taylor Thompson ran as fast as she dared in the heavy, beaded, floor-length Versace gown. She'd chosen it specifically for the River Grove Valentine's Day gala, extravagant even for the high-end affair, but until the tapered skirt was strangling her ankles with each quickening step she hadn't imagined it'd be inhibiting her escape.

She tugged the hemline as high as her calves, steered clear of the ladies' room—no doubt teeming with primped, classy women who were also attending the gala—and ducked into the coatroom.

At least she'd thought it was a coat "room."

Now that she'd shut the door behind her, the tight, dark space felt more like a coat *cracker box*.

No matter. She just needed thirty seconds to herself, away from onlookers. Without having to pretend she didn't know she was about to be proposed to.

God. A proposal.

She'd attended the gala every year save one—the year she traveled to Miami during a college vacation with her friends—so she never thought much of going. She'd never thought of *not* going. It was what the kids of River Grove did.

Here, being wealthy wasn't an option, it was a requirement.

Her family had helped build this town—along with her date's, Brannon Knox's, family. The Thompsons and Knoxes were known for founding one of the biggest tech companies in the nation. The ThomKnox Group was started by her late father, Charles, and Brannon's father, Jack, some twenty-six years ago, when Taylor was two years old.

It seemed that tonight Brannon was attempting a merger of a different style.

"Brannon Knox, what were you thinking?"

To be fair, she should ask herself exactly the same question. When he'd asked her to come as his date tonight, she should have said no. Instead, she'd chickened out, agreeing to *one last* event before having the discussion she should have had with him three weeks ago. The one where she said something to the effect of, "This isn't working. Let's be friends."

Aware she couldn't finish out the party in the closet, Taylor considered her options. She couldn't dart into the ladies' room and face Mrs. Mueller or Patsy Sheffield. They were sweet, and had been nothing but lovely after her father died last fall, but they were also…involved. She didn't need the entire town gossiping about her hiding from her date—and Patsy and Mrs. Mueller would happily start that rumor.

Was it considered a rumor if it was true?

If it hadn't been for her father losing his battle with cancer not so long ago, she probably never would've dated

Brannon. They'd known each other a lifetime, but the attraction simply hadn't been there.

Explaining that to him was never going to be fun. *Sorry, Bran. I only dated you because I was sad and in some way hoped it'd please my father from beyond the grave.* Now with an engagement on the line, explaining to Bran that she should've said no—before tonight—would be more agonizing.

"Dammit!" Fists balled, she stomped one high heel into the floor in frustration. It was hot in here and the room was closing in on her.

Deciding to find a bigger space in which to gather her thoughts, she reached for the doorknob. Wiggling it once, then twice, didn't help. The third time wasn't the charm—the antique knob had an antique lock fixture that had engaged.

"Crap." Sweat beaded on her brow as she jiggled harder, and she suddenly wished she'd carried her clutch in with her instead of leaving it on the table in Addison's care. At least then she would've had the light from her phone.

She wasn't particularly claustrophobic, but the options of suffocating in a coat closet or passing out from panic weren't good ones.

The instant she'd observed Brannon admiring the ring nestled in the Tiffany & Co. blue box backstage, she should have handled the situation. Where was a time machine when she needed one?

She strained to hear music or voices. Not a single sound infiltrated her insulated new home. Giving up on the doorknob, she backed up to throw her shoulder into the panel and bust herself out, when the door swung open, easy as you please.

Silhouetted in the frame was a pair of imposing shoulders in a black tuxedo jacket, long legs in matching trousers, and above that shadowed, sharp jaw she could easily imagine a frown.

Brannon's older brother.

"Taylor? What the hell are you doing in here?" Curiosity lined Royce Knox's voice. Even though he wasn't yelling at her, and even though he scared her about as much as a passing butterfly, her building anxiety pushed forth a gusty breath.

"Royce, thank God." She gripped his forearms. Over the material of his jacket she could make out the corded muscle, the sinew that made up those damned attractive arms. Once, years ago, she'd stumbled on her way to the limo and he'd been there to catch her. She was sixteen years old when she gripped his arms then. They weren't as muscular or thick as they were now, but the fluttery feeling in her belly was the same. When it came to Royce, there was never any question if she was attracted to him. She totally was.

She hadn't missed her father's scolding glower at that party afterward. He'd told her under no uncertain terms to stay away from the older Knox brother. "He's too old for you."

Her father hadn't wanted the older, more serious Knox brother for Taylor. He'd dreamed of a union between her and the younger, more eager one. Brannon.

She yanked her hands from Royce's forearms, unsure if she was more troubled by inadvertently obeying her father's wishes and dating Brannon, or feeling an attraction for Royce she still couldn't deny. It was there, though—pounding in her bloodstream.

"I thought I was going to die in here," she mumbled into the tight, dark space.

A short grunt came from Royce's throat. "Highly unlikely. Bran's looking for you."

"I know." She pictured the engagement ring and her stomach did another somersault. "This was our last date."

"What?" Royce's alarmed question was interrupted by another voice. Bran's coming from down the corridor.

"Has anyone seen Taylor?"

Since the closet she'd sprinted into was around a corner, Bran hadn't seen her or his brother yet. Nor would he. She wasn't ready.

Taylor yanked Royce into the small space and pulled the door shut behind him, lock be damned. Suffocating in here might be better than facing the man who was about to go down on bended knee.

"Hey!" Royce protested as the door clicked. She clapped her hand over his mouth, feeling the barest hint of stubble pushing past a sharp, clean shave—his preference. He reached for her wrist but froze when she gently shushed him. Together, they listened. Her to her erratic pulse sloshing in her ears and just under that, Brannon's receding voice as he continued his search.

She let out the breath she'd held and became aware of two things. Royce's long, blunt fingers covering the pulse point at her wrist and the feel of his warm exhalations on her hand that still covered his mouth.

"This is where my parents were engaged." Taylor's voice was soft with reminiscence. Royce couldn't make out her expression in the dim light but he could hear the sadness. "At the Valentine's Day gala. Mom said it was the most romantic night of her life."

His heart ached for Taylor and her mother. Losing Charles had been hard on all of them. The Knoxes and Thompsons had practically been family since Royce was in grade school.

"That's probably why he did it," she tacked on glumly.

Before Royce could wonder if she'd found out about the surprise, she confirmed with, "Brannon."

Gently, he pulled her hand away from his mouth, the soft scent of her perfume tickling his nose. She smelled good—she always had whenever he'd been this close to her, which was a rare occasion. Charles had seen to that.

"You know," he said. "About the proposal."

"Not until very recently, but yes."

And she didn't sound the least bit happy about it. He couldn't dredge up surprise at hearing that. She'd been dating his younger brother for what? On and off for three weeks? When Brannon came to show him the ring, Royce's reaction had been immediate and it hadn't been favorable. Brannon led with his heart and Royce was more of a numbers guy, so he'd stuck to what he knew and told his brother the truth. *Seems soon in the time line for that, Bran.*

"It's too soon," Taylor echoed now and Royce could swear the feeling in his chest was akin to relief. Bran's plan to propose was a mistake. Anyone should date longer than three weeks before stepping into engagement territory.

"It was supposed to be a surprise. Who blew it?"

"I saw Bran admiring the ring."

"She's a beauty," Royce said of the diamond solitaire that was God only knew how many carats.

"He showed you?" She sounded almost anguished.

He released her wrist and felt for a light switch, which he found after a few failed attempts and moving Taylor one step left and then right. Once the light clicked on he could see three things: empty hangers, plastic bins containing, according to the labels, holiday Decorations, and Taylor's expression: simultaneously distraught and beautiful. The beauty he was used to; distraught was a new look for her.

Shoulder-length dark blond hair swept up for the event,

her lips painted a shade of pink darker than her usual. Taylor fit into the world of class and wealth as well as any of them. They were accustomed to attending events like this one—to being trussed and preening for the elders in their midst. Royce had grown used to the game over the decades. He'd been groomed on how to behave—in life, at work. It came as second nature to him now. He supposed Taylor could say the same.

Even her sparkling gown couldn't hide the ribbon of seriousness strung through her, the ambition she couldn't mask with glitz and glam. That, in part, was why Bran's suggestion to marry her had taken Royce by such surprise. They'd seemed an odd fit from the start. Taylor was like an unofficial sister, a little older than their actual sister, Gia.

But then, he hadn't had a chance to think of Taylor any differently before her father declared her off-limits.

When Bran was insistent about continuing with the proposal, Royce accepted that he might not know Bran or Taylor as well as he'd thought. That maybe they were in love after all.

Until right now. Taylor didn't seem like a woman in love. Not with her breathing approaching fast to erratic and that note of worry in her voice. Royce wasn't the only one who believed an engagement was a bad idea.

"It's hot in here. Try the knob." She didn't wait for him, shoving him aside and twisting the knob back and forth. When that didn't work, she slapped the door, letting out a growl when it didn't magically swing open.

He put a hand on her shoulder, hoping to quell her anxiety, which was due to more than being trapped in a closet. "It's a country club teeming with people, Taylor. Someone will come around in a few minutes. Take a deep breath."

"I can't. I'm wearing Spanx."

Whatever those were. She thrust her bottom lip out and

he fought a smile. She'd be fine as soon as she started breathing.

"Do your best. We've got this. Watch me." He bent to meet her eyes but didn't have to bend much. She was a good eight inches shorter than his six foot four, but today her high-heeled shoes added some height—her lips almost came to his chin.

Her hazel eyes met his, and in the dim light of the closet he could see that she wasn't calm yet.

"Breathe with me," he told her in his gentlest voice.

She let out a shaky breath and took in another, making a soft O shape with her mouth as she blew it out. She did it once more but on her exhale a tear streaked down her cheek.

"I don't want to hurt his feelings, Royce." She gripped his tux's lapels.

"I know." He didn't know, but felt it best to agree.

"It's Dad's fault I said yes to a first date." She tugged harder on his jacket. "I never should've let things go this far. Bran is nice and well suited but…" She shook her head. "I was going to end things this weekend. I only agreed to come tonight to be polite."

"You don't have to explain."

A frown bisected her eyebrows when she repeated, "I don't want to hurt him."

"Taylor." When her eyes tracked to his he saw guilt reflected back at him. "You don't have to say yes to a marriage proposal to be polite." He hooked a thumb under her chin and tilted her face toward his, needing her to understand. "No matter what your father wanted."

She nodded, a small one, her hands still clutching his tuxedo coat. He should've stepped away but instead he lingered, content to have her full attention. Something he couldn't remember having before now.

"It's going to be okay. You'll see." He'd been on the brink of offering a few more generic platitudes, but whatever else was poised on the tip of his tongue never made it out of his mouth.

Not when Taylor put her lips on his and kissed him for all she was worth.

Hell, maybe for all *he* was worth.

Two

Royce told himself to stop kissing her. Told himself that she wasn't for him. She was the Thompson princess, and he the older heir to the Knox kingdom. No matter how poorly suited she and Bran were, or what she'd admitted to Royce in the privacy of the locked closet. He recited those reminders again and again but couldn't seem to leave the sanctity of her seeking mouth.

Her lips were too lush, too ripe. She tasted like champagne and sex. Really great sex. It'd been a while since he'd had really great sex, so he allowed himself a moment to explore. To remember... Maybe *discover* was a better word because he didn't find a single familiar memory to cling to in Taylor's kiss. He only found newness. Excitement. A certain zest... If that was the right phrase.

Ah, screw it.

Who cared what it was called. Now that he'd tasted her, he was inclined to taste her a little longer. To indulge in what he'd been forbidden to claim. Though technically it was Taylor who'd claimed him. He was practically an innocent bystander.

Until he cupped the back of her neck. Until he swept his tongue into her mouth and sampled her deeply—giving in to the yearning that was only seconds old, but felt as if it'd been there a hell of a lot longer.

Royce valued control in all facets of his well-organized life. He'd always assumed it was the way he was wired—he'd inherited his father's shrewd business intelligence, where Brannon mirrored his father's excitement and spontaneity. The attributes had been divvied between the Knox sons equally and were doled out double to Gia—which was unfair, but nonetheless true.

Budgets and financial strategies made sense to him. Royce liked his role as CFO because it was predictable—math didn't have "gray areas."

Taylor *was* a gray area.

At ThomKnox, he'd carved out his dream career by age twenty-three. He was hailed a boy genius in this magazine or that blog post but he didn't care for monikers or attention. He kept his focus on the numbers, which never lied. Gossip websites couldn't claim the same.

Wouldn't they have a heyday if they found out you were making out with your younger brother's date?

That quiet reminder stopped him short of pushing Taylor against the nearest flat surface—the door in this case—and trailing his mouth down her neck and lower. Even though Bran had no claim on her. She'd said so herself. Royce's younger brother was planning to propose and she was planning on dumping him. What more evidence did Royce need that those two were ill-fated?

He pulled away and caught his breath, not knowing she'd robbed him of it until he greedily sucked in a lungful of oxygen.

Her eyes were wide and wild, her mouth opened to say… God, he had no idea… Everything about the kiss made him want to claim her for *himself.* To take what she was generously offering.

For once, practicality failed him. Against his better judgment he leaned in to cover her mouth with his for one more taste. Monday morning would come and he'd deal with consequences. But they didn't matter right now. What mattered was attraction. Set on simmer for years and now boiling over…

Just as he laid his lips on hers and pulled her flush against his body, the door at his back opened. They snapped apart like teenagers caught breaking the rules.

A breeze whooshed in from the force, sucking the air from the room, and judging from the look of panic on Taylor's face, every ounce of air from her body. She backed away from Royce a step.

Brannon stood in the doorway, his expression filled with surprise that faded into rage so fast Royce nearly missed the transition. "I sent you to find Taylor not make out with her."

"That's not—"

"I saw the light under the door," Bran said between clenched teeth. "And now I see the light in a different sense."

Royce had looked out for his siblings for as long as he could remember. He was the responsible one. It wasn't like he couldn't have physically stopped the kiss when Taylor advanced, he just…*hadn't.*

"It's my fault," he said, figuring she could blame him and save herself.

"Now I know why you discouraged me from proposing. So you could have her for yourself."

"Excuse me?" Taylor interrupted, offense radiating off her like her sweet perfume.

"I was going to propose to you tonight," Bran told her, his chin elevated.

"I know," she said. Gently. She was kind. Maybe too kind if she'd been dating his brother for her late father's sake more than her own. Why hadn't she had that pertinent discussion with Bran before tonight? If she'd let him down easy, he never would've purchased a ring.

And if she'd never seen the ring, the kiss never would've happened.

Which shouldn't have happened. But Royce was having trouble regretting it.

"You…knew?" Bran asked Taylor, his face turning an impressive shade of red.

"I saw you with the ring and I… I ran away. Royce found me. I didn't mean to… I… I always wanted to kiss him."

"You did?" Royce and Bran asked at the same time. The brothers exchanged irritated glances.

"I planned on breaking up with you this weekend," she told Brannon, her focus solely on him. "In my head it was already done. I had no idea you were going to…" She gestured at his suit pocket where the telltale bulge of a velvet box confirmed his plans.

"I see." Embarrassment and a hefty dose of hurt outlined Bran's features before he turned to stalk down the corridor.

"Brannon, hang on." But before Royce could come up with some sort of suitable argument, Taylor touched his arm.

"Don't. This is my fault." She chased after Bran, moving as quickly as she could in her gown and heels. Royce leaned on the doorframe and watched her go. He slowly became aware of two women outside the ladies' room all but clutching their pearls. A member of the waitstaff had also witnessed the argument, but averted his gaze when Royce met his eyes.

Taylor caught up to Bran as he reached the exit and then they both walked outside. Royce rooted his feet to the floor. Taylor wasn't his. She never had been. And whatever had happened in this *Twilight Zone* slice of time never *should've* happened.

He'd been caught up in a moment—answering the call of attraction. One he hadn't known was there. He should've resisted. He knew better. His black-and-white worldview served a bigger purpose than simply ticking boxes on some cosmic checklist. Those rules and guidelines also kept the most important things where they belonged. In this case, kissing Taylor could shake the strong foundation of his very family tree. That had never happened before.

Nor would it, he vowed. Not on his watch.

Three

So, Saturday evening could've gone more smoothly.

The only explanation Taylor had come up with for the moment of insanity in the closet wasn't a pretty one. She'd kissed Royce because she wanted to. Simple as that. One opportunity and a little forced proximity was all it'd taken for her to fulfill the dormant fantasy. The kiss hadn't been thought out or rational. But since when was the heart rational?

Brannon Knox had nearly *proposed to her*. He'd taken first place for irrational!

As a result of her unplanned make-out sesh with Royce, the breakup with Brannon happened in the worst possible way. The kiss had put the final nail in that coffin. Actions speaking louder than words and all that. From the time her father declared Royce a no-go zone, Royce had taken up a certain amount of space in her world. He grew to be somehow bigger than life. Celebrity-like. Too far away to ever truly grasp. Which had amped up the attraction tenfold.

Royce had been inaccessible until that stray moment in private at the gala. She'd never been in his circle, not really, because he *was* older than her. Yes, they saw each other at work often and yes, they'd had meetings—even private meetings—but her professional side was every bit as rigid as Royce's. She'd never imagined a scenario that would lead to her kissing him in a coat closet. Kissing him ever.

Ugh. Slumping at her desk, she dropped her head into her hand. She wanted to die.

"Hiya, toots." Gia Knox, the younger sister of the two brothers who had been on Taylor's mind all morning, entered the corner office and shut the door. Taylor had gone to school with Gia—well, until college parted their paths. Taylor hadn't had the brains to land MIT, but few did. Bran hadn't been accepted. Royce hadn't wanted to go there, not that his father had minded. Jack had a streak of whimsy mixed in with his business acumen, like grenadine in Sprite, and had encouraged each of his children to follow their hearts.

"Good morning." Taylor kept her reply measured, not sure how her best friend felt about what had occurred Saturday. Taylor spent Sunday with her phone off, cleaning her apartment. As if that would purge any stray guilt.

"They're both duds if you ask me," the only Knox daughter said with a wink. Her long dark hair spilled over the shoulders of a scarlet dress that kept her curves contained and professional. She was a Knox genius in Jennifer Lopez's body.

She was Taylor's closest friend and the one person she'd considered running to after stepping in it Saturday night. The last place she'd wanted to be was that ballroom in a sea of people, especially with Brannon. He'd been so angry… Justifiably.

That night when she'd followed him outside to explain, he'd spun on her, his voice sharp and unyielding.

"Royce, Taylor? Really?"

"Brannon, it wasn't—" She'd cut herself short of muttering a clichéd retort, though it was true. It really *wasn't* what it looked like. What it looked like was that she and Royce were sneaking off to make out in the closet. In reality Taylor's emotions had become tangled up in a rogue wave of attraction. "I never meant to hurt you."

From there the conversation had stalled, Bran's face dawning with the understanding that she'd seen the ring and fled. He hadn't stuck around to hear her reasoning for kissing Royce, which was probably for the best. What else was there to say?

"Do you hate me?" Taylor turned from her laptop to face Gia, who gave a blithe blink and dragged the guest chair closer to Taylor's desk. She sat, leveling Taylor with chocolate-brown eyes a touch darker than Royce's.

"I *adore* you." Gia offered a pitiable head shake. "I had no idea Brannon was going to propose until he huffed back into the party snarling about how he'd made a mistake."

The blood rushed from Taylor's face. What had he told Gia? What had he told *everyone*?

Gia's hand covered hers. "I stepped out of the ballroom and into a private room with him, so don't worry about the gossip mill. Royce saw us and joined, and Bran gruffly admitted he'd made a mistake planning to propose at such a big affair. I had no idea he'd planned on asking you to marry him, Taylor. I thought you two were completely *caj*. Which I told him, by the way. Royce said he went to find you for *the Big Ask* but instead discovered you locked in the coat closet hyperventilating. Was it one-thing-led-to-another or is there more?"

The lump of dread in Taylor's throat remained, but she told her friend the truth. "I have no idea."

She'd been wondering that herself. Was the kiss the start of something? And if so, how could she navigate those choppy waters? Gia knew the truth and didn't hate her. Royce had greeted her this morning with a gruff "good morning" but he hadn't seemed upset. Was two out of three Knoxes *not* hating her enough?

"Are you okay?" Gia rubbed Taylor's knee.

Great question.

"I'm okay." Basically. "Brannon must hate me."

"His pride is hurt. But you don't have to guilt-accept a proposal."

Almost verbatim what Royce had told her. *You don't have to say yes to be polite.*

"Even if you did guilt-accept a few dates," Gia added.

Taylor watched her friend carefully. Gia had picked up on that on her own. When Taylor had started dating Bran, she felt like she'd crossed an unspoken boundary. How could she ask Gia's opinion or voice concerns over her best friend's flesh and blood? It would have been totally unfair.

"You don't miss a thing," Taylor told her.

"I was shocked when you walked into the gala together. I thought for sure he'd have a date and you'd come dance with me." She pressed her manicured fingernails into her décolletage and fluttered her lashes. "Honestly, I thought you two would've broken it off by now. I could see the distance. Or, well, not the distance so much as…the lack of spark."

"I was procrastinating. I care about him, just…not romantically. Not enough to marry him." She wondered if Gia would be this forgiving if she'd seen what Bran saw when he'd opened that closet door.

Spark City.

When Royce grabbed her up to kiss her for the second time, she'd been overcome. Laying one on him without any notice was one thing. Him reciprocating... That second kiss was heady. Consuming. Sparks zapped her like a free-swinging power line. They'd coursed through her bloodstream and lit up her brain like a neon sign. One that read *Royce Knox can kiss*. And boy, could he. She'd shared a few kisses with Bran over the course of their tepid dates, but none of them had measured up to the kiss in the closet with Royce.

That wasn't due to Brannon's lack of skill or personality. He was fun and made her laugh on a daily basis. He was distractingly handsome, with a dimple punctuating one cheek and a full, generous mouth. He had Royce's hard angles but there was an approachability to Bran that couldn't be denied. The Knox brothers came from good stock—both men were damned good-looking.

But. She'd never been *attracted* to Bran. He was an incredible friend. Or had been before she ruined their friendship with a spontaneous kiss.

If she could have a do-over, she'd have broken up with Bran a week ago—or maybe never would've said yes to that first dinner date. Hurting his pride at the beginning would have been better than at the end.

"I never saw that proposal coming," Taylor told Gia. "I assumed he'd lost interest. We were pretty much back to normal until the gala. He asked me to go with him and I didn't see the harm in it. You know how tedious these events can be."

"Lord, do I. So you two weren't..." Gia made a lewd gesture to indicate sex.

"No! God, no." Taylor couldn't help laughing.

"Hey, it's harder for me to hear than you, ladybug. If you ask me, this sounds like a big misunderstanding."

"I half expected him to politely break up with *me* by night's end." Though *hoped* might be a better word.

"And he would've been so nice about it," Gia said, which only served to make Taylor feel worse. "I'm not saying you weren't! Don't look at me like that."

"I panicked. I never in a million years thought he'd…" She shook her head, picturing the diamond ring in the box. Bran had been admiring the shimmer in the muted overhead light, his face… Wait. His *face*.

"He was looking at the ring right before I ran off. He… He wasn't smiling, Gia. He didn't look happy or excited. He looked… I don't know. Resigned?" And definitely not like a man in love.

"It really makes me wonder…" Gia let her thought taper off before pasting on a slightly insincere smile. "Never mind. Speculation is never good. Who knows what men are thinking?"

Taylor couldn't let her friend off the hook after that teaser. "*What?* What were you going to say?"

"Conjecture. And nothing that would help."

"It's not like you to be coy."

Gia chewed on her lip before she said, "I wonder if the proposal had anything to do with Dad's retirement. Pending retirement. Bran's being engaged would make him appear better suited for the role of CEO than Royce."

"He wouldn't?" But the sentence came out like a question because… *Would he?*

Brannon had mentioned time and again that his father would be stepping down. That he could picture himself in the role of CEO. Their "dates," for lack of a better word, had been consumed by talk of work and Bran's future at the company.

"Dad will retire sooner than we think, Tay," he'd told her one evening over a second glass of wine for each of them. He'd described Royce as his "competition." Bran had also mentioned that he wanted it more, but deserved it less. She'd argued in his defense that he and Royce were equally suited to replace Jack. It was the truth. The Knox boys each had winning qualities and were as dedicated to this company as they were to each other.

"I'm not saying he was using you, Taylor. I don't think he came up with an insidious plan to toy with you to get what he wanted."

"No, no, neither do I." Taylor had known Brannon practically her entire life. Ambition wouldn't cause him to stoop that low.

"But maybe somewhere down deep he thought it'd help to show some stability. Bran is the fun-loving one, after all."

"And president of the company. It's not like he's goofing around."

"Right. And you're COO. A match made in heaven, on paper." Gia tilted her head, her lips compressing. "Your dad always liked Bran for you."

He had.

"I couldn't live with myself if I drove a wedge between Bran and Royce." Taylor sighed.

"That's on them. You weren't the only one in that closet. Whatever amends need to be made, you'll work it out. What's done is done. There has to be a part of you that is glad you don't have to pretend with Brannon any longer."

"You're so understanding."

"Men are babies." Gia shrugged. "They'll get over it."

"I should talk to Bran." The idea of approaching him hung in the air like a foul stench. But they worked together, and closely. She didn't want there to be awkward vibes during meetings or conference calls. She didn't want him to avoid her out of discomfort or pride.

"You will. And you'll say something brilliant and then

everything will be okay. He didn't act like a man in love, Taylor. I don't know why he thought an engagement was the right move, but he wasn't acting from the heart. It was pragmatism and planning if you ask me."

"I should've said what was on my mind that night. That we weren't working romantically. It would have been a relief for both of us."

"You should have," Gia agreed with a curt nod. "But you didn't. And now you have to make decisions starting from the square you're standing in."

A "square" was filled with Royce and her truckload of attraction to him. When she thought about him, apart from everything else, she had to admit it was exciting. Maybe she finally had a chance at a relationship that was visceral and real.

God, how she needed something real.

Even if she never kissed Royce again, she'd had a realization of sorts. She was still sexually attractive. After two years of no dating and her and Brannon's lackluster romance, Taylor had started wondering if she'd ever find someone who curled her toes.

She hadn't imagined that someone would be Royce. Years ago, she'd taken her father's warning at face value. He'd been protective over his baby girl when he'd told her to stay away from Royce. But she was a far cry from a baby now.

"See you in the quarterly meeting."

"Thanks, G."

"You're welcome, doll." Gia wiggled her fingers in a wave and left the office.

Four

Royce stepped into the financial review meeting, unbuttoned his suit jacket and took a seat at the sleek mahogany conference room table. As CFO, he'd be called upon for input but he wasn't running the meeting. That was up to the finance manager, Stella, who had already lined up the projector and was sifting through her notes.

He'd had trouble keeping his mind on work for obvious reasons. Work and play didn't mix. Not that he had time to *play*. Being in charge of the company's numbers was an undertaking he took very seriously.

Gia arrived last as per her usual. She sat next to Taylor, who was at Royce's left elbow. Brannon was across the table, leaning back in his leather chair, tapping a pencil eraser-side down while he glared in Royce's general direction.

Royce ignored him.

"Everyone ready to get started?" Stella asked rhetorically before doing just that. Meetings were a nuisance but necessary to keep everyone on the same page. Especially now that his father was flirting more and more with the idea of early retirement.

Jack Knox wouldn't hit the links right away nor was he interested in building birdhouses in his spare time. No, no. Jack planned on traveling, experiencing life and the world. Royce's old man, now sixty-one, had never truly run out of wild oats to sow.

Bran focused his attention on a paper report while Taylor and Royce consulted their tablets. Gia had a fussy leather notebook in front of her, bejeweled with gems and dotted with stickers. His baby sister wasn't much for formality. Brannon wasn't either, though he did follow along. He rarely used the very electronics their company sold, which made Royce laugh.

Or would have if Bran hadn't been shutting him out for two solid days.

The last conversation they'd had was at the threshold of that closet when Bran had caught Royce and Taylor post-lip-lock. When Royce had come upon Bran and Gia talking later that same night, Bran promptly turned and walked away. Royce understood his younger brother's anger. Seven unanswered text messages later, he'd given up, until this morning.

He'd stepped right into Brannon's corner office and addressed him with a "Good morning, brother."

Brannon had looked up from his laptop to narrow his eyes. Eyes that were lighter brown than Royce's own, and greenish like their mother's. He'd picked up his phone, made a call and started talking, ignoring Royce altogether.

That'd been two hours ago and here they sat, ignoring each other again.

With a sigh, Royce glanced at Gia, who was jotting notes and lounging in her chair at the same time. No doubt her big brain soaked up every word Stella was saying like a fresh, dry sponge. Gia had always been able to pay attention to everything around her. Bran was more easily distracted during boring moments like this meeting, while Royce enjoyed the methodology of a presentation. There was a certain order to it that made sense to him.

Jayson Cooper, Gia's ex-husband who still worked at ThomKnox, was notably absent from this meeting. Cooper was in charge of tech, but he'd sent his assistant, Whitney, to ferry back any pertinent information.

Taylor asked a question, drawing everyone's attention. Royce watched her openly, not a hardship since she was beautiful. He appreciated the way she'd come in today sans drama about Saturday night. She'd always been professional at the office, even though he remembered her differently when they were kids. She and Gia were about the same age, but Royce was six years older than the girls, and only a few years older than Bran. While Royce didn't exactly hang out with any of them when he was younger, social situations mashed them together.

Charity functions, raffles, art shows and galas like the Valentine's Day celebration on Saturday put them in fancy clothes at fancy affairs on the regular. Even when he was a gangly sixteen-year-old and she and Gia had been fifth graders. He hadn't thought of Taylor as more than his sister's friend, including when the girls were teens and attending those same functions in ball gowns.

As he'd aged up, so had Taylor. He could begrudgingly admit that her changes hadn't gone unnoticed. Charles Thompson's candid discussion about how Taylor wasn't a good romantic option for Royce had prompted no argument. Charles was like a second father and Royce respected the man immensely.

But since that very conversation, Royce had noticed attributes about Taylor that he hadn't previously. Physical ones, sure, but also the way she handled her life. She wanted everything and wanted it all at once. Like a kid at a buffet who agonized over how she'd fit a spoonful of everything onto the same plate.

Royce was simpler than that. He did better when his focus was narrow. Unfortunately for everyone, it'd been Taylor who'd narrowed his focus to a fine point on Saturday night.

No matter the reaction to a rogue kiss, the wisest course of action was to set them back on the path from which they'd strayed. They both cared greatly for ThomKnox, Taylor having been thrust into the position of COO after her father passed last fall.

It was a loss she took hard and he noted now, and not for the first time, that those feathered lines around her eyes were a new addition. Grief had taken a toll on Taylor and her mother, Deena, most of all. Jack Knox and Charles Thompson were best friends who didn't always see eye to eye but made the best decisions for the company. Since Charles's death, Jack had been less about the company and more about skydiving lessons, traveling to Africa for safari and scuba diving in the Great Barrier Reef.

His father might be having some sort of late midlife crisis, but Royce supported Jack's decision to retire, regardless of who was chosen for the CEO position. Both brothers wanted it. Bran had a knack for fusing fun and hard work and ending up with a blend both investors and employees enjoyed, so he was a valid choice. Probably the *better* choice.

Approachability was not Royce's strong suit. He was methodical and careful, prepared and concise.

Stella finished answering Taylor's question, and Taylor smiled, her bow-shaped pink lips forming the words *thank you.* Royce felt a pull from the center of his stomach down to his groin.

When Taylor grabbed hold of him and kissed him at the gala, he hadn't expected it. He'd only thought of her over the years as someone he *shouldn't* be kissing. Ever. That kiss had snapped his control in two and ushered in a loss of equilibrium that had changed his world.

Who wouldn't be tempted by that?

But temptation was a temporary dalliance. The moment had passed. He was determined to cram the meddling genie back into her glass bottle, wedge the cork and toss it out to sea. There was no room in a company about to lose their CEO and appoint a new one for squabbling between brothers. Especially over a woman as well respected as Taylor. She was in the upper echelon of ThomKnox. Investors liked stability. Nothing was more important than righting the already upset apple cart.

There was a certain order that Royce liked to keep and though change was inevitable, he preferred to get through it as quickly and painlessly as possible.

Taylor swept a lock of blond hair behind her ear, shifting in her chair so that one long leg slipped over the other. She circled her foot, wrapped in a tall black high heel and he allowed his eyes to trickle up a rounded calf to a supple thigh that vanished beneath the demure hemline of a black dress.

Stella's voice faded into background fuzz and his brain blurred in much the same way. It wasn't hard to admire Taylor before, but now that he'd had his lips on hers, he could easily imagine pressing those lush breasts to his chest and sampling her neck, smelling her soft perfume as he allowed the tip of his tongue to dip into her cleavage…

"Royce?"

By the sound of Stella's voice, that wasn't the first time she'd said his name. He jerked his attention to her, raking over Brannon's grouchy visage on the way. Stella smiled patiently. "The numbers you wanted to share?"

"Yes, thank you, Stella," he replied evenly. He flipped from one screen to the next on his tablet and pulled up the report, but the numbers stopped him cold. They were wrong. This wasn't…

Fantastic.

The report he'd queued up was from *last* quarter, not the careful one he'd been preparing for the bulk of the morning.

"Um… One second." Aware of every pair of eyes in the room on him, he opened a file in the Cloud and hoped to God he'd remembered to back it up there. Then he remembered he'd emailed it to both Brannon and Taylor. All he needed to do was pull up the sent email to access the correct report. He opened his mouth to tell Stella as much when Taylor spoke.

"I can take that question, Stella." Warm hazel eyes swept over him, almost slate gray against the backdrop of her black dress. "Royce and I were discussing that this morning, and there was some confusion as to who was presenting. It appears that the numbers for this quarter showed a nice increase going into next…"

Royce, rapt, listened as she smoothly read the numbers he'd crunched this morning, numbers he'd planned on presenting. He hadn't expected her to take over for him. But she had, sliding in and saving his ass as easily as she'd tugged his mouth down to hers last weekend. Impressed by her knowledge and ease with the topic, he couldn't tear his eyes off her for a solid minute.

When he did, it was only because he felt Brannon's gaze pinning him where he sat. Taking in his brother's ire was nothing new—there were plenty of times when they'd seen the world differently. Their father assured them that it was healthy for brothers to bicker, but Royce didn't think this situation was what Jack had in mind.

Locked in silent battle with Taylor between them, well… There was nothing healthy about it. It was bordering unhealthy. Royce could feel the animosity radiating off his brother and hoped to God no one else picked up on it.

He wouldn't stand for it.

Within ThomKnox were their careers—all of them. The entire Knox family's and Taylor Thompson's, too. His father was retiring soon and her father had left her with bigger shoes to fill as well. They were the next generation of ThomKnox. Time they started behaving like it.

Royce had never, to his memory, missed his cue in a financial meeting—in *any* meeting. The wild card that had changed everything?

Kissing Taylor Thompson.

The last intimate moment they'd ever share.

He had to put this behind him—for the sake of their future. His eyes clashed with Gia's and she quirked her lips in amusement as if saying *Something on your mind, big brother?*

Yes.

And he couldn't afford to have his mind anywhere other than work. The company was about to undergo a massive transition. Either Royce or Brannon would be CEO soon—they'd each been groomed.

The smoother the transition went, the sooner they could return to their regularly scheduled programming.

Royce glanced at Brannon, only this time he'd made a decision. He was going to have a conversation with his younger brother—whether Brannon wanted to or not.

Five

Taylor's mother's papillon, Rolf, stood on his hind legs and pawed Taylor's thigh.

"Such a beggar, honestly." She stroked the dog's fringed, butterfly-like ears.

"Don't feed him your—" Her mother clucked her tongue as Taylor handed over a cube of steak. Her mother was dressed for dinner in a pink skirt and suit jacket, a bumblebee-shaped broach pinned on the lapel and her matching gold jewelry shining. Her budgeproof lipstick was in place, her smooth, straight hair tucked behind one ear.

Deena Thompson fit into the role of wealth easily. Taylor's mother had been raised in a family of wealthy investors and business owners, most of her money hailing from the airline industry.

"He's a *dog*, Mother. He likes meat. Besides he enjoys beef more than me. I'm more interested in the potatoes and asparagus." Both of which she'd eaten already.

Dinner had been served rather formally in her mother's

dining room. The table that stretched the length of the room was better suited for a packed Thanksgiving dinner, which her parents had hosted on numerous occasions, but this was where Deena Thompson liked to dine, so here they sat.

"He's a little dog, and I won't have him fat." Deena cocked her head to the side, sending her medium-length blond hair over one shoulder.

"One bite of steak won't hurt him, will it, Rolfie?" Taylor dropped her napkin on her plate and ruffled the dog's fur, nuzzling his tiny nose with her own. She'd never thought of a fussy toy breed like Rolf's as loving until her dad had been diagnosed. The little dog spent many, many evenings in either Taylor's or her mother's laps, soaking up their tears in his soft fur.

"He does love you," Deena said with a soft chuckle. "I think he believes you're his sister."

"Well. We both have great hair." Taylor gave her last cube of steak to the dog and ignored her mother's scoff.

Taylor was an only child but hadn't felt lonely growing up. She'd had her mother to pal around with, and the Knox siblings were a very big part of her world. Royce, Bran and Gia were raised by busy working parents as well as a team of nannies. Deena, while she'd always had a house staff, had been more than ready to leave the hectic working lifestyle to care for Taylor. Deena considered herself the ultimate domestic diva. She enjoyed keeping a house *and* a staff. She enjoyed catered dinners *and* selecting wines. She also enjoyed crafting in her massive craft room where every shade, pattern and color of scrapbooking paper lined the towering shelves on every wall. Now that Taylor thought about it, her mother's ambition at home *was* a career.

She was under no delusions that she had to mimic her mother's choices. Her work, which she loved, took up a lot of her time. Hiring help to clean her apartment was a no-brainer, especially when she spent her days as COO of a massive company. Sometimes though, she wondered how she'd balance work and family life once she decided to have a child of her own.

"Did you want more than one child?" Taylor scooted Rolf's front paws from her lap as her mother's chef stepped into the room to clear the plates. After they agreed everything was delicious and chose a dessert, he returned with two crème brûlées and tiny glasses of port wine.

Her mother dug into the crème brûlée, either ignoring or forgetting Taylor's earlier question.

"Mom?"

"Hmm? Oh, sorry. Children. We couldn't have any more." She shrugged, announcing it as easily as if she'd just run out of milk.

"What? You never…" Taylor shook her head in confusion while her mother sipped her port.

"No, no, not like that. Not like *couldn't*. Your father was busy with work and so was I. When the company expanded I wanted to hire my part out and stay home with my baby." She smiled warmly and patted Taylor's hand. "You."

"You never wanted to give me a brother or sister?"

"Well, we thought about it. But you had the Knox kids and I had my figure to consider." Deena winked, joking. She was beautiful for a woman of *any* age.

Taylor considered herself lucky to have inherited her mother's athletic build and love of exercise.

"What's bringing this about? Is a certain special relationship advancing? I never asked you about the gala."

Deena had attended for an hour or so before she made her exit. She told Taylor she'd felt inconvenienced by the idea of attending a party for show. Taylor couldn't blame her. Their grieving Charles's passing was a personal matter, and yet the masses felt they should be involved.

"You didn't hear about Brannon's proposal?"

"I didn't say I didn't hear about it. I said I never asked." Deena's eyebrows lifted.

"We broke up that night. Things at work are…strained. He's upset. Understandably."

"Well, you did kiss his brother."

"Mom! You know everything!"

"Patsy Sheffield told me," she said of their gossiping neighbor. "Your father wouldn't like that you're canoodling with the older Knox boy," Deena continued, the crème brûlée spoon hovering in front of her mouth. She cocked an eyebrow. "Did *you*? Like it?"

"He's hardly a boy, Mom." She could still feel the telltale scrape of his facial hair; see the dark look he'd given her before he gripped her waist and tugged her against his solid wall of a body. Taylor's cheeks warmed when she admitted, *"I liked it immensely."*

"Older men." Deena sighed. "There is something about them."

Deena was fifty-four years old, ten years Charles Thompson's junior. When she married Charles, who was selling and making a small fortune in direct sales at the time, Deena's father—Taylor's curmudgeonly but lovable grandfather—hit the roof. It was a story she'd heard time and time again as a little girl, told exuberantly by her father and interspersed with his infectious laughter at how he'd eventually won over his father-in-law. Her mother had laughed with him.

Taylor grew accustomed to the sound of her parents' comingling laughter. It'd stretched from her childhood until her father's passing last year, ending the only way it could—when he was no longer alive to contribute.

She'd recently been contemplating her father's reasoning behind her avoiding Royce. Even when he'd been very ill, he'd reiterated that Bran was a better fit for her and steered her away from the older Knox "boy."

"Well good for you for livening things up," her mother said. "Galas used to be fun, but now they're a drag. I only attended because it was the first time I'd been out since…" She shook her head rather than say the words *your father's death*. "It's expected you show up and look like you're not in a million pieces."

"You're not. And it's remarkable." She reached for her mother's hand and Deena's eyes misted over. "I know you miss him. You must. I miss him like I lost a limb."

"Try losing all of them." Deena's mouth compressed into a tight line.

Dad had been less healthy than his wife—more into rich foods and cigars, and any activity that involved socializing. Taylor smiled a bittersweet smile at the memory of her father's warm personality. After losing him there'd been an absence of charm in her life.

There was a note of ease about Bran that reminded her of her dad, which likely had contributed to her agreeing to go out with him. But the attraction had been a big fat goose egg. If Bran would climb down off that high horse of his, he'd probably admit as much to her. When two people were attracted to each other they behaved like… Well, like Royce and Taylor had behaved in that closet.

Taylor had admired the Knox siblings her entire life— how close they were. She'd been treated like an unofficial sister. Jack and Macy were like a second set of parents. Royce, the oldest, hadn't been around much when Bran, Gia and Taylor were teens and he was in college. But whenever he returned to spend time with his family, Taylor noticed.

Until Saturday night, when Royce's hand had been on

her waist and his lips on hers, she wouldn't have guessed he'd *ever* notice her.

She recalled the silky softness on her fingers when she raked them into his hair. She'd wanted to climb that wall of masculinity to the summit. He'd been a perplexing mix of rigid and pliant during that kiss. Unraveling his straight-edged spine sent a zing of pleasure through her that hummed inside of her still. Had she seen him come unglued before last weekend? She didn't think so.

"I need to talk to Brannon," she told her mother. She'd been saying that a lot lately—to others and to herself. "Royce and Brannon were glaring at each other in a meeting today and I can't help thinking that's my fault."

Royce had been distracted in the financial meeting, and she'd bet she could also take credit for that. He'd been far from flustered, but when his eyebrows carved a deep line in his forehead, she'd read his expression as easily as she had his email. He needed help. So, she bailed him out.

"Brannon was out of line. You two are cute together, but marriage?" Deena shook her head. "I love that boy, I do. Don't get me wrong, I'm not saying Royce is the one for you, but darling, you're not married. You're certainly not engaged. You weren't anything when you shared that kiss except for curious."

And turned on, but that was too crass to mention.

"You're right."

"Perhaps the near-miss engagement is making you think about having a family. You're healing from losing your father. It's normal for your thoughts to turn inward."

"Coffee with the widow's group is helping." Taylor loved her mother but even Deena would be the first to admit that she'd never been what anyone would call "introspective."

"They're a lifeline. As far as your own future, don't pressure yourself. You love to do that, and I can tell you're trying to plot and plan. Let the future unfold on its own instead. See how that goes."

Easy for Deena to say. She loved to go with the flow. Taylor preferred *directing* the flow whenever possible.

"Who do you think Jack will name as his new CEO?" Deena propped her elbow on the table, wine in hand.

"Not Gia. She never wanted to run that company."

"Smart girl." Deena smirked. "I imagine it'll be Royce, don't you?"

"I could see either of them as CEO, but Royce's being older could be an advantage."

"Maybe Jack will name you."

"No." Taylor held out a hand like a stop sign. "I like my inherited position. It suits me. Plus, I like to think that I'm making Dad proud." She was going to say more but a lump in her throat stymied the words.

"Oh, honey." Her mother gave her a quick hug before bending over the table to address her quietly. "He's *so* proud. I know it. Charles always talked about how you're his legacy, Tay. You're like him in all the right ways. None of my underachiever tendencies. If you had a craft room filled with art supplies, you'd have a million-dollar business behind it. I just give them away." She smiled, though, knowing it wasn't a fault but simply the way she was. "When you're ready to start a family—no matter who you start one with—you'll succeed. Plenty of time for that, though."

"Thanks, Mom." Deena Thompson always said the right thing.

"I have a craft room to retire to and I know you're not interested in spending the entire evening with me. I suspect you have work to do even after eight o'clock?"

"You know me well." Taylor was looking forward to it, though. Her laptop was a comfort.

Her mother left the room, Rolf at her heels.

On the drive home, Taylor thought of Royce and what he was doing tonight. If he was home answering emails or tinkering with a spreadsheet. Had he thought of her since the kiss?

He would have had to… Wouldn't he?

Six

"I haven't thought about it, to be honest." Bran's cool expression was the opposite of the lethal one he'd worn when he'd opened that closet door at the gala. Royce guessed his brother would rather not have this conversation at all, but he hadn't left Bran much of a choice. Royce showed up at Bran's house without warning, walking in the second the door was opened.

Over bottles of beer, Royce began the conversation by stating the obvious. *We need to talk about Saturday night.*

Bran tipped his beer bottle against his lips and sucked down a few swallows.

Royce pulled his glasses off, having forgotten they were on his nose since he'd worn them the majority of the day, and tucked them into his jacket pocket. "You've thought about it. I've thought about it. Don't bullshit me."

Bran scowled, the foreign expression now commonplace.

"You can't stay mad at us forever. It makes no sense. Taylor is COO, I'm CFO and you're the President."

"I know our roles."

"Soon one of us will be CEO." A hush fell over the kitchen. They were in direct competition for it, but fiercely loyal to one another. It was a new dynamic and one Royce wasn't sure how to navigate. He loved his brother but he also loved his father. If Jack assigned Royce the position of CEO, Royce would accept it. "You, Taylor, me. We're all integral parts of ThomKnox. If the investors get spooked—"

"*That's* what you're worried about?" Bran snorted, his smile condescending. "Jesus, Royce. I thought you were seducing Taylor in that closet. It's almost a relief to know you're still a cyborg."

"I wasn't seducing her." Anger pinged off his ribs like a pinball, but there was no sense in doing a postmortem. What was done was well and truly *done*. Royce would just say what he'd come here to say. "We're going to make it through this. We're family. But you have to have a conversation with Taylor that makes this okay. *You* were the one who nearly trotted out a proposal in a public place."

Bran's cheeks tinged red with embarrassment or anger—or a blend of both. He raked his hand through his longer hair and it fell every which way but back into place. "What the hell do you suggest I say to her, Royce? 'Sorry you found out I wanted to marry you?'"

"Did you *want* to marry her?" Royce held his brother's gaze, unrelenting. The proposal had been rushed, desperate. Definitely out of character.

"It doesn't matter now, does it?" Bran hedged.

"She panicked. She was practically hyperventilating stuck in that closet. When I found her, she had this wild, frightened look in her eyes and was muttering about how she'd never expected a proposal after only a few weeks of you two seeing each other." Royce lifted his own beer bottle. "She was hiding from you, Bran. Does that sound like a woman who would've responded well to your proposal?"

"Oh, so I should be thanking her for letting me down gently? Before I proposed and she publicly humiliated me?"

"Actually, yes."

Bracing his arms on the counter, Brannon's lip curled.

"The kiss was an accident."

"Looked pretty intentional to me."

It wasn't, but it had awakened Royce's dormant libido like the proverbial sleeping dragon. He worked constantly, content to be alone. If he needed a date for an event, he could find one—save the Valentine's Day gala. He'd run out of time.

The dates he took to a function rarely turned into more. A few repeat dates, maybe. Sex sometimes—he wasn't a masochist. But those dates were handled as efficiently as everything else in his life. The arguments were the same. He didn't have time to date. Women took a lot of time.

See: the current situation.

"What I'm trying to say is that Taylor didn't mean to kiss me."

"*She* kissed you?"

Dammit.

"Did you…enjoy it?" Bran's tone was curious.

"Of course not." Royce forgave himself for the white lie he was about to tell. They needed to move forward not dwell. "She apologized to me after. She was flustered and embarrassed. I was selfishly glad she admitted it first because I was about to do the same thing. She's a good friend, a competent colleague."

"With a beautiful body and stunning mouth," Bran muttered. But it wasn't jealousy that bent his eyebrows. It more resembled suspicion.

"I'm not blind to Taylor's attributes, but she's not a good fit for me." Pragmatism was Royce's best ally.

Bran nodded, but looked like he had more to say. Royce had said all he needed to say.

"Are we good?"

"Sure." Bran nodded. Royce didn't believe it was that simple, but he'd take the reprieve.

"Talk to her." Royce shoved aside his barely touched beer and stood from his seat at the counter. "As her friend, you owe it to her to hear her out. And if you're lucky, she'll let you explain your motives as well. Mistakes happen, Bran. Let's not allow them to cost us what's really important."

"Landing CEO?"

"May the best man win."

"Aw, shucks." Bran flattened his hand over his chest. "Do you mean it?"

Royce had to smile at his brother's cockiness.

"It's your birthright ahead of me, you know. That's not lost on me. Dad handing over CEO is like…the throne. You'd be crazy not to fight me for it."

"There's nothing to fight about. It's Dad's decision and I'll accept whomever he chooses. You're in the running. Throne or no." Royce bowed formally and added, "Your Majesty."

"You're an asshole. I bet Taylor regretted that kiss down to her size 9 Manolos." Bran grinned full out and Royce returned it, glad to be on the same page with him again.

"Without a doubt."

Royce had protected his family to the best of his ability and this was another situation where he'd do what was right. CEO was meant for him, but if Dad chose Bran, Royce would analyze spreadsheets and maintain the important role of CFO at ThomKnox for the rest of his days. Though being CEO would satisfy his own curiosity about what it would be like to step into his father's role at the company, he didn't need to prove anything to anyone.

As he walked out to his car, Royce looked through the window at his brother. Bran was leaning against the wall, his posture more relaxed than earlier, typing into his cell phone.

Hopefully that was Taylor he was texting. And hopefully she'd back up Royce's story about her regretting the kiss. Though he should probably prompt her in case she'd crafted a fictional tale of her own.

In the driver's seat, he fired off a few texts to her before starting the engine and leaving for home.

That ought to take care of everything.

Taylor stepped out of the shower, her hair wrapped in blue terry cloth, another blue towel wrapped at her waist. She'd stood in the steam for a long time to clear her mind. Tonight, rather than work her fool head off, maybe she'd relax. It'd be nice to shut off her work brain, watch TV or read a murder mystery instead of ruminate on Royce and Bran drama.

She used to be an avid dater, but when her father was diagnosed with cancer she put her social life on hold. Charles Thompson was enough man to occupy her time. Taylor didn't want to bring around a date who would meet her father when he wasn't feeling well—a date that might eventually attend a funeral as an awkward plus-one.

Bran had been a safe choice for reentry into the dating world. He'd gone to the funeral. He knew her father. There weren't any tough questions to answer or land mines to sidestep where her family was concerned. He understood her grief and sadness and during one date, when she'd told story after story about her dad, he'd smiled and listened.

Brannon was a good friend. And she hoped he would be again. She didn't like the unfinished business between them.

She took her time blow drying her hair and applying lotion to her arms and legs. She dressed in leggings and an off-the-shoulder long-sleeved T-shirt to thwart California's cool February evening. In front of the TV, she plopped down onto her reclining love seat. She grabbed her phone to turn it on silent before she chose a show to watch and noticed several text messages. One from Brannon. A few from Royce.

She swiped the screen and clicked on Brannon's name first. The text read:

We should talk about Saturday.

It was about time he came to the conclusion they'd have to speak eventually. She opened Royce's texts next.

I explained to Bran that you regretted kissing me and apologized immediately after.

You were panicked and confused. He'll understand.

As Taylor read the texts from Royce, her blood pressure slowly rose.

"I was confused? I *regretted* it?" she said through her teeth. Of all the… She stabbed the call button and lifted her cell phone to her ear. The second she heard Royce's smooth, neutral *hello* she let him have it.

"You told Brannon I kissed you and regretted it? You told him I apologized? To you? You told him I was confused!"

"That's the gist of it, yes."

She pulled in a breath through her flared nostrils. How, exactly, was this her problem? Like Gia said, Taylor wasn't the only one in that closet. "Did you regret it, Royce?"

He'd *clung* to her that night. Pulled her in and drank her kisses like his life depended on them. The way they fit together, even in their formalwear, suggested they'd fit together a whole lot better wearing a whole lot less.

"Of course I regretted it," he answered in the same bland tone.

"No you didn't." He might have shown zero interest in her before that fated closet run-in but not so now. She'd witnessed him taking a painfully slow perusal of her from head to toe in the financial review meeting. "You brought the wrong report to the financial review."

"Thanks for the reminder of my incompetence." He sounded peeved, which peeved her. He wasn't upset about the kiss, but oh-ho! He brought the wrong report! Scandal!

"You seemed distracted at the meeting," she reminded him. "Was there something—" *or someone* "—keeping you from thinking clearly that morning, Royce?"

"Yes." His low growl of affirmation sent her heart into a twirl. She knew it. She knew there was more to that kiss than proximity. "It won't happen again."

It was less of a promise and more an assertion. How could he be so sure? *She* wasn't sure. She stopped shy of blurting, *You looked like you wanted to lick my legs from Achilles to inner thigh.*

An involuntary shudder shimmied up her spine as she imagined Royce's mouth on her legs. His tongue climbing her leg, tickling behind her knee before going higher. It was bad enough she knew what his lips felt like on hers. It'd only made her want more.

Speaking of…

"Did you mention to Bran that after I *threw myself at*

you in a fit of 'panic' and 'confusion' that you swept your tongue along mine until neither of us could think straight?" Heart thudding heavily, she waited. He didn't respond right away, which made her feel smug. She was absolutely right about the effect of that kiss. It'd surprised both of them in the best way possible.

"I was carried away," he murmured.

Satisfied, she smiled as she brushed her hand along the soft suede arm of the love seat. So she had rocked his world. *Not bad, Tay.*

"ThomKnox is facing a very big transition in the coming weeks and months after my father retires. As top brass, our focus needs to be on our shareholders and investors. You don't have to worry about my mouth on yours—on any part of you—again. We can continue at work the way we have in the past. I trust you agree that it's best we appear as one cohesive management team."

The shift from such a personal comment to words as impassioned as a cardboard cutout pissed her off. Royce valued control. This much she knew. But acting like another kiss might disturb the otherwise perfect harmony at ThomKnox? Come on. How cocksure could one man be?

Denying the real attraction that existed between them wasn't only a fabrication, it was cruel. She hadn't had a man in her bed for nearly two years. Two years! She'd put her attraction, her desire for another person, on hold. She'd funneled every ounce of her remaining energy into prayers and good vibes and meditation and research on alternate medicines for her father. Anything to give him another year—another twenty years—on this planet.

None of her efforts had changed what fate had so cruelly set in motion. Her father was destined to die no matter what she did to stop it. It was unfair, and she'd wailed those words at the blank white ceiling of her bedroom on

more than one occasion. And now Royce thought he'd come
along and *mansplain* away how she was feeling when she
kissed him? And worse—claim he hadn't felt the attraction she damned well knew was there.

What a load of crap.

"You can lie to me about that kiss," she told him, "but
you know the truth deep inside."

"The truth, deep or otherwise, is that it shouldn't have
happened. I'm willing to forget it, and I suggest you do
the same."

Seven

After Taylor ended the call with Royce—hanging up on him as he deserved—she didn't have the energy to confront Brannon. First, she was too angry with the eldest Knox brother and didn't want to take it out on the wrong one. Second, and as much as she hated to admit it, Royce was right.

The company was facing a very big transition and it was of the utmost importance that the top brass were one cohesive unit. She and Brannon had both made mistakes. Him, planning a proposal when they'd never so much as slept together and her, not breaking up with him when she knew damn well their relationship hadn't stalled—it never started.

That saying about eating crow swooped by on wide black wings, her father's sage voice echoing in her ears. *If you have to eat crow, might as well do it while it's warm.*

In other words: no more delaying doing the right thing.

She purposefully came in late the next morning to avoid chitchat and the possibility of bumping into Brannon or

Royce on the way to her office. The executive suites had some distance between them in the sprawling building. At least she could ensure privacy for her conversation with Brannon.

After checking their shared meeting calendar and determining he was in, she straightened the skirt of her slate-gray wrap dress and headed to Bran's office.

His personal assistant, Addison Abrams, had worked for ThomKnox since last June and was, according to Brannon, indispensable. She was smart, attentive, and as far as Taylor knew, incredibly kind. Addi was one of the first people in the office to approach her after her dad's death, both with kind words and a touch to the arm that had turned into a gentle hug. Taylor would never forget that small but meaningful gesture.

"Good morning." Taylor checked her slender wristwatch before correcting with a smile, "Late morning."

"It's still morning." Addi's smile was cooler than usual. Typically, she was quick to compliment Taylor on her wardrobe. Maybe gray wasn't Addi's favorite color. The two women didn't converse outside of ThomKnox, but Taylor wouldn't have been surprised if she and Addison someday formed a friendship. "What can I do for you, Ms. Thompson?"

The formality was new, too.

"Everything okay?" Taylor ventured.

Addi's platinum blonde hair was a few shades lighter than Taylor's and wound into a twist at the back of her head. Addi's dress was a bright, sunset orange and would've been appalling on any other woman. But with her high cheekbones, ocean-blue eyes and golden skin tone, Addison was a true Cali girl. The vivid color suited her.

Those blue eyes were icy when she responded, "Everything is fine."

Oh-kay. So much for small talk.

"I'm dropping in on Bran if he's not busy. Is he on a call?" Taylor asked.

The other blonde checked the desk phone where a red light blinked twice before vanishing. Addi sounded inconvenienced when she announced, "Not anymore."

"Perfect. I'll let myself in?"

Addison nodded, her smile forced.

Taylor rapped lightly on Bran's office door before letting herself in. She'd caught the expression of surprise on his raised face through the slatted wood blinds just before she entered. "I'm responding to your text finally."

"In person, no less." He didn't wear a scowl as well as Royce. Bran was better suited for a smile or a mischievous smirk. "Have a seat."

He gestured to the pair of dark leather chairs in front of a glass coffee table and stood to join her. Before he left his desk, he pressed a button on his phone and spoke into it. "Addison, can you send in an intern with drinks…" He let go of the intercom button to ask Taylor, "Is it too early for a drink?"

"Coffee will do."

He dipped his head and pressed the intercom button again. "Coffee. Black for her—"

"Cream and two sugars for you," Addi finished. "I'll arrange it." Her voice was warm when she addressed him. Interesting.

"So Addison isn't unhappy in general, only with me."

Bran didn't deny it. "More like misguided protection. She works for me which means she's automatically on my side."

Addi sent a withering glare through the blinds before stalking off. Taylor wasn't sure Bran had that right. Addi didn't like that Taylor was in Bran's office. With the door shut. Probably she'd heard about the failed proposal and the kiss. Who knew what sort of rumors had been flying around the office?

Bran had already taken his suit jacket off—it was a rare occasion that he wore it—but his tie was knotted at his neck. It was a fun design—yellow with bright orange suns. Taylor had the passing thought that it complemented Addison's dress.

They shared pleasantries about a few emails that had come through regarding a new laptop design until an intern arrived with a tray. The conversation was slightly forced, and given Brannon's stilted responses, he felt the same way. There seemed to be an unspoken rule about civility that almost gave Taylor pause.

Almost.

Bran poured her a cup of black coffee, doctored his own with too much cream and sugar and leaned back in the chair, mug in hand. He was waiting for her to speak, and why shouldn't he? She'd come to him.

"Why do you want to marry me?"

He blew out a soft chuckle. "I don't."

"You *did*," she replied calmly.

"I…" He shook his head, frowning to himself. "Clearly, it was a mistake."

"We hadn't been on an official date in at least a week. And the chemistry wasn't exactly sizzling those two times we kissed."

"Thanks a lot."

"Bran," she said through a laugh. "I'm one of your best friends. Be honest with me."

He stared down at his coffee for several beats before meeting her gaze. "The kisses could have been better. But. That wasn't my fault."

"And you thought an engagement would improve our odds?"

He set down his mug and leaned forward, elbows on his knees. "Engagements can last a long time. How do you know?"

There was something he wasn't saying. Him being coy was getting them nowhere. Gia's comment about Brannon looking like a better option for CEO made sense. And Taylor, despite coming in here to extend an olive branch, couldn't do it knowing that she was nearly proposed to out of convenience.

"Royce lied to you."

Brannon frowned.

"I didn't apologize to him after kissing him. And while I regret the timing—I absolutely should have ended things between you and me a few weeks ago after that awful seafood dinner."

Bran's eyebrows jumped. "We've never had that difficult a time trying to hold a conversation."

"Never," she agreed. "You can tell me why, you know. I *am* your friend."

She balled up her fist and slugged him in the arm. He smiled that cute Brannon smile she'd admired for as long as she'd known him. It might not light her up the way Royce's did, but Bran was still ridiculously attractive.

"CEO means a lot to me. This company means a lot to me. I want a family and kids, but I thought I'd have that before my role at the company changed. Now that it's a one out of two possibility, I felt like…" He shrugged. "I should get the ball rolling?"

He winced, probably not liking how that sounded out loud. But she knew him—had known him her whole life. Gia was right. He hadn't used her. He'd been caught up in the race for CEO.

"So your ambition was in the lead. Admit it. You don't want to marry me."

"It was too soon," he said instead, probably trying to spare her feelings. He might've been blowing by her like a stiff wind lately, but face-to-face, he couldn't be unkind.

"For the record, I don't think you did it on purpose. Your heart is as big and inclusive as your father's. You'd do anything for your family, for this company. Even something as misguided as marriage."

He put his hand to his forehead. "God, Taylor. What *was* I thinking?"

"I should have walked up to you when you were holding that ring and asked what it was." She shrugged. "Instead… I panicked."

Crap. She *had* panicked. One point for Royce.

"And locked yourself in a closet."

"That was an accident."

"Was the kiss an accident?" Bran looked genuinely curious. "You and Royce…" He shook his head. "You two are more mismatched than you and me."

"Well, we both drink white wine and you won't touch it, so we have that going for us."

"Your father proposed to your mother at that gala. And you've been sad. I thought—hell, I don't know what I thought. It was the wrong thing to do."

"So your heart was involved after all," she said gently. He was sweet. No matter what reasoning was behind the doomed proposal.

He stood, taking her hands and helping her to her feet. "Friends?"

"Always."

He pulled her into a hug. When she dropped her arms, he wore his usual mischievous grin. "Damn. That was an awful hug. Dare I say…*disgusting.*"

"Appalling," she teased back. She lifted her mug to take one more sip of her coffee when she caught a flash of bright orange at the window. Addison's mouth was a compressed line, her gaze hard. And hurt.

"There's someone out there for you, Taylor," Bran said. "But not me. Now stop begging me to go out with you. It's embarrassing."

"In your dreams, buddy."

"It's not Royce, either."

"What makes you say that?" She wasn't going to deny there'd been something in that kiss. Something unexpected. Something worth pursuing.

"I don't want to see you hurt. As your *friend*, I'm saying you can do better."

She nodded, hoping that the nod communicated that she agreed. She couldn't exactly *disagree*. Royce had been a pompous ass lately.

"Thanks for stopping by." Brannon opened his office door. Then to Addison he said, "Taylor can't keep her hands off me."

The joke did *not* go over well. Taylor walked away feeling Addison's eyes on her back the entire time.

Jealous much?

She wanted to go back and comfort Addi, to tell her there was nothing going on with Brannon, and there never had been. But she couldn't right that relationship before she fixed another one…

With ThomKnox's stubborn CFO.

Eight

Everything was back to normal by the end of the week.

Sort of.

Royce had been mesmerized by numbers and reports come Friday morning until Taylor marched in, arms flying. And he did mean *marched*.

She'd come in to complain about Lowell Olson—the owner of Box, an elite electronics store. Lowell was in discussions about where and how to shelf ThomKnox products—something Box had never done before.

"Apple is not the only sleek, sexy product on the market, you know. We have a good—no, *better*—tablet right around the corner and he acts like we should pay him double what they're paying for premium shelving!" While Taylor talked, one of the pearl buttons on her silk shirt wiggled loose.

Royce tried to reroute his eyes—honest to God—but they kept flitting back down to that gap showing a swatch of pale pink bra. His body tightened, the memory of the kiss slamming into his gut like a two-by-four. Finally, he looked down at the tablet in front of him and pretended to read the notes he'd taken at yesterday's meeting.

"Are you listening to me?"

He repeated her last sentence back to her. "'Lowell is a buffoon if he thinks ThomKnox can't stand up to any brand on the market. And his company's bottom line is as tiny as his prehistoric brain.'"

She bit her bottom lip, trying to hide a smile. That attraction he'd been trying to ignore? Wasn't working. She'd been carrying on as usual. He'd been barricaded in his office, only attending meetings he was required to attend simply to let the—*whatever* was between them—pass. It would. He'd see to it.

"Was I close?" he asked.

"Spot-on. It sounded funny in your serious tone."

"I'm one-note. Can't help it." His eyes strayed to her shirt again and the bra playing peekaboo.

"You are not." Her smile suggested she saw him differently than a rigid numbers guy. It was oddly appealing.

"Are you looking at my shirt?"

"No." He averted his eyes.

"Royce! You could have told me I was flashing you." She quickly fixed the open button.

"I didn't want you to think I was harassing you at your place of business. You are a colleague and I respect you."

She flipped her hair over her shoulder. "Well, the next time my breasts are on display, or any other body part, please tell me."

He frowned. Mainly because now all he was thinking about was what the rest of her would look like on display.

"Okay."

"Anyway. Hopefully Lowell will come around before the new tablet launches. We need as many eyeballs on it as possible." She pointed to the interoffice mailer she'd dropped in his inbox when she'd walked in. "Can you sign that really fast?"

"What is it?" he asked, opening the envelope.

"Birthday card for Addison."

"Could you have chosen one with more glitter?" He brushed the stray gold specks from his desk before scribbling his name into the card and handing it back to her. "Is there a reason you're taking her card around personally?"

"I need to run off the steam that built after the interaction with Lowell."

"It'll work out."

"I'm also seeing to it that Addison receives her birthday card from me personally." Taylor took the envelope. "As a gesture of goodwill. Well, this and a giant bouquet of Please Stop Hating Me flowers."

"Addison doesn't hate you. She likes everyone." She was bright and smiley and professional. Bran wouldn't shut up about what an amazing assistant she was whenever he mentioned her. Which was usually when Bran was trying to talk Royce into hiring an assistant of his own on a permanent basis. Royce utilized the interns for delegation. A personal assistant seemed too...in his space.

"She shot daggers at me through Bran's office window when she saw me hug him." Eyes rolling to the ceiling, Taylor missed Royce's reaction. He went stock-still, his fist choking the life out of the gold-and-black Mont Blanc pen in his grip.

"You what?"

"I talked to Bran." She dismissed the topic with a hand, like news of *the hug* wasn't a bombshell shaking the walls of Royce's skull. "Addison saw us and I don't think she liked it."

Well. That made two of them.

"I think she likes him, but he's too thickheaded to notice."

"Why were you *hugging* Brannon at all?" The question came out like a thunderclap. He rolled his shoulders and fingered his bow tie, trying to calm down.

"Because Brannon's my friend?" She looked at him like he'd gone crazy, and hell, maybe he had. She'd hugged Brannon before. She'd hugged *Royce* before—he thought. He seemed to remember a few stiff-armed side squeezes over the years. But if Addison was jealous…

"That must've been some kind of hug."

She watched him carefully. A little too carefully.

"I have a lot to go over here—" he gestured to his tablet "—if you don't mind."

Still skewering him with a look, she reached up to finger the button on her blouse, drawing his attention to the silk shirt that touched her body like a caress.

He imagined undoing each of those pearl buttons and sliding the blouse from her skin while covering every revealed inch with his mouth…

"Thanks for the signature," was all she said.

He blinked, snapping his eyes to hers. In a voice of steel, he said, "No problem."

She left and he sagged in his chair. Categorizing Taylor as his coworker and family friend wasn't working. Especially when she was impassioned. Worked up over Lowell or insisting Addison like her again—both made her more tempting.

Royce couldn't allow himself to be tempted. He had to work—and focus on the company's naming a new CEO. Turned out after his lecture about being responsible, Taylor had taken his advice and smoothed out the issue with Bran. He should be glad.

So why wasn't he?

* * *

Royce left the office earlier than his usual six o'clock. His father, Jack, had requested he join him at Rust and Boar, a steakhouse known for its elitist lounge. Fine by Royce. He couldn't concentrate on a damn thing anyway.

Usually over cigars or brandy, or both, Jack Knox made the deals he'd become famous for—the same ones that'd made ThomKnox billions. Jack wasn't one for cigar smoking, though. That'd been Taylor's father Charles's passion more than Jack's. Jack held tight to tradition, however, and liked that even in California, where it rained granola, they could still discuss business over a slab of meat and a stiff drink.

Royce smiled to himself as he recalled the last business meeting that went down in Rust and Boar, mainly because Taylor had come in her father's place. She'd done her father proud. ThomKnox was not and never would be a boys' club. Taylor was as respected—if not more respected—than any man in the company.

He frowned when he thought of how much he liked that about her. How it made her tantalizing in a way other than physically. A woman he should be admiring from afar for her stellar work ethics had somehow worked her way under his skin. It didn't match his ethos and that was possibly more disturbing than anything. Royce was always in control. For Taylor to pop him at the seams… It made no sense.

Stress. He could blame stress. The possibility of being named CEO was a big deal. Brannon and Royce not getting along for a few days was a big deal. Lowell Olsen was a thorn in their sides.

Yes. Blaming stress would work fine.

Not calling himself on his own BS, he stepped inside the restaurant. He spotted his father at the bar, white head tossed back and laughing heartily with the woman next to him. The woman was a very big part of ThomKnox's success and Royce's first love: his mother, Macy.

"Royce!" She threw her arms up when she saw him.

He came close and kissed her cheek. "You're looking beautiful this evening." Then he turned to shake his father's hand. "Dad. Good to see you."

"Our table is being prepared." Jack grinned, his smile bright and genuine. Brannon definitely had that side of Jack—the lighter, more infectious side. Royce had inherited his dad's cunning instincts and head for business.

Can't win 'em all. Besides. Royce was better at rigid and unapproachable. Call it an art.

"Mr. and Mrs. Knox, your room is ready." A suited man, black leather menu boards in the crook of one arm, turned to lead them from the bar to a private window-filled room. Nicknamed "the sun room," the upstairs private room actually belonged to ThomKnox and was often used for special occasions. Royce assumed it'd be where they held his father's retirement party. If Jack ever got around to announcing it.

"What's the occasion?" he asked his parents once they were seated by the window, a breathtaking view of mountains and blue skies in the backdrop. It was rare to have dinner just the three of them. Usually Bran, Gia and, when they were married, Jayson Cooper, were present as well.

"Wine first. Then we'll discuss." Decree made, Jack took his time tasting different vintages before settling on a bottle for the table. They ordered the chef's special of almond-crusted rainbow trout with wilted greens and were halfway through their dinners when Jack was suddenly ready to talk.

"I'm naming you CEO." He made the announcement without fanfare, after forking a bite of trout and chewing thoughtfully.

Royce, napkin in hand, slowly lowered it to his lap and exchanged glances with his mother. Her genial smile suggested she knew what was coming and approved of the decision.

"An announcement will be at the office. I'll hold a meeting and we'll make it official. I wanted you to be prepared. Give you some time to digest the news. I know you're slower to accept change than Bran or Gia."

"Do they know?"

"They will soon," answered his dad.

"Gia doesn't want CEO," his mother chimed in. "She never has. She has aspirations. If you ask me, they're not in marketing. She had to move somewhere after hers and Jayson's divorce."

"Mark my words," Jack said, "she wants to take over the technology department."

"Coop will love that," Royce muttered under his breath. Jayson Cooper wasn't above being ruled by a female, but his ex-wife was next level.

"Brannon wants CEO. And we know that," his mother said.

"But you want it more," his father said.

Royce shook his head, but it was for show. Everything in him leaned forward as if shouting YES. Jack raised a hand to stay anything to the contrary Royce might've said.

"You deny yourself what you truly want. You always have. You're our ambitious firstborn and yet so ready to sacrifice for your siblings," Jack said with a proud smile. "But you can't deny you want this. You're ready."

"It's our way of saying that it's past time to say yes to yourself," Macy added.

"It's also completely selfish." Jack placed his fork and knife on his plate. "You're the one who should be running ThomKnox, no one else. You're the one who can level up with the company. I'm going to be busy building a private resort on an island for your mother and myself to vacation. No time or desire to care about the future of ThomKnox." His father winked to show he was exaggerating.

Hearing the words "no time or desire to care" made Royce's shoulders draw back in pride. He *did* care. He *had* the time. Since graduating high school and doggedly pursuing a college degree he'd been invested in ThomKnox. Not to say that Bran didn't love his family or the business—he did, and so did Gia. But this was about what was right for the company. Who would be more dedicated, more available. That person was obviously Royce.

He wasn't encumbered with a wife or a girlfriend. And now that this was almost settled, there would be no limbo. He could move forward and put the snafu between him and Taylor behind him.

He wanted CEO. Down to his very marrow.

Jack let out a soft chuckle and patted his son's cheek like he had when Royce was a kid.

"There he is," Jack said to his wife. "Told you he'd love it."

Macy nodded. "Yes. You did."

Only then did Royce allow himself to grin. To feel the buzz of satisfaction throughout his entire body.

CEO was his.

He would make his parents proud.

Nine

Taylor hung her silk shirt in the closet and fingered the delicate fabric, her mind on Royce. He'd been checking her out today. His not mentioning her popped button had nothing to do with *respecting her as a coworker*. What was it with men and their complete denial of what was right in front of them?

She shook her head. It'd been a long day. Best not to analyze that stumper. She stripped off her slacks and hung them as well, sliding one hanger then another to the side in search of her favorite pair of comfy leggings.

What was Royce trying to prove today? That she was objectively unattractive? She swiped another hanger, remembering the moment she'd caught him looking. *Really* looking.

"Eating me up with those deep brown eyes…" And then denying it.

Vehemently.

"What's he afraid of?" she asked her closet.

What are you *afraid of?*

Valid point. Why hadn't she called him on it? Why hadn't she confronted him the way she had Bran? Was it propriety? Was it procrastination? Or was it some latent, misplaced loyalty to her father's wishes?

Ding! We have a winner!

It wasn't like her to not go after what she wanted. Until now, however, Royce had never given her a reason to pursue him. He'd never looked at her the way he'd looked at her today. It'd been exhilarating watching him at war with himself, the silent battle pulling the sides of his mouth into a frown. It was as if he'd been giving himself a stern talking-to. Worse, she'd let him off the hook. All because her father had once suggested that Royce was not the man for her. At the time, she'd found it funny. Royce hardly gave her a passing glance.

"Today, it was more than a passing one."

She really needed to get a cat. Or a goldfish. Muttering to herself alone in her apartment was a recipe for a straitjacket. She slid another hanger and encountered a garment she'd forgotten about.

Seth Wheeler had been a longish term boyfriend for Taylor. They'd nearly made it to a one-year anniversary, and she'd believed they might even get married and have a family someday. Her parents liked him and Taylor herself felt stirrings of love after only a month. When Seth finally uttered those three words to her, she'd happily returned them. They were together but separate people, both busy professionals who prioritized their careers. Then Seth, an engineer, had been offered an opportunity in Dubai the very same day Taylor had learned of her father's cancer diagnosis.

Her life abruptly changed for the worse. In so many ways. Seth was ecstatic about the "once in a lifetime opportunity." He was also unwilling to stay in California. Taylor refused to leave her father's side. She'd expected Seth to turn down Dubai. To stay here with her while her father fought for his life.

Seth instead left her behind. He'd been apologetic but oh-so-selfish. "What's between us, Tay, it may not work out long-term," he'd told her. "But Dubai? It's a sure thing."

Mind returning from the past, she fingered the delicate lingerie. She'd purchased the luxurious La Perla slip specifically for her and Seth's one-year anniversary. The black slip sailed over her body like a whisper, making her feel undeniably feminine. The hand-embroidered floral design framing the neckline and the low V-shaped dip in the back made the piece a work of art.

And since she bought it for the way it made her feel, not because Seth would've liked it, she kept it. She told herself that someday there'd be another man in her life who would make her want to slide into the seven-hundred-dollar garment.

As she rubbed the silky material between her fingers, she thought of Royce's reaction to hearing the news that she'd talked to, and hugged, Brannon. Royce had looked like he wanted a few carpenter's nails to gnaw on. She'd bet he was suffering from the same green-eyed monster as Addison.

Royce was *jealous*.

"Like silk, do you?" She pulled down the black velvet hanger, a positively delicious idea popping into her mind. Maybe it was time—past time—to challenge her father's opinion about whom she should or shouldn't date. She loved her father. She respected him. Her dad had the best intentions when it came to her. But he also could've been *wrong*.

Royce wanted her. She wanted him.

What more did she need to do?

Prove it. That's what.

The flirty short skirt showcased her toned thighs. The skinny straps framed her shoulders. The boldness of showing up unannounced wearing it would be Royce's ultimate weakness. No way could he deny his attraction then.

It was past time she did something because *she* wanted to do it. Not what her parents wanted. Not what her friends wanted. She'd been dating the wrong guy in some misguided effort to please her father, for heaven's sake. Enough was enough.

Sparks didn't come along every day. And the ones that flew between her and Royce were so rare, she couldn't remember the last time she'd felt anything like it. Not even with Seth.

She unearthed a snow-white, thigh-length trench coat next, and from the shoebox on the top shelf of her closet, pulled down her highest black heels. The little ankle straps would go nicely with the acres of leg showing beneath the coat.

Wearing only a mischievous smile, she climbed into a warm shower for a quick rinse. Twenty minutes later she was in her car driving to Royce's house.

Uninvited.

Royce arrived home and tossed his key fob into the decorative bowl in the foyer. A lush green plant sat next to the tall narrow table in the entryway, its leaves shined to glossy perfection by his housekeeper. She also left a bowl of lemons on the kitchen counter along with a vase of fresh flowers in the dining room.

He appreciated those kinds of details. Living alone was fine with him, but he liked life breathed into the space that he returned to each day after work. It gave him a sense of not being alone, but he was never required to converse. Which he also liked.

At least he *usually* liked it.

Since his parents had shared the news that he was CEO, Royce had been elated. Practically buoyant. Talk about two emotions he didn't feel often, if ever. His mother had taken a car home and he and his father retired to the bar for a scotch. Jack had reiterated that he would tell Gia and Bran personally, asking Royce not to say anything of their clandestine dinner. "Rumors can destroy a company," he'd warned.

Didn't Royce know it.

"You're brilliant," his father had added. "Hell, all my children are. But you are thoughtful and slow to speak. Careful in the right ways. That is what will make you a great CEO."

Royce had agreed with that assessment. Then his father said something that made Royce frown.

"You're also careful in the wrong ways. Being reckless is okay from time to time. The world won't come off its axis if you do something wild."

His mind arrowed back to—who else? Taylor Thompson. The kiss in the closet that never should have happened. It had been wild. Barely restrained. And while the world wasn't knocked from its axis, it had been given a solid shove.

Taylor was an indulgence. An indulgence he was supposed to have forgotten about by now. An indulgence that should've been satisfied a week ago. An indulgence that was making him itch like he was wearing a new wool sweater. He needed to do *something*, but he had no idea what.

He tossed his jacket onto the back of the dining room chair and removed his cuff links. He didn't typically undress in his kitchen but before he did anything else tonight, he was celebrating. A glass of wine would be nice. Then he could toast to himself.

He bent to pull a bottle of Old Vine Zinfandel from its home in the wine rack and admired the sleek black bottle with the pewter emblem on the neck. His house, normally welcoming and quiet, felt like a soundproof cocoon. He was happy but had no one to celebrate with—he couldn't call up Gia or Bran—so he was stuck with his own company.

Keeping secrets from his siblings didn't sit well with him, though he understood his parents' motivations. They needed to tell Gia and Bran in their own time and in their own way. Royce respected that. He opened the bottle and poured a few inches of the red into a wineglass.

Unsure what to do with himself, he flipped on a table lamp and sat on the new-but-made-to-look-worn leather sofa. Strumming his fingers on his knees, he spotted the remote for the fireplace. In the click of a button flames flickered to life. Wine in hand, he sipped, struck by how odd it was to sit here without work in front of him. He set the wineglass aside, lifted a magazine off the table, also left in place by his housekeeper, and idly flipped through it before setting it aside as well.

He grunted what might've been a laugh. His father was right. Royce really *didn't* know how to unwind.

The doorbell chimed and he jumped off the couch, almost embarrassingly eager to invite whomever it was inside. Even if it was one of his siblings, he could still share a glass of wine if not the reason behind it. Shared wine with company was a hell of a lot better than sitting here alone.

The black-and-white security screen in the kitchen showed a woman standing on his front porch but she was too tall to be Gia. He leaned in for a closer look.

"Taylor?" His first thought was that something awful

had happened. Why else would she stop by unannounced? His second thought, after he'd yanked the door open, was that she was at the *wrong* house.

Her tiny trench coat was belted in the middle and hiding what he guessed was a very short dress. Her legs were smooth and tan, ending in a tall, spiked pair of heels. Her hair was slightly wavy, the same way it'd looked at the office except…bouncier.

Turned out he'd have someone to celebrate with after all.

Be practical. Practicality came as naturally as breathing for him.

But it wasn't easy to be practical with Taylor in front of him looking like sex in stilettos. She teetered, those tall spindles nestled in the crooks of his cobblestone porch. The shoes were black and wrapped enticingly around her ankles with delicate straps and tiny gold buckles. Those delicate straps led to shapely calves, cute knees and up, up to a pair of plush thighs.

An eager part of his anatomy gave a peppy jerk. He warned himself to stop staring—to be practical—but as in his office this afternoon, he was incapable of either.

His eyes reached the short, white, belted coat with big black buttons and continued to dark blond hair framing her beautiful face. A staggeringly gorgeous face. A face he'd have sworn to his brother before last weekend was passably pretty.

A lie.

Taylor, with her slightly parted full lips, high cheekbones dusted pink and long black lashes shielding shimmering brown eyes wasn't "passably" anything.

She was an absolute knockout.

"Good evening." She said it as sweetly as Red Riding Hood, but the twitch in her smile was almost predatory. Before he could warn himself to be practical again, before he could rein in his hope that she'd come here for a reason that was as far away from professional as imaginable, his father's words revisited him like the Ghost of Longing Past.

"You're also careful in the wrong ways. Being reckless is okay from time to time."

No, the world hadn't flown off the axis when he'd kissed Taylor—in fact, things were going his way. Could be this was a sign that he was on the right track rather than the wrong one.

Lucky for her he was a safe Big Bad Wolf to her Red Riding Hood. With a grin he gestured to his foyer. "Won't you come in?"

Ten

Go big or go home.

That'd been Taylor's mantra through drying off after her shower and refreshing her one-and-a-half-inch-barrel curls. From smoothing body oil over her legs and arms to letting the La Perla slip and slide over her smooth, sensitive skin. She'd dug through her underwear drawer and found the matching lace thong. She hadn't worn the thong before either, having categorized it as something she'd wear "someday" like the lingerie.

But now that she was standing in Royce's foyer wearing nothing but silk and lace, now that her hands were nervously tightening the belt on her trench coat, she worried that she'd gone *too* big. That maybe she *should* go home.

"Perfect timing. I had no one to celebrate with and here you are. Can I interest you in a glass of wine?" Royce asked casually as if her showing up at his residence at 10:00 p.m. in do-me heels and a very short trench was normal behavior.

"Sure."

He took her clutch and keys from her shaking hands and gestured to the closet in the foyer. "You can hang your coat if you like."

She worried for a hot second that he had X-ray vision and knew exactly what she wore beneath her coat—that he'd gleaned the real reason she'd come here.

"No. Thank you. I'm, uh…cold."

He dipped his head in a short nod, his expression revealing none of his thoughts. "Red Zin should help with that."

He moved to the kitchen and she walked into the living room. She'd been here once, shortly after he'd moved in five or six years ago. It'd been a great space then but lacked the warmth it exuded now. The cigar-colored leather couch and modern gas fireplace in the center of the wall made her want to curl up in her jammies with a good book.

"Your wine." A balloon-shaped, stemless glass appeared in front of her and she took it, ignoring that her palms were starting to sweat.

Her previous roar of womanhood had turned into a kitten's mew.

How disappointing.

Worse, her confidence was flagging. It was possible she'd read Royce's reaction today wrong. Maybe he hadn't been checking her out. Maybe for him, peeking at her cleavage was no more interesting than…than…the plant in his foyer. Was that so unbelievable? That he *could* resist her?

Ugh.

"Royce, listen…" Setting the wineglass down, she faced him, ready to excuse herself and apologize for barging in. She wasn't prepared to confess the truth, but the excuse of work might be plausible enough to explain away her being here.

Maybe.

"Have you changed your mind about the coat?" His question startled her speechless. She'd never felt so vulnerable in her life.

If she said no, she could blather on about Lowell Olsen some more, saying how she wanted to discuss strategies. Royce would listen patiently, dole out advice and then she'd be on her way home no worse for wear.

But if she said yes… If she allowed Royce to peel her out of the coat and stood before him in her underwear, well… There'd be no explaining away why she was here, would there?

She was at the ultimate point of no return.

He might wrap her up in her coat—or hell, the nearest blanket—and command her to "go home, young lady." Okay, probably he wouldn't say that, but the sentiment would be implied. She was younger than him by six years, and hadn't his age been trotted out as one of the reasons she wasn't supposed to take an interest in him?

It was possible that, aside from the anomaly at the gala, he *still* saw her as his youngest sister's best friend. Not a woman who wanted to strip him out of his suit and spend a good deal of time with him naked.

Fear pressed against the base of her throat as she considered the likelihood that she'd blown his behavior this week out of proportion. Maybe his slow glances weren't interest, but mere curiosity.

"Taylor?" His eyebrows pinched in confusion. This was her chance to undo the potentially cataclysmic choice she'd made to come here. Possibly her last chance to escape unscathed.

But another deeply rooted desire shouted in protest. This was also her last chance to grab hold of what she wanted. She'd never had a rebellious streak. Why not start now?

Royce's hand hovered in midair, poised to take her coat if she was brave enough to hand it over.

"So?" the horned devil on her shoulder whispered, "What's it going to be?" Before Taylor could consult the angel on her other shoulder, the winged-and-haloed hussy nodded her encouragement.

Damned if she did… Damned if she didn't.

"Yes." When the word eked past her throat she couldn't believe she'd actually said it. And when she reached for his hand and placed it over the knot on her trench coat, it was like watching a scene in a movie. "I want you to take it off."

Hand resting over one of his, her heart thundering so loud she could scarcely hear her own erratic breathing, she watched as his other hand joined the first. As his fingers began to gently unknot the belt at her waist…

For once, the pragmatic side of Royce's mind was as silent as if it'd been bound and gagged. There was another side of him, an animalistic side whose instincts trumped reason, that was in charge now.

Knot undone, he opened Taylor's coat, his fingers twitching over what he'd found beneath. Black silk with a subtle shimmer glided over her barely dressed body. She shifted and the material slipped tantalizingly over her breasts, drawing his attention to their hardening peaks.

This was no dress. This was sex sewn together with lace.

He consulted her face for a beat and in her expression found approval—and a question. Did he like what he saw?

"This is a pleasant surprise," he murmured.

Relief washed over her. "I was hoping you'd say that."

"Was there another option?"

"You could tell me to put my coat on and go home."

He couldn't imagine a scenario in which he said that.

He slowly removed her coat from her shoulders. "Is that what you want?"

Her head shook back and forth. *No.*

Good. That sure as hell wasn't what he wanted.

Draping the coat over the back of the couch, he slid his fingers over the impossibly smooth material wanting to touch her bare skin beneath it, which he'd bet was equally smooth. She smelled good, like the bowl of lemons on his countertop—a light citrusy scent that reminded him of summer. She brought her own sunshine on this February night, her eyes bright and earnest, her body arching toward him as he pulled her closer. And when he set his mouth to hers, she responded in the best way imaginable.

She crashed into him lips first, her hands smoothing over his button-down shirt, moving from his pectorals to his shoulders and around to the back of his head, where she gripped his hair.

He sneaked his tongue into her mouth and encountered her equally eager tongue, and the rest of his body moved closer to her as well. Hips first, he ground his erection against her center. A sultry moan sounded in her throat.

He left the haven of her mouth to kiss the gentle curve of her throat before moving to the sensitive skin behind her ear. Hands smoothing over her ribs, he hesitated at the swells of her generous breasts, giving her a chance to push him away. To stop the forward motion that began with her showing up at his house in naught but a scrap of silk and the tallest shoes he'd ever seen her wear.

Instead of stopping him, she cupped his hand and laid it over one breast, tugging his mouth to hers and renewing her efforts to kiss him stupid. With the thumb of his right hand he brushed over her nipple, his left hand joining in so that her other breast wasn't neglected.

She hissed his name on a tight breath, her eyes shut and head dropping back.

"Is this what you came for tonight, Taylor?" Confidence made his voice a growl.

Rarely did he indulge in decadence, save a tall slice of chocolate cake now and then when a craving hit. Taylor wasn't unlike the sinful dessert, her layers exposed. He knew once he took that first taste, he'd devour all of her.

"Yes, but…"

"But?" He lifted his head to watch her.

"I wasn't sure if you'd respond…favorably."

Taking one of her hands, he pressed it against his crotch, straining forward so she could feel just how "favorably" he'd reacted. Her pupils widened, all but swallowing the soft green-brown irises.

"Are you sure this is what you want?" The beast he'd unleashed howled in protest, but he needed her to be sure before they went any further. He'd been swept up before and wouldn't go in blindly again.

"Are you?" She stuck a finger in the knot of his bow tie and tugged. The rasping sound as she slid it from his collar sent goose bumps down his arms. She tossed the tie onto the floor, one eyebrow arched in question. "You didn't seem interested earlier today."

"I was at work." And trying his damnedest to focus. "What did you expect me to do?"

"Fair point." She smoothed her hands over his shoulders. He liked the way she looked at him, like he was a meal and she was starving.

His mind blanked of all thoughts save one: *Take her. Show her how beautiful and brave she is for showing up for you.*

Right when he needed her. Right where he wanted her. Before he'd known it himself.

He bent at the knees to smooth his palms under the lacy, satiny number and over her bare bottom. Thumb tracing the strap of her thong, it was his turn to groan.

He opened his mouth over her breast and lightly bit her nipple through the fabric. She clutched the back of his hair, her reaction an encouraging, "Oh God, Royce."

A wolfish grin emerged as he swept his mouth from her breast and slipped the thin straps off her shoulders. He bared her breasts and shimmied the material past her hips. It fell into a tiny black pool at her feet. One he could've sworn he'd fallen into, and was now careening into oblivion.

Tongue tracing her bare, puckered nipple, he slid one hand beneath the material of her thong, encountering her wetness. She tipped forward to ride his fingers, every slick, smooth glide sending his erection from rigid to damn painful. The torture was exquisite. He returned the favor, his mission to find out how much teasing she could stand. He suckled her nipple as she sighed his name.

"Yes, yes," came her next frantic whisper. She rode his hand in desperation, seeking her release. "Royce, please."

He straightened, his fingers moving double time against her, his eyes burning into hers. He wanted to watch her when she came. Watch her come apart in his hands, revel in the moment she achieved what she'd come here for: a powerful, and he'd bet beautiful, orgasm.

"What do you want, Taylor?" he asked with calm authority.

"This." Eyes closed, she held his shoulders for purchase.

"Describe 'this.'" He knew, but wanted to hear her say it. "Tell me. Please."

It was the *please* that tipped her. Her eyelids opened and her lust-blown gaze landed on his. "You. Touching me."

"Touching you how?" His control ebbed, his cock surging toward the woman who was making him want the one thing he shouldn't. *Her.*

Only now he couldn't remember why he shouldn't. Something about work and transition… Or was it that she was a colleague and they had to be a unified force…

The jumble of words in his head knotted themselves into a tangle. He couldn't focus on anything but the woman in his arms.

"I need… I need…" Her brows bent, her mouth dropping open as her cheeks flushed. He watched her face contort and felt the warm rush of moisture on his fingers. When her knees slackened, he locked an arm around her waist and held her up. She drooped her arms around his neck lazily.

Seconds later, she blew out a breath that ended on a soft, satisfied hum.

"You're gorgeous when you come, Taylor."

An ethereal goddess, to be precise.

Her smile spread on her face like honey dripping off warm toast, her front teeth stabbing her bottom lip as she fisted back his hair. "I bet you are, too."

He liked her boldness. She'd always possessed that attribute but until the gala it'd never been directed toward him. When she kissed him, it sent him into a weightless, uncontrolled spin. He couldn't seem to find "up" again, couldn't make himself care about the consequences he'd held so precious not long ago.

"Only one way to find out," he heard himself say.

Lifting her naked body into his arms, he carried her to the couch. The moment her back hit the leather she began working his belt through the buckle.

Eleven

She'd had no idea what to name the craving that had shaken her for the last week, but now she understood what the hunger had been about. What she'd been hungry for was *him*.

Before Royce sent his fingers into a one-man banjo solo over the most sensitive part of her body, she'd have sworn she was doing fine on her own in that department. What could possibly be the difference between a man's fingers and her own?

Now she had no idea where to start counting. The rough pads versus smooth? The not knowing what he would do next versus her own evenly timed strokes? Or the dirty, delicious way he talked to her during?

Yes. To all of the above.

Aftershocks shook her shoulders as she relived the best orgasm she'd had in literally *years*.

But she couldn't chastise herself for not sleeping with someone sooner. Instinctually she knew that anyone other than Royce wouldn't have delivered as well.

Even after he removed her coat she'd half expected him to turn her down. With him, calm practicality reigned supreme.

Not this version of him, though. He was different tonight. Looser and more open. Eager to please her.

Royce pushed his slacks along with his boxer briefs off his muscular legs. He stood before her, his heavy erection standing against a backdrop of ab muscles she'd had no idea were there. His lips twitched into a smile as he peeled the starched white shirt from his glorious chest. The right amount of wiry hair dusted his pecs and led from his belly button to the part of him she couldn't wait to experience.

The dampness between her legs renewed, a warm trickle sliding through her as she mentally prepared for all that length, all that strength covering her. Clothes in hand, he tucked them against his body and bent to kiss her lightly on the mouth. "Be back."

"Wh-where are you going?" She propped herself up on her elbows, watching his clenching and contracting ass moved away from her and down the hallway.

"Condom," he called as he vanished into the darkness.

Right. Protection. She eased down on the couch, allowing herself a small laugh at her forgetfulness—or maybe it was the sheer joy of getting exactly what she wanted with relative ease.

He didn't stay gone long, padding barefoot back to her. His hand wrapped around himself, he rolled on the protection she was glad one of them remembered. He lowered himself onto the couch and she parted her thighs to accept him. His warm-bordering-hot skin came in contact with her greedy nipples and she gasped at the sensation.

"I like your hair this way." He wrapped one of her curls around his finger. "I noticed it this morning."

"That wasn't all you noticed."

Looking over his shoulder at the high heels still strapped to her feet, he gave her a feral grin. "Lock those around my thighs."

She did as she was told, her body naturally tilting to accept him. When he nudged her entrance she accepted him inch by glorious inch, but made sure she kept her eyes open. Watching him endure the slow torture of entering her was sheer joy, and one he savored. He stretched her intentionally before he began to move. Seated to the root, he let out a sound resembling a growl.

"You looked as innocent as Red Riding Hood on my porch, but there was something wild in your eyes."

"Wild, as in unhinged?" A breath hissed from between her teeth as he pulled out and slid in again—so smooth, so good.

"Wild, as in you're not as safe as you look."

"Are you the wolf in this scenario?" She toyed with his hair, loving talking during sex. Unique, this entire encounter.

"Maybe we're both wolves." His next thrust wasn't as careful as the one before it, brushing her G-spot and causing her brain to skip like a smooth rock over a still pond.

Before she sank beneath the surface she forced him back into focus. "You're the wolf."

He winked. Winked!

"I like you like this," she said, unsure what she'd meant by that until she continued speaking. "Unable to resist me."

"You make it hard, Taylor Thompson."

"Quite the double entendre."

"Keep up that smart mouth and I'll double my efforts."

"Threat or promise?"

He was still for a second. "A threat you'll beg for after how good I make you feel." He kissed her lips quickly. Proving his ability to blot out her mind, he doubled his efforts. Each stroke deeper, more frantic. Her fingernails dragged down the skin of his back, leaving stripes. She fought to hold on to him while slipping off the side of the planet. Voice strained with effort, he said, "Let's see that O face again, Red."

"Let's see if you can bring it, *Wolf*." It was a challenge he accepted.

He nestled one of her knees in the crook of his elbow, lifting her leg and deepening their connection. She couldn't form any words other than "Yes, Royce, yes."

Pleased by her reaction, his smile turned rogue. Refusing to go into the abyss alone, she gripped him with her internal muscles. Surprise colored his face for a beat before he captured her mouth with his.

Seconds later, his head bucked. He bared his teeth, his hips pistoning, the slick skin of their thighs gently slapping. She watched the entire display, smugly satisfied to have her theory proven.

He was *quite* gorgeous when coming.

"They're clean." Royce handed over a pair of leggings and an MIT sweatshirt. "Gia stopped by here to change for the gala and left them. They've been laundered."

He announced it evenly, as if having his clothes laundered rather than doing it himself was a normal, everyday occurrence. She supposed for the Knox family it was. She'd never seen Gia load a washing machine.

When Taylor moved from her parents' house and rented her sizable apartment, she found she enjoyed cleaning her own space. As soon as she was promoted to COO and her hours increased, she hired a part-time housekeeper. With the hours she worked, it was impossible to do it all, but she kept a few tasks on her own to-do list.

One, cooking—the kitchen was a bright, open space

that sparked her creativity—and two, her laundry. It wasn't about finding joy in domesticity, a trait she definitely *hadn't* inherited from her mother. She was particular about her clothes and what didn't have to be dry-cleaned she cared for herself. It didn't make sense for Royce, with his array of starched shirts and suits and bow ties, to stand around doing the wash.

"Thanks." She accepted the clothes, covering herself with the slip first. She was strangely nervous now that they'd had sex, and him standing over her made her feel more vulnerable. "Could you…?"

"Oh. Sorry. I'll give you a minute." His frown returned like it'd never left and she wondered if she'd imagined the smooth-talking, smiling man who'd just turned her inside out.

Neither of them reacted as expected. She'd come here to seduce him, until her spine had turned temporarily weak. He'd reacted the complete opposite—pouncing on her the second she gave the okay.

"No. Wait. Sit down." She lifted her hips and rolled on her thong as discreetly as possible. Royce sat, his eyes glued to her legs. "We don't have to make this weird."

"Too late." His dry tone held a note of humor.

She tugged on the black leggings next, grateful to Gia for leaving them behind. As the clock ticked on, the temperature was dropping. Taylor didn't want to drive home wearing only a slip and a tiny trench coat if she didn't have to.

"No, we don't have to make this weird." He leaned an elbow on the arm of the sofa and raised his wineglass as she pulled the sweatshirt over her head. It was butter-soft and elephant gray, the wide neck falling off one of her shoulders. Royce's eyes didn't leave that swatch of bared skin, where the strap of her slip was visible.

"So." She lifted her wineglass, too, snuggling into the

opposite corner of his couch. "It's taken ten years for you to notice I'm a woman."

He rolled the wine around his mouth before swallowing. "I noticed."

"You did?" That shocked her down to her chilly toes.

He chuckled, his chest expanding within the deep navy blue T-shirt he'd paired with baggy pajama bottoms. His feet were bare. He had nice feet. Big feet, but nice. She'd never dated a guy who wore pajama bottoms, had she? Sweats, yes; boxers, sure; but cotton pajama bottoms with skinny navy blue pinstripes? Not that she could recall.

"I'm surprised you care," he said.

She made a choking sound in the back of her throat.

"Not a blow-off," he amended. "More an honest observation. You were Gia's best friend, closer to Brannon's age than mine. What would an eighteen-year-old want from a twenty-four-year-old, anyway? Did you expect me to scoop you up and steal away your virginity?"

"Joke would've been on you since I'd lost my virginity two years prior." She hoisted an eyebrow, pleased when his lips twitched. "You were twenty-four, not forty-four. It wouldn't have been that unbelievable for us to date back then." But even as she said it, she had her doubts. He'd had his sights set on college girls, not a high school senior who dreaded showing up to every richie-rich function their parents made them attend. He'd had no clue she'd watched him, admiring his breadth and height. The way he held himself. Always the confident one, his walk tall and words evenly spaced. Bran was quicker to laugh and less serious, which she enjoyed in a friendship, but boyfriend material to her was and always would be a man she could count on.

Like my father.

She swallowed the unexpected lump of emotion and swiftly changed the subject. "You could have asked me to be your date at any one of the charity functions I had to be dragged to."

"And here we are a decade later still attending them." His tone hinted that he found them as asinine as she did.

"You don't enjoy going?" She genuinely believed Royce didn't mind attending stuffy functions and donning tuxedos and bow ties. He fit in, drink in hand, genial expression on his face no matter who he was conversing with.

"Hide it well, don't I?" He lifted an eyebrow. The slightly roguish expression went well with his relaxed attire and the sex-warmed buzz vibrating her limbs.

"You hide lots of things well." The words were muttered against the rim of her wine glass. She liked sharing this slice of time with him. In his space, the fire burning in front of them—the one burning *between* them. She liked sharing wine and truths while sitting three feet apart.

"I do what's expected of me. Always have." He shrugged. "Consummate firstborn."

She was sure the last thing anyone would "expect" was for him to take Taylor Thompson to bed—er, to couch. And no one would have put money on her showing up to seduce him, either. A bubble of pride lifted her chest. Finally, she'd taken what she wanted.

"The Valentine's Day gala has always been my least favorite. Until this year. *Coincidentally.*"

She caught his heated gaze and returned it, the air between them practically igniting. He cupped her toes with one large, warm hand.

"Want some socks too?"

"Thanks, but I have to strap those puppies back on." She pointed to the shoes beneath the coffee table, which were about as inviting as an iron maiden. She'd kicked them off when he went to change, past ready to give her toes a break.

"I like them, if it's any consolation." He gave her foot a

squeeze, a gesture that felt familiar even though it'd never happened before.

"I bet I was the last person you expected to find standing on your porch tonight." It'd been outrageous to expect sex simply because she showed up almost naked, but her instincts were rarely wrong.

"The very last. I half thought you were Bran coming to kick my ass. Figured Dad told him…" His lips pressed together like he'd said too much. "Nevermind."

Did he really expect her to let a whopper like that one go?

"What? What did you think Jack told him?"

Tongue swiping his bottom lip, Royce seemed to turn over telling her versus not. He stood and crossed the room to fetch a thin blanket, tossing it over her before he continued, which was sweet.

Wineglass in hand, he watched out the large window behind the dining room table.

"CEO is mine."

She blinked, shocked. She couldn't have been more surprised if she'd found Royce standing at *her* front door wearing naught but a trench coat.

"How…do you feel about it?" She had to ask. She couldn't read his tone or his body language.

"It's my responsibility."

"Do you want it?"

"Of course," he snapped. A warning. Best not to push the topic. They slept together but it didn't grant her entry into his inner circle.

Boundaries were important. They had a lot at stake—more now that Royce was going to be named CEO. Sneaking around wasn't the wisest course of action.

"I should go." She threw off the blanket. "Early day tomorrow. Breakfast with my mom."

He didn't argue, but what had she expected? A heartfelt plea that she strip out of her clothes and follow him to the bedroom? Romance wasn't in the cards for them—especially when she'd started them off on a very unromantic note. Sexy yes, romantic… Not so much.

She buckled her uncomfortable shoes and stood. Royce followed behind her without a second's hesitation. Once they entered the mouth of the foyer, he handed over her clutch and keys. Outside a crisp breeze blew the palm fronds overhead, black against a blacker night sky.

"Good night." Sweeping her hair behind her ears, she guessed a good-night kiss was pushing it. "Congratulations. On CEO."

She turned to walk to her car parked in the driveway when he said her name. Hope rose fierce and full, pressing against her breastbone.

Ask me to stay.

He descended one porch step, all that capable masculine beauty hovering over her. Then he opened his mouth and "Don't say anything to Brannon or Gia" came out.

"Oh. Sure." She nodded. That hope deflated, going limp in her chest and sagging her lungs.

He folded his arms over his chest to ward off the air's chill. "Mom and Dad want to tell them separately. Before the official announcement is made at the ThomKnox offices."

Words failed her.

He nodded, a succinct dip of his chin before he walked back inside and shut the door.

So much for romance.

Twelve

Jack Knox's birthday dinner was held at the Hourglass, a posh fourteen-room hotel in San Francisco that was formerly, of all things, a marble factory. Recently overhauled and designed by Mercury Hill, an acclaimed architecture firm, the building echoed elegance from a hundred years ago while still maintaining a bohemian feel.

The backdrop of the bar was chalkboard-black wood, the floors were a herringbone pattern, and the columns black with contrasting white wood grain. Curved, stuffed chairs in tones of brick red, olive green and deep gray surrounded brass-edged tables dotted with cocktail napkins, on which sat a variety of glasses. Lowball, highball, flutes and the occasional beer glass.

Royce arrived by car, Gia in tow. It occurred to him to invite Taylor to join them, but since he wouldn't have normally asked her to join him, he didn't. The way they'd parted last night left him confused, but then he wasn't great at reading women—this woman in particular.

He preferred his situations black-and-white, like a spreadsheet. Each bit of information in a clearly marked box. Outlined. Precise. Relationships, and women in general, were not so easily contained.

Taylor was about as navigable as a ship in a storm.

They'd had sex—exquisite sex. Did that mean he should call her? Were they dating? The more he thought about it, the more aggravated he became. He'd decided before he arrived to compartmentalize that bit of info. Tonight was about his father's birthday. That was it.

"The man of the hour is on his way!" Bran announced to the crowd, loud enough to be heard by those who had wandered out to the rooftop seating area. He pocketed his cell phone, his smile bright and his shoulders back. It was good to see him not pissed off. Royce guessed their parents hadn't broken the CEO news to him, or else his brother would be a lot less happy. He'd also noticed, during the hour-long drive with his sister, that Gia wasn't in the know, either. She undoubtedly would have brought it up.

"Scotch for you, sir." The bartender served Royce his drink.

"Thank you." Royce had been here for less than five minutes so he hadn't taken inventory of the room. He guesstimated sixty-plus people in attendance for the party that was scheduled to start at eight o'clock, the man of the hour to arrive not fashionably late, but *Jack* late. Jack was on time when he needed to be—he never missed a meeting. But for casual functions like this one he kept his arrival to a fifteen-to-twenty-minute window after the party was scheduled to start. Royce would venture that everyone knew tonight had a twofold purpose for his father: a birthday celebration and a retirement announcement.

Taylor approached him wearing a basic black dress and a smile. Though modest, the frock sent his mind to the gutter. The skirt was knee length and hugged curves he now knew a lot about, and the neckline reminded him of her lingerie—her in it and out of it. Of her undulating beneath him, her mouth open to sigh his name. Of the thong he'd peeled off her long legs. He wondered if she wore a similar undergarment tonight. Judging by the soft outline of her breasts and shy press of her nipples against the fabric, she hadn't worn much beneath the dress.

"Hi," he said. Because *Are you wearing underwear?* wasn't polite.

"You made it." She carried an empty wineglass, apparently catching him on her return to the bar.

"White or red?" He took her glass.

"Rosé."

Leave it to Taylor to choose the undefinable in-between. He found himself smiling as he placed her order.

"Fitting," he said, handing her a full glass of pink wine. But he meant more than her being in the middle of two certainties. "Nearly the color of your cheeks when you came to visit me last night."

Those murmured words took him by surprise— flirting wasn't exactly his MO—but Taylor always drew the unexpected from him.

She lifted her glass to her lips and the heavy gem-studded bangle on her wrist caught the overhead light.

"I've never been here before." She glanced around the room, the brass light fixtures bent to highlight the paintings on the wall, some of them fox-and-hound hunting paintings, others splashy abstracts that complemented the furniture.

"The bar is one of my favorites, and not only because they carry 1926 Macallan." He raised his own glass. "I like the chairs. They look like they belong in a seedy bar, but they're the finest leather, and damn comfortable."

"They snub pretension here."

"There's a painting of dogs playing poker in the men's lavatory."

Her eyes widened. "Really?"

"No." He grinned, enjoying teasing her.

She laughed, demurely tilting her head to the side. The move sent her hair over her shoulder, the blond and brown strands sliding into a unique pattern.

"You changed your hair."

"I had it done today." She sifted a hand through the silken locks and again he was drawn in by the way the various colors fell. "How observant of you."

He opened his mouth to tell her what he'd noticed last night. The pink in her cheeks, the citrusy scent that clung to his skin after she left. The way her hair had tickled his arms whenever he drove into her. The way he woke up this morning with a hard-on, the echoes of her hoarse cries of completion ringing in his ears...

"Hello, good people." Bran swaggered over, beer in hand.

"Bran," Royce greeted.

Taylor put distance between herself and Royce, but Bran didn't seem to notice, leaning in to kiss her cheek.

"You look nice." She nodded approvingly at Bran's casual slacks and button-down.

Royce felt the uncomfortable prickle of jealousy. She hadn't mentioned his suit and bow tie ensemble.

"Ready for anything," Bran said, his gaze seeking the door again for their father's arrival.

Dammit. He doesn't know.

Jack was spontaneous. Liked the spotlight. Even though his father had told Royce he'd announce CEO in a meeting at work, part of him wondered if their father had something a bit more spontaneous in mind.

"There he is!" someone shouted, moving in from the

rooftop toward the front door. Jack entered, their mother Macy on his arm, and lifted a hand to wave.

"Let the party begin!" Jack shouted when someone placed a drink in his hand.

Bran was the first to approach their father and embrace him, Gia second. Royce hung back, allowing close friends and coworkers to go ahead of him.

"Your dad. So *caj*," Taylor said next to his ear.

"What is that?"

"*Caj?* It's short for casual."

"Short for casual? Is it such a long word that we needed to shorten it?"

"Showing your age again, Royce." She winked, standing closer to allow space for the press of bodies that had gravitated toward Jack like he was sun to their planets.

"Which reminds me. I have to be in the car on my way home by nine."

"Oh?" He loved the look of disappointment that swam over her features. Like she'd miss him when he left.

"That's when I watch my true crime shows and work my evening crossword puzzle."

It took her a second to realize he was kidding. "Tease."

He leaned in, mostly to smell her lemony skin. "You started it."

She held his gaze, not bothering to move away from him this time. He liked being close to her. Without anyone in the way. Without any expectations. How rare for him to enjoy anything without expectations.

"Have you seen the rooftop?" he asked.

"But the guest of honor is in here." She pointed at Jack.

"No," Royce disagreed, taking her elbow. "She's right here."

He led them away from the crowd and onto the now-abandoned private rooftop.

Thirteen

The deep navy sky made up her third-favorite part of the ambience on the rooftop lounge. Closing in on second was the modern, square fire table surrounded by chairs. First place belonged to the man who'd walked her out here.

Royce's deep gray jacket was paired with dark trousers, and she caught a peek of suspenders over a crisp, white shirt when he'd turned to lead her outside. The bow tie was her favorite, though. Navy with a silver sheen, yet somehow casual enough to work with the rest of his outfit.

He undid a button on his jacket and pulled out a chair for her. She sat, curling her wine against her chest. Fire or not, the wind hit her and she bristled. A detail he noticed. A moment later her shoulders were covered by his suit jacket. He sat in the chair next to hers and she admired him unabashedly.

Suspenders. White shirt. Bow tie.

Purr.

She was so into him. After the awkward way they'd parted last night she hadn't expected him to be so open.

Jack Knox's laugh drew her attention. Inside, he tossed his white head back, his smile gleaming.

"He doesn't act sixty-something. But you do." She tilted her head at Royce. "Odd."

"Very funny." He canted an eyebrow.

"I didn't tell Gia or Bran, by the way. About us *or the other thing.*" She widened her eyes meaningfully.

"I figured. I rode here with her tonight. If Gia knew, she'd have brought it up. She's not one to keep her feelings to herself."

"I didn't realize you two came together."

He seemed to debate sharing more before saying, "Since her and Jayson's divorce, she leans on me as a travel companion. Don't tell her I told you that. She'll castrate me."

Taylor nodded. Her friend was independent, capable. Gia wouldn't want anyone to know she relied on her big brother for transportation.

"She did ask if there were any further developments where we were concerned." Royce sipped his drink, letting Taylor sweat that out for a few seconds before he shook his head. "I said no."

She didn't enjoy keeping secrets from her best friend, but until Taylor had a handle on what was going on with Royce, she wasn't going to tell Gia anything.

As if on cue, Gia's voice rose behind them. "So this is where the party's at!" She plopped down next to Royce and slapped his knee. "What up, bro?"

"We didn't want to interfere with the ass-kissing. How'd it go?" He swiped her nose with one finger and she glared.

"Don't give me that brownnose spiel. You're the one vying for CEO."

Royce's expression darkened as he exchanged glances with Taylor.

"They should put you in a ring and make you and Bran fight to the death. Like gladiators," Gia added gleefully. "Tay and I would enjoy that."

"There'll be no fighting to the death. Sorry to disappoint you. I will accept Dad's decision."

Gia grew silent, her gaze fastened to her oldest brother.

"What?" Royce's face was a neutral mask, but Gia reacted as if the truth were written on his forehead.

"It's you, isn't it?"

"I— How—"

Brannon's telltale good-natured laugh drifted over their heads next. He walked out, Cooper at his side, and joined their group. Gia kept an eye on Royce, but didn't say more.

An hour later, most of the sixty-eight guests—Addison counted—had left the party for a variety of reasons. The dozen or so of them remaining converged on the rooftop. Additional heaters on stands had been lit to thwart the cold, the flames reflecting off the six-foot-high glass overlooking the city. Above that barrier, a crescent moon stamped the center of a star-pocked sky.

Taylor was still wearing Royce's jacket, which was warm and smelled like him: *incredible*. No one had mentioned it, but Gia had given her a lengthy look that said *we'll talk later*.

Jayson Cooper sat next to Gia, a few inches between the two exes on a short white bench. Bran relaxed in a chair next to Taylor. They were talking about how ill-suited for retirement Jack was, and how gracefully he'd aged.

"I'm glad I inherited the thickness of his hair," Gia said. "But the headful of white can wait."

"What's this?" Cooper touched a strand of Gia's dark brown hair. "Looks like you're getting a head start."

"Stop it!" Gia slapped his hand away.

He grinned, and Taylor shook her head at Gia. "He's teasing you. Your hair is gray-free and beautiful. And still chestnut in color."

Cooper chuckled. "That gets her every time."

"This is why we're divorced." Gia's smile was patronizing.

"That and your inability to admit when I'm right," Coop replied with an easy smile.

Those two. Taylor shook her head, unsure what to make of their bickering. Sometimes it sounded like flirting, other times like they were navigating the difficult landscape of friendship after a divorce.

"I'd like to make a toast." Jack stepped out of the circle of people with whom he was conversing and raised his bottle of water. "And an announcement."

Royce once again looked to Taylor, and she schooled her expression. Only Jack knew what Jack planned on announcing, but judging by Royce's grim expression, she wondered if the CEO announcement would happen sooner than expected.

Jack Knox gestured to the glass wall surrounding the rooftop. "You know… I should've arranged for a group BASE jump while we're all here."

Royce shook his head, unsure if his old man was joking or not. Lately Jack had shown interest in a lot of adventurous pastimes, though diving off a building in a city was illegal, so hopefully he wasn't serious about that one.

"If you're here it's because I've asked you not to leave." Jack switched gears with a jolt. "Not to worry, the staff was polite when they used cattle prods to blast those others out of here early."

In the remaining crowd were Royce's parents, his siblings, Taylor, Taylor's mother, Deena, who'd arrived about an hour ago, Addison, Whitney and a handful of others from the board and upper management. All trusted insiders.

"Thank you for making my sixty-second birthday special." Jack walked through the crowd while he talked. "I never thought ThomKnox would grow to be as big as it is. When Charlie and I started this company we wanted to avoid the confines of a big corporate office while giving ourselves—and the people who work for us—the trappings of a great place life. Then, my children joined the ranks." He cupped Bran's shoulder before resting a hand on Taylor's shoulder next. "And Charlie's daughter."

Her smile was pained yet grateful, with another emotion behind it Royce couldn't place. It uncoiled a sense of longing within him he didn't recognize. He *wanted* to know what emotions had splintered her smile. And why.

Another new reaction to this woman. They just kept coming.

"I didn't expect to be a tech leader, but what I really didn't expect was for Charles to be gone." Jack squeezed Taylor's shoulder and her eyes closed.

Losing Charles was still fresh. Grief rang tuning-fork true when Jack moved to Deena and softly kissed her cheek.

"We've reached yet another fork in the road of Thom-Knox," Jack said. "I'm not getting any younger, and if you ask Macy she'll tell you I'm trying my damnedest to age backward."

"It's true," his mother addressed the crowd. "Just ask our new Ferrari."

The crowd laughed on cue.

Jack held out a hand to quiet them. "It's time for me to go and do some of those things Charlie and I imagined we'd do after retirement. But I am leaving you in capable hands in my absence. Brannon has served as President and our darling genius daughter, who inherited her father's legendary brains, has kept us on the edge of relevance, along with our own tech superhero Jayson Cooper."

"How smart can she be if she let me go?" Cooper draped his arm over his ex-wife's shoulders and pulled her close to kiss her temple.

"You're a moron," Gia told him, but she smiled anyway.

"And Royce." Standing behind him now, Jack cupped his oldest son's shoulder. "Royce has been CFO for as long as I can remember. He's the nerdiest of all of us, and that's saying something for a tech company." More laughter.

Royce's grimace wasn't due to his father's jibes, but at the premonition of where this speech would end.

"He's capable," Jack continued, "he's confident. And as of now, he's your new CEO."

The announcement was made in the same easygoing tone as the rest of the speech. A palpable silence fell as the crowd absorbed the news.

Jack Knox had named his successor.

"I knew it!" Gia was the first to say.

Bran frowned.

"To Royce!" Jack raised his water bottle and a smattering of "cheers" and "congratulations" lifted one after another in clunky refrain.

"Speech!" someone called. "Speech! Speech!"

Dammit, Dad.

This wasn't how the announcement should've happened. There was *supposed* to be a discussion ahead of time with Bran and Gia. They were *supposed* to be in a meeting at work with a bullet-pointed agenda. Jack wanted a BASE jump? This bombshell came close.

"Go on, son. Address your underlings," Jack said.

Royce stood, his glare affixed on his father. "We had an agreement."

Jack shrugged with his mouth. "Things change."

Royce took a long look at the man he'd admired his entire life and realized he was too angry to say anything productive. So instead he turned to Cooper and asked, "Can you give Gia a ride home?"

"Um…" Jayson looked at Gia.

"I'll give Gia a ride home," Taylor offered with a subtle nod. One that said *Go. I have this.*

So he turned on his heel and left.

Without giving a damn speech.

"Two rosés, please," Gia told the bartender at her apartment's lobby bar.

"I can't," Taylor told her. "I'll sit with you, though." The glass and a half of rosé at the party felt like it was still sitting in her throat after Royce's surprising exit.

"No speech then," Jack had said to the crowd, but the comment didn't earn many smiles. Tension was thick in the air. The music started up again and, little by little, conversations restarted. Bran had been silent, his face unreadable. Gia's wasn't as much of a mystery.

They'd stayed only fifteen minutes or so more before Gia hooked Taylor's arm and suggested they leave, too. Fine by Taylor. She'd had enough of the strange evening.

Now, wineglasses in front of them, Gia pushed Taylor's closer. "Just one."

She couldn't turn down her friend. They needed to talk anyway and what Taylor had to say was best discussed over even the most meager amount of alcohol.

"No gray hairs, you swear?"

Taylor held up a palm. "Hand to God."

"Jay." Gia shook her head. "When is he going to back off and get a life?"

"When are you?" Taylor teased, raising an eyebrow.

"Bitch!" Gia laughed the word, giving Taylor a playful shove in the arm before laying her head on Taylor's shoulder. "You'd think he'd have found some new woman to tease."

"You'll always be teased by Jayson Cooper," Taylor said, confident she was right. "Has he even been on a date since you two split?"

"God. I hope so. I hope both of us haven't been celibate for the last year-plus."

"You'd have my sympathy if I hadn't gone *two* years before sleeping with someone." Taylor sipped her wine, not realizing until her friend's mouth dropped open that she'd just confessed the end to her own celibacy.

"*Who?* Who did you sleep with recently?" Gia had been Taylor's own personal cheerleader these last few years. Taylor had confessed she didn't feel anything sexually after Seth left. Her father's diagnosis had only added to her brokenness. Gia had comforted her, saying, "When you're ready, you'll know. No rush."

Taylor took a gulp of her wine, though fortifying herself with the drink meant sticking around longer than she intended. "Before I tell you, you have to promise not to be mad."

"Oh shit. You slept with Brannon?"

"No. I slept with Royce."

Gia's dark eyes rounded. She hadn't been expecting that. "Royce as in my oldest, glorified accountant brother?"

"That's the one. I showed up at his house last night wearing that La Perla slip I've had for way too long."

Gia gaped at her. "Why?"

Valid question.

"My dad."

Her friend's eyebrows rose.

"He cautioned me against dating Royce over the years.

Said he was too old for me. I guess after the kiss at the gala, and the way Royce has been looking at me…"

"He's been *looking* at you? Why didn't you tell me any of this!" Gia's tone was accusatory, and deservedly so. Taylor normally told her friend everything.

"I wasn't sure. He's run a little hot and cold. Until last night. Then it was full-blast *hot*."

"Man." Gia shook her head. "How did I miss that tonight?"

"We're good actors."

"Well, how was it?"

"How was what?" Taylor spun her glass on the bar top and feigned ignorance.

"The sex," Gia said. Loudly. The bartender blinked from his computer screen over to them until Gia addressed him with a stern, "Do you mind?"

"Let's say it was a hell of a way to end the drought," Taylor said meaningfully.

"Wow. I have been in the dark."

"It only happened last night."

"Did you know about CEO, too?" Gia had easily fit those two puzzle pieces together.

"I did. But in Royce's defense, your dad asked him not to say anything to you or Bran. Jack was supposed to tell you and then announce it in a meeting."

"Leave it to Dad to make a scene." Gia chewed on her lip. "I couldn't tell if Bran was okay or not."

When they left, Bran was talking with Addison, and the conversation appeared intense. Taylor wondered if Bran had been using Addi as a distraction to avoid talking to his father.

"Well. Brannon is a grown man," Gia said in conclusion. "And you two are okay, right?"

"Yes, completely. I think you were close when you

guessed he was proposing to win CEO. He'd die before he'd admit that was true."

"I'll strangle him after I strangle Royce for not telling me about CEO." Gia sighed. "Did you eat enough at the party?"

"Not even close."

"No one can survive on canapés alone." Gia waved over the bartender. "What's your best appetizer?"

"I'm trained to say they're all good, but for my money you can't beat the spinach dip or the fried pepper jack cheese bites."

"Both?" Gia asked Taylor.

"Both," she confirmed.

Fourteen

After the new CEO was announced on Monday morning, the offices at ThomKnox were buzzing with excitement—and gossip. Taylor had plenty to handle without the nervous phone calls, emails and sideline chats from the legion of managers she oversaw. The captain of the ship was retiring and with that guard change came a lot of nervousness and fear.

Will this change my retirement plans?

Are there other changes to management?

Will my department be restructured?

And so on and so on.

On Tuesday morning, when she'd dared poke her head out of her own office, she'd witnessed a heated conversation going on in Royce's office. Brannon, Jack and Royce were all in there, and while she couldn't hear their voices, the expressions on their faces through the window suggested they weren't exactly *simpatico*.

The week that was long by Tuesday felt like it'd lasted a

month by Friday's tablet commercial premiere. The executive conference room was packed with upper-crust Thom-Knox management, Jack included.

"This will be my last meeting," he announced. "But I couldn't miss sharing the commercial for our new tablet, the T13. This seven-minute commercial was directed and designed by Downey Design out of Chicago…"

While Jack spoke, Taylor took the temperature of the room. Gia tapped a rose gold pen on her planner, listening—or acting like she was listening. Cooper was leaned back in a chair, arms folded, also listening. Brannon was glaring at Royce and Royce glaring back at him.

So.

There were some unresolved issues.

"Let's have a look, shall we?" Jack shut off the lights and played the commercial.

The video was dark, a ribbon of light sweeping along the edge of a streamlined tablet that looked more like a curvy sports car than a flat computer.

Royce leaned back in his chair and whatever pheromones had been dormant this week permeated the air around her. The room was dark, her senses heightened. She felt him shift infinitesimally closer, and when she heard his rough exhale she recalled the way his warm breath coasted along her neck the last time he kissed her. When he cleared his throat she heard his phantom commands. *Come for me, Taylor. Now.*

Fantasies had plagued her even though she'd been away from him for a week. She considered how right he was about suggesting they keep their distance during such a monumental power shift at work. This was a distraction none of them needed.

It'd been easy to avoid him during the hectic week, but now that they were in this dark room, side by side—

One of Royce's fingers skimmed over her hand and then along her wrist. She sucked in a sharp breath. He tickled her wrist along the edge of her bracelet and she swallowed down a lump of lust. Innocuous, that touch. A mere brush of his skin on hers. And yet she shifted in her seat, distracted and turned on.

She checked to see if anyone noticed. Everyone watched the screen while the voice-over described the stunning new features of the T13. She should be watching, too, but she couldn't concentrate on anything save Royce's hand, now stroking her leg.

He brushed her knee, then higher. The rhythm he set— slow, firm, a whisper of a touch and then a gentle squeeze— was driving her wild. She leaned forward and pretended to write on the notebook in front of her.

The video reached its crescendo as his warm hand slipped beneath her skirt and he gripped her inner thigh firmly. She wouldn't dare look at him. Wouldn't show him the desire in her eyes, igniting her every limb.

Evidently he didn't need the encouragement. He tickled her knee one last time before pulling his hand away. In the dim light, he raised his eyebrows as if to say *Your turn*.

He was challenging her?

Not wise, Knox.

After a furtive glance around the room, she slid her palm over his thigh and higher. He jerked in his seat, feigning a cough while he shifted in his chair. Her Cheshire smile would've been obvious if anyone was looking at her, but they weren't. She palmed Royce's crotch and met his dark gaze in the darker room. His intense expression was highlighted by the glow of the screen. They locked eyes for a beat, then two, before she swept her hand from his hardening cock.

She exhaled slowly, her heart racing, her body warm

and ready. Where was a closet when you needed one? She wanted nothing more than to grab him by the ears and kiss him until both of them were gasping for breath or tearing at each other's clothes. Whichever came first.

Applause jolted her out of her stupor, and the lights slowly rose. Royce looked equally shell-shocked, though a better word might be *horny*.

"Thoughts?" Jack asked the room before taking his chair next to Royce. "Let's start with you, CEO."

Royce, scrumptiously flustered, straightened his bow tie. "I'm intrigued. At first I thought it wasn't for me. A version of this product has been around for years and I've never once been tempted. But this tease—" He gestured to the screen, but Taylor knew exactly what—*who*—he was talking about. "I've changed my mind. It's too sexy to ignore. It's unforgettable. I want more." He slanted a heated look at her. "What about you, COO?"

She ignored the warmth of her cheeks and addressed him directly. "I've had my eye on this one for a while. I was waiting for the right moment to bring it into my life. It could be the game changer I didn't know I was looking for."

The comments continued around the room. Her eyes watched her coworkers but her body was focused on only one person. The man she couldn't keep her head or hands off—the man she didn't want to keep her hands off any longer… Damn the consequences.

The executive team filed out of the conference room, Royce in the lead. He paused to open the door for Taylor, who put extra wiggle in her walk for his benefit. His eyes were glued to her ass, tucked neatly into a navy blue dress. Her tall red high heels were distracting to the nth degree.

Royce waited at the door watching everyone leave. Brannon hung back, as did Jack.

Gia turned to Royce, her attitude set to stun. "Are you guys over your snit?"

Thinking she was referring to him and Taylor, he wisely didn't speak.

"Subtle, Gia," Brannon said. "What'd you expect me to do? Overturn the conference table?"

Ah. She was referring to the heated discussion between Jack, Bran and Royce earlier this week in Royce's office.

"We have a company to run, boys," she said to her brothers. To Dad, she said, "Except for you. Aren't you retired?"

"Yes, and none of this is my problem." He gestured to his sons before leaving the room. "These two need to box it out."

Royce grunted. He and Brannon had argued over the years but it'd never resulted in a physical altercation.

"If you'll excuse me. Presidential duties await." Bran shouldered past them and stalked toward his office, his walk tall and his shoulders back.

They'd be okay. Probably.

The complaint wasn't that Royce had inherited CEO but that he'd kept learning of it a secret. Instead of blaming Dad for the subterfuge, his siblings were content to pin it on Royce. Blame must've come with the new title.

"And you." Gia stabbed Royce with one finger. "Taylor? Were you going to tell me?"

He made sure no one was eavesdropping before responding, his voice low. "No. I don't normally consult you about the women in my bed."

Taylor had told Gia after all. But they were close. It was bound to come out.

"Plus it was only the one time." Though today had been an invitation for more.

His sister offered a saccharine smile. "If you two didn't

think we picked up on your stripping each other with your eyes in that meeting, you really don't have a clue."

"It's unwise. We're CEO and COO. The board—"

"The board can kiss my ass," she said. "This is our company. The Knoxes. The Thompsons. If you're happy—and you can make her happy—who the hell cares what anyone thinks?"

It was as good as having her blessing. He'd had good reasons to be careful, but Gia was right. Who the hell cared what anyone thought?

"You're thinking about it, and I don't want to be around while that happens. Later, bro." Gia headed to the elevator, waving without turning around.

When Royce entered his office, Taylor Thompson was sitting primly on the edge of his desk, her long legs crossed, one red stiletto wiggling in the air. Her devil-may-care smile paired with red lipstick was enough to send him falling at her feet and selling his very soul for one more kiss. One more touch. One more chance to blow her mind.

He wasn't typically led around by his pecker, but here they were. He'd known what he was doing in that meeting. Despite the excuses he gave Gia, the decision to seduce Taylor was cemented in his mind.

"What have we here?" He closed the door behind him, noticing the shades had been pulled. He pushed the lock on the doorknob. It engaged with an audible click.

"Your power's gone to my head." She was still wiggling that foot. He caught her calf in one palm and smoothed his hand over the muscle and down, down, until he pulled her shoe off and dropped it on the floor.

"Same." Repeating the action with her other foot, he said, "You told Gia."

"I…did," she admitted.

"I'm beginning to wonder if I don't care what anyone thinks."

"You cared enough to lock that door." Her cocked eyebrow was a challenge. He ended the stance with his lips on hers, drinking her in. His thirst had been unquenchable this week. When he'd seen her in the hallways talking with Bran or Addison, he'd felt a pinch in his chest he'd been sure was a warning to stay away. But when the lights went down in the meeting he recognized it for what it was.

Want.

A truckload of it.

Touching her hadn't relieved the urge. No. Touching her had been a lit match set to the driest kindling. He'd gone up in smoke and it'd taken everything in him not to pleasure her right there in the damn meeting, teasing her folds with his fingers until his lips could finish the job.

She unbuttoned his shirt, leaving his bow tie knotted at his collar and kissing his bare chest. He caught her head, enjoying the heat of her mouth on his skin.

One night hadn't been enough.

There was no erasing kisses that might as well have been burned into his flesh. She'd consumed him that night, reminding him what real passion felt like—not appreciation, not accomplishment, but real passion for another human being. The gut-shaking, teeth-rattling *need* to bury himself to the hilt, growling her name as he guided her to the pinnacle.

In a matter of seconds, he had her dress unzipped, his hands on her bare breasts, her bra tossed over his computer screen. She returned the favor by opening his pants and gripping his hard-as-steel cock.

She continued what he started in that meeting and he was going to finish it.

Right now.

He dragged his office chair to the side of the desk where she perched. He sat and lowered the chair to the lowest possible height, which brought him eye level with her delicious center.

"What are you doing?" Her voice held jittery notes of excitement.

"Three guesses," he said before pulling off her underwear—a red thong, God help him.

Legs parted, she dropped back onto her elbows and rested her calves on his shoulders. Giving his neglected member a squeeze, he promised to take care of it later. After he kissed his way along Taylor's thighs until he reached the Promised Land.

Oh hell yes.

Not only did she taste as incredible as he'd imagined, but her citrusy smell surrounded him. Her thighs clamped around his ears rendered him deaf save for the sound of her fingers raking through his hair and her sultry moans making a new home in his chest.

He used everything he'd learned about women to please her, sweeping his tongue left and right, up and down, flicking fast and laying it flat and then going slow. As a result, his lemon-scented vixen was having trouble keeping quiet, which made him grin in arrogant male pride.

"How you doin' up there?" he paused to ask but didn't wait for her to answer. Instead he set the pace with his tongue as he tugged her plush hips forward on the desk. He paused only briefly. To say: "Come for me, Taylor."

He wasn't sure if the request worked, but her orgasm followed. Then he was tasting her essence, luxuriating in her sighs of pleasure. She lost her place, writhing and sweeping the phone off the desk. It landed with a clatter that still didn't pull her from her bliss. Another wave hit and she clutched a paper in her hands, crumpling it as her other hand pushed his calculator and his glasses case to the floor.

He eased his mouth away, kissing his way down her legs and lingering at the back of one of her knees. He kissed along her calf and down to her feet, where he gave her big toe a playful lick.

When she sat up her blond hair was wild, her eyes wilder. He was enamored by the sheer wonder of her.

She was as unpredictable as a lightning storm and twice as dangerous. And here he was out in an open field, umbrella held high. With her, he never knew where he was headed. He'd left the black-and-white world of his making and was now wandering in the haze-gray fog of hers.

But there was no erasing what was happening between them. They were best when they were naked together. Even with no time or inclination for a serious relationship, he recognized his physical need for her. It was undeniable. *She* was undeniable.

The tent building behind his boxer briefs as she lowered to her knees in front of him was only partial proof. He rested a hand on her head and she slicked his length and took him into her mouth.

That genie he'd sworn to stuff back into the bottle? Yeah, that wasn't happening. Not when Taylor made his pulse race and his mind blank. Not when she made everything, at least in this moment, feel undeniably, inexplicably *right*.

Fifteen

Taylor always wanted a fireplace in the bedroom, but her apartment didn't have that particular feature. Nor did it have stone floors, Tuscan-style decor or a California king-size bed.

Royce's house did.

She stretched beneath the downy bedding, gold and red, and watched the flames. After another week of barely containing themselves at work, tonight made the third—no, wait, *fourth*—night they'd given in to what they both wanted. He'd come to her house yesterday with takeout. They ate after they'd satisfied another hunger: the one for each other. She'd enjoyed five-star cuisine naked and while lounging in front of the television.

Tonight wasn't dissimilar, though they ate dinner first—and in public—before returning to Royce's house and promptly shedding their clothing. She'd had no idea how domestic he was, in spite of knowing him half her life. But since hanging out with him in his house and hers, she'd seen him cook—scrambled eggs counted—tidy up and, like now, deliver drinks.

He entered the room with a tray holding a bottle of scotch and two glasses. She knew the brand. It was her father's favorite when he was alive.

"I had my first taste of scotch with your dad." Royce placed the tray between them on the wide bed. He wore nothing but black boxer briefs, which had officially stolen the number one spot as her favorite outfit on him. The suit and bow tie combo had been her favorite for years, but oh, how wrong she'd been.

"I was eighteen. Just graduated high school." He handed her a lowball. A few inches of brown liquid surrounded a square ice cube that was almost the same size as the glass. "And a cigar."

"Sounds like Dad."

"Charlie pulled me aside and said, 'Now that you're a man, you should drink and smoke like one.'" Royce's smile was warm. "Never took to the cigars. But I do like the drink. The smoky, complicated nature of it."

"Sounds like you," she teased.

"I thought we'd toast to him."

Her eyes misted over. "You know."

"That today is his birthday? Yes. I know."

"I hate it. Scotch." She sat up, awkwardly covering her naked breasts with the blanket while trying not to spill the drink. "But I'll have it in Dad's honor."

Her nose wrinkled as the liquid streamed down her throat in a trail of fire.

"Ugh. Still terrible," she wheezed. She'd never liked scotch, though she tried to build up a tolerance after her father passed. She'd wanted to feel closer to him and thought that might suffice. No such luck.

"Here." She offered her glass to Royce. "You drink it."

"It's there. The appreciation for it. Go slow. Let it open up. Just take it a sip at a time."

His advice was a good metaphor for them. The appreciation for Royce had been one taste at a time. He'd been slow to open up, too. That first all-in kiss had rocked her world—it was too much at once. After another "sip" of him, he'd easily become an addiction.

They'd given in to the "more" between them. First with sex in his office, then this week where they were behaving like a… Dare she say it? *Couple.*

There was no bridge being burned if they didn't work out. He would return to work as usual and she would make herself forget that the best sex of her life was courtesy of the man she worked closely with every day.

Then again, if things worked out…

The thought made her smile. Her next sip of scotch went down easier than the first.

"The ice helps." Royce was lounging on the padded headboard, a pillow behind his back. He watched the fire but she couldn't take her eyes off his face. The orange glow highlighting a strong, straight nose and angled jaw. The kissable firmness of his lips, and his regal eyebrows.

"Dad trusted me to follow in his footsteps," she said. "My being COO is a tribute to him in a lot of ways."

"But?" Royce tilted his head, reading her tone correctly.

"But, I also wanted a family. My mother never believed that work and family can coexist."

His expression blanked, but he kept the conversation going. "What do you think?"

"I believe I can have it all." She watched her drink, not wanting him to think she was talking about him when she added, "A husband. A family. A career. But I worry about balance. About one area suffering while the other excels."

"Balance is hard," he agreed in the same noncommittal tone.

"My father was all about his career, but still made time for me. He took me to work with him on more than one occasion."

"I remember."

"You do?" She recalled seeing Royce at ThomKnox fresh out of college, when she was a teenager. She had no idea he'd noticed her beyond the moment he caught her in his arms. And then she'd been pretty sure it hadn't registered as an event worth remembering to him.

"He told me to stay away from you," Royce said now.

"Dad?" She'd been lectured but had no idea that he'd gone to Royce, too. "Wow. That's embarrassing."

"It was necessary." He raked his eyes over her body, then touched a nipple that peeked out from the sheet. "Look where we've ended up."

She had to smile, though the news that he was told to stay away from her rocked her where she sat. "My father had a lot of nerve."

"He loved you."

"He was ten years older than my mom, did you know that? And they were great together. Why didn't he think I could handle a relationship with you?" She sensed she was treading on sacred ground. That her father's reasons had been buried with him.

Royce didn't seem to think so. "If I had to guess, I'd say it was stereotypical fatherly protection. He was my age once, and had your mother in his sights. Do you believe he was always the consummate gentleman?"

"Ew." But she had to laugh. Her parents had been very much in love, and Deena was gorgeous. No doubt her father's thoughts about her were less than wholesome. "He liked Brannon for me."

"A safer choice."

She could hear the pride in his voice at being the *forbidden choice*. Bran and Taylor had never had the kind of explosive attraction that Royce and Taylor had.

"Don't be so hard on him," Royce told her. "Your father couldn't bear the idea of you growing up. He could have acted out of self-preservation that had nothing to do with us. God knows my father's done that."

"Jack knows how to draw attention, that's for sure."

Royce watched the fire, silent.

"When we talked about you being named CEO, you said it was your responsibility." She rattled the oversize ice cube in her glass. "Was that all it was?"

"It's my legacy. My birthright. Just as COO is yours. Your dad only wanted the best for you, Taylor. Whatever he said or did while he was here, he said or did with you in mind. You meant everything to him."

"I miss him." She hugged the glass to her chest. A poor substitute for her dad. There would always be a void in her arms.

"So do I." Royce sat his glass aside, gathered her close and kissed the top of her head.

"How did my mom lose him and remain standing?" she asked, not expecting an answer. He didn't offer one, consoling her with a hand moving up and down along her arm. "Is the reward for finally finding *The One* losing them in the end? How is that fair?"

"Losing people we love is par for the course, Taylor. None of us get out of this life alive. Someone always has to go first."

As sad as his words were, they were oddly comforting. She snuggled into him.

"Something I'm learning," he murmured. He touched

the bottom of the glass she still cradled. Her next sip was smoother than the last. "Well?"

"Complex," she answered. It was a good way to describe scotch.

Complex was also a good way to describe the feelings she was developing for Royce. She hadn't thought about The End, not really, but she considered, ever so briefly, the beauty of being someone's forever.

"We have to stop meeting like this." Taylor stepped into the supply closet attached to the copy room. It'd been five days since she sipped scotch in Royce's bed. Five days since he held her in his arms and consoled her. Five days since she realized her feelings for him were deepening.

She'd been trying not to focus on those "feelings," since feelings were fickle. But she couldn't keep from walking toward the glow of the supply closet—especially when the silhouette inside belonged to suited, bow-tied Royce.

He'd been working a lot this week, and late. Tonight was no exception. The executive floor was practically abandoned at this hour. She understood his new position was demanding. This was a temporary state—the shift from one position to the other wouldn't last forever. Soon he could go home before nine at night.

They hadn't had much time together this week and she missed it. Missed *him*, in spite of working with him every single day. When he was with her, he was warm. Open. In the previous weeks, she'd caught a glimpse of who he could be if he weren't shackled to ThomKnox, but that version of him had gone the way of the brontosaurus.

"You're working late."

He looked exhausted—from the shadows beneath his eyes to the rumpled look of his usually starched shirt. "I can't find anything in here." He picked up a box of staples. "I was looking for those clamp things."

"Sounds kinky."

He gave her a tired smile.

She reached behind him for a box of black binder clips. "These?"

"Yes." He took the box. "Thank you. Assistant interviews are killing me. Half the candidates list video games as their past experience and the other half are wildly overqualified. Finding the right person from those two piles is a challenge. No wonder Bran sings Addison's praises all the time."

"You'll find the right one." She fingered the red bow tie at his collar. "In the meantime, how lucky that I stumbled across you in a closet."

"Role reversal of the Valentine's gala." Heat replaced the fatigue in his eyes. He wanted her. Just like that. Nice to know their physical attraction hadn't dampened.

She kissed his frown and his lips softened against hers, the box of binder clips rattling as he wrapped his arms around her and pulled her closer. She raked her fingers into his hair, moaning when his tongue touched hers. She'd never tire of that move.

"How wrong is it to have sex in this closet?" she whispered.

His grin was slow, wicked. "Well, I *am* in charge now."

"Mmm, don't I know it." She let her hands roam while he made out with her long and slow, his movements languid. She guessed he needed to shake off the long-and-turning-longer week, and so did she. No sense in wasting an opportunity to blow off some steam—and each other's minds.

Suddenly, a light flipped on in the copy room, illuminating the shadowed pocket of the supply closet.

"Oh! Sorry, I…" Addison stood, papers in hand, obviously en route to the copy machine. "Oh. My God."

But her *Oh. My. God.* sounded pleasantly surprised rather than accusatory. Taylor unwound her arms from Royce's neck. His hands moved to her hips and he positioned himself behind her. The thick ridge of his erection nestled against her bottom. She would've smiled if she wasn't concerned about Addison's reaction.

If Addi didn't know about Taylor and Royce, she did now. And if Brannon had any leftover doubts about them, one conversation with his assistant would erase them.

"I'll take care of this later." Addison sent them another glance before turning to leave the copy room.

"Addi, wait." Taylor followed Addi to the doorway. There was a distance between them that Taylor didn't like. It niggled at her that Bran's assistant thought of Taylor as "the bad guy." Taylor didn't like being *unliked* by anyone.

"Yes?" Addison faced her.

"You've been upset with me lately. I might be speaking out of turn, but I feel like it has something to do with Brannon."

Addison's cheeks turned bold pink, but she didn't confirm nor deny.

"I don't know what you heard, but Bran never actually proposed to me. He and I decided we were better off friends. Mutually. That hug you saw—"

"Was none of my business. Honestly, Taylor, this is unnecessary."

"You look at Brannon like…" *The way I used to look at Royce.* "Like you're interested in more. Does he know how you feel about him?"

"I—I don't understand what this is about. If it's discretion you're after, you can trust me not to say anything about you and Royce."

"No, that's not it. You and Bran—"

"Have a professional relationship, not a personal one." Addison's smile was plastic. "Who you kiss at work is none of my business. I'm just trying to do my job."

Yowch.

Addison made it halfway down the corridor before Taylor decided to make one last ditch effort at peace between them.

"I think you and Bran would be good together!" she called out. "For what it's worth."

Addi stopped walking and turned her head slowly to the side. She looked half mortified, half nauseous, and then Taylor saw why.

Brannon entered the corridor slowly, his pained expression and Addison's a matching set.

Taylor winced. The road to recovery for her and Addison was about to become even longer thanks to Taylor's big mouth…and the fact that Brannon heard every word that came out of it.

Sixteen

The journey from CFO to CEO wasn't going as smoothly as he'd originally—and naively—believed. Turned out the transition was more complicated than swapping the name-plate on his desk.

Royce was still responsible for his CFO duties while adjusting to CEO. Luckily he'd had a round of interviews today for CFO, and had met with two very promising prospects. He looked forward to finalizing the decision and offloading some of his work.

He'd managed to grab dinner with Taylor one night this week, a far cry from how many nights he preferred spending with her. She was understanding, and had mentioned to him that "these things" took time before reassuring him his hectic schedule was temporary.

"It'll work out. You'll see," she'd said.

Comforting words, but harder in practice than in theory.

He'd promised to leave the office by noon on Thursday to meet her for lunch—just like he'd promised on Friday.

And today. His entire week had been derailed and here he was on a Saturday having missed yet another opportunity to see her.

He picked up his cell phone to text an apology when she appeared in the doorway of his office holding a brown sack with handles.

"Surprise!"

He took one look at the familiar black logo on the bag, one whiff of the enticing smells of garlic, robust tomato sauce and rich oregano, and his stomach roared.

"That smells incredible," were his first words. "As do you." Her wide smile suggested she didn't mind that he'd complimented the food before her.

"I didn't hear from you at noon."

He checked his cell phone for the time. 1:47 p.m.? "I'm sorry. I was going to call. I had no idea how late it was."

"I figured. I had to come into the office and check on a few things, anyway." She glanced at the stacks of paper on his desk that had spilled from his inbox. "You know, you could ask for my help."

He gestured to the eleven windows open on his computer screen. "And subject you to this? I like you too much."

"Who else can you trust with the company's biggest secrets?" She unloaded their lunch onto the low table in front of a pair of guest chairs. She offered a hunk of ciabatta bread and his mouth watered. Garlic was his favorite contemporary Italian restaurant in River Grove. The yeasty, warm bread was a gluten-free person's worst nightmare. He opened the lid on a container. A huge square of lasagna covered in freshly grated Parmesan cheese caused his stomach to rumble again.

"You're serious?" He dunked the bread into the sauce and took a bite. Heavenly.

"I *am* COO. I can handle some of the excess in the short

term. Plus us working closely solves the problem of finding time to see each other. Sort of like date-working." She handed him a plastic fork.

"Scandalous."

"For two of the top brass at ThomKnox, it very well might be." She smiled.

He kissed the corner of that smile. They ate, discussing strategy and how some of his workload could be pieced and parceled out. By the time she stuffed their empty food containers into the bag—he'd helped finish her eggplant parmesan, which he begrudgingly admitted was better than anticipated—he was alive with the excitement of having a plan.

"How's Bran doing?" she asked out of nowhere.

He ignored the rogue spike of jealousy. Royce knew Taylor wanted to be with him, not his brother—her reaction on Valentine's Day had solidified that—so him feeling possessive over her made no sense.

"Bran's busy ignoring me."

"I don't know why he's mad at you. Your father picked you to be CEO. It's not as if you lobbied for it."

He tucked her dark blond hair behind her ear. "It's more about my not telling Bran when I knew. I should've."

"You didn't know Jack was going to announce it at the party." But her tone held a question she spoke when she said, "Did you?"

"I didn't know. But I could've guessed." His father liked the spotlight and he'd much rather go out with a bang than a fizzle.

"You're sure about taking on some of the workload while I'm finding an assistant?" He tipped her chin.

"I'm sure."

"Thank you. And thank you…for the other things."

"Other things?"

"You breezed in here, fed me and took my stress away."

"Yeah, but I was just—"

He kissed her gently, enjoying when she went pliant beneath him. He'd had a hell of a week and having her support meant a lot to him. Even if it was hard to admit he needed it. "I appreciate it. More than you know. That's what I'm trying to say."

He was in undiscovered territory. Having someone to rely on, to trust, had been absent from his personal life for a long time. Taylor made him feel more capable, not less. Having her in his corner was an idea he was already used to.

As long as he kept work first and wasn't distracted, he didn't see the harm. ThomKnox was his number one focus. There wasn't room for much more.

"This feels like an abuse of power." Taylor bit her lip and stared at the curtly worded email on the screen.

"Why?"

She narrowed her eyelids. "You know why. Lowell Olsen is a huge distributor and you're willing to ruin the relationship because I don't like him?"

"No one likes him. Plus, he's bullying you. We don't negotiate with bullies. We'll find a better store."

She hesitated over her laptop keyboard. "But—"

His finger on top of hers, he pressed a button and the "we're no longer interested in placing ThomKnox merchandise in your store" email was sent.

"Oh my gosh. You didn't!" She was elated and shocked and almost—fine, she'd admit it—*drunk with power.*

"I did. And now it's done."

As romantic gestures went, this wasn't hearts and flowers, or chocolates and a puppy wearing a big red bow. But Royce's love language was work. Roughly translated, his ending negotiations with Lowell Olsen felt romantic to her.

She supposed that was expected from a woman in love.

Yep. She'd done it. She'd fallen head over heels for Royce Knox. Of course, she knew better than to share that with him. He'd been buried up to his eyeballs since he'd been appointed CEO and was only now treading water and breathing at the same time. A profession of true love on top of that might send him over the edge.

He took the laptop from her and set it on a pile of papers, mail and folders on the coffee table. "Guess what?"

You love me, too?

"What?"

"Time for dessert."

"Dessert?" They'd shared a very unsexy dinner of pizza and more pizza. It might've been goat cheese and pear with smoked, caramelized onion sauce, but it was still pizza and she'd eaten a ton of it. "How could you be hungry for anything after…" She trailed off as he reached for the waistband of her leggings and began tugging them from her legs. "Royce."

"Dessert," he insisted. "You've worked very hard this weekend and you deserve a reward."

How could she argue with that? She couldn't. Not when he urged her to her back and peeled those pants the rest of the way off. Or when he kissed her belly button, down her thighs and then up to her—*oh.*

His tongue should be bronzed. He was that good.

The skills he had in the boardroom were supersized in the bedroom—or the living room. In any room. She'd been sleeping with him for a little over a month and he'd never failed to render her a boneless mass, her blood sizzling and popping like oil in a hot pan. The man *was* sex, and she couldn't reconcile how well he'd kept the friskier part of himself hidden from her—from the world. Who knew *this* was lurking beneath the veneer of a serious, sometimes-bespectacled number cruncher.

"Yes, *there*," she encouraged, her mind blanking as he tasted her.

"How about *here*?"

She liked to think she'd coaxed out his inner sexy beast. After all, he'd brought out the animal in her. Could she be his secret superpower? Was Royce hers? He knew what she needed physically and had never failed to deliver. She'd been exactly who he needed whether at work or at home. Helping him hadn't been charity; it'd come naturally. The way a couple in love prioritized being there for each other.

Royce's second finger joined his first in the race to her orgasm. Her hips bucked as she tumbled over in record time. Static fuzz descended, blotting out her worries. The words on her tongue as she clutched around his fingers were "Yes, Royce, yes." But if the timing had been different, if she would've allowed her heart to speak for her, those words would have been *"I love you. I love you..."*

In a perfect world, he would've returned that sentiment instead of saying, "Be right back."

As he left the room, she warned herself not to rush him. She wanted him however she could have him, and if that meant she loved him with everything in her without him knowing, then that's how it would have to be. They had plenty of time for him to realize he loved her, too. He had a lot on his plate. That was all.

He returned to the living room, sheathed, but instead of crashing down over her, he lifted her into his arms. Pressing her back against the nearest blank wall, he instructed her to wrap her legs around his waist.

She did as she was told and was rewarded by the long, slick slide of him entering her. Sensitive from his earlier kisses, her channel tightened around him as he moved, giving them both the pressure they desired.

"Taylor. *God*." Each broken word fell from lips she kissed over and over, while her fingers toyed in his hair. She kept her gaze on his face, her truncated breaths sawing from her lungs as they made love against the wall. She had to see the moment he came. Had to witness taking him over the edge of control—control he favored but relinquished whenever he was with her.

It was heady, that power shift.

His hips sped and sweat broke out on his forehead. Loud groans of excitement exited his throat, folded around swear words.

"Harder. Harder," she encouraged. *I love you.*

"I'm there. I'm there." His voice faded into a shout of completion as he pressed her back flat against the wall. She absorbed his weight and strength, kissing his face and neck and tasting the salt on his skin.

He loved her, too. Soon he'd realize it. She wouldn't rush him.

They had plenty of time.

Seventeen

A quick *rap-rap-rap* echoed off Royce's office door but his visitor didn't wait to be invited before opening it.

"I'm *not* not speaking to you." Brannon walked in and shut the door behind him.

Royce pulled his glasses off his nose. "Good. Now get out. I'm busy." He figured Brannon had been keeping busy, too. Their stint of not talking, of not hanging out would end eventually. Even if it had been nearly a month since the meeting where Gia asked about their "snit."

She'd come into Royce's office last week telling him if he hurt Taylor, she'd castrate him. He told her it wasn't serious, which was a bold-faced lie. Not only had Taylor and Royce been sleeping together for six weeks, he'd seen her several times last week and twice this week alone. And they had plans tonight.

As for Bran, he knew that Royce and Taylor were "dating," but that was also a tame way to describe their relationship. Royce had yet to clue his brother in on any details. Not that he'd asked.

"If you're going to insist on staying, at least sit down," Royce told him.

"Why don't you stand?"

"Because I'm working. Didn't we just cover this?"

"We have an appointment at noon." Bran folded his arms over his chest, defiant.

"I have no such appointment on my calendar."

"Write one in and get off your ass. Let's go."

"If you have something to say, why don't you say it and then go back to what you were doing before you came in here to interrupt me with this nonsense?"

"This 'nonsense' is exactly why we're not speaking. And this appointment is one you need to show up for. It's what's going to put us back where we belong."

Royce would do anything for his brother, including going to a mystery appointment so that they could make amends. They *needed* to make amends. They had a company to run—ThomKnox wouldn't function with two out of three Knox siblings. Success required all of them.

He shut his laptop and stood from his chair. "What do I need to bring?"

Bran's smile was smug. "You don't need to bring anything. I have it covered."

Bran's house was a sleek, modern, square utopia. Glass and steel and clean lines made up the design; none of the homier accents like bowls of fruit or vases of flowers here. Odd the way the architecture of Royce's and Bran's homes contrasted the men themselves—Royce's love of spreadsheets and black-and-white areas should have made him better suited to sparse decor. Outside, a huge patio area outfitted with a bar and seating flanked an in-ground pool and a new feature to the yard—one that fit Bran to a T.

"Is that…?" Royce started.

"A boxing ring."

"So you took Dad seriously."

"I figured it'd be good exercise. I've been practicing with the trainer. Know what I noticed?"

"You're no Mike Tyson?" Royce answered drily.

"I noticed that it helps release emotion." Bran pulled on one boxing glove and then threw Royce a pair. "It resolves issues that were formerly unresolved."

"I'm not going to fight you, Bran."

"It's not fighting. It's boxing. It's a sport."

This was ridiculous. What did he hope to solve with the two of them throwing punches?

"What's wrong? Afraid I'll kick your ass?" Bran offered a crooked smile.

Even as Royce assured himself he had nothing to prove to his younger brother, he was baited by that challenge. Giving in to his baser instincts, he tossed his suit jacket aside and pulled his boxing gloves on as well.

After the quickest tutorial ever, Royce and Bran began circling each other in the ring.

"You should've told me Dad chose you," Bran said.

"He asked me not to." Royce held his arms wide.

"Gloves up. I don't want to break your nose." Bran demonstrated by shielding his own face.

"This is stupid." But Royce put his gloves up. He liked his nose the way it was, thank you very much.

"We're in this together, big brother. That means circumventing Dad sometimes. Like when we broke the window in the guest bedroom and moved a plant in front of it instead of telling him what happened."

"We didn't get away with that, either." Bouncing on the

balls of his feet, Royce lifted his gloves in time to thwart an incoming swing.

"Good block. That doesn't change the fact that I would've liked to know what you knew. Rather than sit there with my dick in my hand at the party."

"Pretty sure all eyes were on me. Which I didn't appreciate, you know."

"We could've been a unified front." Bran swiped the air, but Royce ducked out of the way.

"Nothing above the neck, remember? Those were the rules."

"They're more like guidelines." Bran danced in a half circle. "How are you and Taylor doing?"

"What?"

"Don't play coy with me. You and Taylor have been all over each other lately. Beyond the one time Addison caught you in the supply closet, I'm assuming." Bran took another swing and, thankfully, missed. "Didn't suspect you for the falling-in-love type."

"What are you—" Royce dropped his gloves but lifted them just as fast to block a blow meant for his jaw.

Bran laughed, enjoying himself way too much. "Keep your guard up!"

"What are we, teenagers? I'm not *falling in love*. Taylor and I are partners in the most physical sense of the word."

"She doesn't want any more from you?"

Her words from the night they'd shared scotch came back to him. "She wants a family and marriage, but she also wants a career. I'm certain I'm only involved in the last part of that list."

"How certain?"

Royce stilled, giving his brother an impatient glare.

"You're smart, Royce, but dense when it comes to women."

Royce threw a punch and missed, but knocked Bran's footing off. That felt good.

"You're one to talk," he told his younger brother. "Addison wants you and you're a clueless oaf."

"Taylor embarrassed us both when she shouted that we'd be good together. The whole office heard."

"The four of us were the only ones in the office."

"Yeah, well, Addi and I are coworkers *in the most physical sense of the word*. Stop changing the subject."

A few more swings were thrown, but none of them connected. Bran's comments circled Royce's head like a school of hungry piranha.

"What do you know about Taylor, anyway?" Royce finally asked, wondering if Bran was dancing around a point as well as this boxing ring.

"She's been my friend most of her life," Bran answered. "She's always talked about having kids, a husband. A golden retriever, for Christ's sake. That doesn't sound anything like you."

It didn't. But that was never what Royce and Taylor were about.

"Name the flower she's allergic to," Bran said.

"Daisies." It was a guess. Royce swung, aiming for Bran's ribs. His brother slid out of the way, easy as you please. His trainer was good.

"Lilies." Bran smirked. "Do you talk to her, ever?"

Grunting as he stepped out of the way of one of Bran's throws, Royce said, "We must've skipped over that all-important 'do you or don't you like lilies' conversation so crucial to new couples."

"So you admit you're a couple now." Bran stopped moving. Royce threw another punch, but landed against the ropes when his forward momentum took him there.

"I'm sure you two had a lot more time to talk than she

and I do." Royce pushed off the ropes, spun on his brother and swung. The punch connected. Bran clutched his stomach and let out an audible *oof*.

Satisfied, Royce added, "We use our mouths for other pastimes when we're together."

Bran turned and landed the hit he'd been angling for since they stepped into the ring. Light exploded behind Royce's eye and he held up his glove a millisecond too late.

"What the hell!" Royce cupped his eye, which was beginning to feel the same size as his boxing glove.

"Sorry. That was supposed to be your nose," Bran said, not sounding sorry at all.

"What's this about? Do you want her for yourself or something?" Dammit, his eye hurt.

Bran dropped his arms, gloves hanging at his sides, a look of utter surprise on his face. "That's history. You know that, right? Taylor and I patched up what almost happened—what would've been a disaster. This has nothing to do with me trying to win the girl."

"So you're pissed I won CEO and you didn't?" Royce's head hadn't begun to throb yet but he guessed it would start any second.

"No. Goddammit, Royce. I'm pissed you didn't trust Gia or me with that news. We've always been a unit. *Always*."

Royce heard the hurt in his brother's voice. What he said was true. Bran and Gia and Royce were three members of a busy, hardworking family. They were far from latchkey kids, but considering that a staff cared for them during the busy early years of ThomKnox, the three siblings leaned on each other first and foremost.

Bran tore off his gloves. "Taylor Thompson is in love with you, and if you don't see that, you're a bigger idiot than I was." He ducked between the ropes and sat on the steps leading out of the ring.

Royce scrunched his face, aware of the dull thud of a bruise forming. A shiner for the new CEO. *Great*. He stepped out of the ring and joined Bran, whose elbows were resting on his knees.

"I messed up, Royce," Bran said to his shoes. Both of them were panting from their workout.

Royce took a clumsy step, regained his balance and sat next to his brother. "Your heart was in the right place."

"That's just it. My heart wasn't involved at all." Bran sighed. "If you tell anyone this I'll black your other eye."

Royce held up a hand and silently swore his allegiance.

"I thought being engaged to Taylor would give me a better shot at CEO."

Royce frowned. "You're plenty qualified for CEO."

"Yeah, I know. But I wasn't an option in Dad's eyes. It was you the whole time. Part of me knew that. And when you knew that, I wish you would have come to me so that we could've had a moment to absorb it away from all those extra sets of eyes."

Royce's shoulders dropped. He wished that, too.

"I could've hurt Taylor, Royce. She didn't love me, but if she had and I led her on?" Bran shook his head. "She never would've forgiven me for backing out of our engagement. And I would've backed out eventually. I care about her, but marriage? That's insane."

Just hearing the word *marriage* in reference to Taylor made the hair on Royce's neck stand on end. "I doubt she wants to marry me." But his voice wasn't as solid as he'd like it to be. They'd grown close. Shared a lot of intimate nights and slept side by side. She'd brought him lunch and offered to help him at work and, like he'd pointed out a few minutes ago, they were a new couple.

Couple.

He sure as hell wasn't ready for that.

"Next time you talk to Taylor, do me a favor and let her know that Addi and I are not going to date each other."

"Why not? Addison's pretty."

"Pretty? She's gorgeous. But if Taylor keeps teasing her, Addi might quit. You know how hard it is to find a good assistant." Bran was shaking his head again, more adamantly than before. "I rounded the corner after Taylor shouted we'd be good together, and Addi looked like she wanted the floor to swallow her. Trust me, the only thing between Ad and me is professional compatibility. If she liked me, I'd know it."

"Don't be so sure. Not every woman who likes you jumps you in a closet."

Bran crashed into Royce and tumbled him off the steps and into the plush grass, but he was laughing when he did it. The backyard scuffle reminded Royce of the few times they'd wrestled as kids. Never fighting to win anything, always on the same side. Like now.

Bran collapsed next to him, his back to the ground.

"I'm sorry I didn't tell you about CEO," Royce said. "I should have."

"Yeah. Don't do it again."

Royce let out a small chuckle, then fell silent. They lay side by side for a moment, their eyes on the bright blue sky overhead. Royce's head was thumping hard enough to outrace his heart. Partially because of the eye, partially because he knew what he had to do when it came to Taylor.

The position of CEO was rewarding, but demanding. Taylor had been in second place since he accepted the position, and he'd believed that she was okay with it. Now he wondered if that was the case. Would she eventually expect more than he had the ability to give? Did she already expect more?

Bran was right. The Knox trio had always been a unit. He owed his brother and sister the courtesy of *not* tank-ing their family legacy. Hell, he'd swung the felling blow to keep their products out of retail establishments that might've contributed to a significant percentage of sales. Why? Because he'd wanted to please Taylor.

It was time to stop playing house and focus on work—only work.

His chest howled in protest. He wanted her. God, how he wanted her. In his bed, in his life. On his couch. *On my desk*. But when it came to giving her what she ultimately desired—a family—he had no idea when he'd be ready. If he'd *ever* be ready.

His future was predetermined. The success of Thom-Knox rested squarely on his shoulders. Eighteen-hour days wouldn't leave much room for Taylor. She'd accepted his wacky schedule so far, but what about in six months? A year? His dream was coming true, but how long should she wait to have hers? He refused to be the man who would always be telling her, "Let's wait another year…"

His dreams were important, but so were hers. He and Taylor had the physical attraction on lock, but where it counted—when building a life came into the picture, how could he ask her to table her wants and needs for him?

"I smell your brain cooking," Bran said, hands on his own chest and eyes turned toward Royce. "Thinking hard?"

"You might've knocked some sense into me."

"You're welcome." Bran stood, his lighter brown hair highlighted in a halo around his head, part of it falling over his forehead as he looked down. "You need ice."

"You need a haircut."

Bran would probably brag to everyone that he was responsible for the black eye. Just what Royce needed. Bran toed Royce in the ribs and then headed inside. Royce stayed on his back, listening as the icemaker rattled out the cubes that would soon soothe his aching head.

He knew what he had to do when it came to Taylor.

But he didn't want to do it.

Eighteen

No time like the present.

Royce didn't know if flowers were the right accompaniment for what he'd come to say, but he couldn't show up empty-handed for this conversation. He was glad Bran mentioned Taylor's lily allergy. Royce had been sure not to include a single one of them in the bouquet.

His eyes were grainy, his stomach upset—in part due to the decision he felt forced to make, and in part due to the coffee he'd drunk to wake up. He hadn't slept well last night. He'd been awake turning over his and Taylor's relationship. CEO and ThomKnox. Brannon's advice. Gia, and even Jayson Cooper. Gia and Coop had been so in love they'd stunk with it. So in love they made everyone around them roll their eyes. Then they were over.

In a blink.

If a couple like Gia and Jayson could implode when they had true love on their side, what chance did Royce and Taylor have? If he didn't end things with her now—if they continued to blend their individual dreams and it didn't work out—Taylor would grow to resent him. Conversations about family or work would be riddled with landmines. They'd argue. Say things they didn't mean. They'd end in a nuclear-bomb-worthy plume of smoke. He didn't want that.

He wanted her to have a perfect life—a future that she chose, not one that was a compromise. He cared about her—she was practically family—and if there was a chance for her to escape unscathed, he would do what had to be done… While they could still blame proximity and timing on their attraction.

If she was in love at all, it was with the idea of him. Not him. He knew that. But he also appreciated how the lines could blur when sexual attraction was at its peak. Those moments after an orgasm had thrummed through his body like a power line, and he'd definitely felt something intense.

The heart was a tricky mistress, though. He couldn't allow emotion to cloud the surmountable tasks before him. The product launch. CEO. His retiring father. His brother and his sister depended on him. ThomKnox as a whole, including Taylor, depended on him. He didn't take that lightly.

He knew numbers and the math didn't work out when he added Taylor and him together. He couldn't nurture both his job and his personal life. Not right now. Maybe in ten years, but how could he ask her to table what she wanted for *a decade*?

A family. A dog. And, he guessed, a husband who came home before ten o'clock at night after a grueling day at the office.

Obviously, he could provide financial stability and a warm bed—they sure as hell had a good time together— but juggling family responsibilities? His own father was loving, but hadn't often been present. He'd brought Royce to work with him, and then Bran. And then Gia. One might argue they were a part of this company because ThomKnox was where their family congregated. Other than Sunday breakfasts, Royce didn't recall a family vacation where his father hadn't been on the phone taking business calls.

Taylor's father hadn't been that way. He'd worked hard, but he'd also doted on her. Her mother had been equally enamored with her daughter and eventually left Thom-Knox to be at home with her. Taylor wanted the best of both worlds—the job, the family. How had she put it? Balance.

Not his forte.

What if he *never* wanted a family? What if he was content to be CEO and run the company on his own? What if he was incapable of balance? He couldn't ask Taylor to lead half of a life. She'd already lost her father, and Royce wouldn't cost her her future family as well. He cared for her far too much—he could tell by the suffocating knot in his lungs. He cared for her more than he cared for himself, and that was why it was time to call this what it was.

An amazingly fun fling that was doomed from the start.

Flowers in hand, he swallowed down the bile pushing against the base of his throat. He'd never done anything this hard. Not ever. But he knew what he was capable of—and what he wasn't. The perks of being a practical numbers guy, he supposed. It was high time someone was honest about where he and Taylor stood.

The least he could do was be brave enough to say the words neither of them wanted to hear.

Taylor opened her front door and her breath caught. She admired the man on her stoop, easy to do when Royce looked so damn good. It was nice to see him here on a Saturday morning instead of at the office.

Weekends were for croissants and coffee and lounging in her leggings. Royce was a tad more formal in dark jeans.

His button-down shirt was cuffed at the sleeves, revealing his tanned forearms. The bow tie was a nice touch. And sexy. Which she told him with a smile.

He didn't smile. He looked downright miserable, actually. She opened her mouth to ask him why, but he spoke before she could.

"You're allergic to lilies." He handed over the flower bouquet, a beautiful mix of daisies and roses interspersed with wildflowers she didn't recognize.

"I'm not allergic. But I don't particularly care for them." She took a deep inhalation of the bouquet and stepped aside. "I love these. Thank you."

His frown only deepened. "Oh."

Clearly something was bothering him. Whatever had put that lost and lonely look in his eyes, they could handle it together. She loved him, and with loving someone came navigating the occasional bad day.

"Come in. I made sun tea."

"No, thank you." He didn't meet her eyes, regarding his shoes instead. A premonition skittered across her chest on eight hairy legs. "I'm not staying long."

"Okay." She stepped outside to join him, because even the scant distance between them at the threshold of her apartment was too much. He hadn't greeted her with a kiss, another change she'd noticed. That skittering hairy-legged creature climbed her spine.

"You want a family," Royce said in that same flat tone. Her mind scrambled. She wasn't sure where he was going with this, but the circles under his eyes told her it wasn't good. "Kids. House. A dog?"

"Yes. Um. Eventually." She crossed her arms over her chest. If he was about to break her heart, her folded arms were her only defense.

"That kiss in the closet at the gala changed my life," he

said, his tone gentle. "The attraction between us was something neither of us could deny."

Relief came but was short-lived when he added, "I never intended for us to make it this far, or to embark on a relationship. Especially one where you're making plans with me... Plans I can't make with you."

"Royce, what are you talking about?" The flowers in her hands grew heavy, as if each soft petal was sculpted from concrete. She tossed the bouquet on the small chair on her stoop and wondered if she should've sat in the chair instead. Her knees weren't very stable at the moment.

"The tablet launch is happening soon." His words were robotic. Carefully measured. "My first big release as CEO. The hours I've been working are only going to increase."

"So will mine," she said with a half laugh. "It's only temporary."

"Like us."

Temporary.

She'd done the unthinkable: she'd fallen in love. Despite her telling herself not to do it, despite her justifications that she had plenty of time to win his heart.

"You're breaking up with me." Her words were as disconnected as if someone else had said them. She waited for him to refute that statement. Instead, he confirmed her worst fear.

"Yes. While we can still piece ourselves together. Before we end up like Gia and Jayson."

"What the hell does this have to do with Gia and Jayson?" She would love to know. She needed answers and didn't have any. Royce showing up at her apartment, delivering flowers and announcing that he didn't want her anymore had come out of nowhere. "What brought this on?"

"I had some sense knocked into me."

She'd noticed the dark bruise around his left eye. "Oh? Who do I have to thank for that?"

Royce said nothing.

"This isn't about Gia and Jayson," she said. "You didn't bring me flowers—" she shot a disgusted look at the gorgeous bouquet on the chair "—so that you could talk about your sister's failed marriage. Yes, I want a family. I told you that. *Eventually*. Not now."

"You never told me you fell in love with me." His tone was accusatory, and she instantly felt young and foolish, like she didn't know her own mind or her heart. Shame blanketed her like a heavy coat, and even in today's cooler temperature, she was suddenly too warm. Suffocating under the weight of this conversation. "I suspect you didn't tell me how you felt because you feared my reaction."

"I don't fear you at all." She was more afraid of herself. Or more accurately her emotions—the ones that had run ahead of her shouting, *Come on in! The water's fine!*

"You have a lot on your plate," she said, denial setting in. "You've been busy. *I've* been busy. I didn't want to distract you." But they were lame excuses. There'd been plenty of instances where she could've shared her feelings. She just…hadn't.

He was right. She didn't want to scare him away. She worried that putting pressure on him would cause him to shut down, like he was doing now.

"Nothing has to change," she said, desperate to make everything okay. "I'm trying to learn how to balance work and home life, too. We can figure it out together and—"

"How long?"

She blinked. "How long what?"

"How long are you willing to wait to start this family, Taylor? You're closing in on thirty. How long?"

"I don't know. A few years." She'd never had a conversation this intimate with anyone. Not with any guy she'd dated. And definitely not in front of her apartment where her neighbors could overhear.

"What about five years?" he asked. "How about seven? Ten?"

It took her a second to understand he wasn't negotiating. He was trying to prove a point.

"I won't ask you to design your life around me." Some of the hardness left his eyes. He was still in there, the man she fell in love with. The man who'd intrigued her for half her life. The man who'd caught her in his arms when she was too young to understand what her fluttering stomach meant was the same man who had thoroughly won her heart—only to demolish it now.

"Isn't that up to me?" she asked quietly.

"It's up to you and whomever you build a family with. My position as CEO reigns supreme over everything else. I won't be distracted from my legacy. I'm sorry, Taylor."

His apology was somehow more final than the whole of his breakup speech. His mind was made up. He was rejecting her.

It was like a bomb had gone off nearby and deafened her, leaving behind only a high-pitched ringing interspersed with her broken heartbeats.

Royce, task complete, walked to his car. She watched him drive away, and only when he was out of sight did she sag against the door.

There was nothing to say after he'd said it all. He didn't have to say he didn't love her—he knew she loved him and had offered nothing in return. Except the assurance that ThomKnox mattered more than anything.

More than her.

Nineteen

Taylor's first instinct when Gia invited her to spend Sunday lounging at the pool was to answer with a definitive *no*.

She'd spent yesterday miserable and slept terribly on top of it. It was hard to achieve REM in between crying jags. She woke today grouchy and tired, and sad. So incredibly sad. The sadness reminded her of when her father passed away. It wasn't the same kind of grief, but it had the same depth. It choked the joy from her soul.

She'd thought of a million different ways she could've reacted other than standing on her front stoop gaping as Royce's car drove away from her. She should've screamed at him, told him that he was too practical for his own good. She should have grabbed him by that bow tie and kissed him, reminding him what he was giving up. But of course, she hadn't done any of that. What she had done was carry the stupid *lily-free* bouquet into the house and feed the flowers one by one into her garbage disposal while crying.

Like a bouquet was supposed to make up for him shattering her heart?

Did he have any idea how much he'd meant to her? But she knew the answer.

No. He didn't. She'd never told him. She couldn't decide if that made her smart or infinitely stupid. After she'd rid herself of the flowers she curled up with a blanket on the couch and watched TV, desperate for distraction. She cried then, too.

Gia's house looked enormous from the street, but seemed even bigger from the side of the pool where Taylor lounged in a sun chair. It was warm for April—nearly eighty—and the pool was heated. Taylor didn't plan on getting wet, though. It took all her effort to sit here and not seem miserable.

"Spiked lemonade. Perfect for today," Gia announced, swishing outside in a long white cover-up, her bikini revealing each of her enviable curves. "Veggies and hummus?"

"Sure." Taylor forced a smile.

"Okay. Let me traverse through my *enormous* kitchen and see what I can find." Gia had jokingly referred to this house as her "mansion" when she and Jayson bought it. After they divorced, Gia stayed in the house. She'd kept everything, or, more accurately, Cooper hadn't taken anything when he left. Taylor thought of her own situation and frowned. If she'd been married to Royce and then he'd left her, she'd have sold their shared house in a blink. How could Gia be happy in the house she'd bought with her ex-husband?

Despite the sunny day, clouds hovered over Taylor's mood. Her mind on—who else? Royce.

The jackass.

Tears threatened but she swallowed them down.

They'd been blessed with a bright sunshiny day, sparkling blue water, and she now had a pink cocktail with fruit floating in it. She would force a good mood today if she had to. She sipped her spiked pink lemonade, glad for the token amount of alcohol to numb her feelings. Not that a few ounces of vodka in the slim glass would come close to achieving "numb," but every little bit helped.

Gia returned from the house, a plate of vegetables and hummus in one hand. "You know, I wanted to do this last week, but I was so crampy and bloated and pissy, I decided the only company I should keep was my own." She capped that statement with a smile, and Taylor was surprised to hear herself chuckle in response.

"Don't worry, we only have to deal with Mother Nature's ultimate prank for another twenty or twenty-five years," Taylor said.

In her own lounger, Gia leaned her head back. "Don't remind me. It's not like I'm anywhere near wanting kids now anyway. Why must I have to endure that joyous monthly reminder that I haven't had any yet?"

And isn't that exactly what Taylor had told Royce? She wasn't ready yet. But according to him he wasn't ready *ever*. Maybe she should have talked to him about what he wanted in the future—before he'd come to tell her they didn't have one. Maybe she should've told him she loved him as soon as she knew it herself.

Though, if she'd done that, the breakup would've happened sooner. *And while we were naked.* Hopefully one day she'd look back and understand why they didn't work out, and that him breaking up with her was for the best. But today was not that day.

"Oh! Remind me before you leave to show you the print advertising concepts for the T13. They are *amazing*!" Gia described the ads with a flourish and Taylor tried to listen, but another thought had crawled around to the front of her consciousness.

The thought was a question.

When was her last period?

And because she couldn't recall right away how long ago it'd been, or the last time she'd bought a box of tampons, a frisson of panic laced itself around her ribs.

Royce and Taylor had been careful. Very careful. He'd been the one to remember the protection. She'd usually been hovering around cloud nine after an orgasm, though, which meant something could have been overlooked. Condoms weren't 100 percent effective, either—now, were they?

God.

How long *had* it been? She'd been so busy. So distracted...

Gia sat up from her lounger and removed her sunglasses, tucking them into the messy bun on top of her head. "Are you ready to talk?"

"Am I— About what?"

"You're so sad I can feel it like I can feel this sunshine, sweetheart. I was stalling to see if you wanted to bring it up."

"That's not like you." But now that Gia offered to talk about it, Taylor wasn't going to lie about what had happened.

"You're dating my brother and I love you both, so I'm trying to let you two work it out without my involvement."

"I love him, too." Admitting it out loud made Taylor's heart fracture. Damn Royce and his stupid breakup flowers.

Gia's smile lifted her cheeks. "Really?"

"Yes. But he doesn't love me. He broke up with me yesterday."

"What? Why? Like he can do better?" Ire washed away her friend's smile. What was left was Mama Bear Gia. But then her tone softened and she leaned forward a smidge. "Honey, are you okay?"

Taylor shook her head, tears causing her vision to swim. She wiped her eyes beneath her sunglasses. Gia noticed and was next to her in an instant.

"I am going to kill him. I swear." She stroked Taylor's arm. "I already threatened his person if he hurt you. So he should expect it."

"Maybe we were never a good match from the start," Taylor said around a sob. "We were good together, but I want a future that he says he can't imagine. He can't see past CEO. I deserve better than that."

"Damn right you do."

"I'm incapable of being as pragmatic as Royce. I can't outline our relationship in a flow chart. I can't form an opinion based on past occurrences. I fell in love with him. That had nothing to do with pragmatism."

Gia sighed. "Don't I know it, hon."

"Anyway." Taylor sniffled. "He didn't fall in love with me. That's hard to accept. But even worse was that he wasn't willing to try."

Despite Gia's assurances that Taylor deserved better than someone who had to "try" to love her, Taylor felt like her heart was in pieces at their feet. Or at the bottom of Gia's swimming pool. Today, despite her best efforts, she wasn't going to be able to enjoy the sunshine or her pink drink or her friend's plucky sense of humor. Today she was going to have to sit with her heavy emotions and deal with them the same way she would be dealing with them in the future.

Alone.

Twenty

Taylor waited until the following week to confirm that she was, in fact, pregnant.

Waiting had not ushered in her period. She didn't tell Gia—she didn't tell anyone. She'd gone to the pharmacy, purchased three pregnancy tests and took every one of them. The boxes said to wait two minutes for results, but the pair of "you're pregnant" lines appeared instantly for her.

Rocked as she was, she'd called in sick Monday and had gone to her doctor to confirm. She even had a due date. November 27.

She supposed calling in sick was the truth. She'd been sick at the idea of seeing Royce again. It was almost unbelievable that a month had passed. Since then, he'd been cordial, stiff lipped and mostly absent. He must've taken every off-site meeting or opportunity to leave the building because his office door had been locked, the room dark most of the time. So many huge changes lay like fallen soldiers between them. Jack had retired. Royce had become CEO. Taylor had found out she was expecting a baby.

She didn't have the luxury of avoidance the way Royce did. In a month or so, her body would reveal the telltale pregnancy bump and everyone would know. Unless she quit her job, there'd be no way to hide it—a moot point since she was keeping the baby.

There were a couple of musts in her life. One, thriving at ThomKnox. Two, keeping her friendships with Brannon and Gia, who were more like family than friends. Taylor wasn't sure where Royce fit in yet, but she'd made a decision about being a mother and it was only fair to give Royce an opportunity to decide how involved he wanted to be in his child's life. Which meant she needed to tell him there was a decision to *be* made.

Sigh. Life was hard.

She'd never been at once so filled with joy and devastation. She missed Royce, but the idea that her family would be starting, granted a lot sooner than she expected, filled her with unmitigated happiness. At the same time, she was sad that her father would never meet his grandchild. And then there was the overall feeling of solitude, since she hadn't told anyone about the pregnancy.

Telling Royce was the number one item on her agenda today.

She approached his office, surprised to encounter a woman sitting outside of it. She was fifty-something at best guess, her hair and clothing stylish. A smattering of freckles dotted her cheeks, giving her an air of youth, unlike the glasses perched on her nose.

"May I help you?" the woman asked with a stiff smile.

"Hi. I'm Taylor Thompson. You must be Royce's new assistant?"

"Executive assistant," she corrected.

"Welcome to ThomKnox." The woman didn't respond, so Taylor kept talking. "So, if he's in, I need to speak with him."

"He requested not to be bothered, but I can let him know you were here." She pulled a pen and notepad from a drawer and looked up at Taylor expectantly.

"This is important, so I'm going to have to insist." Taylor wasn't in the mood to be delayed. She was tired. She was cranky. She was pregnant. She stepped toward Royce's office door, but the woman stood to block her path.

"I'm the COO of this company," Taylor told her.

"I understand, but his instructions were implicit."

"Not to see me?" Taylor hoped not. That was horrifying.

"Not to see anyone, ma'am."

"You're new here," Taylor responded with a patient smile. "You don't understand how things work. Royce will want to hear what I have to say and it can't wait." When she reached for the door handle, the other woman physically swatted her hand away.

"You will not go in there." The woman arched a prim blond eyebrow. "Not while I'm stationed here under orders. No matter who you are."

Red faced, patience lost, Taylor leaned in. "What about if I'm the mother of his unborn child?" she growled. "Can I go in then?"

At that moment, the office door popped open. Royce looked from his new assistant to Taylor, frozen in place.

"Sir?" The woman addressed him.

"At ease, Melinda." His calm facade returned. He was too good at calling up that blank look when he needed it. "Taylor. Come in."

That wasn't how she'd wanted him to find out, but there was no going back now. He shut the door behind her and gestured to the leather sofa in his office. He lowered into the chair across from it rather than sit next to her.

"She's intense." Nervous, Taylor smoothed her hands over her skirt.

"I guess I should have been more specific about who to exclude from that request."

"Would I have been excluded?"

His brow furrowed. "Of course."

She supposed that was some relief. At least he didn't hate her. "I have three positive pregnancy tests and a report from the doctor in my purse." She took the bag off her shoulder and began riffling through the contents.

"Not necessary." He stayed her with a hand. "I believe you."

"I didn't do this on purpose."

"I don't think that," he said calmly. He was too calm for her liking. She didn't know what kind of reaction she expected, but it wasn't this.

"I'm keeping the baby. You'll be involved in your child's life if you want, of course. I'd never shut you out. But I understand you're busy and I know that your new position as CEO is demanding. I'm prepared to do what it takes to continue my own position here, including working from home on occasion after the baby is born."

Royce blinked. "Okay."

"Your level of involvement is totally up to you. I won't saddle you with a family if you're not ready." And according to the last visit he'd paid her on her front stoop, he wasn't anywhere near ready.

He dipped his head to acknowledge her. Silence fell, the only sound Melinda's voice through the door when she answered the phone.

The tide of emotions—anger, sadness, loss—could be blamed at least partially on Taylor's physical state. Hormones caused tumultuous emotions, right? She refused to cry in front of Royce. Even though he'd broken her a little. Hell, maybe a lot. The fallout wasn't complete yet. But she wouldn't whimper in front of him like a lost puppy. She had to be strong. She'd have a family of her own soon—just the two of them if the shell-shocked expression on his face was any indication of how well he was taking the news.

"We have time to sort out the details," she said, hoping to prompt a response.

"Okay," was all he said.

"Okay," she repeated. "Well. I guess I'll be going."

He followed her to the door, his eyes on her purse as she pulled it over her shoulder.

"Hopefully leaving will be easier than coming in," she sort of joked.

"I'll let Melinda know you can come in anytime you like," he said. "Maybe I'll even include Bran and Gia on that list."

Neither of them smiled as he pulled open the door.

"Thanks for coming by," he said formally when she stepped out. Hopefully he'd said that for Melinda's benefit. Him being this distant, this cold, this unresponsive was awful.

She was the woman who'd once drawn a response from him that was borderline out of character. She'd kissed him in a closet two months ago and uncovered a man neither of them had known existed. Not only had they not returned to the way they were before the kiss, but they'd arrived in a place they'd never been. With her as cordial and distant as he was.

Awful. Just awful.

Back in her office, she sat on her chair and stared blankly at the computer screen. Then she logged on and opened her email and started working.

Maybe what they needed was time apart. Time to digest that they'd soon be parents. And judging by Royce's reaction—time to accept that they'd be parenting apart as well.

Twenty-One

Time should have quelled the pain.

It should have, but it hadn't.

Royce had turned over the last personal conversation he'd had with Taylor every day since it'd happened, and had arrived at the same exact conclusion every time.

He'd blown it.

She was pregnant and he hadn't reacted well to that news, either. To learning he was going to be a father and could "choose his level of involvement." Like this was a video game and he had the option to choose his starting level. In his defense, he hadn't had time to react considering he'd had an audience—his tart assistant. Had he been eased into the news rather than overhearing it, maybe his reaction would have been more favorable. Then again, who the hell knew? He had zero experience hearing he was going to be a father before last week.

God. A baby. The fact that he would soon be a parent to a living, breathing human being still hadn't sank in. Probably because he was excellent at compartmentalizing.

The baby wouldn't be born for months. No reason to rush to a decision. Plus, he'd told Melinda not to disturb him because he'd had a packed week ahead of him. It hadn't been hard to fill his time with myriad tasks considering he was still wearing the CFO *and* CEO hats.

Though now that he'd completed his round of interviews with three very qualified candidates for the position of Chief Financial Officer, and the follow-up interviews were scheduled with Brannon and Taylor, Royce was left with a lot of time on his hands. With nothing but quiet in his head so that he could figure out how he felt.

How *did* he feel?

Elated.

Devastated.

Buoyant.

Enraged.

Ridiculously happy.

But that happiness was a balloon that couldn't fully inflate, as if there was a microscopic pinprick letting out a stream of air. Arguably he was the "prick" in this case. Which pissed him off more.

He'd funneled that anger, that rage, and aimed it directly at the version of Taylor in his mind. How dare she make plans and exclude him? She'd told him he could be involved as if it was optional. Like he would be too busy to spend time with his son or daughter?

Son.

Daughter.

He'd have one or the other come winter. It was terrifying. Exciting.

Inevitable.

Bran let himself in without so much as a knock, interrupting a rare bout of silent time and earning a solid scowl from Royce.

"I waited until Melinda went to lunch to sneak in." Bran shuddered theatrically. "She's scary."

"She's thorough. What do you want?" Royce asked, tired. "If this is about the follow-up interviews, I'll indulge you."

"It's about Taylor."

"In that case, you can go." Royce was only half kidding.

"Much as I'd like to leave you alone with your righteous anger," Bran said as he lounged in a chair in front of Royce's desk. "I'm going to have to call you on your bullshit."

"Did you misunderstand me? I don't want to talk about Taylor with you."

The pregnancy was common knowledge. Not only did Melinda and anyone within earshot overhear Taylor, but Royce had immediately told his siblings. Gia was hurt that Taylor hadn't come to her, but Royce wasn't taking his chances where his brother and sister were concerned. The last time he'd kept a secret from them, it'd blown up in his face.

"Taylor informed me that I can choose my level of involvement. As if my *not* being involved was an option," Royce grumbled anyway, ignoring his own earlier statement that he didn't want to talk about it. The truth was he *did* need someone to talk to. "How could she say that to me? Did what happened between us mean so little to her?"

Bran laughed, which sent Royce's anger soaring. "Do you hear yourself, man? How much could she possibly have meant to you if you dumped her on her doorstep?"

"I did what had to be done."

"Listen, I'm as surprised as you are that Taylor is expecting your baby. But can you blame her for making a plan? Her life is about to change irrevocably."

"Well, so's mine!" Royce roared.

"Gia thinks you're lucky Taylor told you at all."

"Oh, you and Gia are talking about it now, too? Maybe the three of you should get together, decide my part and let me know."

"Don't be pissed at me. I happened to be there while Gia was ranting about what a moron you were. You know I always love a good conversation about what a moron you are." Bran smiled, but then quickly grew serious. "Do you have any idea how miserable you've been lately, or have you been ignoring that too?"

"I'm fine." If *fine* felt like he'd lost the outermost layer of his skin or like his heart had been mashed into paste with a crowbar, then sure, Royce was fine.

"You were *fine* when you were dating her," Bran said. "Or didn't you take time away from your busy schedule long enough to notice?"

His brother picked the wrong moment to needle him. Typically, Royce was able to be the bigger man. He knew when to let things go, and when to pursue them. He was the ultimate at picking his battles. Just not today.

"You don't get to do this, brother," Royce said, his voice low. "Not while I'm grappling with impending fatherhood. Not while I'm trying to hire a new CFO—a role that was mine for a decade plus. Not when I'm reeling over the woman I love not caring if I'm involved in our child's life or not!"

The door to his office opened and Gia stood in the doorway, wide-eyed, her hand resting gingerly on the handle.

"Hey, sis." Royce leaned back in his chair and threw the pen he'd been holding onto the desk. "Come on in and have a seat. Or should I call a staff meeting and announce to everybody what I'm going through?"

She traded wary glances with Bran, and then they both turned their eyes to their older brother.

Royce, beyond frustrated, huffed one word. "What?"

Gia's eyebrows rose.

"Why are you both staring at me?" Royce tried again.

"The woman you *love*," Gia said. "You heard that, right?" She elbowed Bran's arm without looking at him, instead studying Royce like he was a specimen in a petri dish.

"I think I heard it. I'm stunned stupid." Bran blinked.

Royce didn't know what the hell either of his younger siblings were talking about. What he didn't need right now was either of their opinions. What he needed was for them to leave him alone so he could—

Love.

Had he said that?

"Oh my God," Gia said to Bran. "I'm pretty sure he just realized what he said. Do you think he didn't know before we pointed it out?"

"I'm not sure. Let's watch and see what happens." Bran folded his arms and stared at his brother. Royce's collar felt hot. His bow tie, usually nestled comfortably in that collar, was strangling him. Cutting off the blood supply operating his brain.

He hadn't been using his brain during that outburst. He'd been speaking from his heart. And his heart had definitely not consulted his brain before those words had exited his mouth.

"I'm in love with Taylor," he said for the first time out loud. Admitting it to himself while admitting it to his brother and sister. "I've been miserable without her. I felt like… Like I was sinking, with cinder blocks tied to my feet. No matter how hard I struggled to pull myself to the surface, the weight kept pulling me down."

"Sounds like love to me," Gia said softly. Her saying

anything softly was a rarity, so Royce paid attention. "I felt like that after my divorce. I'd like to tell you it gets better. I want to tell you that the sinking, drowning feeling fades. I don't think it does. I think you just learn to think about it less often. To grab little bits of air when you can."

"Meanwhile, I wish I could tell you that you deserve this. That you entered territory you shouldn't have gone anywhere near." Bran shook his head. "But I can't. Taylor did something to you. She changed you. In a good way. Even though I'm the one who suggested you break up with her."

"You ass!" Gia punched Bran in the arm.

"Ow! I know, okay?" Bran rubbed his arm, grumbling about Gia's pointy knuckles before turning back to Royce. "My point is that a baby…a baby is a big deal. And if you're in love with the woman carrying your baby… Royce. You're going to be a father."

"You're going to be a daddy," Gia sang in a syrupy voice. "I'm going to be an aunt. I was upset Taylor didn't tell me about the pregnancy tests at first—that I had to hear it from you, of all people."

"Hey." Royce frowned.

"I was being selfish," Gia continued. "This isn't about me. Taylor dealt with the news the best way she knew how. You should be glad she isn't cutting you out of your life."

"That's Taylor. Selfless," Bran said, and Gia nodded her agreement.

"Putting herself last," Royce added. "She was trying to make this easy on me. I didn't deserve it."

"That's true," his sister said. "But you can always make it up to her."

"Have you decided what you want?" Bran asked Royce. "Taylor's letting you choose your level of involvement. Did you?"

No.

He had compartmentalized. He'd ignored everything but work. He *hadn't* dealt with it. And he clearly needed to deal with it. He'd had no idea what was in his head or his heart until his outburst.

"I need the room." Royce stood and walked to the door. "Please."

Bran and Gia filed out, Bran slapping Royce on the shoulder as he left. "Sorry."

"Don't be." Royce would figure out something. He wasn't sure what yet, but there was no way he was living his life without the mother of his child. Without the woman he loved. He would figure out a way to win her back—to erase this painful memory and replace it with only good ones.

His cell phone chirped a reminder for the advertising conference call starting in five minutes. The last of the details before the launch. Horrible timing. Every time he turned around, he was putting his life on hold for Thom-Knox.

There was a tired argument in the back of his mind about how this was his legacy and how he had to be here, that without him, ThomKnox would go belly-up. Only now it sounded like one excuse on top of another. Royce despised excuses.

Despised that he was making them.

"Fuck it." He tossed his phone onto the desk and shut his office door, locking it behind him.

"Where are you going?" Bran asked as Royce blew by.

"Not here." He stepped into the elevator and pressed the button for the ground floor.

Bran caught the doors before they closed. "What about the conference call?"

"Handle it. I have to do something."

Royce would never forget the look on his brother's face as long as he lived. Pride stretched Brannon's smile as he moved his hand away, his last gesture a nod of confirmation as the doors slid shut.

Royce was through making excuses.

Through living without the woman he loved.

A plan formed as the elevator slid down the shaft and by the time he exited into the lobby of ThomKnox, his mind was racing along with his heart.

He didn't know if his idea would win her back, but he had to try. His last thought as he climbed into his car was, *I'll try anything. Everything.*

Taylor belonged with him. It was past time he told her so.

Twenty-Two

Taylor loped into her mother's house for dinner, weighed down by everything life had thrown at her over the last month. Not only had Royce been further ignoring her, she'd felt a chill coming from Gia.

Taylor hadn't meant to exclude her friend in the announcement of her pregnancy, but even Gia should understand why Taylor had gone to Royce first.

Gia would come around. Bran had been keeping his opinions to himself and Taylor hoped it wasn't because he'd chosen sides. She wanted her baby to be born into a family overcome with love for their new addition, not upset over how the news was announced.

She'd been battling morning sickness lately too, so when she stepped into the house and the smell of garlic and grilled fish hit her nostrils, her stomach did a barrel roll. She sprinted to the half bath and emptied her lunch into the toilet, gripping the sides of the porcelain bowl.

"Good gracious, Tay!" Her mother rushed in and

snagged a decorative hand towel from the ring, wetting it under the sink. Deena helped Taylor to her feet only to push her down on the now-closed lid as she flushed. "What on earth…?"

Deena dabbed the corners of Taylor's mouth, refolded the cloth and patted Tay's overheated cheeks. That mothering gesture was something she'd done when Taylor was young. Deena had always taken care of her. Just like Taylor would take care of her own child soon. With or without Royce Knox.

"What happened? Do you have the flu?" Deena examined her closer and then pressed the back of her hand to Taylor's head. "Not too warm. But you look pale."

Taylor hadn't told her mother yet, and evidently Deena hadn't heard from anyone. Now was as good a time as any. At least Taylor knew her mother would be happy for her.

"I'm having Royce Knox's baby," she announced, looking her mother in the eye. "Fish and I aren't friends right now." Even the word *fish* made her stomach toss. She took the towel from her mother as Deena righted herself. Her mother's face broadcasted five different emotions simultaneously.

Joy won.

"I'm going to be a grandmother? I'm going to be a grandmother! It's—it's amazing!" She clapped her hands together. "How far along are you?"

"Nine weeks or so. I'm due November 27." Taylor allowed herself to smile, too.

Deena's response was pure and congratulatory. No judgment. Exactly how a mother should react. "Oh! I can make baby announcements! I have the cutest scrapbook paper I've been saving. Yellow ducks! Probably not enough for all the people we'll have to send a notice to, though." She put her hand to her chin in contemplation. "What if we send half ducks and half bears? A few sailboats? Is that tacky? Oh, who cares!" Deena crushed Taylor into a hug and mentioned again how excited she was to be a grandmother.

An hour later, Taylor and her mother finished their dinner—fish free, thanks to her efficient chef. They turned down dessert, and Taylor passed on the port in favor of a club soda with lime.

Only then did Deena broach the subject of—

"And Royce?"

"I'm not sure yet. *He's* probably not sure yet. He's been very…stoic." That was a nice way to say he was acting like a horse's ass. "It didn't work out between us. Before the pregnancy, I mean."

"Oh." Her mother frowned. "You didn't mention it."

"I've been processing."

"I understand. You've been through a lot."

Taylor appreciated her mother not guilting her for keeping her news to herself. That small grace was huge.

"I'm not sure how involved Royce will be. When I told him he kept repeating the word 'okay.'"

Deena clucked her tongue. "Well. You have my support. My undying support."

"ThomKnox is his firstborn. I should have known better than try and compete. I hope he'll make room for one more." She put her hand on her stomach.

"I hope so, too, dear. Your father made room for you. Always."

Taylor's heart grew heavier. "He was a good dad."

"The best," Deena agreed.

They changed topics, Deena discussing the announcements and when to have a baby shower. They ended up in the craft room choosing scrapbook paper with ducks or bears or sailboats, and also a few sheets with little blue whales with starfish stuck to their bellies.

At one point Deena asked if Taylor would like to move back home. The answer was an easy *no way*, but she wouldn't break her mother's heart by saying so. She instead promised Deena ample opportunities to babysit once Taylor returned to work after maternity leave.

Regardless of Gia's reaction, Bran's nonreaction and Royce's *underreaction*, Taylor chose to be happy. And if this pregnancy meant sacrificing the man she loved in order to give her son or daughter an amazing life, then that was exactly what she was going to do.

Twenty-Three

The day of the tablet launch had arrived, and Taylor, while nauseous, made her way into the offices only thirty minutes late.

She hadn't known what to expect on the day of Royce's first product launch, but certainly not what she walked into. Basically the same office she'd left at five o'clock last night. Most of the staff was in their offices, a few chatting casually in the break room. Even Bran waved a casual hello as she passed by.

Royce's office was dark but his aggressive assistant was in her chair, sitting guard outside his door. Taylor had seen his office dark a lot lately, but she didn't expect it today. He should've been here brighter and earlier than any of them. Deciding it wasn't worth the run-in with Melinda, she bypassed his office without speaking.

In her own office, Taylor opened her email and settled in for the day, expecting a meeting alert on her calendar for upper management. There wasn't one, but there was a calendar announcement that alerted her to Royce's absence.

He wasn't coming in at all today?

That was insane. The first product launch of his career as CEO and he bailed? Barring open-heart surgery, she couldn't imagine he'd skip work today. She might question the state of his romantic heart, but she doubted the actual organ was in anything less than working order.

At that moment, someone rapped on her closed office door.

"Come in."

A pretty blonde stepped inside.

"Addi. Hi."

Addison averted her eyes for a moment before meeting Taylor's. "Do you have a moment?"

"Of course." Taylor stood and rounded her desk.

"I won't be long, I just…wanted to apologize." Addison folded her hands primly in front of her periwinkle-blue dress. "I've been awful to you and I'm not quite sure how to make up for it. You might not think I was awful, but it's how I define *awful* for myself. I'm happy for you. For you and your baby. I don't want there to be any ill will between us."

Taylor smiled softly, moved. "I owe you an apology, too. I didn't mean to embarrass you when I pointed out that you and Bran looked good together."

"Oh, don't— That's not—" Addison dismissed Taylor with a quick shake of her head. "Anyway. Thank you for the birthday card and flowers. Belatedly. And congratulations on your pregnancy. Also belatedly. You can count on me if you need anything. I liked it better when we got along."

"Me, too." Taylor liked Addison and was glad there wouldn't be any further discomfort where the two of them were concerned. Plus, points to Addi for addressing the elephant in the room. Taylor hadn't been that brave.

Addi wished her luck on the product launch and left, but before Taylor could shut the door, in walked Gia, with an uncharacteristic look of chagrin decorating her face. Without a word, Gia wrapped Taylor into a hug. It went on for nearly a minute. Taylor hung on to her best friend for purchase and tried to keep the tears at bay. She succeeded, but only because Gia pulled away before emotions overtook her.

"So, I'm a horrible person and I owe you an apology." Gia shrugged matter-of-factly.

"False," Taylor replied. "Your timing is curious. Is there a line forming out there or something?" If so, Royce should be at the front of it—the only person in it, in fact.

"I'm thrilled for you. I was upset that I had to hear about my niece or nephew from Royce instead of my best friend, but that was on me, not you. I shouldn't have been so cool toward you."

Taylor noticed her friend's distance, but Royce was Gia's brother. This entire situation had to have been hard for her, too.

"Royce is your brother. I understand your loyalty to him."

"I'll always choose you." Gia smirked, and even if it wasn't 100 percent true, it was still nice to hear. She chewed on her lip for a second before asking, "Have you spoken to Royce today?"

"No. Why?"

"No reason," Gia answered quickly.

"Do you know why he opted to take off on launch day?" Taylor asked, her suspicion rising.

"I don't." Gia's eyes were shifty, her lips buttoned tight.

"Maybe I'll check with Bran. God knows Melinda won't give me any information."

"Good idea," Gia said, not offering any details. "I have to go. It's not every day we launch a new tablet." She rushed out of the room.

That was strange. And the second time in as many minutes that Taylor had been approached by someone who wanted to make amends.

Taylor followed her out, heading to Bran's office next. "Do you also have an overdue apology for me?"

"Sorry, toots. We covered that already." He winked. He wasn't wrong. There was nothing between them but a solid friendship, one she treasured.

"Why is Royce out? I know you know."

"He's at home." Bran looked her straight in the eye. "Called me this morning and said he was taking off the rest of the week."

"The rest of the *week*?"

"Yep, left his cell phone here and everything."

"It's his first product launch!" Had Royce gone crazy? This was the most important release of his career, and if not the most important *ever* at least the most important *right now*.

"He's not okay. And if you don't know why, then you never really knew my brother."

Well. She certainly didn't appreciate that.

"Maybe you should go check on him."

She folded her arms over her breasts. "Did he ask you to tell me that?"

"Nope." They had a miniature standoff.

"He's mad at me," she guessed. "Is he not showing up because he's mad?"

"Nope." Bran's eyebrows raised.

"Is he sick?" The calendar didn't specify that he'd taken a sick day, but maybe he didn't want anyone to know.

"Sort of," Bran answered, his tone gentle. "Not the way you think, though. He's sick about a lot of things."

"He's not the only one. Morning sickness is my new BFF."

Bran stood and came to her. "I'm sorry things have been strained between you two. I'm not sure Royce knows what to do with so much change this quickly. And before you challenge me on it," he said when she opened her mouth to offer another *me too*. "I know you've had a lot of change, too. You should know that when Royce came over to break up with you, I might have encouraged him to do it."

"What?"

"Unintentionally," he added. "I was concerned you two weren't on the same page. That you were developing feelings for him. I was also pissed off at him for not telling me he was named CEO the second he found out. It was immature."

"And you blacking his eye wasn't?"

Bran smirked. "That was an accident."

"Uh-huh. I'm not allergic to lilies, by the way. I just don't like them."

"Oh."

"Yeah, 'oh.' You don't know everything." But as much as she wanted to lay into Bran for his contribution, she couldn't. "Not that I blame you. The decision Royce made was ultimately his. You can't make that man do anything he doesn't want to do. He chooses what's most important to him."

Bran smiled at that—an out-and-out grin. "You're exactly right. He prioritizes those he loves. You know, I could actually use your help. Can you go to him? Remind him how important it is for him to be here today? I'd hate for him to wreck the role of CEO now that he has it. You have a better chance of convincing him to come in than I do."

"I don't know…" Bran was her friend. This company was important. But what good would it do for her to go to Royce's house if he didn't let her in?

"You're the COO. Second in command," Bran reminded her. "There's no one else."

"Low blow." Bran knew how much this position meant to her. She wasn't willing to shirk on her responsibilities any more than she would let Royce do it. "Fine. I'll do what I can to flush him out of hiding. But you owe me."

"I owe you," Bran agreed, palms up in surrender.

Royce could blow up his personal life but she wouldn't allow him to take ThomKnox with him. This company meant too much to him—to all of them—and she wouldn't be the reason, even inadvertently, that the CEO didn't do his job.

Twenty-Four

In Royce's driveway, Taylor gaped at the sheer amount of boxed furniture sitting in the open garage. A desk, chair and several bookshelves in flat-pack boxes, leaned in a stack on the wall opposite Royce's sports car.

She walked through the garage and into the house, where she found more boxes, packing foam peanuts scattered over the floor and discarded plastic. One box showed a photo of a bassinet, another box contained a playpen, and yet another, a high chair.

She picked her way around the mess, through the living room and past the couch where she and Royce had first made love. And then toward one of the back hallways where she heard what sounded like an electric drill.

Followed by a very loud swearword.

"Royce?" she called, but the drill was whirring again, her voice lost under the sound. She followed the noise to one of the back bedrooms, and found him sitting on the floor, the remnants of what might have been a crib, if he were handier with a drill, lying around him like giant matchsticks. He looked up at her, visibly stunned to see her there.

He wore a gray T-shirt and light blue jeans, his hair in disarray, she guessed from pushing his fingers through it. She didn't think she'd ever seen him like this. The T-shirt and jeans, sure, but never disheveled. Never with dark pockets under his eyes suggesting he'd been up all night worrying, and never with naked, pained vulnerability reflected in his eyes.

"Taylor." There was enough shock in his voice that she knew Bran had told her the truth. Royce hadn't been expecting her.

"It's ThomKnox's first launch day with you as CEO. What are you doing?" she asked.

"I could ask you the same thing." His smile was crooked as he gestured with the drill. "I'm putting together a crib. *Trying* to put together a crib."

By the looks of it, he wasn't doing a very good job.

"I'm a shitty carpenter."

"Why are you putting together baby furniture?"

His eyebrows pulled together. "Because we're having a baby."

We.

The fault line in her heart was quaking, like she might achieve a ten on the Richter scale from whatever he said next. Falling apart wasn't an option. Nothing had changed, not really. Sure, Royce had bought baby furniture, and was having some sort of breakdown given he was assembling it instead of going to work, but that only proved he'd decided to take responsibility for being a father. It was good news, but it didn't change their relationship.

Though none of his behavior should surprise her. She

hadn't expected him to deny responsibility for his own child. Maybe he'd just needed time to process.

"Now it's your turn," he said. "What are you doing here?"

She glanced around the room—at the torn box and Styrofoam, the miscellaneous pieces and a well-wrinkled instruction book. What was she supposed to say?

"It's okay. I should probably go first anyway." He straightened from his crouched position and set the drill aside. He was taller than she remembered him. More capable.

It was her heart that reached out first; the love she felt for him still so prevalent. She hadn't been at his side for over a month. One long, miserable month while she'd decided how to handle a pregnancy on her own—without him. How to handle her life without him. It was proving much harder than she'd imagined.

"So, I was wrong. That's the gist of it," he said, sliding his hands into his back pockets. "My priorities were out of order. I thought ThomKnox came first. I thought loyalty to my family came next—my father, my siblings." He shook his head sadly. "You, Taylor, are the one who comes first. I've never… This is embarrassing…" He trailed off for a moment. "I've never been in love before. I've always been the practical one. The responsible one in my family. Love seemed frivolous. An indulgence. I never gave myself breathing room because I didn't want to let everyone down. It was the role I gave myself, I suppose."

She didn't know how she managed a response, but she did. "You were the one with the legacy."

"Yes." He took one step closer to her. "It took me a longer while to realize how wrong I was about that. You, Taylor Thompson, are my legacy. You are the love of my life. I can't celebrate any ThomKnox milestone without you.

We made a baby. It's a miracle." His smile was bright, like the sun coming out after a long rain. She'd never seen him so happy.

"It is pretty incredible." She felt her lips tip into a smile of their own.

"I should've reacted better when you told me. I just… I had no idea what to do. I was overwhelmed. But now I'm not. Now, I know."

"You know?"

"Yes." He gripped her biceps. "I want to make a life. With you. ThomKnox is important, but I can work from home sometimes if you need me to be with the baby while you're at the office. You don't have to shoulder this alone. I don't want you to be alone. Hell, *I* don't want to be alone. I want you here, with me. In this house. In my life. In my bed."

Oh, how she wanted that, too. Was her dream of a family and Royce loving her too finally coming true?

"That's what the office furniture is for. So you can set up an office wherever you like. If that's at home with our baby, then that's where your new headquarters are. And if you'd rather return to the office, well, then I'll stay home with our son or daughter."

Our son or daughter. That phrase opened her up and laid her bare. How could she say no to the man she loved? He was inside her, still—he'd been a part of her this entire time. Royce was saying not only that he wanted this family, but that he would sacrifice his own legacy to support hers.

"Our paths have always been laid out before us, Taylor. But we don't have to walk the path our fathers intended. We can still honor them, whether they're here or not." He gave her arms a gentle squeeze, tender emotion shining in his eyes. "We can do the job we were put on this planet to do. Mine isn't, as I previously believed, to be CEO.

My job is to love you. I'm going to make up for failing at that. I swear."

"You're doing great so far," she whispered. Happiness bloomed in her chest, dangerous and full. He was in love with her? His *job* was to love her? It was everything she wanted to hear, but… "Royce, if you're having some sort of breakdown or early midlife crisis—"

"It's not a breakdown. It's an epiphany. I've always seen the world as black and white. Your father knew that about me—that my inability to handle emotion well was my downfall. That was why he warned you away from me." Royce smiled gently. "What he didn't know was that you, Taylor, had the ability to change me. To open me up to love. You're my first. I also want you to be my last. I'm happier in the gray with you."

Was Royce right? Had her father only been trying to protect her from a future he'd predicted?

"Do you love me, Taylor? That's the only missing piece. That and the sincerest of apologies, which I'll do right now. I'm sorry I broke up with you. I'm sorry I ended what we had without giving us a chance. I said I couldn't envision myself as a family man, but the truth was I never tried. I overlooked the gift you would've given me—your heart. I love you so much. So much I tried to use an electric drill." His throat bobbed in a rough laugh. "We've had separate dreams for too long. It's time we build a new dream together. One that we choose ourselves, not the one predestined for us."

"I like the sound of that." She swiped the tears from her eyes as he pulled her into his embrace. She went, wrapping her arms around him and knowing he was right about them needing to build a dream together. They would change their fathers' plans, but only slightly. They would run ThomKnox their way. Together.

Against her lips, Royce murmured the words she never thought she'd hear from him. "Move in with me. Marry me. Have my baby."

"Okay," she said simply. And it was simple. She loved him and he loved her, and the rest they would make work. But she couldn't let him fail. They had time to work "them" out. His legacy still mattered. "But the launch…"

"Do you think Gia and Bran would let ThomKnox go down in flames?"

"No."

"Do you think if you aren't there, that they'll let you fail as well?" He tipped his head.

"Absolutely not." Bran and Gia were more than friends. They were family. And now that Royce had proposed— soon they would *literally* be family. And soon Royce and Taylor would begin raising their own.

"Neither do I. Besides. I can't go to the office. I have a crib to build."

"And a bassinet." She let out a soft laugh. "Why didn't you hire somebody to do all of this?"

"I wanted you to see I'm capable of being the man you need me to be. I'll be a good father, Taylor. Like mine. Like yours."

"I know you will. I always knew you would. I'm sorry I ever made you believe otherwise. I love you."

"I love you." He kissed her. She'd never doubted his ability to love his child. She'd only doubted herself. The day he'd brought her those doomed flowers, she should have told him she loved him. She wondered if he would've known then that he loved her.

"I'll be a better husband than I was a boyfriend," he told her. "When I put my mind to something, I always succeed. And with your love in my corner, how could I possibly fail?"

She kissed him, tasting the resolve on his tongue, feeling the passion in his touch. Surrendering to him when he carried her into the next room and they made love long and slow. It didn't quite make up for a month apart, but it was a good start.

A good start that would have the happiest of endings.

They'd see to it.

* * * * *

TEMPORARY WIFE TEMPTATION

JAYCI LEE

To my tall, dark and handsome husband.
You'll always be my favorite hero.

One

In reality, Garrett Song, Hansol Incorporated's VP of Business and Development, was just a man. A creature of flesh and blood. Yet from everyone's awe and fascination, he might as well have been the Dark Knight.

His grandparents had founded Hansol Incorporated, and it was now one of the top fashion retailers in the country. It was the Song family's hard work and dedication that accounted for its success, and Garrett was a Song through and through. His workaholism was renowned in the industry, and Natalie Sobol had witnessed it firsthand. Well, not in person, but through emails and phone calls.

Prior to transferring to Los Angeles a month ago, he'd worked out of the New York office. When the VP of Human Resources there had gone on medical leave last year, Natalie was appointed the interim VP to manage her key duties. She'd worked remotely from the LA office, and reported to Garrett Song for eight weeks. He was exacting but unerringly fair, and she respected his keen intelligence and dedication to the company. And she could swear there was a wicked sense of humor beneath his curt, dry words.

Now that he was in LA, Natalie couldn't fathom why he couldn't find half an hour to review and sign the HR documents to finalize his transfer. A pang of disappointment and anger jarred her equilibrium. Did he think his royal status put him above ordinary employees? Had she misjudged him so abysmally?

"Well, tough," she muttered, tapping her pen against his empty personnel file. Everyone had to abide by the company's policies and procedures. Even the company's heir apparent.

It was a good thing she was skilled at putting arrogant executives in their places. She hadn't become the youngest HR director at Hansol by cowering from her responsibilities. *Hell, no.* She would lay down the law this minute. After placing a neat stack of unsigned documents into his folder and tucking it under her arm, Natalie headed for his corner office. No matter how entitled he felt, he should be able to sign documents placed right under his nose.

After the briefest of knocks, she stepped into his office and shut the door behind her with an audible click. From the slim metal-and-glass desk to the single abstract painting on the otherwise bare wall, it was a great deal more stylish and far less pretentious than his counterparts' offices.

His head was bent over the desk, dark hair glinting in the sunlight from the window. Her heart stuttered with the sudden awareness; she was finally meeting Garrett Song in person. *This isn't a social visit, Nat.* She marched up to his desk, her sensible pumps clacking on the floor like the beat of a battle drum, but he didn't bother looking up. *Ugh. Is he waiting for a formal announcement of my arrival?* She raised a fist to her mouth, but the "ahem" never made it past her throat.

"Yes?" Garrett Song raised his head and his dark brown

eyes locked on hers. She felt hot and cold at once, her heart tripping over itself. The grapevine had been on fire due to his renowned good looks, but she hadn't been prepared for his magnetic presence. The man was breathtaking and she was reminded, with shocking intensity, that she was very much a woman.

You didn't come to drool over him. You came to reprimand him.

"Mr. Song, I'm Natalie Sobol." She stuck out her hand, relieved to see how steady it was. "It's a pleasure to finally meet you in person."

"Ms. Sobol." He nodded, accepting her proffered hand. "The pleasure's all mine. I haven't forgotten your invaluable work as the interim VP of HR. You're truly an asset to our company."

His compliment brought color to her cheeks, and sparks skipped along her skin as her body responded to the warmth of his hand. She noticed how his broad shoulders and muscular arms strained against the confines of his dress shirt. His upper-class polish barely contained his raw strength and sexuality. Did he ever let his control slip? Let his powerful sensuality burst through? Natalie suddenly wanted to be the one to shatter his control.

"What can I do for you?" he asked.

Startled out of her reverie, she tugged on her hand to break contact. For a second, it felt as though he tightened his grip, but then she was free. With her expression restored to polite indifference, she placed the folder on his desk. It didn't matter that he made her blood rush; he was an executive of Hansol and she was its HR director. It would be unprofessional of her to so much as smile too warmly at him.

"What's this?" His eyebrows drew together and his gaze turned glacial as he scanned the papers inside.

"Your personnel file." Natalie cleared her throat and

drew her shoulders back. "And a written warning for violating company policies."

"I can see what it is, Ms. Sobol. What is it *for*?" He enunciated each word with care.

"All employees are required to sign their employment documents within two weeks of hiring, or in your case, transfer. You've been here over a month, but you still haven't signed them. As the HR director, I have a duty to write you up for violating a company policy."

He stared at Natalie as though she'd sprouted a third eye on her forehead. Then, he leaned back in his seat and crossed his arms over his chest, making everything bulge and strain against his shirt. *Gah*. It was so much easier to work with him when she didn't have to look at him.

"Of course, if you sign the documents here and now, I won't put the written warning in your personnel file." Her words tripped over each other. She'd taken on many executives as part of her daily dose of kick ass, but none of them had melted her bones before. She stomped down on the lust raging low in her stomach.

"Correct me if I'm wrong," Garrett drawled, "but that sounds curiously like a threat."

"I don't see how doing my job comes across as a threat to you." Her words were laced with iron. "It's imperative I enforce company policies consistently across the board."

"If you want to insist on going strictly by the book, you're violating a company policy right now. Employees are entitled to a verbal warning prior to a written warning. Isn't that correct, Ms. Sobol?"

She already knew he was well versed in the company policies, but she was impressed nonetheless. Unfortunately for him, she knew them better.

"HR gave you countless reminders. Those were more than adequate preliminary warnings. But if you prefer the process to be more official, I'll be sure to invite you to my office for your next verbal warning."

"I appreciate your dedication to Hansol." His full lips quirked into a sexy grin in an abrupt shift in mood. *Or tactic.* "Why don't I sign the documents now? Please have a seat."

Damn it. She was dying to get out of his office—she didn't understand her reaction to him and she didn't like it—but he'd effectively trapped her. Gritting her teeth, she sat down and clasped her hands on her lap.

Virility radiated from him. She'd seen good-looking men before, but she hadn't been so attracted to a man since... well, since forever.

He worked his way through the short stack of papers. His shirtsleeves were rolled past his elbows, exposing solid forearms that looked smooth and tanned, as if he spent his days in the sun rather than in an office building. She bit her lip, unable to stop imagining the rest of him. He had a light smattering of hair on his muscular chest that tapered off above his smooth, sculpted abs only to resurface below his navel as it darkened toward his...

Stop! Natalie couldn't lust after Garrett Song. She would be a hypocrite to even think about an office romance. She was the HR director, for heaven's sake.

"That wasn't too hard." He gave her a rueful smile. "I apologize for the delay."

"Apology accepted."

Natalie jumped to her feet, eager to escape him, but he proceeded to tap the papers on his desk, straightening them with exaggerated care. Then he placed the neat stack in the folder in slow motion before holding it out to her. The man was immensely irritating.

Not trusting what she might say, Natalie snatched the folder from him and speed walked out of his office. Her unannounced arrival and abrupt departure might've convinced him she was strange and rude, but better that than throwing herself across his desk and begging him to ravish her. *I bet he's an excellent ravisher.*

Besides, he could have his pick of beautiful women out there. He'd never be interested in someone ordinary like her. Even if he got bonked in the head and became interested in her, she had Sophie to think of.

Sophie.

Her hormone-frenzied thoughts ground to a halt. The air rushed out of her lungs as grief rushed in, raw and real. It hit her out of nowhere, as it often did since that fateful car crash over a month ago.

Traci was gone.

Natalie rushed the last few feet to her office and shut the door as a ragged sob escaped her lips. Traci's husband, Parker, the older brother Natalie had always wished for, had died on impact. Her older sister had hung on until she reached her side in the hospital.

"Promise me," Traci had said as she gripped her hand.

"Anything." The last member of Natalie's family had been slipping away. "Just don't leave me."

"Raise Sophie as your daughter." Her eyes bore into Natalie's, frantic and terrified. "Promise. Me."

"I promise," she had pledged.

Her sister's dying wish meant little to the law. Lily and Steve Davis, Sophie's paternal grandparents and next of kin, would become her legal guardians by default. The chances of the court granting Natalie's adoption application were abysmal, especially with the Davises opposing the adoption. They were good people, but Sophie was their last link to Parker, and they intended to take her to New York with them even if it meant a drawn-out custody battle.

Meanwhile, a social worker had told Natalie that two-parent families in a high-income bracket had better chances of adopting. Too bad she couldn't pull a wealthy husband out of a hat like a fluffy, white bunny.

Natalie would do anything to give her niece a happy, carefree childhood. She and Traci knew what it meant to grow up without a mom.

With a forlorn sigh, she reached for her mouse and clicked through the forty-seven emails she'd received while she was in Garrett Song's office. One in particular caught her attention.

"What?" She rubbed her eyes and read the email again. She had to be hallucinating from her desperation. "No. Freaking. Way."

The current VP of Human Resources was retiring at the end of the year, and the company wanted to promote internally. The position had a six-figure salary with generous benefits—*Sophie, I could send you to a Montessori preschool!*—and the opening was in *New York*. Surely, the Davises would be open to negotiating custody if they could remain a large part of their granddaughter's life.

It was about time Fate threw her a bone.

If she could get the promotion, then all she needed was a husband to seal the deal. Without warning, an image of Garrett Song filled her head. His strength. His raw masculinity. Her breath caught at the visceral intrusion and heat gathered at her center before she shook it off.

What did Garrett have to do with anything?

For the first time in his nearly two months at the LA office, Garrett left work early. His grandmother had summoned him, saying she wanted to see his face before she forgot what he looked like. It was his grandmother's passive-aggressive way of telling him she wasn't happy with his biweekly visits.

She lived with his father and his younger sister at their family home in Pacific Palisades. The fact that he didn't move back in when he returned to Los Angeles was still a touchy subject with her. Customarily, Korean folks lived with their parents and grandparents until they got married. Garrett planned on dying a bachelor, and getting his own place now was a good way to start acclimating his elders to the idea.

He navigated the surface roads to avoid rush-hour traffic but eventually got on the freeway and joined the other cars crawling five miles per hour. Stuck in the mind-numbing commute, Garrett's thoughts wandered to Natalie Sobol as it had done numerous times in the last several weeks.

Hell.

He dragged in a deep breath, his shirt stretching across his chest.

When she first walked in, he'd thought—with a flash of annoyance—that she was one of their Korean-American models, tall and beautiful. He was too busy to listen to her lie about getting lost on her way to the design department, a classic but unimaginative ploy used by women to get intimate with his wallet. But as she drew closer, he'd noticed her startling whiskey eyes, creamy skin and hourglass curves, and forgot his irritation and suspicions. She was stunning, and desire pumped through him.

Then she'd introduced herself.

For the briefest moment, he'd lusted after Hansol's HR director. Someone he enjoyed working with and valued as an employee. He and the VP of HR had even discussed Natalie Sobol as her potential successor.

Restless, he changed lanes and advanced a half-car's length. She wasn't even his type. He preferred the sophisticated women from his own circle who understood no-strings-attached affairs. Everyone knew the rules and no one got hurt.

He cringed and shoved his fingers through his hair. From her button-up shirt to her knee-length skirt, she'd been the picture of professionalism. Oddly, rather than turning him off, something about her meticulous demeanor had made him want to…dishevel her. Undo her buttons and hike up her skirt—

He slapped his cheeks like a drowsy driver fighting the sweet temptation of sleep. Having the sudden hots for an employee was inconvenient and messy. Their HR director, at that. As a rule, Garrett never dated anyone in the company.

And the timing was diabolical. A scandal so close to his CEO appointment could have consequences more dire than mere personal humiliation. It could destabilize the entire corporation, and sabotage his plan for a partnership with Vivotex, the largest fashion group in the world. His family had worked too hard and sacrificed too much for him to risk the company's reputation and the livelihood of thousands of employees over his libido.

And his grandmother. The eighty-year-old was still as sharp as a surgical knife but she was growing frailer than she let on. If she lost face because of him, she would give herself a heart attack by sheer force of will. A small one, just enough to cram a healthy dose of guilt down his throat. *Damn it.*

His self-control had shifted as he held Natalie's eyes. He'd wanted to kiss the woman with a white-hot lust he couldn't comprehend. As far as he was concerned, Natalie Sobol was the devil incarnate sent to toy with him, and he planned to avoid her at all costs.

He arrived at his family home with fifty minutes left until his meeting with a potential business partner, Clark Nobu. He was the backbone of Vivotex's board of directors, and earning his trust would boost Hansol's chances for a partnership.

"Hey, Gare. Colin's taking me to one of his new clubs." His sister, decked out in a black sequined dress that was six inches too short, skipped down the staircase and pecked him on the cheek. "Bye, Gare."

"Good seeing you, too, Adelaide," he said dryly. Their cousin Colin ran several successful nightclubs in Koreatown and Hollywood. A self-made man. Garrett respected that, but the family branded him as the black sheep. "I'm rooting for Colin but he can't avoid Grandmother forever."

"I know." A somber shadow clouded Adelaide's eyes. "And I'm rooting for you, *oppa*. Good luck with Grandmother."

"Yeah, thanks. Have fun, kiddo." He frowned at her back as she hurried out of the house.

After their mom died, Garrett had done his best for his baby sister, but there was only so much a fifteen-year-old boy could do for a seven-year-old girl. By the time their dad emerged from years of grief, Adelaide was a petulant high-school kid who switched boyfriends like pairs of old shoes, seeking affection and comfort from superficial relationships.

Adelaide was smarter than him, though. Watching his father fall apart after his mom's death hadn't been enough to teach him the destructive force of love. It had taken Samantha to nail home the lesson and bleed him dry of sentimental delusions. Even years after their breakup, the mere thought of her singed him with a flash of betrayal and humiliation.

Garrett knocked and entered his grandmother's room. It didn't contain any Western furniture, such as a bed or chairs. Rather, she sat with her back ramrod straight on a thick floor mattress with her Samsung laptop set up on a low table beside her in a fusion of the old and the new.

"Hal-muh-nee." He bowed at his waist, then kneeled in front of her on a *bang-suk*, taking his usual position on the comfortable floor cushion. "How was your day?"

"The usual. Incompetent idiots running around like their asses were on fire." She was fluent in English but she spoke to him in Korean. An outsider would be thrown by the conversation conducted in two different languages—as though there was an invisible translator between them translating English into Korean and Korean into English at lightning speed. "Did you eat?"

"I had dinner at the office."

"Good. Sit down more comfortably."

That was code for him to settle down for a long conversation. Garrett shifted to sit with his legs crossed in front of him and waited for her to speak.

"We have half a year until you're appointed CEO. I trust you're diligently preparing for your new duties."

"Of course, Grandmother." They both knew he was ready to run the company. He'd been trained for the job since he was a child.

She nodded and breathed deeply. If he didn't know better, Garrett would've thought she was hesitating, but that was preposterous. She wielded her authority with unwavering confidence.

"When we announce you as Hansol's new CEO at the press conference, we will also announce your engagement."

"My what?" His heart lurched as he studied his grandmother's face. *Did she have a stroke without anyone noticing?* "Are you feeling all right?"

"Of course I'm all right." She waved aside his question with an impatient shake of her head. "As I was saying, we will announce your engagement to Jihae Park of the Rotelle Corporation in Korea."

His blood chilled as disbelief turned to outrage. Every minute of his life had been micromanaged to mold him into the perfect heir. Edges that didn't fit into that box were sliced off without mercy. Skateboarding was for hooligans. Golf was more appropriate. Basketball could get too rough. Tennis reflected higher culture. *Now she wants to decide who I marry?*

His parents' marriage had been a union of two wealthy Korean-American families and their businesses. They had found love and happiness in their arranged marriage, but when his mother succumbed to cancer, the warmth and laughter in their home had faded away. Garrett and his sister's childhood had been dominated by the sterile, suffocating demands of upholding their family name.

"Am I being married off to the woman or the corporation?" He forced his voice to remain calm.

"You…" Her eyes widened to reveal an unnatural amount of white around her irises. "You dare talk back to me?"

A stab of guilt pierced his heart, but Garrett clenched his fists and pressed them onto the hard floor in front of him. His grandparents had built Hansol from the ground up, working sixteen-hour days in front of sewing machines, their eyes going blind and their fingers deteriorating with arthritis. After a decade of single-minded determination, Hansol opened its first retail store and took its place as an up-and-coming fashion retailer in mainstream America, but his grandfather passed away too soon to see his dream realized. To Grandmother, Hansol was more than a company. It was her late husband's soul.

"I've obeyed you without question my entire life because I know of the sacrifices you've made for our family, but an arranged marriage is out of the question." He'd rather crawl across sizzling lava than become a bartered stud for the Song family. "Please reconsider, *hal-muh-nee*."

"Min-*ah*." As his grandmother addressed him by his Korean name, her stern features softened imperceptibly. "I arranged the match with your best interest at heart. Jihae is a lovely, accomplished child from a well-respected *jae-bul* family. She will make a good wife and mother."

"My best interest? And it has nothing to do with having a *jae-bul* granddaughter-in-law who will bear you *jae-*

bul grandchildren?" The only way to obtain the power and authority of a *jae-bul*—the rich, pseudoroyal families in Korea—was through birth or marriage. No matter how successful, the Songs were still part of the nouveaux riches, not a *jae-bul* family. "Grandmother, I respect our heritage and want the best for Hansol, but I could uphold our family name without a *jae-bul* wife."

"Such insolence. Defying your elders." She bowed her head and shook it slowly as though she was too ashamed to hold it up. "This is my fault. After your mother died, I did my best to raise you and your sister right, but it's obvious I failed you."

Garrett swallowed a roar of frustration. Reasoning and pleading wouldn't get him anywhere with his grandmother. She was ruthless and obstinate, and she would hold her ground until it crumbled beneath her. It was time to reclaim his life.

"You haven't failed. You raised us to stand up for ourselves and to fight for what we believe in." His voice shook with colliding emotions. Taking a deep breath, he straightened his back. He wasn't the scared young boy who'd lost his mom. He was a grown man and it was time his grandmother accepted it—even if he had to lie to get it across to her. "I'm already engaged to another woman, and I will fight for her."

For the second time that evening, she was at a loss for words, but only for a moment. "Well, you need to tell the *other woman* the engagement is off. There is no harm done, yet. The press is unaware of either engagement."

"No harm done? I was taught that honor should be upheld at all costs. Casting aside the woman I love to marry another with wealth and power is not honorable."

"I am your grandmother. Do not presume to lecture me about honor." Her slight figure trembled with outrage. "If you do not marry Jihae, I will stop you from ascending to the CEO position. Don't forget I am the majority share-holder."

"And I'm the most qualified CEO candidate, and the only one who could deliver the Vivotex partnership. If you vote against me, you'll be voting against the company." Garrett stood and bowed to her. "I'm keeping my promise to my fiancée. I trust you to act with Hansol's best interest in mind."

With those last words, he left the house with long, fast strides. There was rebelling and there was *rebelling*. He was surprised his grandmother hadn't passed out. Then again, she wouldn't be Grace Song if she showed weakness in the face of adversity.

Garrett planted his hands on the hood of his car as vertigo blurred his vision. Not only did he now have to find a fiancée, but he also had to marry her. If not executed flawlessly, his plan could split his family apart, and Hansol could take a blow. There was no room for error.

Once he secured the partnership with Vivotex, his grandmother wouldn't oppose his CEO appointment. She would never put her personal agenda ahead of the good of the company. Hansol meant too much to her. But Garrett wasn't safe from her interference with his personal life until he married his imaginary fiancée.

Where can I find the perfect bride? He slid into the driver's seat with a mirthless laugh. *Now there's one question I never thought I'd ask myself.* His brief dalliance with self-pity and panic ceased as he focused on how to pull this off. His partner in crime had to be someone discreet, practical and desperate enough to agree to a fake marriage. Simple. Raking his hand through his hair, he stepped on the accelerator and made a sharp left, heading toward Melrose.

A real marriage was the last thing Garrett wanted to inflict on himself. It made little difference whether it was an arranged union or a love match. Marriage was a senseless gamble. He would never risk the kind of love that could break a man and his family.

When Garrett drove onto Melrose, the traffic stopped, killing any breeze he was able to enjoy. As soon as he saw the club's valet sign, he shot out of his car and tossed the key to the parking attendant.

He grimaced as he stepped into the meat market known as Le Rêve, and headed for the private VIP room. Garrett usually steered clear of places like this, but Nobu was a widower who thrived on the kind of excitement Le Rêve had to offer.

Garrett was relieved the VIP room was empty. But the civil war he'd instigated with his grandmother wrapped him in a fog of anger. How had it to come to this? He pinched the bridge of his nose as tension built in his temples. When his phone buzzed in his back pocket, he sighed with resignation, knowing it was Nobu canceling.

I'm tied up in a work emergency. Not getting out of here until past midnight. My apologies. I owe you one.

Garrett was officially off the clock. He huffed a humorless laugh. If he married that Korean heiress, he would never be off the clock. Even the most intimate aspects of his life would be intertwined with Hansol. He was tempted to grab a stiff drink, but he didn't get drunk in public and rarely did so in private. Control was much too valuable, but tonight, his was dangerously close to shattering.

Where the hell would he find his convenient bride?

Two

The cool silk of the dress caressed Natalie's bare skin as she inched forward in line. She winced at the reminder that a slip of fabric was all that stood between the world and her rear end. Sighing, she crossed "going commando" off her bucket list.

"You. Lady in red."

When no one stepped up, she craned her neck to peer behind her. Maybe the bouncer meant the blonde in hot pink? After three seconds, Natalie realized he meant her.

"Come on through, gorgeous." His smirk was a tooth short of a leer.

According to her internet research, Le Rêve's Hulk look-alike bouncers upheld the less-is-more philosophy. Her dress was definitely less. The strap of her scarlet mini flowed into a bodice that exposed a third of her right breast, and the back of her dress... Well, there wasn't one. Natalie didn't recognize herself in the mirror, especially with her dramatic eye makeup, but she couldn't afford to be modest. Getting in mattered too much, especially as it was a Friday night and everyone was dressed to kill.

Forcing a smile, she sashayed past Hulk Number One and ascended the steep staircase in her four-inch stilettos. Natalie reached the top without falling on her face or mooning the crowd. *Yes-s-s.* She pulled back her elbow in a discreet fist pump.

Lily Davis had called at 4:00 a.m., sobbing and hiccupping a jumble of words, including "Sophie," "high fever" and "vomiting." Natalie had instructed Sophie's grandparents to take the baby to the nearest emergency room from their hotel and rushed over to meet them. By the time the doctor explained that it was a twenty-four-hour virus a lukewarm bath would've eased, she'd missed her interview for the VP position.

Stupid rookie mistake. She should've researched the symptoms online instead of panicking like that. But the damage was done. Natalie had no luck rescheduling her interview. The hiring committee had decided staying with her sick niece in the ER rather than showing up for the interview proved she lacked the commitment for an executive position. They'd waved aside her explanation as though she was making a my-dog-ate-my-homework excuse. She gritted her teeth at the unfairness.

What had happened this morning could ruin the one chance she had at adopting Sophie. But it wasn't over yet. It couldn't be over. Garrett Song was the future CEO of Hansol. Surely, he could convince the hiring committee to give her a second chance. Ambushing him at a nightclub wasn't the most professional move, but she had run out of options.

According to his calendar, he was having a business meeting at the club, which also meant there was a good chance of his leaving for a business trip the next day. This might be the last chance she had to talk to him face-to-face for a few weeks. There was no time to waste, so Natalie had resorted to desperate measures.

Squaring her shoulders, she ventured deeper into foreign territory. Her lips parted at the sight of beautiful people writhing and rocking to the DJ's mixes. They made sweaty, drunk and horny look attractive. The blinking strobe lights and reverberating bass pulsed in rhythm with her jackhammering heart. Natalie unclenched her clammy fists. *Just find him, ask him and leave.*

But first, she needed liquid courage.

Icy blue accent lights slashed artfully across the circular bar, its central column of spirits reaching high to the distant ceiling. *How in the world could they get those bottles down?*

Natalie shook her head to rein in her wandering thoughts, then froze. She'd spent an hour taming her black curls, but they were already straining against the five hundred bobby pins holding them down. She had half an hour, tops, before she turned into Medusa. At the hottest club on Melrose. *That's just swell.*

Hustling through a tiny space between revelers, she managed to snag a stool, then waved for a bartender. A boyish mixologist with tattoos hugging his biceps gave her a nod and a wink, as he performed a hair-raising cocktail stunt involving two jiggers and a tumbler for another customer. After all the juggling and shaking, the pink liquid he finally poured into the martini glass was underwhelming. Even the fresh mint and cucumber garnish—added with a flourish—couldn't save it.

When Biceps made his way over to her, she took a deep breath and broke his heart. "Double Scotch. Neat."

"Any particular brand?" he asked, pouting at the sheer uncoolness of her order.

"Bowmore. Twenty-five years old."

"Nice." His eyebrows drew up and he flashed a grin. "A beautiful woman who knows her whiskey."

She smiled back, glad she'd dodged the showman's bullet, but her relief was short-lived.

"Power up!" he hollered.

"Power up!" his compatriots echoed.

A few customers clapped excitedly as a small skateboard-like contraption with handlebars zoomed around the liquor column on hidden tracks and stopped where Biceps waited. He stepped on and secured a harness around his waist, becoming the center of attention as he spiraled upward. Grasping the bottle of Bowmore from the top of the column, he descended like a rock star.

By the time he handed her the Scotch, her cheeks were burning and she seriously considered hiding under the bar. It was bad enough being at a club, not wearing much at all, without a bunch of strangers staring at her.

Forcing herself to relax, she took a long sip. The whiskey caressed her throat and kindled a fire in her stomach. She closed her eyes and smiled at the simple pleasure. When she opened them again, Biceps was standing in front of her, sporting an odd gape-mouthed look. Then, sudden realization flamed her cheeks.

"Oh, jeez. I'm so sorry." She hurriedly grabbed her credit card from her clutch and handed it to him. "Here you go. Thank you."

Looking a little embarrassed, he enveloped her outstretched hand in his. "The drink's on me, beautiful."

"That won't be—"

"My name's Kenny and I get off in three hours. Can you stick around?" His lips curled into a boyish smile. It was only when his gaze lingered on her cleavage she realized he was hitting on her.

"I can't, um… I…" Natalie had no idea what to do. She wasn't used to getting hit on at a bar.

"Thanks, Kenny," a deep voice rumbled behind her. "I got this."

Natalie stiffened in her seat as the hair on her arms stood on tiptoe and a shiver ran down her spine. The deep, rich voice did strange things to her body, but she wasn't sure she approved of the stranger's high-handedness. Either way, she couldn't face him until she reined in her galloping pulse, so she downed the Scotch in a single tilt.

"As a matter of fact, why don't you put her drink on my tab?" A strong, long-fingered hand passed a hundred-dollar bill to Kenny, who dropped her hand and accepted the tip with a grudging shrug, bowing out to the alpha.

Okay. She definitely did not like that. Natalie spun around to give the arrogant stranger a verbal ass kicking, but the sharp challenge froze and died a quiet death on her lips.

The stranger with the sexy voice was none other than Garrett Song, and he was even more magnificent outside of the office. He was closer than she'd thought—only a few inches separated them when their gazes collided. The amusement flickered out of his eyes and a charged silence tightened around them.

Natalie vaguely heard Kenny's curt "two double Scotch, neat," but she remained fixated on Garrett's jet-black hair, strong jawline and full lips. *And my, oh, my, those fiery eyes.* Her gaze flitted down to his broad shoulders, chest and long, muscular legs. The conservative dress shirt and slacks couldn't hide the power of his body.

Her heart fluttered like a dragonfly taking flight under his insolent perusal. His face didn't register a hint of recognition, which wasn't surprising. Natalie didn't resemble the woman he'd seen at work.

Natalie drained her second drink without breaking eye contact. She uncrossed her legs and slid off her seat, her calf accidentally grazing the side of his body. She was about his height in her four-inch heels, so they faced each other squarely. His heat embraced her, and his masculine scent, like an autumn wind, beckoned her closer.

She couldn't follow her instincts to climb her boss like a tree even if her inner thighs were slick with desire. She would act professionally. Natalie would state her business and not take no for an answer. She opened her mouth but promptly closed it shut.

Apparently, she'd forgotten how to speak.

Garrett was lost from the moment she swiveled in her seat.

She had glided into the club as he was leaving. Then his legs had brought him to her without his permission. Her sculpted body was meant to bring men to their knees. And her dress seemed like it had been painted onto her lush curves.

The sight of her made him weak with lust, but her air of vulnerability made him want to shield her from other hungry eyes. His fervent urge to possess and protect the woman tripped all kinds of alarms in his head, but his brain had decided to take an inopportune hiatus.

"Dance with me," he said.

Her eyes widened and his pulse quickened in anticipation. She looked familiar but he wouldn't forget a woman like her if he'd met her before. He held out his hand and she stared at it, her head cocked like a curious bird. After a pause, she placed her hand in his. It was warm, smooth and delicate. The thrill of their connection gripped him by the shoulders and shook him alert.

As their feet touched the dance floor, Garrett wrapped his arm around her waist, cradling her right hand against his chest. They swayed softly to the music while the crowd gyrated around them. He brushed his fingertips against her bare back. Her skin was like warm silk. As a gnawing hunger filled him to the brim, Garrett laid his palm on her lower back and pressed her body flush against his. A tremor ran through her.

God, she feels so good. He struggled to make sense of her—the stark contrast between innocent wide eyes and a body that radiated raw sensuality.

"Who are you?" he rasped.

Her eyelids fluttered at his question as though he had awakened her from a dream. She shook her head briskly and a veil shifted across her face. Suddenly, he recognized her and his arms fell to his sides.

"You…you really don't know who I am?" she said, unease crossing her lovely features.

That thrill. He'd only felt it once before, and he belatedly realized this was the same woman who'd made him feel it the first time.

Was her voice this velvety when she barged into my office?

"Should I know you?" He stalled to figure out what her game was.

Samantha had been his first lesson in gold diggers, but she certainly hadn't been his last. Naturally, Garrett considered himself something of an expert on the issue, and Natalie Sobol didn't fit the profile. He trusted and respected her. She had backbone and integrity, which made her damn good at her job. Even so, she must've orchestrated their run-in to get something out of him.

"I'm…" She cleared her throat and drew back her shoulders. Regrettably for him, the small adjustment managed to thrust her glorious breasts forward, nearly derailing his focus. "It's Natalie Sobol, Mr. Song."

"Call me Garrett," he said, leading her by the arm to the relative privacy of the outdoor balcony. "While we're getting familiar, care to tell me what you're up to?"

He couldn't make out her expression in the moonlight,

but he heard a sharp intake of breath. To his surprise, she didn't pretend their run-in was a coincidence.

"I came here to ask you for a second chance." She spoke quietly, but her words carried the weight of determination.

"A second chance at what?"

"VP of Human Resources. I missed my interview because of a family emergency, but I'm confident I could do the job better than anyone else."

So that was her game. His lips twisted. "How do you suppose I fit into that?"

"Please. All I ask for is a chance to get my interview. You'll soon be our new CEO. The hiring committee would listen to your request." She swallowed, hesitating for a second. "Please believe me when I say I would never dream of imposing on you like this if I had any other choice. I need that job."

She was good. He'd long outgrown any disappointment at being used for his money or connections. But he almost believed this woman. Sympathized with her. Garrett hadn't allowed anyone to manipulate his emotions since Samantha, and his brief slip infuriated him. It made him want to test her.

"And are you offering something in return?" He didn't bother disguising his disdain.

She gasped and her hands clenched into fists. He watched through hooded lids as pride, anger and mortification splashed across her features. Then, she breathed slowly through her nose before replying in measured tones.

"I'm offering to be the best VP of Human Resources Hansol has ever had." She arched an eyebrow in cold challenge. "Do I need to offer anything beyond that?"

When he didn't respond right away, Natalie turned her back on him and strode toward the door with the poise and dignity of a queen. *Damn it.* He caught up with her and grasped her arm, trying not to notice her warmth.

"Wait."

It was true. She was a perfect fit for the position, especially with her experience as the interim VP. She wouldn't have needed his help if she hadn't missed her interview. Maybe he'd misread her. It was difficult to think with so much of his blood pumping away from his brain.

"Are you willing to consider my request?" Her tone was clipped, but at least she was talking to him.

He understood the hiring committee's refusal to reschedule her interview—reliability was the bare minimum requirement for an executive position—but Garrett respected her decision to put her family before her promotion. He was only too familiar with putting his family ahead of his own needs.

Garrett froze. It couldn't have been more than a few hours since his declaration of independence. What if the key to his freedom stood in front of him? Natalie's appearance was timely enough to be eerie. She was intelligent, pragmatic and *desperate*—maybe even desperate enough to accept his unconventional proposal.

"Yes, and you can help me in return."

"You need my help?" Her eyes widened in surprise, but not alarm. He was gratified she didn't jump to an unsavory conclusion despite his earlier brutishness.

Garrett scanned their surroundings. They had some privacy in their corner of the patio, but a popular nightclub wasn't the place for a lengthy discussion of his plans.

"I need a wife."

"You want me to find you a wife?" Her eyebrows scrunched together as though she was struggling to untangle an intricate knot.

"No. I want *you* to be my wife."

Her eyes grew impossibly wide, and he was struck once more by her alluring beauty. Her contrasting layers—demure and sizzling, uptight and witty—intrigued him. She was intoxicating. But for this arrangement to work, he couldn't go there. Something told him sex would mean more than an enjoyable pastime to Natalie Sobol, and messy emotional entanglements could make even the most rational people reckless. No matter how tempting, she was off-limits.

"In exchange for getting me an interview?" she asked.

"You won't need one. The job is yours if you accept my offer."

"I don't need you to hand me the position." She lifted her chin, narrowing her eyes at him. "I could get it on my own if I get my interview."

"I wouldn't hand you the job if you weren't qualified. Why don't we say your performance as the interim VP was your interview and you passed?"

"I could have the job? Just like that?" She arched an elegant brow, communicating both her skepticism and distaste.

"If you marry me as soon as the wedding can be arranged, I'll promote you to the position at the end of the year." She did a poor job of hiding her eye roll, and Garrett rushed to clarify. "The marriage obviously won't be permanent."

"Obviously." Her expression told him none of it was obvious. "Just out of curiosity, how long is not permanent?"

"Good question." Garrett hadn't thought through the details, but it had to last long enough to convince his grandmother that the marriage was real. But, most importantly, it had to last until he closed the Vivotex partnership and was appointed as the new CEO. *It will happen. It has to.* His grandmother had been grooming him for the position since the day he was born. It was her greatest wish to see him become Hansol's CEO. Once he sealed the Vivotex deal, she could give in without losing face. "About seven to eight months until your new position opens up. Perhaps a few months longer. But definitely no more than a year."

Natalie sighed deeply, and raised her eyes to the night sky. "Why?"

"It involves a sensitive and complicated family issue." She deserved to know everything about his unorthodox proposal, but not here. "I trust you'll keep this conversation confidential until we can discuss the details somewhere more private."

"Anything else?" She met his gaze, but her voice sounded distant and tired.

"You have the key facts," he said, tension edging into his words. "Will you marry me?"

She stared back at him for a few seconds then shook her head. "That's probably *the* worst proposal ever made. Like catastrophically bad."

A bark of surprised laughter escaped him. "You're probably right, but this is the most efficient and effective solution to both of our problems. If—"

She held up her hand to stop his words, and he obeyed her silent command out of shock. He was accustomed to deference from executives twice his age. He long admired her strength and confidence but being on the receiving end of her imperious attitude was startling.

"This scheme of yours is beyond ludicrous." She heaved a ponderous sigh, making the milky mounds of her breasts rise and fall. It took Herculean effort to keep his eyes focused on her face. "But I'm desperate enough to consider it."

"Good call," he said with equal parts irritation and relief. To his chagrin, her reluctant not-quite-assent stung his ego, but his rational side was relieved she would even consider his preposterous proposal. Natalie Sobol was practical to a fault, but this time it worked in his favor.

"I highly doubt that," she said with a quirk of her red lips.

Of course she did. The more she thought about it, the

more dubious everything would seem. He couldn't give her too much time to think things through. "Given this is a time-sensitive situation, you have until tomorrow at midnight to give me an answer."

"Tomorrow? You're impossible." With an exasperated glare, she spun away and stalked toward the staircase inside. His mouth curved into a grin. He'd spiked the ball into her court and she wasn't the kind of person who would back down from a challenge. He was looking forward to her next move. Before he could turn away, the sight of her softly swaying hips recaptured his attention and his smirk morphed into slack-mouthed admiration.

When she disappeared from sight, Garrett leaned against the railing and frowned at the starless sky. *Why is she so desperate that she'd consider giving up a year of her life for a second chance at a promotion?*

Three

Natalie shut down her computer after a long day and stretched her back with a groan. She was determined to catch up on the projects that had fallen behind while she was on bereavement leave. Challenging work kept her mind sharp and focused, and made a great excuse for avoiding Garrett. Her heart leaped at the mere thought of him, as though it was startled awake by his magnetic pull. *Gah.*

After tidying up her desk, she left the office and drove home on autopilot with tension tightening her shoulders and pain drilling into her temples. A bubble bath and a glass of wine should take care of that. But as soon as she sank into the fragrant bath, Garrett invaded her thoughts. The way his hand had trailed down her naked back and how her softness had molded to fit his hard lines. She sighed as she ran the washcloth down her legs, her oversensitized skin trembling with pleasure. Her body begged for release, and the warm water and her slippery skin tempted her hands to slide up her thighs.

"No, no, *no*." Natalie scrambled out of the tub. She would not pleasure herself daydreaming about her boss.

Why the heck did he want a temporary wife anyway? His proposal was pure, unadulterated madness. They would have to live a lie for the duration of the contract. And how could she weather the vicious rumors that were sure to come? There had to be another way to secure Sophie's adoption.

With Tin Man–stiff shoulders and a migraine, Natalie sprawled out on the living-room couch and glared at her ceiling. There was no other way. If she agreed to Garrett's crazy scheme, she and Sophie could move to New York in seven months. *Maybe a few months longer if her and Garrett's objectives weren't met by the end of the year.* But still, Natalie could start a new life in no more than a year. The custody battle alone could last longer than that and would likely bankrupt her.

With Garrett's help, Natalie could convince the Davises to reconsider contesting her adoption application. They couldn't want a drawn-out custody battle any more than she did. Even if they continued to contest the adoption, having a wealthy husband with a recognizable name would support her position that Sophie would have a secure, stable home. And with her promotion, Natalie could afford a nice place and excellent childcare for the baby even without a rich husband.

More importantly, something about Garrett Song centered her. True, he made her hormones streak naked across her mind, but on a deeper level she trusted him. He was too arrogant to say something he didn't mean and he valued his word too much to go back on it.

As for the anticipated gossip, Natalie could handle the ugliness for a few weeks. The wedding bells would soon soothe her coworkers' ruffled feathers. An office fling was fodder for gossip, but love and marriage wrought oohs, ahhs and well wishes.

With a long, frustrated growl, Natalie sat up on the couch. She needed to handle some time-sensitive work before making a decision about Garrett's proposal. She reached into her bag to retrieve her laptop, but her hand came out empty. In her rush to leave the office—and Garrett Song—she'd forgotten it. *Grr.* She exhaled with enough force to collapse the third pig's house.

Reining in her temper, Natalie left for the office. From her Koreatown apartment, it took only fifteen minutes to reach downtown Los Angeles.

When she got there, Natalie tapped her toes as the elevator crawled up to the fifty-fifth level. Once she arrived on her floor, she sidestepped through a six-inch gap in the elevator doors, while rummaging around her purse for her office keys. Half of her head was crammed into her tote when she walked straight into something big and solid. She wobbled and a pair of strong hands reached out to steady her.

She didn't need to see whom she'd run into. Her body already recognized Garrett Song. Fire kindled where he held her and blazed across her skin. Keeping her head bent, she focused on slowing down her pulse.

"I'm sorry. I didn't know anyone was here." Natalie tried to back away, but his hands stayed firm on her arms. She raised puzzled eyes toward his face and her voice caught in her throat—his gaze was boring into her with unsettling intensity.

"Are you all right?" Garrett's voice sounded husky.

When she nodded, he stepped back and folded his arms across his chest.

"I forgot to bring my laptop home." Nerves on hyperdrive, Natalie babbled on with her explanation. "I need to finish up some work tonight. A good HR director never rests."

He didn't respond and continued staring at her, as if trying to decide whether he was amused or bored. She couldn't help noticing how well he filled out his jeans and T-shirt. He looked younger, more approachable, in his casual outfit. Without her consent, her eyes traveled down to the sculpted pecs pushing against his white shirt. He could've been used as the mold for one of those anatomically correct Batman suits. Dual forces fought inside her—part of her wanted to run as far from him as possible, but a troubling and foreign part of her wanted to run straight into his arms.

"Okay." Natalie willed her lips into a polite smile, making sure no hint of her inner war showed through. "Have a good night."

"I was on my way out to see you." His expression was unreadable but his eyes looked predatory. "I believe we have unfinished business to discuss."

Her drumming heart bruised her ribs, and her mouth opened and closed in her best goldfish imitation before she could form her next words.

"Tell me why."

"Why what?"

"Why do you need a temporary wife?"

She might think he was overreacting or being a coward for taking such drastic steps to escape his grandmother's control. Some people had a difficult time grasping how sacred family, duty and respect were in his culture. Perhaps Natalie had been raised similarly and would understand. He was accustomed to derision for what others perceived as weakness, but he didn't want her to see him as some stunted man-child.

"My grandmother arranged for me to marry a woman I've never met based on her family's wealth and connections."

"She did what?" Natalie's voice rose an octave, her expression a mixture of shock and indignation. "There are so many things wrong with that sentence. Your grandmother chose someone for you to marry? Based on the woman's *family* assets, not the woman herself?"

Garrett smiled at the protective edge that had crept into Natalie's voice. "Yes to both, but Grandmother insists the woman herself is also satisfactory."

Natalie's eyes flashed. "Satisfactory to *her* standards. You haven't even met your *betrothed*."

"She isn't my anything. Have you forgotten that I've asked *you* to be my wife?"

"But… I still don't understand why you want to marry me."

"Are you familiar with Korean culture?"

She sighed with a sheepish shrug. "I'm half-Korean, but all I know about our culture comes from K-drama."

He cocked his head and stowed away that information to explore at another time.

"As the eldest member of our family, my grandmother commands absolute respect and obedience from her children and grandchildren. I couldn't flat-out refuse to marry the heiress she chose. That would be like spitting in her face. So I told her I was secretly engaged to someone else and I couldn't go back on my word to my fiancée."

"Hmm." Natalie's eyebrows drew together as she digested his explanation. "And your grandma's okay with that?"

"Of course not. She threatened to stop my CEO appointment if I don't break off the engagement."

"I need to sit down." She looked dazed. "What are you going to do?"

"First, we're moving this conversation away from any prying ears." With his hand on the small of her back, Garrett led her to the privacy of his office, and settled her onto a sofa. Once the door was shut behind him, he continued,

"Then I'm going to get married as soon as possible because my grandmother will meddle with my personal life until I do."

"But what about the CEO job?"

"You could help with that, too. I'm working on a partnership with Vivotex. It's nearly done but I still need to convince some key executives over there. Presenting myself as a family man could strengthen my credibility, and help me win their trust. Once I get the partnership sealed, the board wouldn't dream of electing another CEO. They need to do what's best for Hansol, as does my grandmother."

"That all makes sense in an upside-down kind of way."

"I'm glad you think so," he said quietly, relieved she didn't think less of him.

"If I marry you..." A burst of triumph spread through his chest, and the caveman possessiveness reared its head again. He opened his mouth to speak but Natalie cut him off. "If I do, I have some conditions."

"Conditions?" He wasn't fond of conditions being placed on him, but he didn't have a line of contract brides waiting to marry him. "Name them."

"I won't share your bed," she blurted. "My professional life and my personal life never cross."

"Agreed," he said, but his eyes raked hotly over her body against his will. With effort, he focused his gaze on her face. Consummating the marriage would complicate an already complicated situation. "It'll simplify the dissolution of our marriage. An annulment is more efficient than a divorce."

"Good. And I also want to ask you to not have...relationships while this lasts." She flushed a bright shade of pink.

"What kind of relationships?" It both surprised and amused him to watch her squirm and blush.

"The extramarital kind involving sex with people who

aren't your wife." She jutted out her chin in a show of defiance that was becoming familiar to him.

"Ah, that kind."

"Yes." Natalie rolled her eyes. "That kind."

"Agreed." Unable to resist, he teased her with a grin. "I presume you will do me the same courtesy?"

"Of course. It's important we convince the world our marriage is real. Not only for you, but for me, as well." Her expression grew fierce. "I'm fighting to adopt my niece. She was orphaned when my sister and her husband died in a car crash."

"Your niece?"

"In my heart, she's already my daughter, but her grandparents are contesting the adoption. It's already difficult for a single woman to adopt, but if the child's next of kin contests it, it becomes nearly impossible. The Davises aren't heartless people, but they want Sophie with them in New York." Natalie gritted her teeth, near tears for a brief, heartbreaking moment before she regained control. "I thought if I became the new VP of HR and transferred to New York in December, I might be able to convince Sophie's grandparents to withdraw their opposition to the adoption."

"That's why you agreed to do this." His gut lurched at the realization.

Her desperation to get the promotion and her agreeing to consider this marriage—it was all for her niece. It would complicate everything. He couldn't let Natalie get under his skin, especially with a little girl in the picture. But he couldn't turn his back on her. It went against his very core to abandon a mother fighting for her child. Also, on a logical level, his time to search for a contract bride was up, and he wouldn't find anyone more invested in pulling off their fake marriage than Natalie.

"Yes, so if we do this, I'm going all in. Marrying you will boost my chances of becoming Sophie's mom, but if anyone finds out our marriage isn't real, then I could lose her."

"I understand." He understood only too well how important a mother was to a child. He couldn't let Natalie bet her future on the promotion and the goodwill of Sophie's grandparents. His name, wealth and influence could help her adopt her niece. "I'll do everything in my power to help you get custody of Sophie."

"Thank you." A tremulous smile lit her face.

She was so beautiful. Dangerously so. Heat unfurled low in his stomach, and resisting the need to touch her made him dizzy.

"Anything else?"

"Just one thing. Is it absolutely necessary for us to be seen in public together?" Her words picked up speed, tripping over each other. "I was hoping to avoid situations where I'd have to come up with spur-of-the-moment lies. I'm the worst at lying."

"I need you to attend functions with me. There's no way around that."

"Couldn't you tell them I have a headache or something?"

"For months on end?" He raised an eyebrow at her.

"Fine." Her shoulders drooped and she narrowed her eyes. "I could smile and play along, but you're in charge of making stuff up on the spot."

"Deal."

"Okay." Her sigh was tremulous but her beautiful features hardened with determination. "I'll marry you."

The silence stretched and Natalie shifted on her feet. *Damn.* He couldn't tear his eyes off her, and awareness shrouded them like moist, tropical heat. *What is it about this woman that drives me crazy with desire?* Whatever it was, he couldn't have her. Maintaining distance was crucial to avoiding complications when they annulled the marriage.

Even so, his gaze dropped to her lips and his breath hitched to find them wet and softly parted. Garrett swayed toward her without conscious thought, and Natalie tilted her head, leaning in. The evidence that she wasn't immune to the dizzying attraction chipped away at his willpower. He couldn't have sex with her, but there was no harm in kissing her.

Like hell there wasn't. She was a good woman and he wasn't a complete bastard. She'd agreed to the contract marriage, but her decision was an emotional one, a sacrifice for her niece. She was probably more vulnerable than she let on. Their lips were only a breath apart when he pulled back and shoved his hands into his pockets.

As he drew in a steadying breath, Natalie closed the distance between them and pressed her lips against his. Surprise held him immobile but she was warm and intoxicating. When a sound that was somewhere between a moan and a whimper escaped her, he lost the fight for control. He deepened the kiss with a low growl, and Natalie pushed her body against him. Burying his fingers roughly in her hair, he tilted back her head to better taste her.

Something cold and alarming seeped through his mind even as he leaned back on the wall and nestled her between his legs. Her skin smelled like vanilla and sweet musk, and felt like silk beneath his hands as they slid down her bare arms before settling on her hips. Her cool fingers skimmed his stomach just under his shirt and he hissed at the intense pleasure.

His reaction to the simple touch shocked him out of the moment. Garrett broke off their kiss. Natalie stumbled back from him with her fingers pressed against her lips. Their gazes crashed and held, their panting breaths filling the silence.

Natalie didn't seem aware that her fingertips were brushing back and forth across her lips, pink and swollen from their kiss. The movement was hypnotic—a seductive lure that could capsize his meticulously planned life. He couldn't give his body the chance to win the battle.

"I'll make some arrangements and contact you soon."

"Okay," she said in a husky whisper, her hand finally dropping to her side. She gave her head a vigorous shake and inhaled deeply. "Um… That was good practice. Some public displays of affection will be necessary. I'm glad we got the initial awkwardness over with."

"Initial awkwardness?"

In all fairness, he had brushed aside their kiss, but to hear her call it "awkward" pricked his pride.

"Yeah, well…" she said. "Our first kiss shouldn't be in front of an audience, so I'm glad we got that over with."

"I approve of your strategy. Good night." With a curt nod, he spun around.

When he reached the parking structure, he made for his car with long, impatient strides, intent on leaving the building as soon as possible.

He slid into his Aston Martin and sped through downtown LA with the windows down, putting much-needed distance between himself and whatever the hell had happened back there.

When he was certain he could speak in a normal voice, he called Michael Reynolds, his oldest and closest friend, as well as Hansol's PR specialist. Garrett needed to think things through, and Mike was his most trustworthy sounding board.

His friend picked up on the second ring, sounding winded. "This better be important, Song. You interrupted my dinner with two of your senior executives. I'm missing the good parts of their prostate exam stories."

"So you ditched them?" Garrett smirked.

"I don't know what you're talking about."

"You owe me one, Reynolds."

"I know. Thanks."

"By the way, this *is* important." He pulled up to the Ritz-Carlton. "I'm getting married."

"What?" Mike's voice rang across the lines. "To who? And why haven't I met her?"

"You know my grandmother. We kept our relationship under the radar so she wouldn't worry." Garrett left his explanation vague to avoid lying to his friend. "I'm marrying Natalie Sobol."

"*The* Natalie Sobol?" Mike said after a lengthy pause.

"I didn't realize she was famous." As the valet drove away with his car, Garrett walked into the hotel lobby. "You know her well?"

"I've met her a few times at Hansol's functions, but her reputation precedes her."

"And what reputation is that?" He stepped into the elevator and pressed the button to his penthouse.

"How do you think a twenty-eight-year-old became a regional HR director? Actually, she was twenty-six when she was promoted."

"Well, she's exceptionally bright and competent."

"She certainly is, but that's not all." Mike's voice held a note of awe. "That woman's got nerves of steel."

"I believe that." Garrett chuckled under his breath.

"She's known as the Ball Buster."

"The what?" He tugged his tie loose. "What the hell did she do to earn that title?"

"About a year ago, someone in middle management wasn't playing by the rules." By the sound of it, his friend was cupping his hand over his cell to whisper. "Natalie investigated the allegations and found evidence he'd been giving preferential treatment to male employees. She fired his ass and convinced him to sign a release stating he won't sue the company. She laid down the law."

"That's my woman." Garrett grinned as he got off the

elevator. The city lights greeted him through the panoramic windows of his penthouse.

"So how should we handle this from the PR side of things?"

"We need to release a statement announcing your engagement."

"That's a given." Garrett dropped onto his leather lounger and kicked off his shoes.

"But first, you should 'sneak around' with your fiancée and make sure to get caught. Invite the public into your 'clandestine' romance."

"The public might dig that, but Hansol employees will be out for blood. We need to announce the engagement as soon as possible. The venom will leach out and everything will become rosy and romantic as soon as marriage enters the picture. How long do we have to sneak around?"

"Two weeks."

"Fine, but she's moving in with me within the week." Two weeks would give his grandmother time to wreak havoc on his plans. He had to make the first move.

"Impatient, are you?" Mike chuckled. "Luckily, that's a good PR move. A fast-paced, secret romance is even more popular."

"Perfect. Let me know what else you need from my end." Garrett pinched the bridge of his nose, running through the list of things to get done the next day. "You can go back to your little party now."

"What?" Mike sounded panicked. "Don't you want to have a long conversation about your bachelor party?"

"Not happening."

"I was worried Samantha ruined you for love and happiness. Now that you have Natalie, I'm sure you're thankful for the narrow escape," Mike said without a hint of levity. "I'm happy for you."

"Thank you."

Garrett ended the call and leaned back on his seat. Love and whatever happiness it might bring weren't worth the risk of heartbreak. The last time he'd let his guard down—worn thin by buried grief and loneliness—Samantha had happened.

Trust and sentimentality inevitably led to pain and loss. Logic and reason, however, had never let him down. He could almost understand why his grandmother devoted her every waking moment to Hansol after his grandfather died.

His engagement to Natalie had nothing to do with love and happiness, or out-of-control attraction. She was his partner in a project to change their lives. He would get his CEO position and a personal life that belonged to him, and she would adopt her niece and start a new life in New York. They would both get what they wanted and walk away content.

This might *actually* work.

Four

Natalie smacked her palm against her forehead. She was so dazed from their kiss she'd returned home without her laptop. Color flooded her cheeks and her heartbeat kicked up a notch. *Would kissing him always make her want to rip off his clothes?*

Miserable and mortified, she shuffled down the hall and knocked on her neighbor's door. Mrs. Kim was her friend and confidante. Natalie wouldn't have made it through her sister's death without the older woman's kindness and wisdom. If anyone could help sort out this mess, it was her.

Mrs. Kim cracked open the door then swung it wide with a welcoming smile, but Natalie's smile wobbled at the corners. Her neighbor's only reaction was the slightest tilt of an immaculately shaped eyebrow. Then she nodded her head as though she'd reached a decision.

"Soju."

Natalie had been accepted as part of Mrs. Kim's exclusive "in" crowd by fearlessly tilting back the potent liquor, matching the older woman shot for shot.

She didn't know a whole lot about her neighbor except that she lived a quiet and solitary life. When Natalie had first met her, she'd guessed her to be in her midthirties, with her trim figure and smooth skin, but she soon learned that Mrs. Kim was well into her fifties. Natalie was beginning to think that *soju* was the secret to her youth.

The two women settled in at the kitchen table and Mrs. Kim poured them each a drink. She hissed in appreciation of the soju's kick, and lifted her shot glass for Natalie to refill. Once her glass was filled to the brim, she took the bottle from Natalie and refilled hers. "You know *Forrest Gump*?"

Natalie blinked several times. That was random. Nineties cinema was not a frequent topic of their conversations. "Do you mean that Tom Hanks movie?"

Mrs. Kim nodded.

"Yeah, I've watched it on TV before."

"Well, he was wrong." Mrs. Kim poked the air with her index finger. "Life is *not* like a box of chocolates. You'd never find a piece of crap in a chocolate box."

Natalie nodded somberly, then they downed their shots. She would've found the observation hilarious if it hadn't made so much sense. Life could bury you in a mountain of crap, but the worst you could do with a box of chocolates was bite into a piece with nasty pink goo inside.

"Still no headway on Sophie's adoption?" Her neighbor's eyes were soft with understanding.

"No," Natalie whispered, desperation clogging her throat. "The odds are stacked against me, but I can't let her go."

"And now, you have a man," she said matter-of-factly. Sometimes she could swear Mrs. Kim was a psychic. "That complicates things even more."

Complicates things? That's such a genteel way of describing the mess I'm in.

"I don't exactly *have* him." There was no use denying there was a man. Mrs. Kim jutted her chin at Natalie to continue, then poured more shots into their glasses. "I'm just engaged to him."

To her credit, Mrs. Kim swallowed her *soju* before she coughed and sputtered, "You're what?"

"I got engaged to Hansol's VP of Business and Development."

"Fancy."

"He's also the heir apparent to the entire freaking company."

"Holy crap."

"Exactly. And you know what else? He's melt-your-clothes-off hot, and for some reason that really pisses me off!" Natalie slammed her palms on the table. *Shoot.* Mrs. Kim was twice her age. She shouldn't be disrespectful. "Sorry. I mean he's very handsome."

"Don't be a prude. I'm not that old. He's sex on a stick. I got it," she said. "And you're not *pissed off.* You're just *turned on.*"

Natalie emptied her glass and glowered mutely at her.

"How did all this come about?" Mrs. Kim studied her face with concern.

"Suddenly." Natalie couldn't lie to her but couldn't tell the truth, either. She inhaled a fortifying breath. "We…understand each other, and marrying him will help me adopt Sophie. I think it'll be a mutually beneficial arrangement."

"And that's enough for you? Sometimes doing what we think is best for our children comes at a cost, Natalie."

Mrs. Kim sighed and opened up another bottle of *soju.* She raised it and glanced at Natalie, but she shook her head. She had urgent matters to deal with first thing in the morning, thanks to *twice* losing her wits over Garrett Song.

"There was someone…after my husband died, but I ended things with him to focus on my kids. Overcompensating for being a single mom, I guess. But now…" Her unflappable neighbor sighed, a small, forlorn sound. "My children have grown and left—as they should—and I'm a lonely old woman with only bygone memories to warm my bed."

"Mrs. Kim… I…"

Natalie didn't continue. She was in no place to comfort Mrs. Kim. She was too afraid to give her heart to anyone, knowing she didn't stand a chance of keeping him. The one guy who'd wanted to stick around was a narcissistic jerk from college. No man worth having seemed to want her. Natalie poured Mrs. Kim another shot and lifted her glass for a refill. They raised their glasses in solemn silence and drank to bygone memories.

Unlike Mrs. Kim, who had loved and lost, Natalie didn't even have memories to keep her warm. She only had a sexless marriage to an unfairly hot husband to look forward to.

Natalie didn't hate giving presentations *too* much. She just had a hard time breathing and got a wicked headache. Even so, it beat "hanging out" and "socializing." The actual event was never as bad as expected. She had to focus on that. Today it was just a quick office-etiquette seminar.

"You look bulletproof," Garrett said, close to her ear. "Why the power suit?"

She squeaked, nearly jumping out of said suit. Immersed in her mental pep talk, she hadn't heard him approaching in the hall. Her hand on her chest, she scanned their surroundings and didn't see any prying eyes on them.

Even when her mind grasped she wasn't in mortal danger, her fight-or-flight instinct raged inside her. The man next to her was dangerous. Seeing him, and in such close proximity, made her heart play hopscotch in her chest.

Natalie reined in her hormone-induced reaction. She lived in the real world with real problems, like bills to pay and a daughter to adopt. She didn't have the luxury of lusting after her future husband.

"Good morning," she said as she continued swiftly down the hallway. "Did you need something?"

"Not at all." He fell in step beside her, his face a careful blank. "I'm just stretching my legs."

She couldn't help stealing a peek at his long, muscular legs, and heat rose to her face. Her gaze roamed over him, lingering on his strong jawline and full lips. When her eyes met his, amusement glinted in them. He was well aware of her perusal, and quite enjoying himself.

"Go stretch them somewhere else," she said through clenched teeth.

He chuckled, the corners of his eyes crinkling. Rather than casually parting ways, as she'd hoped, he took her by the elbow and led her toward the landing of the emergency stairway. Too startled to react, she allowed the door to click shut behind them. She huffed an exasperated sigh and slumped against the wall.

"Why did you bring me out here, Garrett?"

"We need to discuss our sleeping arrangements."

"What—what do you mean?" Awareness stormed through her, making her knees weak. After their kiss, she'd imagined sharing a bed with him. It involved very little sleeping.

"I want you to move into my place as soon as possible."

"No," she blurted in a panic, her heart jumping and stuttering.

Garrett shrugged. "If you'd rather buy a new place, I'll have my Realtor call you."

"It's not that." She pressed her palm against her forehead. "Why do we have to move in together already?"

He arrogantly raised an eyebrow. "Our engagement will be announced soon."

"I haven't forgotten, but I don't know what the rush is. I could move in after the wedding."

Garrett raked his fingers through his full, dark hair, tousling it into a sexy mess. "My grandmother isn't going to give up on the arranged marriage easily."

"And that's why we're getting married. I haven't forgotten."

"Knowing her, she's going to use all her influence to stop our wedding. Maybe even leak my 'engagement' to Jihae Park to the press."

"Why would she do something like that?"

"Then it won't be just the CEO seat on the line for me. I'd be responsible for burning bridges with Rotelle Corporation and publicly humiliating a young woman." Garrett squeezed the back of his neck. "But it'd be a risky move on my grandmother's part since Hansol will receive negative press if you and I still went ahead with our wedding. Neither Grandmother nor I would do anything to harm Hansol, but I don't know how far she'll go. We've never been on opposite sides of a conflict before."

"When are we announcing the engagement?" she asked, her teeth tugging at her bottom lip. Their conversation sounded more dramatic than a scene from a soap opera. She'd be sitting on the edge of the couch stuffing popcorn in her mouth except this was actually happening to her. Cue the *Twilight Zone* music.

"In two weeks." Garrett rubbed a hand down his face.

"Couldn't we move it up?"

"We have less than two weeks to warm up the public to the idea of us. When we announce our engagement, we need people to feel like they're part of the romance. If we blindside them with it, they'll feel duped. That won't win us any fans."

She nodded as his words lit up a dark corner of her heart. *He's protecting me.* He lived in the limelight and could charm the press with a grin and a witty remark, but Natalie would be vulnerable to the public's scorn. She soaked up the warmth of the knowledge.

Wait, no. This way lies trouble. Natalie couldn't let her loneliness fool her that his kind gesture meant anything more than what it was. She and Garrett had a purely business arrangement and she shouldn't forget that.

"You'll be an open target to your grandmother's manipulations. Are you sure about waiting?"

"No." Garrett shrugged and pinned her with his gaze. "That's why I need you to ruin me for the Korean heiress."

"Ruin you?" Natalie was horrified at how far his grandmother would go to control his life. It had to be suffocating to bear so much pressure. Yet, he was risking so much to protect her reputation. "I don't know… I've never ruined a hotshot billionaire before."

"It's simple." His lips quirked in amusement. "Move in with me."

"But how does moving in together ruin you?"

"Jihae Park's family, as well as my grandmother, will be scandalized if we moved in together before our wedding. At least superficially, propriety and virtue are still important in Korean culture, especially to those *jae-bul* families. If I'm lucky, her family will call off the wedding first. At the very least, my grandmother won't be able to make any engagement announcements of her own."

"Virtue?" She blinked and searched her mind for the right words. "My moving in with you will compromise your virtue?"

"And yours." He grinned mischievously.

She gulped. *Yes, he would definitely be a good ravisher.*

"Fine. I'll think about ruining you." She rolled her eyes to hide how much the thought of tainting his virtue aroused her. "If we're done here, I have a presentation to give. You can leave in fifteen minutes."

"What?"

"I don't want anyone seeing us come out of the stairwell together." She could do without adding "stairwell quickie" to the gossip fodder.

"You want me to waste fifteen minutes of my time out here?"

"Not at all." She wished she could snap a picture of his expression. She could look at it for a good laugh whenever she was having a bad day. "You can sit on the stairs and productively check your emails if you'd like. Just don't come out for fifteen minutes."

Natalie scanned the hallway before slipping out and shutting the door in Garrett's stunned face.

His fiancée had locked him out of his own company.

Garrett glanced at his watch, feeling ridiculous hiding in the dimly lit stairwell. He waited exactly five minutes; that was all she was getting. Even so, he made certain the hallway was empty before he left his confinement.

After shutting his office door behind him, Garrett sank into his desk chair and sifted through a pile of documents, then tossed them back down. They were getting married in a few weeks and would be living under the same roof for months. What was there to think about?

Growling with frustration, he pushed back from his desk and stood, making his chair skid drunkenly. Enough nonsense. She was moving into the penthouse by the end of the week. Coming to a decision, he placed several calls to make the arrangements, then strode out of his office with determined steps.

Natalie was back from her meeting and was sitting with her nose nearly pressed against her monitor, as though she wanted to fall into the computer. And she was singing softly under her breath. He leaned a shoulder against the door frame and listened for a few seconds. Then, he recognized the song.

"Are you singing 'YMCA'?"

Her bottom shot an inch off her seat and her cheeks turned red.

"What now?" She studied him with wary eyes.

"I need you," he said, deepening his voice. Her mouth rounded into a plush O and he allowed himself a satisfied smile. If flirting was what it took to get her attention, then he wasn't opposed to engaging in some harmless fun. "Have lunch with me."

"Lunch?" Her eyes darted around her office, as though she was searching for an escape route. He watched her, wondering what excuse she'd come up with to wiggle out of it. She took a deep breath and squared her shoulders. "Sure. Let me just log off."

"You will?" Garrett's eyebrows shot up. He didn't think she'd give in so easily. "Great."

Recovering from his surprise, he walked beside her through the cubicles. Natalie kept a respectable distance between them and lengthened her strides as though trying to escape the surreptitious glances of curious employees.

"See you in the lobby," she said in a terse whisper and made a sharp right.

Her barely audible words and sudden change of direction caught him by surprise and he almost turned to follow her. Catching himself at the last moment, he made an awkward pivot to continue down the hall.

It'd been inconsiderate of him to just show up at her office. They needed to be seen together in public, but they didn't need to give the employees an exclusive sneak peek. Natalie still had a day or two before the rumors flew at work.

By the time they reunited in the building lobby, her

cheeks were back to their creamy white, and her features were as serene as a placid lake. Away from prying eyes in the elevator, something perverse in him wanted to disturb the calm surface of that lake. He would press her up against the back wall and slide her prim blouse off her shoulders. He would finally discover the exact shade of the tips of her lovely breasts... *Are they pale pink like a soft blush against her translucent skin? Or creamy brown like sweet caramel?*

Garrett shifted on his feet, his trousers growing uncomfortably tight. *Hell.* If he didn't stop his adolescent fantasizing, he was going to have to walk to his car with the swagger of a cowboy after a long day on the saddle.

"This way." He led her toward the parking elevator.

"We're driving?" she asked, meeting his gaze for the first time since they'd left her office.

"Yes. I'm taking you to my place."

"Oh." Natalie swung around to gape at him, then nodded slowly. "Is it far?"

"No." He wondered what she'd think about his choice of residence. "I live at the Ritz-Carlton on Olympic Boulevard."

Other than a slight tilt of her eyebrows, she didn't reveal her thoughts. "People know who you are over there, right?"

"Right."

She nodded absently and was quiet on their walk to his car.

As soon as they pulled out of the parking structure, Natalie freed her hair from her customary bun and shook her head to make the curls bounce around her shoulders. Garrett forgot to watch the road as he stared at her undoing the top three buttons of her blouse. When she bent to rummage through her purse, he caught a glimpse of her lacy white bra and his blood rushed south again. He was ogling her, his jaw slack. *Damn it.* He snapped his mouth closed, and returned his attention to the road.

"Is this better?" She scrutinized herself in the car mirror after painting her lips a deep pink rose.

"Better how?" He wouldn't have been able to pull off the cool-guy act even if his voice hadn't cracked. There was no use denying it. He was going to spend the entire afternoon obsessing over her perfect pink lips and wondering what other parts of her matched that shade.

"I figured you were taking me to your place so we could be seen together before our engagement announcement. You mentioned it was important I look the part, but this is the best I could do on a moment's notice."

"Don't worry about it. You look nice." *Nice? What am I? In sixth grade?*

Garrett drove the car into the hotel's circular driveway, and opened Natalie's door himself. When he helped her out of her seat, she stood on tiptoes and brushed her lips against his cheek. She seemed to have thrown herself into the role. While he stood in shock, she wrapped her arm around his waist and glanced up at him. Snapping back to attention, he pulled her to his side and kissed her hard, letting his hand slide up to rest an inch beneath her breast. It was all for show, of course.

He lifted his head before his control slipped again. Natalie stood and blinked her wide eyes, and he felt a surge of pride. Grinning broadly, he wrapped his arm around her shoulders and they strolled into the lobby. Seeming to emerge from a fog, she smiled prettily at him, back in character.

As soon as the elevator doors closed behind them, she dropped her smile and he dropped his arm from her shoulders. Natalie was so pumped from the performance she was practically shuffling her feet, reminding him of a scene from *Rocky*. An image of her in silky red boxing shorts and a tight black tank top flitted through his mind. *Goddamn it. Is there anything this woman does that I don't find sexy?*

They reached his penthouse before he did anything fool-ish, and were met by the spectacular views of downtown that stretched all the way to the Hollywood sign. The gusty spring winds had carried away much of the smog, and all of Los Angeles stood clear and arresting before them.

"Come on." He beckoned her with a tilt of his head. "I'll give you the five-cent tour."

Natalie followed him with her bright eyes scanning the condo, but her attention kept drifting back to the city view. The condo itself wasn't much. Three bedrooms, three and a half bathrooms, a couple dens, a kitchen and dining room, two libraries and an exercise room. The two of them should have enough space without feeling too cramped.

"Um… Is this where we're going to live after we get married?"

He hadn't given much thought to what Natalie would need or want. He was, without a doubt, an insensitive tool. "I don't have a particular attachment to the place. We can move if you'd like."

"No. I wouldn't dream of imposing on you like that. I'll only be here a while." Natalie waved her hands.

"You don't need to feel like a guest while you live here. It'll be as much your home as mine." If Mike or Adelaide heard him, they'd be shocked. Garrett valued his privacy as though his life depended on it.

"That's very kind of you." Her lashes fluttered shyly. "Thank you."

"You're welcome," he whispered. Her sincere words touched and humbled him "Thank you for rescuing me from an unwanted marriage."

"Don't thank me, yet. You won't be safe until I ruin you for good." Her mischievous smile made him hold his breath. "I'll pack over the weekend and move in by Sunday."

His breath left him in a hoot of laughter, and he enveloped her in a bear hug and swung her off her feet. She squealed and held on to his shoulders.

"Garrett, put me down," she said in a voice breathless with laughter.

After another spin, he steadied her onto the floor, keeping his arms loosely wrapped around her. He couldn't stop grinning. To his surprise, he very much looked forward to playing house with Natalie.

Five

Garrett was picking her up in fifteen minutes and she was still in her bra and panties. Natalie enjoyed big shindigs as much as she liked rolling around in a patch of poison ivy. She was agonizing over her attire for the dinner party— her bed was littered with half a dozen dresses. Garrett had sent them to her, and they were all beautiful, fashionable and—no doubt—expensive. She had to look the part, but he'd gone overboard.

It was their official "first date" and Natalie's insides were tangled into knots. They had gone out to lunch almost every day to strategize about their next moves, and let the paparazzi take pictures of their "secret romance." But this evening, she was accompanying Garrett to Michael Reynolds's birthday get-together to convince his friends what a happy couple they were.

Five minutes late, she eeny-meeny-miny-moed a black, strapless dress from the pile and slipped into it. She wore her hair in a loose updo, away from her bare shoulders.

As a finishing touch, she sprayed her favorite scent on her wrist and behind her ears. After a pause, she spritzed her cleavage.

With a last look in the mirror, Natalie rushed down the stairs and out of the building. Garrett had parked his car close to the entrance and stood outside, leaning back against the passenger-side door. He looked sinful in a tailored gray suit with a navy shirt, unbuttoned at his throat.

"Sorry I'm late." She sounded breathless. It had to be from running down the stairs, not because of how handsome he looked.

Garrett glanced up from his phone and froze as something hot and predatory flared in his eyes. He opened his mouth then closed it to clear his throat. "You look beautiful."

"So do you." The words popped out of her mouth before she could stop them, and blood rushed to her cheeks.

The corners of his eyes crinkled as his lips tugged to the side in a sexy grin. "Thank you."

"You're welcome," she mumbled, sliding into her seat while he held the door for her.

Natalie was surprised that Michael Reynolds was Garrett's oldest, closest friend. She knew Michael as a laid-back man with an easygoing smile, always cracking jokes. He was so different from the reserved, intense person Garrett was… It was difficult to imagine them as friends. But then, she didn't really know her soon-to-be husband all that well.

Forty-five minutes later, Garrett pulled up to a South Pasadena estate with a huge front lawn. The circular driveway was packed with luxury vehicles. Valets in bow ties and black jackets rushed around to take the guests' keys.

"This is his house?" Her voice rose at the end. She'd expected a casual get-together. Sure, she figured rich people would have fancy hors d'oeuvres and a Dom-Pérignon fountain or something, but not *this*.

"Yes," Garrett said, then switched off the ignition and stepped out of the car.

Natalie followed suit when one of the valets opened her door. Smiling her thanks at the man, she took Garrett's arm and whispered, "You said it was a 'small gathering.' This is a freaking wedding reception."

He furrowed his brow. "He's a publicist so he invited some influential acquaintances, but it's hardly a huge party. There can't be more than a hundred people here."

"Good Lord. What have I gotten myself into?" She dug her fingers into Garrett's forearm, which was muscular as hell. *Big party. Hot man.* She wanted to run off into the night.

The other guests were in their element, drinking and laughing, taking all the opulence for granted. Natalie was grateful to be wearing her new designer dress. Even so, she felt like she was on the wrong planet.

She rubbed shoulders with rich, powerful people at work and held her own, but that was her job and she knew what she was doing. This was a completely different beast. Small talk and mingling were not her forte. Garrett led her through the throng, stopping frequently to greet people he knew. As promised, she smiled and nodded in the right places, relieved she wasn't expected to talk.

"Mike." Garrett clapped the host on the shoulder. "Are you old enough to drink yet?"

"No, but I shaved for the first time today," Michael Reynolds said with an easy smirk. His smile broadened when he turned to her. "I'm glad you could make it, Natalie."

"Happy birthday, Michael." She dropped her voice to a conspiratorial whisper. "And let me know if you need a fake ID. I know someone who knows someone."

"I see you speak my language." Michael chuckled. "And call me Mike."

Natalie laughed with him and the knot in her chest loosened a notch. She didn't know their host well, but he had an openness to him that she liked.

She glanced up at Garrett when his arm snaked around her waist and he drew her close, but he addressed his friend without meeting her eyes. "You're a bad influence on my fiancée."

"I think it's the other way around." Mike lowered his voice and winked at her. "Congratulations, by the way. As his oldest friend, I thank you in advance for putting up with the grumpy son of a bitch."

Natalie snorted. "You're very welcome."

When Mike walked away to mingle with the rest of his guests, Garrett dropped his hand from her waist. She shivered at the sudden loss of heat.

"Are you cold?" A small frown marred his smooth forehead.

"No. I'm fine, but I could use a drink."

"Bowmore?" he said, one side of his lips tipping up.

"Just a glass of champagne." Her stomach fluttered—she was surprised he remembered her drink from Le Rêve. "I need to stay sharp for our audience."

Garrett resisted the urge to glance over his shoulder to check on her. Natalie was a grown woman and he didn't need to protect her from being swarmed by admirers. Besides, she was the one who had proposed they refrain from *other* relationships, so she wouldn't do anything to hurt his reputation or hers.

Earlier, at her apartment, he'd caught fire at the sight of her in her little black dress. It was demure compared to the one she'd worn at Le Rêve, but it hugged her hourglass figure and highlighted the curves underneath just enough to tease his imagination.

He walked to the bar for his Scotch and grabbed a flute

of champagne from a server on his way back. As he'd anticipated, Natalie was now surrounded by a group of men and he lengthened his strides to reach her.

"Sorry to keep you waiting, sweetheart." He pressed a light kiss on her lips and handed her the champagne.

"Thank you." She leaned her head against his shoulder when he pulled her to his side, playing her part like a pro.

"Natalie was just taking us to task about USC's new head coach. It seems neither he nor I truly understand college football," said one of Mike's college friends.

"Is that so?" Garrett raised an eyebrow at her and she shrugged.

"Taking you to task is a bit harsh." She hid her grin against the rim of her champagne flute as she took a long sip. "It's just that I have a *better* understanding than you guys."

The audience winced and guffawed at her cheekiness. As Natalie continued with her lecture, all the men listened intently, as did Garrett. She was funny and down-to-earth, and her mind was quicker than lightning. Lost in her words, Garrett belatedly noticed the crowd had grown. Her champagne glass was depleted and her smile was becoming strained.

He leaned down close to her ear. "Tired?"

"And hungry."

"All right, gentlemen. I'm whisking away my date now. I'm tired of sharing her."

When the crowd finally dispersed, Natalie slumped against him with a groan. "I need food, champagne and somewhere to sit."

A server walked over with a tray of bacon-wrapped shrimp and Natalie snatched a couple of them. She popped one in her mouth and mumbled around her food, "Not necessarily in that order."

Garrett laughed and guided her toward the French doors

leading out to the garden. Natalie ate every single hors d'oeuvre she met along the way and finished another glass of champagne.

"Holy cow. Is everything really, really delicious, or am I just famished? I would totally go back for that crab cake if my feet weren't screaming at me to get my butt on a chair."

He glanced down at her zebra-print high heels. They did amazing things for her legs but didn't look remotely comfortable. "There's a bench around the corner."

"Oh, thank God." She kicked off her shoes as soon as she plopped onto the seat.

Garrett shrugged out of his jacket and draped it around her shoulders before sitting next to her.

"Thank you," she murmured, gazing at the garden. "It's so beautiful out here."

"Is it?" He and Mike had grown up tearing apart that very garden, but Garrett had never sat still and taken it all in, like they were doing now. "I guess you're right."

"Mmm-hmm."

He studied her profile, her high, regal cheekbone and the graceful curve of her neck. Half of her hair had escaped the loose knot behind her head and fell down her back and shoulders. He wanted to sweep aside her hair and feel the softness of her skin, which he absolutely should not do.

"So how do you know so much about college football?" He tore his gaze away from her and stared at an old maple tree ahead of him, hard enough to make his eyes water.

"Long story."

"We've got time." He made a show of checking his watch. "I'll give you ten minutes."

Her laughter filled the garden, then ended on a wistful sigh. "My dad and I, we weren't very close. The only time he didn't mind my company was when we watched college football together. He was a huge fan. I don't think he even noticed I was sitting there half the time."

Garrett understood what that felt like. As soon as he finished graduate school, he'd thrown himself into his work. It was satisfying in its predictability and it created a common ground for him and his father. His dad had stepped down from the CEO position when his mom died, but returned to Hansol a few years later as an executive VP.

"I thought if I learned enough about the sport, he'd like me a little better." Her shrug told him it hadn't worked, but Natalie told her story without an ounce of self-pity—like she owned her past, hurt and all. His respect for her deepened. "But soon I noticed I wasn't faking my enthusiasm anymore. I'd grown to love the sport. Who knew it'd come in handy at an intimate birthday party for a hundred people?"

"You certainly won over quite a few of them."

"I did?" Her eyebrows shot up in genuine surprise.

He huffed out a laugh. "Why did you think that crowd was hanging on to your every word?"

"Watch yourself, Garrett Song." Natalie narrowed her eyes and pointed a finger at him. "I know where you live."

He snatched her hand and tugged her to her feet. "Yes, and you'll be living there with me starting Sunday."

"Ugh." She hooked an index finger in each of her shoes, not bothering to put them back on. "Do you ever stop thinking about work?"

"Yes." He cocked his head and pretended to consider her question. "But only when I'm thoroughly distracted."

Her lashes fluttered and color saturated her cheeks, and his gut clenched with heat. She could definitely become his most dangerous distraction.

Six

Still groggy from sleep, Natalie stepped out of the shower and wrapped herself in a warm woolly bathrobe, yawning until her eyes watered. Garrett hadn't brought her home until past one last night, and she hadn't fallen asleep until close to three. She yawned again.

It took a while for her brain to piece together that someone was knocking at the door. *It's not even eight, for God's sake.* Natalie cracked open the door a sliver and peered into the hallway. All traces of the sandman's influence evaporated at the sight of Garrett standing outside with two steaming cups and a brown paper bag.

He looked damn gorgeous and relaxed in his black T-shirt and jeans. He'd obviously had a good night's sleep. She'd had a fitful slumber only to wake up at the crack of dawn. Not fair.

"I bring strong coffee and warm croissants." He held up his offerings. "May I come in?"

Her stomach rumbled on cue, and Natalie opened the door wider. "My stomach welcomes you."

As Garrett closed the door behind him, Natalie remembered she was naked underneath her robe. *Stay calm.* She smoothed out her face in an expression of serenity. At least she hoped she looked serene. She could be bright pink *and* calm, right?

She waved for him to follow and led him into her small kitchen. "You can put those over there."

After setting his burden on her kitchen table, Garrett leaned a shoulder against the wall and focused his attention on her. His gaze drifted down her throat to the deep V of her robe, and her body warmed and softened in response. He might as well have been drawing a line of fire down her skin.

Could they really keep their hands off each other living under the same roof?

Things would get so much more complicated if she succumbed to the temptation. What if she got needy and clung to a man she could never keep? *God, no.* She was a grown woman and her brain dictated her actions, not the hot, aching center of her body.

"Have a seat." *Damn it.* She sounded breathless. "I'll be right back."

Her blush deepened and she licked her lips. *Crap.* There was something erotic about him seeing her fresh out of the shower with her wet curls sticking to her cheeks. Natalie scurried into her bedroom and leaned against her closed door. After stuffing her screaming hormones in a deep, dark corner of her mind, she threw on some tights and a soft tunic and went out to meet her fiancé.

Garrett had pulled out two small plates from her meager collection and set out their breakfast on the table.

"Plain or chocolate?" he asked when she sat down across from him.

"I'm not a crazy woman." She snorted and rolled her eyes. "Why would I pass up on chocolate?"

He chuckled and passed her the chocolate croissant, then took the plain one for himself.

Her croissant was still warm and melted chocolate oozed out when she took a bite. Her eyes fluttered closed.

"Mmm…"

She used her fingertip to dab the excess chocolate from the corners of her mouth and licked it off. No napkin was getting a single smudge of her chocolate. She was half-way through her breakfast before she noticed how quiet Garrett was.

When Natalie glanced at him, he was glaring at her with his croissant untouched. She squinted at him. "Are you re-gretting not taking the chocolate one?"

"No. I don't like sweets," he said in an oddly husky voice.

They enjoyed the rest of their breakfast and coffee in companionable silence. He offered to clear the table, but she waved him aside and put their plates in the sink, which was only two steps behind her.

"Okay. What brings you by so bright and early?" Natalie beckoned him to walk with her to the living room and plopped down on the couch. He followed suit, taking up her ancient sofa with his muscular thighs and broad back. The heat radiating off him made her breath hitch.

"We can't announce our engagement without an engage-ment ring." Garrett lifted Natalie's hand from her side and retrieved a ring from his pocket. "It was my mother's."

"Your mother's?" she gasped. It was absolutely stun-ning. The ring consisted of an antique emerald surrounded by small diamonds set in a rich gold band. "Are you sure you're okay with me wearing it? Shouldn't you save it for when you propose to someone you actually want to marry?"

"Unless you've forgotten, I asked you to marry me,"

he said. "I wouldn't have done that if I didn't want you to agree."

"You know what I mean. I think you should save your mother's ring for someone you love. Someone you want forever."

"Then the ring will never see the light of day." He let out a short, humorless laugh. "I don't intend to marry for love and forever. Not everyone buys into that fairy tale. Certainly not me."

A chill ran down her spine at the finality of his words. "Well, this is lovely. Thank you. I'll return it to you when this is all over."

"Don't worry about it," he said tersely. "We'll deal with it when the time comes."

"Okay," she said slowly. A solid wall had fallen across his expression at the mention of love and forever. Someone really must have done a number on him. "You know I'm moving in with you today. You could've waited until tonight."

"Call me old-fashioned. I wanted to put a ring on your finger before you ruined me."

Garrett left Natalie's place after loading his car with the few boxes she'd managed to pack. Even though she was leaving behind her furniture to sublet the apartment, they would need to make several trips to move her belongings over. She'd shooed him out of her apartment so she could pack her stuff *her way*.

It actually freed up some much-needed time for him to visit his family. He wanted to tell his father about his engagement in person, even if he'd already heard his grandmother's version of the story. Garrett and his father's relationship had improved over the past few years, but he wasn't sure where his old man would stand on the issue of his only son's marriage.

As he anticipated, the Song family's housekeeper, Liliana, informed him that his grandmother was "indisposed"—she smiled sympathetically at him—so he was free to search out his father. He found him in the study, nursing a glass of Scotch. When Garrett raised his eyebrows as he took a seat across from him, his father lifted the glass in mock salute and took a healthy sip.

"It's past noon. That means it's not too early for Scotch."

"Does Dr. Ananth know about your minute-past-noon Scotch rule?"

His dad was on a medical leave at the behest of his cardiologist. Garrett doubted whiskey was part of the doctor's treatment program.

"Don't you start on me, too. I have enough trouble keeping Adelaide off my back."

"You should be glad she cares enough to nag."

Regret and vulnerability passed over his father's face, but they were gone too quickly for Garrett to be certain. "I have a feeling you're not here for father-son bonding time." His dad leaned back in his leather chair and steepled his fingers in front of him. "What's going on?"

Well, Dad. A hell storm is brewing, and I'm in the eye of it. "I'm getting married."

"To which fiancée?"

"I only have one." Garrett's fists clenched on his knees. *Dad did know about the arrangement with Jihae Park. He just didn't bother standing up for me.*

"Not according to your grandmother. Are you sure you want to defy her?"

"No, but I'm sure I want to marry my fiancée, not a complete stranger."

"Your mother and I…" His voice grew thick and he couldn't continue. There was no need. Garrett knew his parents were strangers when they married.

"It's not about whether or not Jihae Park is a good match

for me. Or whether she and I might find happiness in an arranged marriage." Garrett breathed deeply through his nose. "The point is I already chose my wife, and it is my decision alone. I will not be a pawn for the Song dynasty."

"So be it." His father's voice rang with a note of determination, and he straightened in his seat, drawing back his shoulders. Garrett couldn't tell whether his dad was determined to stop the wedding, or would help him stand up to Grandmother. "Well, tell me about your young lady."

"She…" Garrett cleared his throat, caught off guard by his dad's sudden interest. "Her name is Natalie Sobol. She's Hansol's HR director in the LA office."

"Ah, yes. I've met her on a few occasions. She's an intelligent and competent young woman. Isn't she Korean-American?"

"Yes, on her mother's side."

"Good, good." He nodded absently, then added, "But you took an unnecessary risk dating a subordinate."

"She's not a *subordinate*," Garrett said with tight control, fighting against the resentment churning in his stomach. "She's my fiancée and your future daughter-in-law, not some second-class citizen."

"I never implied that she was. The fact is you're an executive and she's your subordinate employee. It all worked out but that doesn't mean it wasn't risky."

"Isn't it a bit late for doling out fatherly advice?" *What the hell is wrong with me?* Garrett's emotions were too close to the surface. He dragged his fingers through his hair, and tried again. "I wanted you to hear this from me. Her sister passed away recently, and Natalie's fighting for custody of her niece, so she may have an adopted baby soon."

"A baby?" The initial shock on his father's face gave way to comical excitement, as though his birthday wish had come true. "You're going to be a father."

"Natalie needs to win custody first."

Garrett shied away from the thought of becoming Sophie's *fake* stepfather. The deal was between him and Natalie, but his father's unexpected response made him wary about how his family would react when they dissolved the marriage.

"How old is the baby?" An odd little smile tugged at his dad's lips.

"About six months."

"Well, when do I get to meet them? Dinner tomorrow evening?"

"If Natalie's free." It was Garrett's turn to be shocked. He'd gotten a lecture when he said he was marrying an *employee*, but when he added a baby into the picture, his old man turned to mush. "But Sophie's with her grandparents, so I can't guarantee you'll see her tomorrow."

"I see." His dad's shoulders drooped half an inch. "Did you already tell Adelaide the news?"

Garrett nearly groaned. "Not yet."

He and his father exchanged a rare look of understanding. Adelaide was going to flay him for keeping Natalie and Sophie a secret. Unfortunately, he couldn't tell her it was new to him as well. He would have to appreciate the irony on his own while his baby sister put him in his place.

Seven

The weeks leading up to their wedding had spun past her in a tornado of improbable events. Now Natalie found herself standing in the Song family's garden. It had been transformed into the most enchanting wedding venue she'd ever seen. The shimmering Pacific Ocean, the mild spring breeze and the deep orange sunset held an otherworldly beauty that stilled her breath.

And Natalie wanted to sob her heart out. She shouldn't be here. She didn't belong in this world of riches and luxuries. She didn't belong with Garrett.

Traci, I miss you so much. If her big sister had been here, she would shake Natalie by the shoulders and tell her to run the hell away. From the lies. *But then, if she was alive, I wouldn't have thrown myself into this ridiculous scheme just so I could adopt Sophie.*

The sudden surge of resentment knocked the wind out of her. None of this was Traci's fault. No one had twisted Natalie's arm to marry Garrett. Even the man himself hadn't unduly pressured her. She couldn't deny that his arrogant certainty swayed her, but in the end, the choice had been entirely hers. *God, I wish I could go back a month and slap some sense into myself.* Well, she didn't have a time machine, and she had a part to play.

Adelaide and the wedding coordinator had pulled off a miracle in a few short weeks. But finding a suitable venue on such short notice had proven impossible until Adelaide convinced her grandmother to allow the wedding to proceed in their home. For the sake of privacy.

Natalie sighed wistfully at the dusty pink and cream calla lilies—the color of her bouquet—and the rest of the flowers in fresh spring colors that were in full bloom throughout the garden. If she ever got married after this madness ended, her real wedding would pale in comparison to her fake one.

"Natalie!" Adelaide linked an arm through hers and tugged her back inside. "Garrett just got here. What if he saw you?"

"I'd say hi," Natalie mumbled under her breath.

Adelaide had had her locked up in a guest bedroom all afternoon while a makeup artist, a hairstylist and a seamstress poked and prodded Natalie. As exhausting as it had been, her reflection convinced her the hours were well spent. More than anything, she truly loved her wedding dress. It could've been a French heirloom from the 1920s. The silk inner dress hugged her figure, but the shimmery lace overlay shifted and swirled around her like Salome's seven veils.

"You know it's bad luck for the groom to see the bride before the wedding." Her soon-to-be sister-in-law huffed and threw her an exasperated frown.

"Sorry."

Adelaide and their father, James, were probably shocked by Garrett's sudden news, but they welcomed her with open arms. His grandmother, however, had refused to meet Natalie, much less attend the wedding.

She wasn't vain enough to expect everyone to like her, but Garrett's grandmother had decided she didn't like her without bothering to meet her. *I guess a middle-class woman without a family could never be worthy of her grandson.* Her absence stung even more since she'd chosen to stay in her room, mere steps away from the ceremony. Natalie couldn't imagine how hard his grandmother's rebuff might be for Garrett. Sure, their marriage was a ruse, but Madame Song didn't know that.

"People have heard of bridezilla, but I bet they've never heard of sister-in-law-zilla." Adelaide said, ushering Natalie back inside. The joke brought her out of her sullen thoughts.

Alone in her bridal suite, Natalie paced in circles, too nervous to sit. She stopped in front of a settee where her bridal *hanbok* sat, wrapped in a box. The traditional Korean dress was worn on special occasions like weddings and New Year's Day.

Natalie never had one of her own, but had always wanted one. Her mom had eschewed all things Korean when she moved to the States with Dad, a soldier who'd been stationed in Seoul. But Korea was once her mom's home, and learning about its culture made Natalie feel connected to her.

She opened the box and ran her fingers over the dress. It had a deep yellow cropped top and a crimson empire-waist skirt with hand-embroidered flowers and butterflies fluttering across the bottom of the voluminous skirt and on parts of the sleeves.

Her sister-in-law had hired a well-known seamstress to make the *hanbok*, hoping her grandmother would come around and attend the wedding. If she did, Garrett and Natalie were to change into their *hanbok* after the wedding ceremony to observe a short tradition where the eldest members of the groom's family bless the newlyweds by throwing dried jujubes for the bride to catch in her skirt.

Natalie had thought Adelaide was messing with her with the whole jujube thing, but online research verified the tradition. Plus, she learned that the jujubes symbolized children. The more jujubes the bride caught, the more children the couple would have. Natalie had laughed herself to tears imagining Garrett and her batting the jujubes away.

Lost in her musings, Natalie nearly jumped out of her skin when Adelaide knocked softly and poked her head in. "Hey, sis. They're ready for you."

Adelaide was quiet for once as they walked to the garden. She held Natalie's icy hand in her warm one. Before they reached the guests, she leaned in and carefully hugged Natalie so she wouldn't disturb her makeup and intricate updo.

"Thank you for marrying my brother. He seems cold and aloof, but he's a really good guy and I can see glimpses of his old self when you're with him. And I'm so happy I finally get an older sister."

"You're going to make me cry before my grand entrance." She breathed in a shuddering breath. "I'm happy to have a sister again."

Too soon, Natalie stood at the start of the silken road, but her feet refused to budge. She hadn't been close enough to her father to miss him at this moment, but she wished she had a strong arm to hang on to. There were too many eyes on her, making her want to run in the opposite direction.

She searched the crowd. For what, she didn't know. Not until she found him.

Garrett's heated gaze bore into her and the knot in her chest broke, allowing her to breathe again. The ringing in her ears faded as he came into focus. He was breathtaking. His unruly hair was swept back, accentuating the hard angles of his face. The fitted tuxedo made his shoulders look impossibly broad. He exuded power and certainty, and for this moment, lie or not, he stood waiting for *her*. His eyes didn't leave hers for a second, and she held on to his gaze to guide her to his side. She didn't remember taking a single step until she reached him at the altar and he enfolded her icy hands in his.

"You look beautiful." His whisper caressed her ear and she shivered with awareness.

Natalie focused on the heat of his body and her skin prickling in response. Anything but the dread that threatened to consume her if she acknowledged it.

The ceremony washed over her like a flitting dream and she made the oldest, most sacred of vows with no hope of keeping them. For someone who was allergic to lying, she sure was getting good at it.

Garrett wrapped Natalie in his arms and they swayed to the music. Like the night at Le Rêve, his blood sang as their bodies touched, but this time, it was more than desire. Temporary or not, she was his wife—his alone.

"We're finishing our dance at last," he said before his possessiveness overwhelmed him. She gave him a ghost of a smile, but fatigue lined her features. He tucked her head under his chin to hide his frown. After their dance, he led Natalie back to their table and reached for her hand. "Are you all right?"

"Of course." He studied her face, his thumb drawing slow circles on her wrist. She was pale under her makeup with dark blue half circles under her wide eyes. Seeming to notice his concern, she forced a smile. "I'm fine, Garrett."

He grunted, unconvinced by her reassurance, but the stubborn jut of her chin said there was no whisking her away for an early night. With a resigned sigh, he turned his attention to the crowd and sucked in a quick breath.

"Sophie has my father wrapped around her little pinkie."

She looked adorable in her cream-colored dress with pink and white flowers dotting the skirt, and his dad held her like a precious treasure. When he lifted the baby high in the air, she rewarded him with a squeal and an infectious giggle, peppered with wet raspberries. His father laughed out loud for the first time in what seemed like years. *How will Dad take it when Sophie and Natalie leave for New York in the winter?* Something close to dread stabbed at his gut.

"She's a charmer." Natalie watched them with a soft, sweet smile, then met his gaze and held it. "And, Garrett, it'll be okay. Sophie and your family won't have a chance to get too attached. She's with her grandparents, and what little time I have with her I'll be guarding greedily."

Her voice trembled slightly. She obviously didn't want anyone to get hurt, either, especially their family. She continued to search his face, worry and vulnerability in her expression. He nodded, unable to trust his voice, but his heart twisted when she gave him a tremulous smile.

This was their wedding day—alluding to the end of their marriage left a bad taste in his mouth. Capturing his bride's hand, he planted a kiss on her palm, wanting to distract her from her thoughts. He flashed a wolfish grin when she gasped and turned a lovely pink. For good measure, he brushed his lips against the sensitive skin of her wrist, and a shiver ran through her.

"Garrett," she breathed.

Her voice was low and husky, and reckless lust flared in him again. He'd made sure their first kiss as husband and wife was short and chaste. But sitting so close to her, her soft fragrance entangling his senses, he wanted to claim her—to have a real wedding night. *Damn it.* He dropped her hand and sat back in his seat. When he saw Mike waving him over, Garrett rushed to his feet. "Duty calls."

"Does your duty entail joining that group over there with

everyone holding a bottle of champagne?" Natalie said with a wry smile. "I think there's a bottle with your name on it."

His best man held a bottle in each fist and lifted them over his head, confirming her suspicion. "It's not easy, but someone has to do it," Garrett said.

She laughed and gave him a gentle push toward them. "Well, go then."

"I'll be back." Without thinking, he dropped a kiss on the tip of her nose, the easy affection startling him. That bottle of champagne was sounding better by the minute.

When Garrett reached his friends, he grabbed a bottle out of Mike's hand and tipped down a good quarter of it.

"Thirsty?" His friend quirked an eyebrow at him.

"Very."

"Oh, what the hell." Mike shrugged and followed suit. "Gentlemen, Garrett beat us to it and drank half his bottle already. Let's drink to our unexpected groom. May you not be an ass to your stunning new bride so she will tolerate you till the end of days."

"Thank you for that touching speech." Garrett lifted his bottle to his friends and drank.

Shouts of laughter and cheers rang through the crowd, and much imbibing ensued. His emotions back in check, he risked a glance at Natalie. Her chair was empty and a flash of irritation hit him. He'd run from her a moment ago and now he wanted her where he'd left her. He conceded he was being an ass. Still, his gaze sought her out in the crowd.

He found her on the dance floor, being twirled by his father. He was smiling down at Natalie and she was biting her lip as though she was on the verge of tears. Garrett's stomach lurched in alarm. After shoving his champagne bottle at Mike, he rushed to her side.

When he reached the dance floor, her smile was still a bit watery but she didn't seem upset and his dad was chuckling.

"May I cut in?" Garrett said.

"Of course. She's all yours." After kissing Natalie on the cheek, his father strolled off.

"What happened?" He watched his dad join Sophie and Mrs. Kim—Natalie's firecracker neighbor. He'd met her during the move, and survived her intense grilling.

"What do you mean?"

"Why were you about to cry?"

Her mouth opened, then closed. "How did you know?"

"I saw you." He brushed aside her question impatiently. "Tell me."

"Your father just welcomed me to the family. He said... I was his daughter now." Her voice broke, and tears sprang to her eyes. "I don't even remember my mom, and my dad couldn't stand me. Even with Traci gone and Sophie's adoption in the air, your dad made me feel like I was part of a family. Like I wasn't alone. What he said was a gift—a gift I don't deserve—but I'll cherish it forever."

Garrett didn't know what to say, so he pulled her close and held her against his chest. *What can I say? Enjoy it while it lasts?* Things were getting a hell of a lot more complicated than he'd anticipated, and he had a sick feeling in his stomach that hearts would be broken before this was over.

And he hated himself for praying his heart wouldn't be one of them.

Eight

Garrett pressed her against him, and Natalie forgot everything—the lies, the uncertainty, the guilt. The warmth of his embrace and the sweet strains of the ballad gradually eased the tension from her shoulders.

"Kiss, kiss, kiss!"

Natalie jolted back to reality at the thundering chant of the tipsy wedding guests and the sharp chiming of forks striking wineglasses. She peeked over Garrett's shoulder to see they were surrounded by his champagne-chugging buddies. She buried her face into his chest again and groaned.

"Let's give them the kiss, then we can leave," he said, lifting her chin with the crook of his finger.

Natalie looked up at him with an exasperated sigh. By the grim line of Garrett's mouth, he wasn't too thrilled about it, either. He lowered his head slowly, brushed her lips with the softest of touches and began to draw away, but the gentleness of his kiss knocked down her defenses. Too tired to fight, she pressed herself against him and pulled his mouth back with greedy fingers tangled in his hair.

Garrett stilled for a moment, but with a moan, he took control of the kiss. Nipping and tasting her bottom lip, he sought entry with the tip of his tongue. She complied and he deepened the kiss, his fingers digging into her hips. The slick slide of his tongue against hers as they tangled and danced made her light-headed, and she slid her hands down his arms and spread her fingers across the shifting muscles of his back.

Garrett's breath caught sharply in his throat, then he pressed his hand against her back and pulled her flush against his body. Catcalls, shouts and applause rang far off in the distance, but Natalie was too busy to acknowledge the sound. An unmistakable hardness pressed against her stomach through the soft material of her dress, and she whimpered, rising on tiptoes to get closer to him.

Then she was rudely torn from him and held at arm's length. Garrett stared at her with an unreadable expression on his face, his hands gripping her shoulders. They stood silently, both breathing hard.

She'd forgotten where they were and why they were kissing in the first place. She might not have stopped if Garrett hadn't pushed her away.

Natalie wanted to become a little rodent so she could scurry into the nearest mouse hole. Not only was the situation mortifying, but she also couldn't let this happen again if she wanted an easy-peasy annulment.

Tonight had to be a fluke. They'd kissed plenty of times since their engagement. Yet she'd successfully resisted the temptation to tangle tongues with him. The wedding wasn't *real*—at least not for the bride and groom—but she was only human. How could she help but notice how beautiful and romantic everything was and get a little carried away?

"Let's go." Garrett's voice was gruff but his expression was impassive.

He had put their kiss behind him. And why not? It was just another kiss to him. Not just that, but it was a fake kiss. He couldn't help that he was an excellent kisser and his fake bride couldn't take the heat.

In a blur of smiling faces and well wishes, they bid their guests and family a hasty goodbye and headed for the Ritz-Carlton. Since it was only a marriage of convenience, they'd agreed a honeymoon was unnecessary. Besides, she had a baby to adopt and he had a partnership and a CEO seat to secure. It was time they focused on the important goals.

"Here we are." Garrett waved away the valet as they arrived and opened her car door for her.

He put his hand on the small of her back and led her into the hotel lobby. Once the elevator door closed behind them, he dropped his hand and stepped aside, putting some space between them. Natalie annoyed herself by missing the heat of his body next to hers. As soon as they reached the penthouse, Garrett headed to the foot of the stairs.

"You did well today," he said, loosening his tie and the top buttons of his shirt. Her eyes were riveted to the hollow at the base of his throat, which had been revealed by his unintentional striptease.

"Thanks?" Natalie said, bemused by his review of her wedding performance. "Good night."

Garrett stalked off without a backward glance. She blinked. *What the heck just happened?* She stood alone in the vast emptiness of the living room and looked around. The city lights twinkled, taunting her that the people out there were actually living their lives, while she was putting hers on hold for months.

Natalie sighed, bone-deep tired from being lonely. This had to be the most *un*romantic wedding night in the history of contract marriages. In the romance novels she read, the fake couples at least played chess or watched *Die Hard* together.

Her husband watched her descend the staircase with hooded eyes. Natalie was wearing a floor-length column dress in emerald silk with a sweetheart neckline that lovingly cradled her breasts. Her hair fell down her back with a single barrette sweeping to keep the curls out of her eyes. Gold shadow dusted her lids and her lips were painted Old-Hollywood red. She looked damn good and hoped to find at least a spark of appreciation in Garrett's gaze.

"Hey," she said, joining him at the foot of the stairs.

He wore a tailored tuxedo that emphasized his broad shoulders, narrow hips and long, muscular legs. Pure female appreciation fluttered in her chest, then died at his next words.

"We're late."

Right. There was no time to waste on complimenting his wife.

"Of course," she said with sweet sarcasm. She was exactly four minutes late. "Sorry for holding you up."

Garrett raised his eyebrows in response, and Natalie fumed inside. They'd been married for thirteen days and twenty-one hours, and she was beyond tired of her husband's cool apathy toward her. They were going to a charity ball that Clark Nobu and Sebastian Diaz were attending, and she wanted to help Garrett make a good impression.

Maybe she should come down with a sudden, blinding migraine. Natalie suppressed the childish impulse. A deal was a deal. She would do her best to help Garrett. No matter how infuriating he was.

Silence had been a staple during their short marriage, and it followed them on their drive to the ball. Most days, Garrett left for work before she woke up and came home after she went to bed. She hardly even ran into him at the office. Being busy was one thing, but she didn't understand why their conversations had become so stilted. Couldn't they be business partners who talked to each other?

"What's our plan?" She hoped strategizing would break some of the tension between them. "You said Sebastian's attending with his wife, but what about Clark? Is he married?"

"No, he's a widower."

"Oh, no. That poor man."

"Life goes on."

Something in Garrett's tone sent chills down her spine. *Is it because James is a widower, too?* She could let it go and enjoy the stifling silence again. Or not. She sensed an old hurt there and found herself wanting to ease it.

"How did your mom die?" she asked softly.

Every muscle in Garrett's body tensed, and Natalie thought she might have crossed the line he'd drawn between them.

"Cancer."

"I'm so sorry." She knew the pain of having someone she loved being stolen from her too soon. "I didn't know."

"Not many people do." Garrett kept his gaze on the road. "It wasn't a long battle, though. She went quickly."

"How old were you?"

"Fifteen."

"Oh, Garrett." Natalie reached out and put her hand on his arm.

"My parents were crazy about each other," he continued in a voice so low she almost didn't hear him. "My father... he broke down, as though someone cut off his life source."

"You had to grieve for both your parents."

His eyes snapped to her, and in that moment, the vulnerability and loneliness of the fifteen-year-old Garrett stared out at her. Natalie's heart bled for that boy.

"I want you to introduce yourself to Sebastian Diaz and his wife. They're visiting from Spain. Sebastian is a substantial shareholder and the COO of Vivotex. His opinion carries tremendous weight," Garrett said, regaining his composure and severing the brief connection they'd shared. Natalie pulled her hand from his arm, knowing her touch was no longer welcome. "I know everything about him on paper, but I don't know what really makes the man tick. Meeting him socially might show you something I haven't learned."

"What about you?"

"I'm going to chat with Clark Nobu, the head of Vivotex's US headquarters."

"Sounds like a plan," she said with false bravado.

Her emotions collided with each other hard enough to give her whiplash. Empathy, anger and hurt churned in a primordial soup in her stomach, but she focused on the most pressing emotion at the moment. Nervousness. Major panic-inducing nervousness.

Natalie clenched her teeth, determined not to let Garrett see through her calm facade. She'd never been to a ball before and he planned on leaving her on her own. Before it could take form, she stomped down on the twinge of resentment prickling inside her. He had no reason to know she felt like Cinderella five minutes before midnight. Even if he did, she didn't need him to protect her. If her designer gown turned into rags when the clock struck twelve, she'd rock it as the grunge-chic look and rescue her own behind.

They arrived at the famed Music Center, the venue for the charity event, and maneuvered through the glamorous mob to enter the grand hall. The modern building emanated subdued opulence through deep, dark wood and rich royal blues.

Garrett scanned the crowd from the elevated entryway, then guided them down the steps. He placed his big hand over her cold fingers curved on his tuxedo sleeve. The night air brushing her bare shoulders had chilled her, but his touch warmed her up—far too efficiently. When he lowered his head and nuzzled her ear, a shiver ran down her spine and her toes curled.

"I'll come find you in an hour." Unlike the intimacy of his touch, his voice was cold and businesslike.

Her body's response to his proximity and his apparent immunity to hers made her temper flare. Before she knew what she was doing, she snaked her hand around the back of his neck and tugged so she could capture his startled mouth in a hot, demanding kiss, daring him to respond.

Garrett didn't back away from the challenge. He crushed her body against his and cupped her face as he deepened the kiss, his tongue plundering her mouth with frantic, deep plunges. Even as her body softened and opened in response, her mind retained a strand of reason. She'd made her point and she needed to end the kiss before her self-restraint broke.

Natalie managed to maneuver her hands against his chest, which proved challenging since there was no room between them from chest to thigh. *God, he has magnificent pectorals.* She leaned back at the waist at the same time she pushed against his chest with all her strength.

Garrett barely budged but lifted his head an inch away from hers. His eyes were molten onyx, filled with undisguised longing, and her blood pumped in triumph. But she couldn't fall back into his arms if she wanted to retain her pride.

"Okay," she said, her voice husky but functioning. "I'll see you in an hour."

After a featherlight kiss on his cheek, his wife sashayed away, her perfect round ass taunting him. He was able to swallow after three attempts, but it was only when she was out of sight that his lungs expanded to capacity. Her warm, vanilla fragrance had clouded his mind the moment she stepped into his car earlier. But standing with his arm around her had given him a whiff of the warm musk that could only be called pure, delicious Natalie. Combined with her dress and red, pouty lips, the woman was lethal to his sanity.

Garrett had been avoiding Natalie since their wedding, unwilling to gamble on his self-control holding out if he got too close. But there was an unexpected side effect to depriving himself of his wife's company. The suppressed desire slammed into him ten times stronger the moment he laid eyes on her.

He scowled with frustration at the ridiculous predicament that he couldn't make love to his own wife. A server passing by gasped and hurried past him, mistaking herself as the target of his displeasure. He released a deep breath and rearranged his expression to one more suitable for the event, then strode in the opposite direction from Natalie. He had a partnership deal to secure.

Clark's formidable intellect and shrewd instincts were unmatched in the industry. He also happened to be a decent human being by all accounts. Both of them being in the fashion industry, they'd exchanged pleasantries in the past. Even without an official partnership between their companies, Nobu would be a valuable ally.

Garrett found him leaning against the bar nursing a drink. "Just the man I was looking for."

"Song." Clark assessed him with a shadow of a smile. "Eager to claim that drink I owe you?"

"We're on the same wavelength." He saw no point in playing games when the other man would see right through them. "The partnership already looks promising."

"It's always looked promising. The problem is the timing and the execution."

"The shared vision is the crucial factor." Garrett grinned. "The rest is technicalities."

"I would like a preview of your plans for the *technicalities*. People say your genius is in the details."

"That's quite a reputation to live up to, but I appreciate your vote of confidence." He raised his glass in salute.

His conversation with Clark flowed easily and soon they were on their second glass of Scotch. Garrett scanned the throng of partygoers, hoping to catch a glimpse of his wife, but she was nowhere to be seen.

"I know you're new at this so I'm going to give you some unsolicited advice," Clark said. "Does your wife know anyone at this party?"

"Not to my knowledge."

"And you left your brand-new bride to fend for herself amid all this massive hoopla? I hope you're looking forward to sleeping in the guest room tonight."

Garrett chuckled at the irony, pushing aside his prickling unease. He recalled her brief panic over the size of Mike's party, but she'd single-handedly won over that crowd. He had no doubt she was charming her way through this ballroom full of guests. Even so, anxiety tugged at him.

"Natalie is far too independent to need me hanging around her all night."

"You poor, clueless bastard."

They went in search of Natalie and found her a few steps outside the ballroom with Sebastian Diaz and his wife. From the booming sound of Mr. Diaz's belly laugh, she was having a successful night.

"Maybe I misspoke," Clark whispered, and walked ahead to greet the Diazes.

"Sorry to keep you waiting, sweetheart." Garrett slipped his arm around Natalie's waist and dropped a chaste kiss on her red lips, unwilling to torture himself with anything more.

"I missed you, darling, but your lovely friends have kept me from wilting away." She smiled sweetly at him and leaned her head against his shoulder.

Even though her affectionate greeting was for the benefit of their audience, he couldn't help pulling her tighter against him, drawn by her warmth. "Sebastian. Camilia. It's good to see you."

"Good to see you as well," Sebastian said. "I'm glad I got to meet your beautiful bride."

"I hope you were behaving yourself," Garrett replied, and the older man burst into another guffaw. "Natalie, I want you to meet Clark Nobu. Clark, this is my better half."

Clark smiled and lifted her hand to his lips. "It's a pleasure to meet you."

"Nice to meet you, too." Natalie blushed, lowering her lashes.

Garrett frowned and tightened his fingers around her waist. Widower or not, Clark had a reputation with women.

"Please forgive me for detaining your husband. He was eager to come back to you."

"That doesn't sound like him. He knows I don't need a chaperone." She arched an eyebrow at Clark and glanced at Garrett. "Don't you, my love?"

Clark's eyes widened and Garrett grinned. "Of course I do."

"Well, I still say your husband's a madman for leaving your side." Clark winked at Natalie, drawing a bright smile from her.

Breaking the man's jaw wouldn't help Garrett win his support, but refraining from the satisfaction wasn't an easy call. *Where the hell did that come from?* He forced himself to breathe and unclench his fist.

"I have a prior engagement but I hope to see you again soon, Natalie." Clark turned to Garrett and said in an undertone, "And, Song, please have your secretary call mine to schedule our meeting."

"Absolutely. Looking forward to it," said Garrett with a firm handshake.

After bidding everyone good-night, Clark disappeared into the crowd. With a surge of protectiveness, Garrett stepped behind Natalie and wrapped his hands around her waist. Her proximity and warmth eased the brief unease that had seeped into his veins. He'd never been much for public displays of affection. But it was different with Natalie. He had difficulty controlling his urge to be close to her. To touch her.

At that moment, Natalie glanced over her shoulder at him, her amber eyes wide and beguiling. He had to kiss her—to taste those sinful crimson lips. Garrett dipped his head to do just that when Camilia's voice jolted him back to the present.

"Natalie is such a charming young lady, Garrett. And I'm so excited we share a common passion," said Camilia. "Tennis!"

"Tennis?" He smiled vaguely and arched an eyebrow at his wife. Their faces were mere inches apart and he couldn't bear to pull away from her.

"Yes. Well…" She tensed against him and her eyes grew wide and plaintive. "I'm better at talking about the sport than playing it. Camilia is much more active in the game than I am."

"I'm not the one who played on the varsity team." The older woman wagged a finger at Natalie.

"In high school."

Undeterred, Camilia clapped her hands in front of her chest. "I have a wonderful idea. Sebastian was invited to Hansol's retreat next month. We just *have* to play doubles."

"I haven't held a racquet in a decade," Garrett said. "It

wouldn't be fair for us to go up against pros like you and Sebastian."

"Nonsense." Sebastian waved aside his objections. "It'll be a friendly game. Nothing brings people closer than enjoying a sport together."

"How could we refuse if you put it that way?" Natalie said before he could think of a judicious refusal. He narrowed his eyes at her too-innocent air.

"You can't unless you want to break an old man's heart."

"Sebastian, I would never do that in a million years," Natalie said, her eyes twinkling. "You have yourselves a doubles match."

Garrett felt a stunned grin spread across his face. His wife had hustled the Diazes into a tennis match.

Nine

"Garrett… *Garrett!*"

What the hell? Garrett ran down the stairs, bolting over the last half flight to reach Natalie. She was standing in the middle of their kitchen, pale as virgin snow.

"Are you hurt? What's going on?" He grabbed her by the shoulders and scanned her from head to toe for injuries.

"Norma is going to blacklist me after tonight. I'm sure of it. And it's all my fault." Her voice broke on the last word and tears filled her amber eyes.

Satisfied that she wasn't physically hurt, Garrett shoved his hand through his hair and swallowed a frustrated growl. Norma Rice, Sophie's social worker, was coming over for dinner tonight, and Natalie had been a nervous wreck all day.

"Breathe, Natalie. Whatever happened, I'm sure it's not that bad."

"I burned the main course. She's coming for dinner but all she's going to get is a salad."

"Didn't you say you were making shrimp scampi? How do you burn…?" Garrett coughed to cover his laugh. "I mean, I'm sure it's fine. A little char adds flavor."

She slammed the pan on the counter and Garrett winced. The contents of the pan were burned beyond recognition. They wouldn't even be able to salvage the pan, much less their dinner.

Natalie would've been the first one to laugh at herself under normal circumstances. Not tonight. She was wound so tight, Garrett was afraid she'd snap before the social worker got there. With a sigh, he unbuttoned the sleeves of his shirt and rolled them above his elbows.

"What are you doing?" Her eyes widened as she watched him.

"Helping."

Opening the fridge, he checked its contents. Garlic, parsley, lemon and white wine. She'd only bought ingredients called for by the shrimp-scampi recipe, but now the shrimp was history.

"I can manage," she said, straightening her shoulders. "I know you have work to do before Norma gets here."

"You also yelled bloody murder, calling me down here. I'm cooking and you're demoted to being my assistant."

"You can cook?" Her stubborn refusal to accept help gave way to a hopeful lift of her voice.

"Like angels can sing." He shot her a wide grin before laying out the ingredients on the counter and setting a big pot of water to boil. "We'll have spaghetti *aglio e olio*. Do we have crushed pepper flakes?"

"Crushed pepper?" Despite her protest seconds ago, Natalie smiled, unable to hide her relief. "Let me check."

"And the salad, did you already make it?"

"Make the salad?" She snorted. "Even I can dump out a salad kit and squeeze dressing over it."

"You bought a salad kit?" He grimaced. "Get out a

lemon and grate off some lemon rind. We'll try to salvage the salad the best we can."

He chopped a handful of garlic cloves and the Italian parsley. When the olive oil was warm in the pan, he added the garlic, then turned off the heat after two minutes. The simple pasta needed to be served immediately after it was prepared.

Natalie had gained some color back in her cheeks and seemed calmer after having a task to focus on. She had grated the skin off a dozen lemons but Garrett let her carry on.

"Are we serving dessert?" he asked.

"What? You bake, too?" Her expression was an amalgam of admiration and envy.

"Hell, no. I don't do measuring cups or tiny spoons."

"Okay." Natalie's smile was small but genuine. She had her panic under control. "Then we'll just go with the ice cream and berries I bought."

Garrett was suddenly struck by the domesticity of the moment—the two of them making dinner together, waiting for their guest. The odd twist in his heart was accompanied by a jab of fear. Before he could analyze his feelings, Sophie cooed through the baby monitor.

"Sophie's up," he said. Their attorney was a skilled negotiator, and the Davises agreed to allow the baby to spend two days a week with him and Natalie soon after their wedding. "I'll get her ready."

"Would you?" Natalie pressed a shy kiss on his cheek. "Thank you so much. Her outfit's on the nursing chair."

"No problem." His voice was gruff as he fought the urge to pull Natalie into his arms.

When Garrett reached the nursery, Sophie stood waiting, holding on to the railing of her crib like a prisoner doing time behind bars. But her chubby face split into a huge grin when she spotted him.

"Gah-gah!" He wasn't too thrilled about sharing the famous singer's name, but he was getting used to being called Gah-gah. With that sweet smile, anything she said was fine by him.

"Hello, sweetheart." Garrett lifted her out of the crib and over his head until the sound of her giggles filled his heart. "We're counting on you to charm Ms. Rice tonight. You can handle her, right?"

"Gah-gah."

"Okay." He took that as a yes and stared at the pink dress set out for her. "You're going to have to help me here. Does this ruffly thing go on your head or your bottom?"

Sophie tried to stuff it in her mouth, where it definitely didn't belong. He contemplated shouting for Natalie but he refused to admit he was an idiot who didn't know how to put a dress on a tot.

By the time they came back downstairs, Natalie had set the table with a centerpiece of trimmed daisies and a yellow table cover he'd never seen. It looked warm and charming, like someplace a real family would eat. It filled Garrett with a yearning he thought was dead. *No. None of this is real.* It was an illusion that a soft breeze could extinguish. Something that would end in less than a year.

But all thoughts fled when a glowing smile lit Natalie's face, and a thread of inevitability tugged him toward her. She leaned in and kissed the baby, and he wrapped his free arm around her waist. When her startled eyes met his, Garrett slowly lowered his head to kiss her, and she rose onto her tiptoes to meet him halfway.

Before their lips could meet, the elevator buzzer rang to announce the arrival of their guest. With a gasp, Natalie took a step back then another, and he stalked her, step by step, until he caught himself. He ran his fingers through his hair as the clacking of his wife's shoes rang down the hallway. After a deep breath, he joined her to welcome their guest.

"Norma, I'm so happy you could make it," Natalie said, her nervousness so subtle that he could barely detect it.

"I'm Garrett Song. It's a pleasure to finally meet you." He shifted Sophie into his other arm, and extended his hand with a broad smile. "My wife has told me so much about you and how hard you're working on behalf of Sophie."

"Oh, well…" The social worker's round, ruddy face turned blotchy with a fierce blush. "It *is* all about the little ones. I just do the best I can for them."

"Of course, and I thank you for it." He nuzzled the little girl's soft cheeks and enlisted her charms. "Sophie, say hi to Ms. Rice."

"Puuuu," she said, not skimping on the spittle. Natalie's eyes widened in alarm when Norma harrumphed and proceeded to dry her face with a lacy handkerchief.

"Well, then." He cleared his throat. "Would you like a glass of wine, Norma?"

He led them into the dining room and settled Sophie in her high chair. Then he poured two generous glasses, offering one to the social worker and the other to his wife. Natalie gazed longingly at the crisp, chilled chardonnay, but she hesitated. He sighed and thrust the glass into her hand.

"I'm the designated parent tonight, so no wine for me," he said. "Sophie's a good sleeper but she's teething right now, so she might wake up at night."

Norma nodded enthusiastically, making some of her wine slosh over the rim of her glass. Garrett caught Natalie's eye and winked, and his wife mouthed, *thank you*. As she breathed in the crisp, chilled chardonnay and smiled, warming the entire room with her light, he stared at her, slack jawed.

Hell.

"I'll bring out the salad," he said in a rush.

When the kitchen door swung shut, Garrett ran cold water in the sink and splashed some on his face. His body hadn't stopped burning since the gala. Every time he reined in his desire, her scent would waft past him or her smile would capture his attention, and he had to start all over. He breathed deeply through his nose until he had his body under control. Natalie had been amazing at the gala even though he'd abandoned her like a jerk. The least he could do was win over the social worker.

He served the first course, with cubes of tofu for the baby, and refilled the wineglasses. There was a lull in the conversation as the adults watched Sophie smash some tofu in her fists before transferring it to her mouth. She beamed proudly even though most of it ended up on her face.

"When did she start finger foods?" asked Norma.

"A few weeks ago," Natalie said, cleaning Sophie's face and hands with a baby wipe.

"She certainly is an enthusiastic eater." The social worker smiled fondly at the baby. Garrett caught Natalie's eyes and laughed at the understatement, while Sophie stuffed more tofu into her mouth.

Once the adults were finished with their salad, he cleared off the plates, waving aside Natalie's offer to help.

"I just need to toss together the pasta with the sauce. Keep Norma company." He dropped a kiss on the top of Natalie's head and heard Norma sigh from across the table. "Honey, is Sophie having her star pasta tonight?"

"Mmm-hmm." She hid her smile on the rim of her wineglass.

"We still have your homemade marinara sauce for the baby in the freezer, right?"

Natalie choked on the chardonnay but pulled herself together. "Right."

"I still rely on Natalie for most of the parenting duties," he said with a rueful look aimed at Norma. "I'm completely dumbfounded and humbled by what an amazing mom she is."

Garrett was laying on the loving husband act a bit thick, but Norma seemed to be gobbling it up. And he found himself enjoying his role for the night.

He brought out the main course and they all dug in to the meal.

"Everything is so delicious." Norma dabbed her mouth with the cloth napkin. "This pasta looks simple but it's so flavorful."

"Thank you. We're so glad you like it," Natalie said.

"Yes, my wife is a fantastic cook." *I wonder if I went too far with that one.* Natalie stared at him like he was crazy, and he decided he'd done just fine.

"Darling, would you help me put these dishes away before I bring out the dessert?" Her eyes shot daggers at him and she jerked her head for him to follow.

"Of course, my love."

The kitchen door shut behind them and she rounded on him. "What are you doing?"

"Helping you win custody of Sophie," he said mildly, fighting back a smile.

"I really appreciate your help—I do—but do you have to ham it up so much? She's going to see right through us."

"Did you see the woman's face? We have her completely charmed."

"You mean *you* have her charmed." Natalie sighed, inexplicable sadness flitting across her face.

"What's wrong?" He frowned, bewildered by her sudden mood change.

"Nothing's wrong. The day must be catching up with me." She gathered the ice cream and berries on a platter. "Let's go back out before Norma wonders where her dessert is."

Once dessert and coffee were served, Natalie lifted her

drowsy daughter from her high chair. "Norma, would you excuse me while I put Sophie down?"

"Of course," said Norma, smiling from ear to ear. "Please, don't rush on my account."

"Don't worry, honey. I won't let our guest become bored," Garrett said and earned himself a warning glance from his wife.

"So, Garrett," Norma said, her voice suddenly firm, after Natalie left the room with the baby.

His gaze shot back to the social worker. He'd been staring after the swing of Natalie's hips, and he had to clear his throat before answering. "Yes, Norma. Could I offer you anything else?"

"No, I couldn't eat another bite," she said. "I have a couple of questions for you."

His shoulders tensed. Had she saved the hardest part for last? Without Natalie there, she could easily catch him in a lie when it came to Sophie. "Go right ahead."

"You must be very busy with work. Are you gone from home often?" Norma's gaze became laser sharp and she leaned in for his answer.

Garrett had to improvise fast. "I do work long hours, but I try to be home for dinner at least twice a week. I can't avoid business trips but delegate when I can."

"Don't you think it'll be hard for Natalie to bear the brunt of the child rearing?"

"My father and sister adore little Sophie, and will help out often while we're in LA. Once the adoption is finalized and Natalie's ready to transition to New York, the Davises will want to spend as much time as possible with their granddaughter. If we get custody, that is."

Norma stared at him with narrowed eyes. A lesser man would've broken out in a cold sweat, but Garrett held her gaze with the most congenial expression he could muster. *Does the woman even blink?*

"How about the rest of the time? Both of you will be working."

"Natalie is leaning toward a Montessori nursery. Sophie is impatient to learn how to do things on her own, and a Montessori program would foster her independent spirit." Garrett paused to study the social worker's reaction. She wore an unfaltering poker face so he decided to hedge his bets. "However, I feel a bit overprotective, and would like to hire a nanny for the baby until she's around two. We're still figuring things out."

"Will you be moving to New York at the end of the year as well? Or will you be a weekend dad?"

"I'm absolutely moving to New York with my family." It was a bald-faced lie but a part of him was thrilled by the idea.

This isn't real, Song.

"Hmm," she said, releasing him from her scrutiny. He had no idea if he'd passed or failed the test.

"Sorry to keep you waiting." Natalie hurried down the stairs, the front of her blouse wet and crumpled. "Sophie decided I needed a bath, too."

"You're doing a wonderful job with her." Norma smiled and patted his wife's shoulder. "I hope you and your family are happy together. You deserve it after everything you and that sweet child have gone through."

"Thank you." The corners of Natalie's answering smile wobbled. "That means a lot."

"Well, then. It's time for me to head home to my family," Norma said, rising from the table.

"It was a pleasure having you over," Garrett said as he and Natalie led Norma down the corridor.

Natalie fidgeted beside him as they made small talk waiting for the elevator. As soon as the elevator doors closed, her excitement burst free.

"Did you hear her?" She jumped up and down with her hands clasped in front of her chest. "She called us a family."

Her amber eyes sparkled in her flushed face and happiness radiated from her. Garrett stared at the beautiful woman in front of him with overwhelming pride, and a familiar grip of possessiveness strummed through his veins. Steeped in her joy and relief, Natalie didn't seem to notice anything odd about his silent appraisal. Then, with a suddenness that surprised an "oof" out of him, she threw herself at him, winding her arms tightly around his neck. His arms instinctively wrapped around her as he chuckled into the wild tumble of her curls.

"Easy, there."

"Garrett, I…" Her words were muffled against his chest so he leaned back, loosening her death grip from his neck. He sought her eyes but she lowered her thick lashes with endearing shyness. "Thank you for tonight. You were wonderful."

"It was nothing." Her genuine gratitude felt undeserved. Considering what was at stake, Garrett only wished he could've done more. Even so… "Wonderful, huh?"

"Don't let it go to your head." Her attempt at a stern expression failed miserably. "But, yeah. You kind of were."

He wouldn't have been able to hold back his ridiculous grin even if he'd wanted to, and her answering smile was blinding. It took a moment for him to remember he still held her in his arms. The soft swell of her full breasts pressed against his chest, and her warm vanilla fragrance assailed his senses. He dropped his hands from her waist and took a hasty step back.

"Do you have an extra one of those?" he said, pointing at the baby monitor. "I should keep one in my room tonight in case Sophie wakes up."

"Why would you…" Natalie's eyes widened and she

waved her hands in front of her. "No. Really, there's no need. I…"

"I wasn't asking for permission. I wouldn't have offered you wine if I hadn't intended to keep my word." He strode to the counter and picked up the baby monitor. "You're exhausted. Go to bed and don't get up. I'm on baby duty tonight."

Garrett Song was a good man. A kind and wonderful man. He'd won over Norma and secured them an ally. And her husband's calm, rational arguments had convinced the Davises to consider supporting her adoption application in exchange for moving to New York after her promotion.

They didn't discuss any specifics about Garrett moving to New York since their marriage would probably be annulled before then. Besides, the Davises' main concern was having Sophie near them.

The very competent—and expensive—lawyer Garrett had hired was managing the legal angles in court. Against the odds, Natalie might really become Sophie's mom in every sense of the word.

With everything proceeding smoothly, Natalie was ready to tackle whatever the day hurled at her.

But not this.

Madame Song had invited her to her home at seven o'clock. Sharp. The woman hadn't even shown up for their wedding, which was literally in her backyard. What could she possibly want with Natalie now?

There was no time for introspection. Besides, Grace Song would tell Natalie exactly why she was summoned with unapologetic frankness. She vacillated about calling Garrett. Perhaps he had some insight about his grandmother's unexpected invitation, but he had a hectic schedule and she didn't want to bother him. In the end, she settled on sending him a quick text.

Meeting your grandmother. Will call you later.

She had less than two hours to get herself ready to meet the infamous Song matriarch, and she had no idea what to do. Mrs. Kim would know. Throwing everything she could grab into two giant shopping bags, she drove straight to her old apartment building.

"Mrs. Kim." Natalie was close to tears when her friend opened the door. "I need your help."

"Oh, for heaven's sake. Come inside." Her friend stepped back from the entrance and pointed to her sofa. "Put those bags down there and have a seat."

"Garrett's grandmother wants to meet me but I don't know what I'm supposed to say or do when I see her. I don't even know what I'm supposed to wear."

Mrs. Kim sifted through the bags Natalie had brought and gasped as she held up her bridal *hanbok*. "Oh, it's beautiful. A new bride should wear her *hanbok* to visit her husband's family for the first time."

"I need to wear all that fabric and present myself to her without falling flat on my face?" She'd packed it just in case, but was hoping she wouldn't have to wear it for her first audience with Garrett's grandmother.

"Breathe, girl." The older woman appraised Natalie with her head tilted to the side. "Now let's get this *hanbok* on you."

Once Mrs. Kim tugged, spun and muscled her into the skirt, Natalie gasped, "Is it supposed to be this tight?"

"Well, yes." Her friend pulled the ties another half inch tighter around her bust. "Your girls are lovely but not really ideal for a *hanbok*. If I don't bind you snugly enough, the cropped top is going to flap up in the front, and it'll look all wrong."

"Great." One of the few things she remembered about her mom was her telling everyone about how *big boned*

Natalie was. It took her years to accept her body, big bones and all. Even though the *hanbok* gaped and stuck out in places, she refused to feel bad about her figure. "I guess I'll have to forego breathing to make a good impression on Grandma Grace."

Mrs. Kim snorted. "I dare you to call her that to her face."

"Why not? Her name is Grace and she's Garrett's grandma," Natalie said with false bravado. *Yeah, I could never call her that. Your Supreme Highness is more fitting.* They'd never actually met, but she'd seen Grace Song from a distance a handful of times at the office. "What am I supposed to do with all this fabric?"

"The edge of the skirt winds around you to the left, so you could gather it in your left hand. Don't get confused and grab the right side. Women of ill repute used to wrap their skirt to the right. But don't quote me on that. It might be an urban legend, but let's just play it safe and go with the left side."

"Women of ill repute? What the literal hell?" Tears stung the back of her eyes. "How am I supposed to remember all this? I should just wear my skirt suit."

"Want to give her a nice view of your thighs and maybe flash her a little?" Mrs. Kim huffed. "You're going to have to kneel on the floor, so a pencil skirt is out of the question. I don't want you to hyperventilate so I won't even tell you about the formal bowing, where you have to cross your ankles and lower yourself to the ground and sit gracefully without falling on your ass—"

"Stop! You. Are. Not. Helping." Natalie immediately regretted her outburst. "Actually, you're a lifesaver. Thank you."

"You didn't need me. Well, maybe for the *hanbok*." Mrs. Kim clasped her hand. "Just be yourself, sweetie. She'll love you."

* * *

"Hi, I'm Natalie," she said to the kind-faced woman who answered the door at the Song family's mansion.

"I'm Liliana. She is waiting for you."

Natalie followed the housekeeper down the corridor, holding her skirt up to her *left*, grateful that they weren't going upstairs. When they reached a door near the back of the house, Liliana smiled warmly. "Good luck."

"Thank you. I really·need it."

She knocked hesitantly on the door, wondering if she'd be judged by the tone of her knock. Maybe she should have knocked more confidently.

"Come in."

Natalie took a shuddering breath and drew back her shoulders. *You got this.* She opened the door, marched in and promptly tripped on her skirt. She saw herself falling in slow motion before she landed on her hands and knees with a thump.

Mrs. Song was by her side with lightning speed and ran her hands over Natalie. "Are you all right, child?"

The wind was knocked out of her and the throbbing in her knees told her she'd be black and blue the next day, but she wasn't broken or bleeding anywhere. It took her a few seconds to get her bearings.

"I'm fine, Mrs. Song. I'm so sorry."

"Grandmother." The older woman leveled Natalie with a stern gaze, settling herself back into her seat. "You are married to my grandson. You will address me as 'Grandmother.'"

"Yes, Grandmother." She might have hit her head on the floor. *Is Her Supreme Highness really asking me to call her 'Grandmother'?* Natalie worried her bottom lip, having no idea what to say or do next.

"I have not forgiven Garrett for his impudence. He dishonored me by asking for your hand without my approval."

"I—"

"You do not interrupt when an elder is speaking. I see you have much to learn about our family's ways and traditions."

Natalie opened and closed her mouth. She was a bit peeved at the scolding, but she was more interested in learning about Garrett's grandmother than smart mouthing her. Grace Song seemed nothing like the cold, calculating woman she'd imagined her to be.

"Ever since his mother died, Garrett never once disobeyed my wishes. But an iron curtain fell across his heart, and I couldn't reach him. As the eldest son of the Song family, it is his duty to bring honor to the family name, and I used his sense of duty to motivate and propel him. I could find no other way to keep him from disappearing entirely. I thought an arranged marriage was his only chance to find warmth and companionship." Grace Song met Natalie's eyes and clicked her tongue. Probably because Natalie was pressing both hands over her mouth to stop herself from blurting, *What?* "Did you have something to say?"

"No, ma'am. Please continue."

"Marrying you was the first choice he made for himself in over a decade. An important, life-altering choice. Even though he chose the wrong way to do it, I hope it means he is finding his way back to us." The older woman's eyes glistened but Natalie didn't dare believe that it was from tears.

"Thank you, Grandmother. I know he misses you and hated opposing you—"

"Well, he did oppose me and he will not be easily forgiven."

"I… But…" Her gut told her Mrs. Song missed Garrett as much as he missed her.

"I want my grandson to become the man he was meant to be, but he should never have turned his back on his elders.

He should not have kept you a secret from me. He will make penance and win the CEO position without my support."

He'd hurt her. She thought Garrett hadn't trusted her enough to ask for her support, but he couldn't have told her about Natalie since there was no whirlwind romance or secret engagement. Lies and more lies had created a rift between Garrett and his family, but telling his grandmother the truth might destroy all chances of reconciliation.

Ugh. The cell phone she'd stuck inside her calf-high stocking—traditional Korean elf-toed things—had been vibrating for the last half hour, and she was getting nervous that it might be an emergency.

"I'm so sorry, but I need to check my phone. Someone has been calling me nonstop since I got here."

Natalie spun on her bottom to face away from Grandmother's sour expression and dug out her phone from under her skirt. She heard the older woman tsk again, and blushed with embarrassment. At least she hadn't stuck it inside her bra.

It was Garrett. He'd called eight times and texted a dozen increasingly urgent messages. Basically, he wanted to know if she was okay, and demanded she call him. Natalie sighed and shook her head. Did he think she was going to slip and reveal their secret? She peeked over her shoulder and hurriedly sent her husband a text.

I'm still with your grandmother. Everything is fine.

Liliana entered with a serving tray, and as they shared a lovely cup of tea, Natalie decided she felt eight percent less intimidated by Garrett's grandmother than she had half an hour ago.

"Will you be staying home now that you're married, *ah-ga*?" the older woman asked, setting down her teacup.

Grandmother had started calling her *ah-ga*, which was

how an elder addressed a new bride in their family. She said the literal translation meant "baby," and it made Natalie feel warm every time she called her that. It was silly to be touched by such a small thing, but learning about her heritage from her *grandmother* was more than she'd ever dreamed of.

"What? Oh, no. I've worked too hard to get where I am, and I plan to go even farther. I hope I can be one of those supermoms who do everything and a half."

Grandmother's lips tightened into a straight line. "Wouldn't Garrett benefit from you staying home?"

"You of all people should understand that a woman's place isn't necessarily at home." It wasn't easy to say, but it had to be said.

"Such audacity," the older woman said, but a faint smile softened her face. "But yes. I know very well that at times it takes a woman to build an empire."

Natalie wanted to be just like Grandma Grace when she grew up. They were still smiling at each other, both a little shy and surprised by their unexpected connection, when Garrett flung open the door without knocking and skidded into his grandmother's room.

It was as though he was expecting to face a raging battle. Instead, he found two sets of shocked female eyes focused on him. His heroic stance faltered and confusion took its place. "What's going on?"

Grandmother's expression turned stoic and hard, and Natalie wanted to whack Garrett on the back of his head. *What is wrong with him? Did he think his grandmother was roasting me over a pit?*

"Grandmother invited me to tea, honey. You should greet her properly and join us."

Garrett's mouth dropped open and his head swiveled back and forth between the two women before his gaze settled on his grandmother.

"*Hal-muh-nee*, have you been well?" His tone was endearingly hesitant.

"You know that I've been anything but," she said with artful hauteur. "I see you're practically glowing with health. Marriage must agree with you."

"Yes. It does," he said, his lips pressing into a stubborn line.

Mrs. Song didn't give him permission to sit, and a tense silence filled the room.

"Please rest, *hal-muh-nee*. We'll be on our way." Garrett lifted Natalie to her feet. "Let's go."

Afraid to stumble and fall again, Natalie allowed herself to be tugged out the door. It was only when they were on the freeway heading home that she realized she hadn't said goodbye to Grandmother.

She stole a peek at her husband's profile. A muscle jumped in his jaw and his knuckles were white on the steering wheel.

"What were you doing there?" His voice was a low growl, and there was more than a small amount of anger in his words.

"She asked me to visit, and I've been wanting to meet her. Grandmother and I were getting along just fine until you barged in."

"Grandmother?" He shot a surprised glance at her.

"Yes." Natalie couldn't hold back her smug smile. "I'm to address her as Grandmother, and she calls me *ah-ga*."

"You…she…what?" Garrett's head snapped toward her; he looked dumbstruck.

"Grandmother asked me to visit her once a week from now on, and she wants to meet Sophie as soon as possible."

Her husband opened his mouth to speak, but changed his mind and turned his gaze back to the road. But not before Natalie saw the pride and admiration in his eyes.

Ten

Hansol was famous for pampering their employees with an annual retreat at a luxury resort. This year the two-night retreat was being held at Ojai, a small town reminiscent of Provence that improbably flourished in California's desert climate.

Ojai was one of Natalie's favorite places in California. It was so serene and beautiful, and the richly scented air provided continuous aromatherapy. The hacienda-style villa she'd be sharing with Garrett was gorgeous, but it only had one bedroom. Natalie's mouth went dry at the sight of the prominent king-size bed in the center of the room. She averted her eyes and made quick work of changing into her swimsuit.

Garrett had a meeting at the office, so he'd arranged for one of the Song family drivers to bring her to the retreat. A part of her had been relieved he couldn't drive with her. Something had shifted between them after her visit with his grandmother. They somehow ended up having dinner together almost every night of the week, and talked for hours, laughing like old friends until they…weren't. Their attraction would combust without warning and they would find each other mere inches apart, breathing heavily. Starving for a kiss. But one of them—Garrett more often than not—would come to their senses in the nick of time.

She was afraid that someday soon she wouldn't be able to pull away. Wouldn't want to. Natalie wanted her husband with such urgency that she was on the verge of exploding. She'd never desired anyone like this before. Not even Peter Klapper, the college boyfriend she'd fancied herself in love with. But he'd soon lost his appeal when she discovered his selfish, narcissistic nature.

The problem with Garrett was the more time they spent together, the more she liked and admired him, and her attraction only grew. Natalie released a long breath. Everything was going to be fine. As long as they didn't get within four feet of each other, she should be able to suppress her lust for her hot-as-hell husband. But they were sharing a suite for the next two nights. Tight quarters in romantic Ojai meant trouble. Horny, sizzling trouble. *Crap.*

She headed to the pool using the map she got from the front desk. She got a bit turned around and wound up taking the long way there, but she fortunately didn't run into any Hansol employees to witness her directional challenges.

She scanned the pool area and spotted a secluded corner that was perfect for her. After spreading out her towel on a lounger, she perched on the edge, ready for some sun worship. The soft melody she was humming under her breath sputtered and died as her jaw dropped.

Garrett was in the pool, swimming toward her with powerful, fluid strokes. When he reached the end by her chaise, he rested his forearms on the edge and grinned at her.

"When did you get here?" The husky tenor of his voice made the innocent question sound like a caress.

Only his glistening hair and muscled torso were visible to her, but Natalie couldn't drag in a full breath. Garrett was here and he was wet. The light sprinkling of hair on his forearms clung to his skin, and his jet-black hair rained drops of water. Mesmerized, Natalie followed the water sliding down the slopes of his broad shoulders, and wished her fingers could trail after it.

She'd never understood why people thought *wet* was sexy. Now she could write a thesis on it. The amusement sparkling in his eyes made her realize she was staring at him with her mouth open. *Kill me now.* She should be thankful she wasn't drooling.

"Less than an hour ago." To stop herself from staring at him, she focused on unbuttoning the linen shirt she'd thrown over her swimsuit and shrugged out of it. "What are you doing here? I thought you couldn't make it till later tonight."

The silence stretched on between them as his gaze bore into hers with an intensity that stole her breath. His cocky grin was nowhere in sight; instead, he looked at her with the thirst of a man lost in the desert. Confusion clouded her brain and she hid her face by digging in her tote for her sunscreen.

"Did you just get here, too?" Natalie asked to break the tension.

"Yes." Garrett cleared his throat. "Just."

"We must've crossed paths at the villa."

"Right. I saw your luggage in our room when I arrived."

Silence settled around them again as Natalie smoothed white lotion down her legs. It smelled like an orange Creamsicle. She succeeded in avoiding Garrett's eyes for as long as she could.

But she finished all too soon, leaving only her back undone. *Would it look odd if I dislocate my shoulder trying to get sunscreen on my back?*

"Here." Garrett pushed himself out of the pool. "Allow me."

Despite the hot sun, a chill tripped down her spine like tumbling dominoes.

"Th-thank you."

Natalie handed him the tube as he settled his glorious wet body next to hers. She gasped and hunched forward. She wasn't sure what startled her more—the coolness of his hands or the electric shock his touch set off.

"Sorry. The water was pretty cold." He tugged her back toward him. "Now, hold still."

He started at the curve of her neck then slid his hands down to the top of her shoulders. Cupping one, he circled his other palm down her back. His touch grew hot against her skin, and it was all she could do to keep from leaning back and purring.

"Your skin's so fair. Almost as transparent as fine china." His breath warmed the back of her neck. He leaned in closer, putting his lips at her ear. "Would you break if you're not handled gently?"

"I'm stronger than I look," she said. And right now, she wanted to test her strength with something hard and fast.

Natalie twisted around to face him, her breathing uneven. He perused her body, an arrogant tilt to his lips, and a flush of arousal spread across her bare skin. He wanted her. That much was certain. Emboldened, she met his gaze and held it before she lowered her eyes to stare appreciatively at his chest, so smooth and strong.

She'd wondered countless times what he would look like under his dress shirts, and her imagination had not done him justice. The dips and grooves of his well-defined abs begged to be touched. He allowed her to study his body, sitting so still that she wondered if he was breathing. Her hand reached out of its own accord and she pulled it back with a sharp gasp.

She was treading a dangerous path and needed to retreat several paces. It could only lead to heartbreak. He'd made it clear their marriage would be short-lived. If Natalie followed her instincts and gave herself to him, she would be the only one to blame for her regrets.

"I'm going in for a swim," she said, hoping the water was very, very cold because she was burning inside and out.

He stared at her for a few seconds, letting the electrified air float around them. Her cheeks turned an adorable shade of coral, which told him that she wasn't immune to the desire raging between them.

For a moment, he thought she was going to touch him. The image of her delicate hands on his naked torso almost made him groan.

"I'll see you later," he said, his voice curt. "I need to take care of a couple matters before dinner tonight."

"Okay, bye."

She dipped her toes in the pool, testing the water. He needed to get the hell away before she got wet. Garrett hurried toward the pool gate as quickly as he could, which wasn't very fast because the mindless part of his body refused to stand down. He hoped he was being inconspicuous as he placed his T-shirt in front of his tented board shorts and concentrated on deflating the tent.

Aunt Margo's sadistic cheek pinches. My old mangy mutt with his perpetual drooling. The food poisoning I had last summer. Just. Don't. Think. About. Her.

Natalie had cast a dangerous spell over him. He saw nothing else when she was near. Years of hard work, his family's legacy and the responsibility of ensuring the livelihood of thousands of employees were the foundation on which he'd built his adult life, but he forgot everything. He became a being of want and need. He had no control over it.

He had to devise a hands-off strategy for this weekend.

Making certain he hardly spent a moment alone with Natalie had worked so far, but his desire howled in his veins even when they were apart. *If I have this much trouble not touching her out in public, how the hell am I going to keep my hands off her tonight?* Resisting her allure would be torture—exquisite but agonizing torture. He needed a chastity belt for men.

By the time he reached the hotel lobby, Garrett had himself under control and pulled on his T-shirt. Hansol's employees crowded the air-conditioned sanctuaries of the indoor bars and restaurants, and their objective was loud and clear—consume vast amounts of alcohol and make public spectacles of themselves.

People were convinced what happened at company retreats didn't count in real life. For Garrett, who had been in the public eye his entire life, every second counted.

"Mr. Song, sir! Come join us!"

A few of the more inebriated employees tried to wave him over. These were the same employees who practically clicked their heels and scuttled away when he passed them in the office.

Garrett gave a curt nod and walked on, but he envied them with sudden intensity. He longed to forget about family expectations, and honoring your elders over your own desires. He wanted to burn away the scars of his childhood, his cynicism and his self-preservation instinct. He wished he could forget everything and be *reckless*. Get drunk in public, and make love to his wife…

A humorless laugh escaped from him. He was Garrett Song. Control was everything.

The moment he stepped into their villa and saw Natalie—lovelier in her shorts and T-shirt than any other woman he'd ever seen—he forgot all about work, plans or legacy.

When he'd run into Natalie at the pool, the walls he'd

meticulously constructed to shield his desire collapsed like a fortress made of smoke. His mind had been congested with yearning and hunger, and he couldn't turn to his work for refuge. Instead, he'd gone to the hotel gym to work out until his muscles screamed and he forgot how much he wanted to take his wife to bed. Unfortunately, his dick didn't care how tired the rest of his body was. One look at her and it was all too alert and ready for its own brand of workout. There was no denying he wanted her more than his next breath.

"Hi." She took a few uncertain steps toward him, eyeing him warily. "I was just about to make some tea. Would you like a cup?"

"No, thank you." He stalked her until she backed into the edge of the sofa.

He let his eyes roam her face, then down her body, soaking in every curve and flare. By the time his gaze returned to her face, all he heard was the thunder of his pounding heart. He raised his hand and smoothed his thumb across her cheek. Her lashes fluttered and her lips parted on an indrawn breath. He froze, his mind and heart battling.

In halting movements, he buried his fingers in her hair and drew her to him. With a shaky exhale, he brushed his lips against hers in a fleeting, reverent touch. He withdrew just enough to meet her eyes and waited. His whole body shook with longing and fear—of what, he didn't know.

Natalie held his gaze, peering steadily at him before leaning in. She kissed one corner of his mouth, then the other, each fleeting touch sending tremors down his spine. With a whispered sigh, she fully claimed his lips, pressing her body against his. He stood still, his hands hovering near her shoulders—to push her away or to hold on to her, he didn't know.

When she squirmed against him, demanding a response, Garrett caved with a guttural groan. His mouth sought hers while his hands skimmed her sides and hips before reaching back to cup her round ass. She mewled in approval as her fingers dug into his back. Natalie caught fire in his arms and he couldn't get enough. His tongue flicked, teased and plunged into her warmth, desperate to possess her.

Garrett growled, picked her up by the waist and braced her against the wall. He rolled his hips against her until they both moaned. Another minute of this and he was going to lose it in his pants like a goddamn sixteen-year-old. He drew back an inch and cursed under his breath.

Natalie took advantage of the brief pause to step out of his reach. He blinked at the sudden loss of heat and lifted his hands to bring her back to him.

"We shouldn't have done that," she said in a husky whisper. Her breathing was shallow and uneven, but her expression was cool and detached. "We're both sexually frustrated from our forced celibacy, but we can't lose sight of our agreement."

She was absolutely right, but it gutted him to hear the words—the same words he repeated to himself whenever she was near. Well, no more.

"I'm beyond frustrated," he said. *And damn the agreement.*

Her eyes widened, as if she'd heard the unsaid words. It was time to stop hiding from the inevitable. He was going to make love to his wife tonight, and to hell with the consequences.

Eleven

Natalie couldn't quite put her finger on it. Garrett wasn't acting any differently than usual, but she got goose bumps every time he glanced at her. He exuded the air of a panther who was leisurely circling his cornered prey.

She was probably imagining things after the heated episode earlier. The need to touch and be touched had risen like a primal instinct, and her body had screamed to take him inside her. Breaking away from his arms was harder than she could've imagined, but she'd been certain he would've done the same thing once his cool logic pierced through the fog of lust. She'd withdrawn from his embrace in the nick of time, self-preservation coming to the rescue.

Natalie sat on the couch and tied her shoes with excessive care. She heard Garrett moving behind the closed doors of the bedroom, and willed herself not to imagine him changing. She grabbed the remote and flipped through the channels. Every time she peeked at the clock, it seemed to be standing still, as though its hands were bound by invisible string. It was almost time for their tennis match with the Diazes. She wanted out of the oddly charged villa before she jumped her husband.

"Are you ready?" he asked as he strode into the living room. He wore a black polo shirt and shorts, looking thoroughly fit and masculine.

"Yes." She bolted to her feet and shot out the door, her heart beating erratically at the sight of him.

The sun was making its leisurely descent and the cool breeze felt lovely on her warm cheeks. They rumbled toward the tennis court in a golf cart, and some of the tension left her shoulders. It had just been a kiss—a long kiss with some heavy petting, but just a kiss nonetheless. She would put it past her. A glance at her husband's calm, easy expression said he already had.

When they arrived, Garrett tipped the driver while Natalie glanced toward the court. The Diazes were already there, stretching. These people meant business.

"I see them over there," she said, waving.

They had to be well into their fifties but looked as lithe and athletic as people half their age. They were decked out in matching white outfits as though tennis was their second career. Natalie's pulse leaped with excitement. *Worthy opponents.*

Garrett grimaced by her side, not half as excited as she. But she didn't buy his claims of being rusty at the game. Her husband's every movement spoke of strength and agility. If he'd forgotten how to swing a racquet, he was going to pick it right back up during the warm-up sets.

"What's your plan?" His eyes danced with mischief. "Should we throw the game to stoke Sebastian's ego? That should help me gain his support."

Natalie gasped. "Don't even joke about something like that. The only way to seal the partnership is to annihilate them and earn their respect."

"Annihilate them?" Her husband arched an eyebrow.

She shrugged, fighting a blush. "Or just kick their butts a little."

"I don't know how we got talked into this."

"Here are the newlyweds," Sebastian said as he and Camilia approached.

"You'll go easy on us, right?" Garrett smiled and shook his hand.

"Not a chance," the older man said.

Camilia hugged Natalie, squealing like a young girl. "I'm so glad we could do this."

"Me, too," Natalie said. Traci used to tell her she got too competitive sometimes, but it was all good, harmless fun. She just really liked to win, and there was nothing wrong with that. "Should we hit some warm-up balls?"

To her disappointment, Garrett actually was a bit rusty. His serves were poetic, but his backhand needed work. And Camilia and Sebastian were even better than Natalie had assumed.

"Damn it, Garrett." Natalie tried to keep the impatience out of her voice but he gave the Diazes an easy point. "That was your ball."

"Sorry, honey." His lips twitched. "I got distracted. Your skirt is way too short for me to be on my game."

What has gotten into him?

"Thank you, Natalie," Sebastian guffawed from across the net.

It was a close second set. Her limbs ached and her lungs burned. They could still win if they took the next set. Garrett hadn't made any more careless mistakes, but she had a feeling he wasn't putting in his full effort.

She glanced over her shoulder and saw him spinning his racquet in his hand, looking damn fine in his fitted polo and shorts. The man had seriously muscular thighs and his biceps flexed and bulged with every movement.

He caught her checking him out and his face split into a slow, sexy grin.

Everything happened in a split second, but she saw it in slow motion. They were all tired, which was probably why Camilia's next serve veered to the wrong side and came straight toward Natalie. She just had to lift her racquet and shield herself, but she was too focused on her husband to react in time. The ball caught Natalie squarely on the forehead. She fell onto her bottom and sat dazed with a hand over her injury.

"Natalie." Garrett was by her side in an instant and peeled her hand off her forehead. "Are you okay?"

"Oh, my goodness." Camilia had reached her side. "Are you all right, Natalie? I'm so sorry."

"Don't worry. It startled me more than anything," Natalie said, but her voice sounded faint.

Sebastian, who'd disappeared from the court when it happened, now sprinted to them with a bag of ice. "Here you are. Put this on."

"Thank you, but I'm fine."

Garrett grabbed the ice and placed it gently on her forehead, ignoring her protests. Natalie got her bearings back in a few minutes. The mild throbbing told her she was going to have some bruising the next day, but she was otherwise perfectly fine.

"That's all, folks," she said, waving her hands to dispel their worried expressions. "The show's over."

Natalie wanted to get off the cold ground, but before she could stand, Garrett reached under her and lifted her as though she didn't weigh much more than Sophie. She squeaked but reflexively grabbed onto him.

"Oh, my," Camilia said, fanning her face. "Maybe I should get hit in the head with a ball so Sebastian would carry me like that."

"There's no need for such extremes." Sebastian reached

out to grab her and Camilia slapped his hands away, laughing.

Garrett met Natalie's eyes with a smile that made her heart vibrate like a windup alarm clock. "Feeling okay?"

"Yes, I'm fine. You can put me down."

He shifted her in his arms but ignored her request. "Okay, you kids. I need to take my wife back to our villa."

"Of course," Sebastian said, pausing from their horse-play. "Please call us if you need anything. And let's play a round of golf next week to talk about your proposal in detail."

"Thank you. That sounds great. I'll call you Monday," Garrett said, and turned to leave.

"I'm sorry about knocking you down." Camilia waved, her smile bright and affectionate. "Good night."

"Wait." Natalie remembered something very important. "We didn't finish the game. We don't have a winner yet."

"Why don't we call it a tie?" Garrett said.

"A tie? But that's so…not winning." Natalie deflated in her husband's arms.

"Well, why don't we say we won?" Garrett's warm breath tickled her ear. She sighed and a shiver ran through her, awareness simmering between them. "We won Sebastian's support."

"I guess you're right." They'd not only secured their business goal, but also gained the Diazes' friendship. It was a double win.

Garrett looked down at her with a perplexed frown, but his eyes twinkled with humor. "When am I not?"

When the golf cart stopped in front of their villa, Garrett reached for his wife.

"I'm really okay," Natalie protested.

He ignored her and carried her through the door. The significance of the act hit him a moment later. How appropriate to carry his bride over the threshold on their long-overdue honeymoon.

Natalie gazed at him with wide, vulnerable eyes. He was hit again with how alluring she was—so innocent yet sensual. In an instant, his blood turned molten with raw desire. Once inside, he lowered her to the floor, letting her body slide slowly down his.

All his reasons for not touching her were still valid, but he couldn't fight what they had anymore. Their kiss earlier had proven that. Whenever he was near her, she came into sharp focus and everything else ceased to exist. Call it a cruel twist of fate, but their attraction was beyond their control. And they were caught in its vortex again.

"I'm going to collapse in bed after a nice bath." Her soft voice trembled and she hastily turned away from him.

Garrett followed her into the master suite, and she spun around with wide eyes.

"Did you need something?"

Her jaw went slack as he lifted her up again and carried her into the bathroom. He set her down by the tub and stared into her eyes before reaching around her to turn on the faucet.

"I, uh…" Her words trailed off as she bit her lip. He added some bath salt to the steaming water, making lavender and citrus steam rise around them. "What are you doing?"

"Drawing you a bath."

"I can manage," she said.

"I know."

"This isn't a good idea, Garrett."

"I know." He did, but he didn't give a damn anymore.

She stared at him with wide eyes, a pulse fluttering under the translucent skin of her neck. His gaze not leaving hers, he reached around her and carefully lifted her top off over her head. Natalie moved pliantly beneath his hands as though she was in a trance. Her shirt on the floor, he linked his fingers into the waistband of her skirt and smoothed it down her thighs, letting it pool around her ankles. His breath caught at the sight of her curves dipping and flaring in a way that could drive a man crazy. Her eyelids fluttered as though she was waking from a dream, and she lifted her arms to cover herself.

"Don't," he said, his voice gruff. "Let me look at you."

He reached out and lowered her arms back to her sides, and Natalie didn't stop him. With a shuddering sigh, he unhooked her bra and slipped it off, his hands skimming the soft skin of her arms. She trembled against his touch, and his gut tightened with desire. He stared at her bare torso. He'd never seen anything more beautiful.

When his thumbs brushed across her breasts, she groaned and arched toward him. He stilled for a second, relishing her response, before he kneeled to tug off her panties. He reverently ran his hands down the sides of her hips and her outer thighs.

"You're so perfect," he whispered, rising to his feet.

She blushed and lowered her lashes. His heart was pounding with need as he lifted her into the tub, his sleeves getting drenched in the process. He shrugged out of his dripping shirt, and Natalie's lips parted as her eyes roamed his chest approvingly.

Then she sighed, tilting her head back into the water, her eyes closing in wordless invitation. Garrett struggled to swallow, his mouth as dry as the sand dunes. He lathered the soap in his hands and lifted her arm, so soft and smooth, then moved onto her other arm. Her chest rose and fell more quickly underneath the water, but she didn't open her eyes. He washed her legs, then moved down to her feet, awed by the masterpiece that was Natalie.

By the time he reached her torso, he was trembling. He groaned as he smoothed his palms over her breasts, and

Natalie pushed against his hands, her hips lifting under the water. He wanted to heed her silent plea, to reach between her thighs and watch her fall apart for him.

For a moment, he wanted to be the man who burned for her, and she the woman who caught fire at his touch. No past, no future. No fear, no heartache.

Gritting his teeth, Garrett hooked his arms under her shoulders and knees, and lifted her out of the water. Her eyes were wide with confusion but he said nothing. With shaking hands, he dried her off, wrapped her in a towel and stepped back from her.

He wasn't going to seduce her. She needed to know what he was offering, and if she declined, he had to walk away. She should refuse him for both their sakes, but his body begged her to accept him.

Twelve

"I want you." His voice was a whispered caress, and the intensity of his onyx gaze speared through her defenses. "But this marriage, it still ends once our objectives are reached. If I make love to you tonight, I'm taking your body and giving you mine, nothing more."

Garrett stood before her, his hands in his shorts, his ruined shirt discarded on the bathroom floor. What would he look like if his shorts fell next to his shirt? She had a feeling he would be as magnificent as he was everywhere else.

If I make love to you tonight...

Natalie knew herself. She wouldn't be able to sleep with him and not become emotionally attached. The line he'd drawn was the only thing protecting her from... *What exactly do I need protection from?* It wasn't until Traci had died that she understood the agony of loss. She hardly remembered her mom, and her father was as distant as a stranger. But Natalie hadn't minded. Not really. Because she'd had Traci.

A chunk of her heart had been torn from her and buried with her sister. If the pain of losing her sister didn't kill her, then she could survive anything. Like the end of a fake marriage. Everyone left one way or another. In this case, at least she'd see it coming. She could prepare herself.

And no matter what happened between them, Garrett wouldn't end their marriage before Sophie's adoption and Natalie's promotion. He was a man of his word.

Don't I deserve to experience true passion?

She had never felt this way about anyone before and probably never would again.

Isn't it better than living the rest of my life wondering what it would've been like to make love to him?

"I understand." Natalie's heart skipped like a stone thrown across calm waters. "And I want you, too."

A predatory light flared in his eyes, but he didn't lean down for the kiss she was expecting. She could see him holding back, fighting for control. Then she understood. He was as helpless as she was against their crazy attraction, and that vulnerability tipped her over the precipice.

Natalie closed the distance between them and kissed him. Garrett stood as still as a sun-warmed boulder, but his lips parted against hers, inviting her to explore him.

So she did.

She kissed his hot, smooth lips, and she wanted to venture further—to taste more of him. When she eagerly sucked his bottom lip into her mouth, Garrett moved. With a low groan vibrating in his chest, he pushed her up against the wall and flicked his tongue across her lips. He took advantage of her startled gasp to deepen the kiss. His heat, his smell and the carnal pleasure of his touch invaded her. His lips and tongue teased and danced with hers. So wet. So hot.

An onslaught of sensations blanketed her and instinct took over. She plunged her fingers into his thick, dark hair and pushed herself up into his kiss. She hummed with satisfaction as the evidence of his desire pressed against her stomach. He moaned and slid his hand down the back of her thigh, then hitched her leg around his waist.

Lust burned through her veins. Pure, basic and animal. The hunger to touch and be touched threatened to consume her. The tepid kisses she'd experienced in the past hadn't prepared her for this man.

He ravished her lips as his hands explored her body. She braced her hands on his chest and a decadent sigh escaped her as her fingertips met his hot, bare skin. Desperate to feel him against her, Natalie dropped her towel to the floor. With an impatient growl, Garrett cupped her breasts and dipped his head to run kisses across the sensitive skin.

Instinct was a funny thing. She'd never been touched like this—the few men she'd been with were clumsy and awkward in comparison—but she knew exactly what she wanted. Gripping handfuls of Garrett's hair in her fists, she held his head against her chest and arched her back, demanding more. She whimpered when his tongue licked one taut peak. When she scraped her fingernails across his scalp, he groaned and took her fully in his mouth.

At first, she didn't even hear her phone ringing. It was coming from the bedroom.

Then she heard his phone ringing from his pants on the floor.

"Don't answer it," she breathed.

When the hotel phone rang in chorus with their cell phones, panic sliced through her lust-addled brain.

"Oh, God."

The last time every phone near her started ringing had been the night Traci died. Cold fear replaced the heat of desire. She recognized this dread. She'd felt it that night, too. Natalie ran to her phone and picked it up.

"Yes, this is Natalie." She was shivering so violently her teeth were clacking against each other.

"You need to put this on." Garrett wrapped her in a bath-robe and stood behind her with his hands on her shoulders.

"What happened?" she asked in a hoarse whisper.

"Natalie…" Steve Davis's voice broke on the other end of the line. "It's Sophie… Lily was carrying her down the stairs and her hip gave out. She managed to break her fall but she lost her hold on the baby…"

"How badly is Sophie hurt?" Natalie's mind went bright white. Garrett cursed then wrapped his arms tightly around her waist, his chest solid behind her back. She leaned back, grateful for the support.

"Mostly scrapes and bruises." The poor man choked back a sob. "But Lily's worried Sophie might have bumped her head. They're running more tests on her to rule out a concussion."

Natalie didn't recall the rest of their conversation. Once she hung up the phone, Garrett turned her around to face him and wiped the tears spilling down her cheeks with the pad of his thumb.

"Sophie fell down the stairs." Her voice sounded distant and foreign. "She might have a concussion."

"God…" Garrett didn't try to comfort her with empty words. He pulled her into his arms and held her until her trembling subsided.

Then he snapped into action, punching numbers into his phone and barking out orders. Natalie heard him men-tion a helicopter. They needed to go to Sophie—the sooner, the better.

As she stood rooted to the spot, Garrett pulled on his clothes then proceeded to dress her, maneuvering her limp limbs into compliance. "Sophie needs you."

The helicopter ride took less than half an hour, but it felt like a lifetime. As they landed on the hospital roof, Garrett kept his eyes on Natalie. She'd stopped crying but she was too still and quiet. Tugging her head into his chest against the rush of the propeller's wind, he ushered her downstairs.

When they got to the waiting room on the pediatric floor, they found Lily weeping silently into Steve's shoulder. Adelaide and James sat close together. When Lily spotted Natalie, she walked toward her, limping slightly, and hugged her tightly.

"I'm so sorry. It's all my fault. I'm so sorry."

"It was an accident. It's not your fault." Natalie stepped back from the older woman and scanned her. "Are you okay? Did you hurt your hip again?"

"No. I'm fine." Lily didn't sound too happy about that. "I should've protected the baby, but I couldn't hang on. I'm sorry, Natalie. I was so selfish to keep her with me…"

"Not now. She's going to be okay," Natalie said, blindly stretching her hand behind her. Garrett knew she was looking for his hand, so he took hers and squeezed. "She has to be."

There was so little he could do for her. Natalie usually acted as though her spine was made of steel, but when the phones started ringing in Ojai, she'd crumbled like ancient clay. He'd never be able to forget the horror in her eyes.

Garrett wished he could've done something to spare her from the pain. He'd never felt more helpless in his life. Over the next couple hours, he stayed by Natalie's side and held her whenever he could, but she seemed leagues away. She sat motionless, as though she was an empty husk of herself, all the blood gone from her face. Only the sporadic fluttering of her lashes indicated she was alive.

Garrett dragged his hands down his face and shot to his feet. He stepped out of the waiting room and stood uncertainly. He didn't want to leave her, but she didn't seem to notice when he walked out.

Just ten minutes. He'd stretch his legs and come back. After no more than five minutes, he hurried back to Natalie with a cup of hot tea in his hand, hoping it would warm her up. As he neared the waiting room, he heard loud sobbing. Pain shot through his heart. It was Natalie. He ran the rest of the way and came to an abrupt halt at the entrance.

Natalie and Adelaide were hugging, laughing and crying, while a doctor in blue scrubs stood nearby. His dad stared at the ceiling with red-rimmed eyes, his lips pressed tight. When Natalie spotted Garrett at the door, she launched herself at him, barely leaving him time to move the hot tea out of the way. Leaning against the door frame to balance himself, he held her tightly against him.

"She's okay. All the tests were normal." Her voice was muffled against his shoulder, but her relief was palpable.

He squeezed his eyes shut. *Thank God.* They stood wrapped around each other until he heard a small cough. He opened his eyes to find the mild-mannered doctor smiling at them.

"Mrs. Song, you can come in and see Sophie for ten minutes," he said. "She needs rest but I'm sure she misses you."

"Thank you." Natalie's hand flew to her mouth as her eyes filled with fresh tears. Then she hesitated and turned around to face the Davises. "Would you like to see her first?"

Lily had her face buried in her hands, and Steve mutely shook his head. They needed more time to pull themselves together. Natalie bit her lip, concern for the older couple clouding her exhausted face. Garrett was standing behind her with his hands on her arms. Small tremors shook her frame and he wanted to pull her back into his embrace.

"Will you come with me?" She looked over her shoulder at him.

"Of course." His voice caught in his throat.

When they entered the room, the baby looked so pale and small in her hospital bed that Garrett wasn't surprised to hear Natalie's choked sob. She ran to Sophie's side, cooing soft words he couldn't make out, but the little girl smiled in her sleep. Garrett stood back as long as he could, but when Natalie's body shook with the force of her sobbing, he went to her and placed his hand on her shoulder.

"Let Sophie sleep. Come with me." He helped Natalie to her feet and tucked her to his side, then quickly glanced back at Sophie. "Sleep tight, baby girl. We'll be back soon."

Garrett had to twist their arms to make the rest of the family go home. In fact, they wouldn't cooperate until Adelaide put her foot down.

"Sophie's okay. We're not helping anyone by becoming sleep-deprived zombies," she said, packing up her things. "Natalie, you have my number. I'm here if you need me."

"Thank you."

Adelaide hugged Natalie then kissed Garrett on the cheek. His father followed Adelaide's example. He squeezed his shoulder on the way out and Garrett nodded his understanding. His father was there for him, too.

With a sigh of relief, Garrett turned to Natalie and helpless anger surged inside him. She hugged herself tight but her teeth were still chattering. *Damn it*. He dragged his fingers through his hair.

"She's okay, Natalie. She's going home tomorrow." With her grandparents… The Davises seemed stricken and unsure of themselves, and frustration filled him. Sophie should be with Natalie. They should see that now.

"I… I know…" she stuttered through the tremors. "But I keep thinking…what if I'd lost her?"

"Hush," he said. He sat down beside her and tucked her close to his side. She snuggled her face against his chest. "But you didn't lose her. Focus on that."

Natalie didn't answer but her shivering eased. Then her soft deep breaths told him she'd fallen asleep in his arms. He kissed the top of her head and let his eyes drift shut, holding on tight.

Thirteen

"Sophie!"

Natalie bolted upright, blood pounding in her ears. She gradually registered her surroundings, and her heartbeat regained its normal rhythm. Sophie had been discharged midmorning, and went back with the Davises to their extended-stay hotel. And Garrett had marched Natalie straight to bed as soon as they got home.

What time is it?

The room was pitch-black, but she didn't know whether it was because of the blackout blinds or because it was the middle of the night. She could've been asleep for two hours or fourteen.

Swinging her legs off the bed, Natalie waited until her eyes adjusted to the dark. A spill of light leaked under the door, and she made her way toward it. She twisted the handle and poked her head out, conscious that all she wore was an oversize T-shirt.

The light was coming from Garrett's room. Soft mur-

murs drifted through the open door, so she tiptoed over, holding her breath. He was on the phone. Suddenly aware she was creeping around the house, eavesdropping on her husband, she rolled her eyes and turned to head back to her room.

Natalie stopped short when she heard Garrett say Sophie's name.

"Good. Sophie has a mighty spirit inside that little body, Steve," he said, his voice deep and warm. There was a pause as he listened to the other end. "Yes, she's okay. Just exhausted. She slept through the afternoon. And how's Lily holding up? It wasn't her fault. Natalie doesn't blame her. No one does."

He was checking up on the baby and comforting the older man. Warmth spread through her body and every locked door in her heart burst open with her love for her husband. Natalie almost gave herself away with a sob.

Pressing herself against the hallway wall, she clapped her hand over her mouth. Willing her shaky legs to function, she made her way back to the master bedroom and sank onto the bed. She swiped at the hot tears trailing down her cheeks. It wasn't easy accepting she was probably the stupidest woman in the world.

She'd loved him all along—from that first heart-pounding moment in his office. She'd just been too naive and scared to see it. When she heard soft steps in the hall, she wiped her face with the back of her hand and went out to meet him. At least she knew what she wanted now.

"Natalie." Her name left his lips in a rush of breath. He scanned her T-shirt-clad body before he jerked his gaze to her face. A muscle jumped in his jaw, but he rubbed the back of his neck and gave her a strained smile. "You slept through the day. Why don't you go back to bed till the morning? Or are you hungry? Do you want to eat something?"

But his grin faltered as he walked up to her. He cupped her damp cheek with his hand and tilted her face toward the light.

"What's wrong?"

Without answering his question, Natalie turned her head to brush a kiss on his palm and smiled at him.

"Natalie, you're not…" She silenced him with a finger on his lips.

"Oh, Garrett, but I am." He thought she was too vulnerable so soon after the accident, but Natalie had never been more certain of anything in her entire life.

When she tugged him into her room, he followed with hesitant steps. She reached behind him and clicked the door shut. His Adam's apple jumped in his throat and he watched her with something akin to panic in his eyes.

"We don't have to do this tonight." His voice was strangled and his eyes greedily roamed her body.

Arching an eyebrow, she drew her T-shirt over her head. Garrett's breath left him in a whoosh and she smiled in triumph. She did that to him.

Right now. In this room. There is no one but him and me. A man and a woman. Husband and wife. I'll make him mine.

She didn't know who took the first step and didn't care. Somehow, they were on each other like a whirlwind, mouths and hands moving frantically. Natalie tugged impatiently on Garrett's clothes, desperate to feel his skin pressed against hers, his hard contours against her soft curves without any barriers. He made quick work of tearing off his clothes, then pressed her against his naked body.

God, he feels so good.

But she pushed back from him, wanting to touch him. She spread her palms flat on his chest and caressed his smooth heat, relishing the wall of muscle beneath her hands. Curious to see if she could do what he'd done to her, she ran her thumbs over the small peaks of his chest and he tilted back his head with a guttural moan. She snatched her hands away, worried she'd done something wrong.

"Don't stop," he said, putting her hands back on his chest. "Touch me."

She swallowed but did as he demanded. Slowly, she ran her fingers down to the ridges of his stomach, and his body jerked in response. He was clearly holding himself in check; she could feel his body humming with suppressed desire. But when she pressed her breasts against him and ran her hands down his broad back, his control snapped.

Garrett wanted to take things slowly so they could enjoy each other, but the longing he'd been holding back swept in like storm waters breaching a dam. Natalie seemed to be overtaken by the same storm, and she was fierce and demanding in his arms.

He explored her mouth with burning thoroughness, entangling his tongue with hers. Drinking deeply from her, he lifted her up and carried her to the bed. Her fingers dug into his shoulders as he eased her onto the mattress. Her magnificent breasts rising and falling fast, she beckoned him with the crook of her finger, a seductive smile curving her swollen lips.

Garrett reached for her, his hands roaming up the sides of her thighs and around to her back. With one swift motion, he positioned himself over her, and her softness cushioned the hard planes of his body. The contact made him catch fire. He kissed the side of her neck and ran his tongue along her heated skin, enjoying the way his name escaped her parted lips in a breathless rush.

"Garrett...please," she whispered.

He grabbed a condom from the nightstand and sheathed himself with shaky hands.

"Look at me," he commanded, positioning himself at

her entry. Her eyes widened as he touched his hardness against her. She was so lovely in her passion that his heart throbbed and he ached with the need to claim her.

She held his gaze. "I want you, Garrett."

Unable to hold back any longer, he crushed his lips against hers and swept his tongue inside her sweet mouth.

"I fought this so hard," he said, pulling his mouth from hers. "And waited much too long. I want you so much it hurts."

"Then take me."

With a moan torn from deep within, he buried his face in her neck and plunged into her in one swift thrust. Garrett froze when a sharp gasp escaped from her. He glanced down and saw Natalie had her eyes closed tight, her bottom lip between her teeth. *What the hell?*

"Sorry. I'm okay," she gasped. "It's been a long time."

Her moist, tight warmth drove him mad but he didn't move a single muscle as he bore his weight on his forearms. When he continued to hold still, her eyebrows drew together and she shyly swerved her hips.

God. He groaned, searching for his precious control. "Do. Not. Move. Give me a second. I want to go slow for you."

"But I don't want you to go slow."

"Damn it, Natalie." He'd plowed into her like a beast when he should've coaxed her body into accepting him with more ease. "I hurt you…"

"Not hurt. Just startled." She cupped his cheek in her palm and stared up at him. "Please."

His blood thundered so hard in his veins that Garrett could hardly hear her. His mind battled with his body as he searched her face.

"Please," she said again, then rocked her hips against him.

Garrett shuddered in her arms, and began to move

slowly, looking intently into her face. Gripping his shoulders, Natalie moved with him and set a faster rhythm until he broke. With a groan, he planted his hands by her head, rising onto his arms, and drove into her to the hilt.

He thrust faster and she matched him stroke for stroke. It was almost too much. She was close but he didn't know if he could hold back. Then, Natalie cried out his name and arched her pelvis off the bed. Seconds later, he collapsed on top of her with a hoarse cry.

As their panting eased, Garrett rolled onto his back, taking her with him. He held her head against his chest and ran his hand down her hair.

"Natalie?"

"Mmm?"

"Are you all right?"

"Mmm-hmm."

"Good."

He tilted her chin up with his finger and studied her face, struck by her beauty inside and out. The delicate skin underneath her eyes was pale and bruised. She was still exhausted from yesterday's ordeal, and he held her tighter, the need to protect her surging in his blood. With a sigh, she molded her body against his and her breaths grew long and steady.

He absently drew circles on her naked back. It was surreal how right all of it felt. *Mine.* Nothing in his no-strings-attached sexual philosophy explained his possessiveness. The mere thought of her having another lover scraped him raw. At least for now, she was his and his alone.

But this hunger... He had to believe it would pass. Natalie had no place in the life he meant to lead. He'd been content to pour himself into Hansol, and to find satisfaction in his professional accomplishments within the confines of his duties. Garrett had never wanted a real marriage. He couldn't change who he was. He couldn't offer Natalie anything more than what they had. *She understands that. Doesn't she?*

And yet, the future he'd accepted as written in stone now seemed like a flimsy note on the back of a cocktail napkin—crumbled and blowing across the sidewalk.

Fourteen

The last few times Adelaide had seen her brother and sister-in-law, Garrett couldn't stop touching Natalie—tucking a strand of hair behind her ear, entwining his fingers through hers, pulling her close to his side with an arm wrapped around her shoulders. Since their mom died, he'd held himself cold and aloof, becoming unreachable. Untouchable.

With Natalie by his side, her brother had finally shed his iron armor, and exuded warmth from his pores. And he became a puddle of goo when Sophie was around. The little girl had recovered from the fall scare faster than the grown-ups and was back to her energetic, rascally self.

Adelaide's heart burst with joy to see him so happy, but a small, lonely part of her shivered with fear. Garrett was her constant. His love unconditional. No matter how much she screwed up, he would have her back. *Have I lost him?* Adelaide cringed with shame. She wasn't the spoiled princess people made her out to be. She should stop acting like one.

She hadn't lost a brother—she'd gained a sister. A wide smile spread across her face—Natalie was the best big sister imaginable.

Humming under her breath, she stepped out of the elevator at Hansol headquarters and strode past the reception desk.

"Hi, Cindy," she said, waving goodbye at the same time.

"Hello, Ms. Song," said the receptionist with a grin. "Bye, Ms. Song."

Natalie was a sushi fiend. It was a surprise visit but she'd never turn down sushi no matter how busy she was.

"Adelaide." When she entered Natalie's office, her sister-in-law jumped up from her chair and rushed over for a hug. "What a wonderful surprise."

"Are you talking about me or the *nigiri* plate I brought you?" She lifted the bag holding three paper boxes from a hole-in-the-wall restaurant in Little Tokyo.

Natalie's eyes glazed over. "I love you."

Adelaide laughed shyly, pleased by her warm reception. "I got some for Garrett, too."

"Oh, no. He's in a meeting for the next few hours."

"That's fine. He's always in a meeting." She sat at a small, round table by the window and waved over Natalie. "Eat up. We have to finish his portion, too."

"Not a problem." Natalie sighed happily, her chopsticks poised over the box.

Full and happy, they sipped green tea in comfortable silence until Adelaide saw her sister-in-law frown. "What is it?"

"Garrett has been looking tense and haggard lately," Natalie said, her hands wrapping around her mug. "Do you know if he's worried about something? Is anything wrong at work?"

"You don't know?" Adelaide stared at her, shocked by her question. Her brother hadn't told his own wife about the whole mess. Keeping his baby sister in the dark was one thing, but his wife? *That idiot.* Why did he insist on bearing all the responsibilities alone?

"What don't I know?" Natalie sat up in her chair. "Garrett hasn't said anything to me."

"He's my brother but he's so stubborn sometimes." Adelaide threw up her hands. "He didn't tell me anything, either. I doubt he even told our dad. He thinks he's 'protecting' us."

"Adelaide, just tell me."

"I did some digging around. Everyone thinks I'm a spoiled little princess with an unimpressive IQ, so it's easy for me to go under the radar and gather intel." Everyone underestimated her, including her own family. Michael was the only one… She shut down the thought, annoyed she'd let him slip in again. He had nothing to do with this. Nothing to do with her. "It's Vivotex. They're considering a partnership with Yami Corporation, a small-time fashion manufacturing company. They don't have the brand recognition or the manufacturing capacity for any kind of partnership with Vivotex. Yami must have a powerful backer to catch Vivotex's attention, but we don't know who that is. My gut tells me this mystery powerhouse is using Yami as a pawn for its own plans."

"What if Garrett can't close the deal?" Natalie paled, her brow knitting with concern. "Will your grandmother really block his CEO appointment?"

"I hope not." When she was a kid, Adelaide used to fight her grandmother like a hellcat over everything—big and small. But somewhere along the way, they reached an unspoken truce. They were too much alike—strong willed, opinionated…and breakable. *Anything that doesn't bend inevitably breaks.* "I can't tell what she's thinking sometimes, but she has never let me down."

"Do you think it'll help if I beg her?" Her sister-in-law grinned but she wasn't entirely joking.

Tenderness flooded Adelaide's heart at how dearly Natalie loved her brother. It was no wonder Garrett followed her around like a puppy with hearts in his eyes. They were so perfect together. Adelaide could only hope she too would someday find that kind of love. Before she could turn wistful, she smiled brightly to reassure her big sis.

"My big brother is meant to be the next CEO." She squeezed Natalie's hand. "Try not to worry."

Natalie worried until Garrett came home that night.

"Hello, Mrs. Song." He walked up behind her and wrapped his arms around her waist. "What are you up to?"

"Making dinner."

She gave the cherry tomatoes one last rinse and reached out to turn off the faucet. Garrett had been nuzzling the sensitive spot behind her ear, but went still at her answer.

"Dinner?" He sounded more than a little alarmed. "Are you sure? Remember last week…"

Her face flamed. She remembered all too well. Filled with a sudden urge to test her domestic talents, Natalie had tried making lasagna and nearly set the kitchen on fire. Oddly enough, the lasagna had come out unscathed from the fire—as in completely raw.

His apprehension was warranted, but that didn't mean she'd let him get away with it. Natalie elbowed Garrett in his side. He grunted under his breath and she turned around to face him. He was gingerly rubbing his stomach, but his eyes were sparkling with laughter.

Her elbow had met rock-hard obliques. She doubted he'd even felt the jab. Still, contrite for her violence, she kissed the side of his neck then buried her face against him. He smelled so yummy, musk warmed against male skin.

"I'm only tossing a bag of salad." She straightened to

finish the job. "I ordered pizza for the main course, so you can stop worrying."

Garrett pulled her back into his arms and kissed her. She hadn't seen him all day and she'd missed him. She parted her lips and pressed herself to him, making him groan and slide his hands up the back of her shirt. Familiar heat spread through her and she had a second before losing all rational thought.

"Um, Garrett?"

He grunted and lifted her up onto the counter.

"Garrett." Natalie laughed and squirmed in his arms. They needed to talk about the Yami Corporation situation. It was ridiculous for him to carry all that weight by himself. "We need to talk. I want…"

He didn't seem to hear her and continued trailing kisses down the side of her neck. By the time he reached her collarbone, she couldn't remember what she'd wanted to talk about. She wrapped her legs around him and whispered the only words she could form. "I want you."

"Good." His voice rang with arrogant satisfaction. He cupped her breast with a possessive hand and something fierce burned in his eyes before he kissed her with heat and desperation. When he filled her, she cried out, marveling at how whole she felt, and never wanted to let go.

After the storm passed, Garrett lifted her down from the counter. He was bare chested and she wore nothing under her oversize T-shirt. She plucked her panties off the floor, not bothering with her jeans. When her husband reached down for his shirt, she kicked it away with her foot. "You're fine. It's casual Friday at the Song penthouse."

"Is that so?" A wolfish grin spread across his handsome face as he folded his arms across his naked chest.

Her eyes glazed over as she ogled his bulging biceps. *Gah.* Natalie hurried to the opposite side of the kitchen counter so she wouldn't jump him. Her stomach growled loudly, reminding her she'd been putting together dinner. *Yes, a woman cannot live by sex alone.* She needed pizza.

Garrett chuckled under his breath as though he knew her inner struggle of pizza versus sex. "Have a seat. I'll finish the salad."

She sat on the counter stool and made herself comfortable. Natalie decided there was nothing better than watching her shirtless husband cook for her. They chatted comfortably, warm laughter punctuating their conversation.

This was happiness. Unshed tears pricked her eyes and her lips curved into a tremulous smile. *So this is what it feels like to be whole.* Love swelled to the brim and lapped perilously at the edge of her heart. Unable to hold back any longer, she opened the dam and let it spill over.

"I love you."

"Could you pass the salad?" Natalie asked in a small voice.

"Sure." Garrett passed her the salad bowl, careful not to let their fingers touch.

"Thank you."

The conversation at the dinner table was scintillating. It might've had something to do with him all but ignoring her declaration of love. Her words had brought something fierce and hungry to life inside him, but he'd smothered it ruthlessly. *What else can I do?* He could never give her what she wanted. What she deserved. He shut his eyes and mind against the torrent of emotions threatening to breach the walls of his heart.

"Garrett." His eyes flew open at Natalie's whisper. "You don't need to worry. I haven't forgotten our agreement. I'm not asking anything of you."

"Hush." Garrett shut out what her words implied. She deserved more but he was going to hold on to her—letting her go would wreck him. He brought her hand to his mouth, kissing each knuckle before placing a lingering kiss on her palm. Her lashes fluttered and her lips parted in response. Without warning, he scooped his wife off her chair and headed upstairs, taking two steps at a time.

"What are you—"

"Hush." Blood pounded in his ears. His panic fueled his desperation. *Mine.* He laid her down on the bed, then ripped his pants off with rough impatience. She watched him with sad, wide eyes, and his heart slammed against his ribs. "Your turn."

He reached around her and pulled off her T-shirt with shaking hands. When he reached her hips, he linked his fingers into her lacy underwear and tugged it down. Then she was naked before him, and she was perfection.

Garrett lowered himself, covering her body with his. Molten heat flared at the contact. He claimed her mouth, sucking and nipping, drinking in her intoxicating taste like a man starved. She writhed under him, and everywhere her body touched his, a fire started. As he explored her, she made those small sounds of passion that never failed to drive him mad. He slid one hand down her silken curves. A guttural groan tore from his chest when he found the hot, moist warmth of her center.

"Look at me." When her eyes focused on him, he gave himself to her the only way he knew how. "Do you see what you do to me?"

"Yes." She whimpered and grasped his buttocks as he pulled his fingers from her.

"I can't get enough of you." Unable to hold back any longer, he surged into her. "I've never wanted anyone like this before. Only you."

"Please, Garrett."

"You're mine." Wanting to prolong her release, he slowed his rhythm even more. "Tell me you're mine."

"I'm yours."

Her words slashed the last of his control. He raised himself on his arms and drove into her again and again until she screamed his name, her internal muscles clenching around him. His hips bucked once, twice, then he shouted his own release and collapsed over her.

After a long while, Garrett lay with his forearm over his eyes, listening to the steady rhythm of Natalie's breathing. He'd made love to her with a desperation that should have alarmed him, but he had no space for any thought other than her words. *I love you.*

They made love every night, giving and receiving pleasure he had never experienced before. It wasn't love but it was real and tangible. Was it enough for her?

In the last few months, having Natalie by his side had grown into an unwavering need. Subconsciously, he'd been pushing aside the fact that their marriage would end soon. Thinking about it made his stomach twist and churn. His soul rebelled, screaming, "She's mine." Did he want to hold on to Natalie?

He had no answers. At least, none he could face head-on.

Garrett watched Natalie get dressed for work. She twisted around in front of the mirror examining the fourth outfit she'd shimmied into this morning. Not that he was complaining. Watching her dress—and undress—was hotter than a striptease.

"Are you sure?" she asked him for the tenth time that morning. "Adelaide talked me into buying it but I just don't know."

"Yes." Garrett twirled his wife in a pirouette. "And my answer will still be yes when you've asked me for the twentieth time."

Natalie finally settled on a black wrap dress rather than one of her severe business suits. It highlighted her curves instead of hiding them, but the tight fit had her fidgeting like it was crawling with somersaulting circus fleas.

"You look beautiful." Garrett kissed the tip of her nose. "And professional. You'll be great today." Presentations never ceased to frazzle her even though she was fantastic at them.

When she drew in a breath, he pressed a finger to her mouth to stop the objections he knew were coming. But the feel of her parted lips and her intoxicating scent threatened to derail him from the point he was trying to make.

"Our wedding pictures were featured in *Focus* magazine. Everyone has already seen your lovely figure. I assure you the employees won't treat you differently because you decided to let your hair down a little."

"You really think so?" Natalie raised hopeful eyes to his.

"Yes, I know so." Garrett paused for a beat. "They'll treat you differently because you're married to me."

"You're terrible." She punched him in the arm as surprised laughter burst from her.

He loved the sound of her laughter. Garrett pulled Natalie into his arms. "Stop being so nervous. Your presentation will be great, and short, and you'll be back to your daily routine, whipping people into submission."

She narrowed her eyes at him. "I don't whip anyone into anything. I just make sure that company policies are carried out with uniformity and consistency."

"Of course, Mrs. Song. You better move your butt, or you're going to be late," Garrett said, checking the clock.

"Oh, shoot. Okay." Natalie hopped around putting her heels on, then rushed to the door. Garrett picked Sophie up and trailed her hurried steps. "Bye. See you tonight!" Natalie called over her shoulder.

He cleared his throat loudly and held Sophie out in front of him. Natalie had almost left without giving her a kiss.

"Oops. Sorry, sweetie."

She turned to go after brushing her lips on the crown of the baby's head. But Garrett wasn't going to let her get away that easily. He shot out his free arm and crushed her to him. Shifting Sophie to one side, he kissed Natalie deeply, sipping in her soft moan. He stepped back before he tore off her carefully selected outfit, and she stood looking slightly dazed.

He reached out and patted his wife's perfect bottom. "Go!"

Natalie blinked then scowled at him again before rushing out the door.

"Didn't Mama look pretty today?"

"Yup!" That was Sophie's it word these days. It actually sounded more like "yah-pu" and involved some spit spewing on the "pu."

"Mama will do great today, right?"

"Yup!"

He'd volunteered to take Sophie back to the Davises' since he didn't have any meetings lined up till ten o'clock. This was the first reprieve he'd had in weeks.

Yami Corporation's interference in the Vivotex deal was an unexpected nuisance, but Clark and Sebastian were the loyal allies Garrett hoped they'd be. They'd successfully convinced the majority at Vivotex that Yami's overtures were merely distracting them from closing a profitable partnership, and that Yami couldn't offer what Hansol promised.

Garrett had worked night and day to finalize the details of the contract. It was grueling work but the deal was within reach, and he thrived on the knowledge. Once the deal closed, the CEO position and everything he'd worked for—including his independence from his grandmother—would finally be his.

The real headache in the fiasco was that there was someone inside Hansol leaking confidential information regarding the Vivotex deal. Every leak had given Yami Corporation an edge in the bid for the partnership. But corporate espionage was a dangerous game to play, and a small-timer like Yami wouldn't have the guts to start a war with Hansol. It meant there was someone else behind it all, and the unknown puppet master knew how to play the game well. Garrett had to catch the spy to find out who the real threat was.

Fifteen

Soon Natalie was going to look like the bride of Frankenstein. Her curls were beginning to stand from the static Garrett was generating.

"Garrett." He glanced at her, but continued to pace around his office. "I know you're nervous, but please stop pacing."

"I am not nervous."

"Of course not. You're just trying to create alternative energy with your feet." He scowled, but she just grinned from her perch on his desk. "Oh, look. It worked. I see smoke coming from your shoes."

He strode menacingly toward her, arms outstretched to catch her. Laughing at him, she let herself be caught and pressed up against him.

With a forlorn sigh, Garrett buried his head in her neck. "Okay. Fine. I'm feeling some nervous excitement. But mostly excitement. Hardly any nervousness."

"*Of course* you are. Well, there's no need for any nervousness because Vivotex is here to sign that contract. It's going to happen."

"Damn right, it's going to happen."

Garrett straightened up. Natalie wanted to pull him back to her and hang on for dear life. The grains of sand were falling in the hourglass. She cherished every moment she got to spend with him, but her heart bled knowing every second that passed meant she was that much closer to losing him.

But she couldn't think about that now. Natalie glanced at the wall clock and hurried toward his chair to retrieve his suit jacket. "Settle down, cowboy. You only have five minutes until the meeting."

She held the jacket open for him and he put it on. After running her hands over the nonexistent wrinkles on the suit, she straightened his tie and smoothed back his hair. With everything in place, she stared at her beautiful husband, taking in every inch of him, memorizing him.

All hints of his nervousness were gone, and he stood before her strong and confident. He was ready and she had to be, too.

"Are you satisfied with what you see, ma'am?" Garrett's lips tilted into an arrogant grin. Without fail, Natalie's heart sped up and desire sparked to life.

"There's no time for flirting, Mr. Song."

She made an effort to be stern, but she probably sounded breathless and flustered. With a low, husky laugh, Garrett pulled her into his arms and held her tight.

"You're right. That'll have to wait until tonight."

She walked with him to the door but stopped uncertainly. "Garrett."

I love you. I love you. I love you.

The words burned her throat, but she held her silence, knowing he wouldn't want to hear them. So she forced a cheeky grin and gave him two thumbs up.

"Go get 'em, tiger."

* * *

The Song family home rang with laughter and celebration, but the endless pop of champagne corks sounded hollow to Natalie's ears. She was so proud of Garrett, but emotion still choked her as she scanned the scene of the party celebrating the Hansol-Vivotex partnership. Garrett's eyes sought hers often, so she did her best to smile for him. But amid the strains of piano music and laughter, she was feeling overwhelmed.

"Ah-ga." Natalie spun at the sound of Grace Song's voice.

"Grandmother. I'm so happy you decided to join the celebration." During their weekly visits, Natalie had begged her to attend. "You must be so proud."

"I expected nothing less from my grandson." The older woman's voice sounded wistful. "His mother should be standing by James's side tonight. I wish she could've seen the man Garrett has become, and the family he's built for himself."

Natalie's chest tightened and hot tears stung her eyes. In her own reserved manner, Grandmother was telling Natalie that Garrett had chosen a good wife…that she accepted her. *Thank you, Grandmother. And I'm sorry for lying to you about our marriage.*

"Well, Grandmother. You should be doubly proud on his mom's behalf then."

A gentle smile lit Grace Song's face and she placed a warm hand on Natalie's cheek. "I am, and you should be, too."

When Grandmother made her way back to her guests, Natalie stared at her husband to memorize every detail about him. With their days numbered, she couldn't hold back. Her hunger and longing saturated her soul and she longed to reach out to him. As though heeding her silent call, Garrett turned to her from across the room, an answering fire flaring in his eyes. She didn't know if it was her nerves playing tricks on her, but he seemed more restless and edgy than he'd been before the contract was signed. She watched him rush through his rounds, tilting back the flutes of champagne offered to him. Despite her insistence that he should go and celebrate, she was desperate to have him by her side and all to herself.

After spending the shortest acceptable time with his guests, Garrett abandoned them and strode toward her with long, impatient strides. "Miss me?" He raised a hand to cup her face.

"Desperately." She placed a lingering kiss on his palm and a tremor ran through him. *Good, because I'm trembling, too.*

"We're leaving," he rasped in her ear, his hot breath caressing her skin.

A thrill of anticipation slid down her spine and gathered mass at its base, where Garrett rested his hand. They stepped out into the night, but instead of heading to his car, he led them toward the garden at the far end of the property.

"Garrett, where are we going?"

"Somewhere private." His voice was low and dangerous.

She quickened her steps to keep up with him, frantic to touch him. To possess him. To mark him as hers.

Soon they were sprinting through a topiary maze with sharp turns and narrow passageways. The maze stood at least two stories tall and the half moon hardly pierced its depth. She'd never be able to find her way out, but Garrett seemed to know it even in near darkness. He stopped at what had to be the heart of the maze, where there was a beautiful but aging pagoda.

"What is this place?" Natalie whispered, not wanting to disturb its eerie peace.

"It used to be my sanctuary." Garrett's voice sounded far away. "No one knew how to find it but me."

"What would you do out here?" She leaned her cheek against his chest as he wrapped his arms tightly around her.

"Nothing exciting. I would just read a book or stare at the clouds." His hand made idle circles on her back. "It's not what I did that made this place special."

"Then what was it?"

"As a kid, you don't have much that you could truly call your own, but this place was mine. It existed only for me."

"I didn't know you could be so possessive," she teased.

"Oh, yes. When I have something rare and special, I want it all to myself." His hands became bolder, dropping to her backside.

"And now? What do you want all to yourself?" She wanted to hear him say it. Even if it wasn't love, she wanted him to claim her as something rare and special, and only his.

"You." His answer didn't sound like a word but a primitive growl. "You're mine and I want you."

Right then, Natalie became a flame, burning wildly for him. She kissed him wherever her lips landed, tearing ineffectively at his clothes. With a suddenness that shocked her into momentary stillness, he picked her up and carried her up the stairs of the pagoda. When he set her on the ground, she slid down his powerful body and felt his unmistakable hardness.

"I need you," he said before crushing her mouth with his. His kiss was erratic and wild; there wasn't a hint of his damn control in sight. He groaned, pushing her against a wooden pillar. "Natalie."

His hand moved under the hem of her dress to her panties. Reaching her center, he growled in satisfaction. "You want this. You want *me*."

"Yes, Garrett. I want you."

He spun her around to face the pillar and pulled her hips back, bending her at the waist. Her arousal was blinding and she didn't know how long she could wait. She heard Garrett unzip his trousers and tear open a condom packet.

Natalie was frantic when he pushed inside her with a moan. His fingers bit into her hips as he withdrew from her and plunged back in, deeper than before. She knew he was trying to slow things down for her but his maddening pace was going to kill her, so she tipped up her rear and pushed against him, setting a pace more to her liking. She felt his control break and she laughed in triumph.

"Natalie."

Too far gone for finesse, he worked frantically to bring them to their climax, his shout coarse and wild in the night.

Garrett made a conscious effort not to grip Natalie's arm too tight as he led her out of the maze. She darted uncertain glances his way, but he didn't trust himself to look back at her. He'd ravished her like a madman in his childhood hideout, but the thought encroaching on his triumph had rattled him to the core. He had no excuses left to hold on to Natalie. She'd held up her part of the bargain, and Sophie's fall had rattled the Davises enough to withdraw their opposition to the adoption. Once the adoption papers were approved by the court, there would be nothing left to prevent Natalie and Sophie from walking out of his life.

But she loves me.

"Garrett—"

"Home." He cut her off more brusquely than he'd intended, and he turned to give her a stiff smile. "We'll talk at home."

He had to eradicate the notion of a temporary marriage from Natalie's mind. He'd put it there in the first place, but things had changed—*he* had changed. Garrett admired and respected her. Burned for her. Couldn't that be enough? There were relationships based on far less.

And she said she loved him. Something warm and aching tore through his heart at the thought. He was afraid his past wouldn't allow him to love her like she deserved, but he could offer her and Sophie everything they could ever need. They would never have to worry about money again. He would move to New York with them, and work out of the office there. He would show his girls the world, promise them a future they never dreamed of.

Would that be enough for Natalie? Would she give up her chance to find someone who truly loved her?

But that was just it. Their relationship was more than sex and companionship. They were incredible together. He had never experienced anything even remotely close to the connection and pleasure he felt making love to Natalie. Their passion. That was rare and special. Not only that, but they could also talk to each other and truly understand what the other person meant…as if they had a distinct wavelength that existed exclusively for them.

What they had might not be the stuff of fairy tales, but they were good together. He might not deserve her, but he would fight to keep her.

Sixteen

Garrett had been traveling often the last several weeks to prepare for Hansol's first joint venture with Vivotex. The trips were short, no more than a night or two at a time, but Natalie felt as though her time with him was being stolen from her.

Natalie took heavy steps to the parking structure, dreading going home to an empty house. Lost in her melancholy, she jumped when her cell phone rang. It was Garrett. She let the phone ring a few more times, trying to work up a cheerful "hello." After a deep breath, she picked up.

"God, I miss you." His words sounded as though they'd been torn from him.

Natalie halted as tears blurred her vision. He'd only been gone for two days, but she missed him with a physical ache. She held back the words on the tip of her tongue. *I love you.* She didn't regret telling him she loved him, but he never acknowledged her confession. And every time she said those words again, he would disappear behind a wall of indifference. At least he missed her. That had to mean something.

"I miss you, too," she said. "Hurry home to me."

"Soon." The single word, a promise filled with longing, stole her breath.

"Garrett."

"I'm headed to my next meeting." A small pause. As though he was waiting for her to say something. Then he sighed softly. "I needed to hear your voice."

"I'm glad you called." She swallowed back her emotion with some difficulty. "Go. Don't be late for your meeting."

Natalie hung up before she said more than she should. She slid into her car clutching the phone to her heart, and jumped when it rang again, thinking for a second it was Garrett calling back. Laughing at her foolishness, she glanced at her screen. It was the family-law attorney Garrett had retained for her.

"This is Natalie."

"Mrs. Song, this is Timothy Duffy. I have some great news."

Natalie's heart dropped to her stomach. "Yes, Timothy. I'm listening."

"Congratulations. You're a mom," he said with a smile in his voice. "The judge signed the adoption papers."

"Oh," she gasped and tears strangled her voice. "I'm a mom. I'm Sophie's mom."

"You certainly are. I've notified the Davises, and as previously agreed, they will have a week to relinquish physical custody of the baby." She could hear the smile in Timothy's voice. "I'll email you the details. You should go celebrate."

"Yes. Thank you."

Her phone fell from her limp fingers and tears streamed down her face as her heart tore into two pieces. One part of her heart was so very happy that Sophie was hers and she was Sophie's. The other half broke and bled. The adoption had been the one last thing that held Garrett to her.

She remembered his words from Ojai only too well. *I want you. But this marriage, it still ends once our objectives are reached. If I make love to you tonight, I'm taking your body and giving you mine, nothing more.*

But they'd come a long way from that night. Hadn't they?

One thing was certain. She couldn't go on like this. She had to tell him she didn't want their marriage to end—she wanted forever with him.

The next evening, Natalie waited in front of the elevator, her heart thumping against her rib cage. The adoption papers were tucked away in her nightstand drawer. She planned on telling Garrett everything—about Sophie, about wanting them to be a real family and about forever. Her ice-cold hands fisted at her sides.

When the elevator opened, Garrett caught her in his arms and spun her around before kissing her senseless. Her fears and worries melted away. He was home and that was all that mattered.

"Did you miss me?" He leaned his forehead against hers.

"Nah." *So much it hurt.* "Not really."

"I'll make sure to remind you what you've been missing."

"Is that a promise?" She looked up at him through her lashes, biting her lower lip.

"Damn it, Natalie," he groaned with a pained expression on his face. "I still have calls to make…"

Natalie laughed and danced out of his reach. "Well, you started it."

"Real mature." He stalked toward her, his eyes shining with intent.

Then his phone rang.

He cursed with gusto and growled when he checked the

caller ID. He pointed at Natalie and mouthed "later" before he answered and stomped toward his office.

Natalie smiled at his back, pleased with his obvious frustration. He really had missed her, and she planned on showing him how much she'd missed him. As she went into the bathroom to take a shower, she pushed aside the thought that they were running out of time.

After putting on a black chemise over her damp skin, she emerged from the bathroom, ready to share the news of Sophie's adoption. But when Garrett strode into their room only to freeze at the sight of her, all rational thoughts fled her mind. His heated gaze was filled with yearning and another emotion she couldn't define. Something akin to desperation...fear. Something primal and possessive filled her veins and she sashayed toward her husband. She had to have him. Show him with her body that they belonged together.

"Now, pay attention," she purred, unbuttoning his shirt and pushing it down his shoulders. "Because I'm going to have you my way."

"Is that so?" He arched an eyebrow and had a ghost of a smile on his lips.

"I didn't say you could talk."

"Natalie…"

He groaned, tilting back his head when she went down on her knees to pull off his slacks. Garrett swayed and planted his feet more firmly as her hand skimmed the outline of his erection on her way up.

"Take off your clothes," he ordered through clenched teeth.

Natalie just smiled and pushed him down onto an armchair. He lunged for her but she fluidly evaded his hands.

"Shh." She placed a finger over her mouth. "You aren't paying attention."

He growled.

With her gaze glued to his face, Natalie stripped off her clothes, standing barely out of reach. She had no idea how to perform a striptease, but judging by the fierce, unblinking attention of her husband, she was doing quite well.

Naked, she strode to the chair and straddled him, then took his hard length in her hands, making him hiss.

She positioned herself over him. "Do I have your full attention?"

"Yes," he rasped.

"Good."

She took him all the way inside her and he groaned against her neck, his hips surging to meet her. Natalie rode him with wild ferocity. Her body knew his intimately and she set a rhythm that would drive him mad. Drive her mad. And like the countless times before, they were caught in a storm neither of them could control.

Afterward, he carried her limp body to bed and they lay down facing each other. She stared at him, feeling too raw and vulnerable to hide the love from her eyes. He stared right back at her with an expression that made her insides melt.

"Wait here."

With that sudden command, he got out of bed and pulled on some pajama pants.

What a shame to cover up such a fantastic ass.

After digging through his suitcase, he strode back to her with a small box in his hands and sat on the edge of the bed.

"What is it?" she said.

He scratched the back of his head and cleared his throat. If she didn't know better, she would've thought he looked nervous.

"I have something for you." He held out the box to her and sat still as a statue as she opened it.

Her hand flew to her mouth and tears filmed her eyes. They were earrings. Emerald with diamond inlays. They looked exactly like his mother's ring, which Natalie wore every day.

"Oh, Garrett. They're beautiful." *But what does this mean?* she wanted to ask him.

"Put them on." His voice was gruff, tense.

"I…" She couldn't put them on. Not when the adoption document sat less than a foot from her. Not before she told him everything. "Garrett, I can't take them…"

"Why?" The absence of emotion in his voice shot fear through her heart.

"It's—it's too much. And you—you might want the ring back soon…" She trailed off, hoping he would correct her. Tell her he wanted to stay married to her. She didn't need a declaration of love. Not yet, anyhow. But she wanted to know this was more than just a business arrangement to him.

Instead, he shrugged and a mask of indifference fell across his features. Did he understand why she couldn't accept the earrings? Did he not care that their time together would soon end? Her heart clenched painfully.

"It's been a long day." He eased down and turned his back to her. "Let's get some sleep."

The distance between them seemed to stretch out endlessly, and Natalie lost the nerve to tell him about Sophie. Because when she told Garrett the adoption was finalized, she was going to bare her soul to him. Tell him that they were already a family. That they belonged together. Forever. But not tonight. Not like this. They didn't have long left, but they still had tomorrow. She would tell him everything tomorrow.

"Okay. Good night."

Out of habit, Garrett's eyes shot open at 4:00 a.m. Then, remembering he'd left his calendar open for the morning, he was about to let his eyelids droop closed when he bolted up, the sheets slipping down to his waist. His wife's side of the bed was empty.

He couldn't believe he'd slept at all. She'd refused the earrings because she intended to return her ring to him. Natalie was planning to leave him. She said soon, but she couldn't be gone already.

Garrett groaned. He'd had the earrings specially designed to match her engagement ring, so he could ask her to never take it off. *Did she understand my intent? How could she when I didn't tell her any of it?* Instead of waiting for her to come back to bed, he strode over to the en suite bathroom.

"Natalie?"

Considering that it was dark inside, he wasn't too surprised when she didn't answer. Maybe she'd gone downstairs for some water. After pulling on the first T-shirt he could grab from the dresser, he jogged down the stairs. The downstairs lights were on and he sighed in relief. He opened his mouth to call her name, but his phone beeped from the room.

Damn it. Who could it be at this hour?

He hesitated before he turned around to get his phone. The timing told him it might be an emergency.

It was a text from Mike. Call me. It's urgent.

"What is it?" Garrett demanded once he had Mike on the phone, impatient to get to Natalie. "Can it wait?"

"We found him." Mike's voice was grim. The spy. His friend was the only person Garrett trusted enough to help with the investigation, but he could deal with that later.

"Good. Is that it?"

"No." The pause on the other end lengthened and Garrett frowned, his gut telling him something was very wrong. "It sounds bad, but I don't want you jumping to any conclusions."

"Spit it out, Mike," he said through clenched teeth. "I'll make my own decisions."

"Starting a few months ago, someone named Peter Klapper was buying up all the Hansol stock he could get his hands on. If he acquired enough shares, he could've swayed some key votes to block your CEO appointment, but the oldest members of the board wouldn't let go of theirs. The board of directors is a curmudgeonly lot, but no one could question their loyalty."

"Who is he?"

"He works for Yami Corporation. He's been climbing up quickly. A clever and ambitious guy, but he's been gambling and amassing quite a sizable debt."

"So he's a puppet for a deep pocket."

"Right. We traced multiple electronic transfers into his bank account. Hundreds of thousands of dollars at a time."

"Did you find the origin of those transfers?"

"Not yet, and Klapper disappeared without a trace."

"Goddamn it. We need to hunt down the mole inside Hansol before he runs, too."

"We're close to finding that link. It's someone in the LA office." Mike sighed. "And the investigator found something out."

"What is it?" Garrett shoved his hand through his hair.

"Peter Klapper and Natalie went to college together. They dated for a few months…" Garrett's heart slammed into his rib cage. "They kept in touch for a while until a couple years ago, and the investigator claims Natalie hasn't been in a relationship since she broke up with Klapper. He thinks she might've been carrying a torch for him…"

"And he approached her to resume their affair and use her as his informant," Garrett said, finishing for him.

"Look, Song. That investigator is playing Sherlock Holmes and failing badly. His theory is so far-fetched and flimsy I was tempted not to tell you, but I refuse to keep information from you." Mike's voice rang with fierce conviction. "I know you've been burned by Samantha, but you need to remember Natalie is nothing like her. I don't know what the story is, but don't shut her out. Talk to her—"

Garrett hung up. He'd heard enough.

The pieces—the nightmarish pieces—started fitting together. The spy. It was Natalie. She'd been feeding Klapper the information. Garrett had been stupid enough to let a woman use him again.

Why, Natalie? What did the bastard offer you?

Garrett could've given her anything that Klapper offered and more. She had to have known that… Then it hit him square between the eyes.

Love. Peter Klapper had offered her love. A real family for her and Sophie. The one thing Garrett made clear he couldn't give her. The room spun at the realization. He shoved away the searing pain and focused on his cold, numbing fury.

He found her in the living room, sitting with her feet tucked under her and staring out at the city lights.

"Natalie."

A sweet smile lit up her face when she saw him. It nearly broke him. *Lies. All lies.*

"What are you doing up?" she said.

"Mike called. We found the spy."

"You caught the spy?" Natalie gasped, her hands rising to her chest. "Thank God for that. Who was it?"

Her feigned relief knocked the wind out of him. He'd never told her about the spy or the investigation. "You knew there was a spy."

"Yes, I found out recently. I wish… I wish you'd told me, Garrett." She sounded both hurt and frustrated. He narrowed his eyes as his fury built. "You didn't have to worry alone."

"I didn't tell you because it's none of your business," he snarled like a wounded beast.

She gasped then looked away. "I—I see."

Oh, she is good.

"Do you, Natalie?"

"What?" Her eyebrows drew together. "What's wrong?"

"Wrong? Well, that depends on one's perspective. I suppose it's for the best I found out sooner than later. Before I made the mistake of my life."

"What are you talking about?" She stood and walked toward him. His gaze flickered to a manila folder that fell from the couch. She cupped his face in her hands. "Garrett, look at me."

"What did he promise you, Natalie? Did he tell you he loves you?"

"Who?"

"Peter Klapper." He watched for her reaction. Guilt? Fear? All he saw was bewilderment.

"How do you know Peter?" She cocked her head.

"I had the misfortune of being the target of his corporate-espionage scheme."

"Peter? Corporate espionage?" Finally, her face reflected the horror he'd been expecting and her hands dropped to her sides. "But how? He used to be a little full of himself, but I can't imagine him doing anything illegal. Besides, he doesn't have any money or connections."

"He doesn't need money. He's just a pawn for someone who has it. As for connections, you supplied those for him, didn't you?"

Natalie stumbled back from him. "What are you saying?"

"Do you love him?" He took a step toward her and she retreated a step. "Is that why you betrayed me?"

"Me?" Her hands flew to her mouth and the blood

drained from her face. "You think I stole information from you to help Peter?"

"Are you trying to tell me it's a coincidence he was your lover?"

"Yes. He *was* my lover for a brief time. It was a long time ago," she said, her voice soft and trembling. "Tell me. Are you playing six degrees of separation or investigating corporate espionage?"

"I am not playing a *game*. I'm confronting my *wife* about being unfaithful to me," he roared, pain searing his heart. "Did he tell you he loves you? Did he promise you forever?"

"Listen, goddamn it." She took a step toward him with her hands outstretched, and this time, he stepped back from her. "I love *you*. Only you."

"Of course. *Love*." A ragged laugh tore from his throat.

Her eyes widened and she swayed slightly on her feet. He fisted his hands to stop himself from steadying her. A part of him shouted for him to stop. To listen. To think. But he couldn't do any of that. The pain and fear he'd run from for so long nipped at his heels, and if he stopped, those feelings would catch him—hurt him.

"I've never said those words to another man."

"Words. Mean. Nothing," he spat.

She hunched forward as though he'd hurt her physically. Her eyelids flickered and her lips parted but no words came out.

Samantha had said she loved him. They were only twenty but he'd asked her to marry him and she'd accepted. All those lonely years after his mom died... He thought she would fill that void. But when she found out his trust fund couldn't be accessed until he was twenty-five, she'd left him for a guy who had immediate cash to burn. Words meant nothing.

"Are there any more secrets you kept from me?"

"Yes." He flinched even though she had whispered the word. "I was going to tell you, but I was too afraid to find out what it would mean for us."

"Find out what? What were you going to tell me?"

"Sophie's adoption was finalized." Her shoulders shook but she held his gaze. "Everything we bargained for—your deal with Vivotex, Sophie's adoption… We did it. We won. Now there is no reason for us to stay married… except I couldn't bear for us to end. I wanted forever with you."

"I don't believe you, and I sure as hell don't believe in love and forever." His head spun and he barely managed to stay on his feet. "It's over."

He wanted to snatch the words back as soon as they left his mouth. It wasn't over. He would beg her to leave Klapper.

But her blood drained from her face and she stood eerily still. Fear gripped his throat. *No. Please, no.*

"You're right." Her voice was steady and strong when she spoke at last. "It really is over."

Natalie walked past him with her chin held high. Every nerve in his body screamed for him to stop her but he couldn't. Time must have passed because the next thing he knew, Natalie was standing in front of him again, fully dressed and holding a suitcase in her hand.

"I'm leaving."

"You can't leave now." *Not ever.* He dragged his hand down his face. "It's not even light out."

"What I do isn't any of your concern. Not anymore," she said, her face drawn but resolute. "If you don't mind, I'll ask my friends to pick up the rest of my things later."

He swayed slightly and widened his stance to steady himself. She seemed to be waiting for him to say something, but he could barely stand, much less speak. *Oh, God. What have I done?*

"Goodbye, Garrett."

It was the final nail in the coffin, and he felt shrouded in darkness. He welcomed the oblivion as he listened to Natalie leave with a quiet click of the door.

Seventeen

Natalie barely made it to Mrs. Kim's apartment before her knees gave out and she crumpled to the ground. Her friend was at Natalie's side within a second.

"What's wrong?" Mrs. Kim supported her by the waist and led her into her living room. "What happened?"

A sob broke from Natalie and sorrow enveloped her. Hot tears streamed ceaselessly down her cheeks until she felt wrung dry. She lay down on Mrs. Kim's couch and closed her eyes. Consciousness was exhausting…

The next time Natalie opened her eyes, it was dark out. She'd barely made a sound, but Mrs. Kim was at her side.

"You need to eat something." The older woman set a bowl of cereal on the coffee table. "I need to go to the market to make you a proper bowl of *jook*, my famous Korean porridge, but I couldn't leave you alone."

Natalie shook her head and flinched. It hurt. It hurt everywhere.

"Fine. Let's start with some water, shall we?"

Mrs. Kim held a cup to her lips and she swallowed. Once. Twice. "No more. I can't."

"Give yourself a few days to grieve, then no more." Mrs. Kim pressed a kiss to Natalie's forehead. "Think of Sophie."

Natalie sat up and looked at the bowl Mrs. Kim had brought her. She never knew Cheerios could expand five times their size by soaking up all the milk in the bowl. Natalie settled in to witness the entire process—without curiosity, without interest. It was food she was meant to eat, but couldn't.

I don't believe you.

She clenched her eyes shut.

It's over.

Her mom had abandoned her and her dad couldn't stand her.

Stupid, lonely girl. You should've known Garrett would never love you back.

The dark, gaping hole in her soul spread—patient in its malice, in its cruelty. Soon it would swallow all that was good and bright in her. She looked forward to it because maybe then she could find some peace. A peace for the dead.

Only the mother in her would survive. She would eat, talk and breathe as long as Sophie needed her.

"What the hell is going on, Garrett?" Adelaide burst into his office and opened the blinds, letting in a shaft of blinding sunlight. "Have you turned into a vampire?"

Garrett hadn't slept in days and it felt like a sledgehammer was pounding inside his head. Sunlight didn't help, so he'd closed all the blinds and shut off the lights.

"Leave. Now."

"I had a feeling he would be a wreck," Mike said, closing the door behind him.

"You told me they might've had a fight, but this is ridiculous," she huffed at his best friend.

Garrett didn't see any reason to talk to them, so he kept
abusing the keys of his laptop, even though the document
on his screen made no sense. Nothing made sense.

"Where's Natalie?" Adelaide said, stepping deeper into his
office. "I've been trying to reach her for over a week, but she
hasn't responded to any of my texts except for the first one."

He jerked up his head and met his sister's eyes. "What
did she say?"

"All she said was sorry." She leaned toward him, bracing her hands on his desk. "Where is my sister?"

Sorry. Sorry for what? Unbalanced laughter built in his
chest.

"*Hal-muh-nee* is worried sick. It isn't like Natalie to
ignore her calls." When Garrett didn't respond, Adelaide
shook him by the shoulders. "What's wrong, *oppa*?"

Mike gently withdrew her hands from him, and leveled
him with disappointed eyes. "I told you not to do anything
rash, Song."

"Screw you, Reynolds." His voice was a low croak. He
couldn't remember the last time he ate or drank anything
other than Scotch.

"Shut up and listen. We found the mole. Peter Klapper seduced a naive new hire in the media department—"

"I know it's not Natalie," Garrett interrupted.

"What? You thought Natalie was the spy? Are you freaking crazy? Please tell me you didn't accuse her of being the
spy." His little sister sounded furious and scared at once.
Her voice trembled when she said, "She was worried about
you, Garrett. She didn't know anything until I told her. Oh,
God. You broke her heart, didn't you?"

"Hush. It's going to be all right." Mike wrapped his arm
around Adelaide's shoulders and dropped a kiss on the top
of her head.

"*Hal-muh-nee* needs to know what happened, but I can't tell her on my own. You'll come with me, right, Michael?"

"Of course," he said in a soothing voice. Then his face turned stoic as he addressed Garrett. "Go find Natalie and fix the mess you've made. I'll deal with the mole and track down the puppet master."

"Look for connections to Rotelle Corporation and Jihae Park." Garrett had suspected Rotelle's involvement for a while.

"Your almost-fiancée Jihae Park?" Adelaide wrinkled her nose. "It was just an informal agreement between the elders. Why would they go through so much trouble to give you grief?"

"Her *jae-bul* family probably hasn't lost a single thing in their life," Garrett said with a humorless laugh. "They felt slighted so they sent her to the States to give me hell."

"If that's true, she played you exceptionally well," Mike said, frustration clipping his words. "You fell right into her trap all because Natalie dated Klapper when she was a college kid."

Garrett gripped his hair in his fists. "Get out."

"You deserve to be happy, Garrett. Both of you do," he said, concern infusing his voice. "Don't throw this away."

"Out!"

"Come on." Mike steered Adelaide toward the door.

"But we can't leave him like this." His sister sounded like she wanted to pummel some sense into Garrett.

"Give him time."

"Time for what?"

"Time to get it through his thick head that he's in love with Natalie."

"He doesn't know he's in love with her? How could…?" The door shut quietly behind them, muting Adelaide's next words.

Garrett tried to inhale. Maybe he needed to exhale. He

couldn't do either because he already knew. He was in love with Natalie and he'd done everything in his power to push her away to protect his sad, scarred heart.

Did I ever believe she betrayed me? No. Natalie was incapable of the duplicity he'd accused her of. It came down to fear. He was afraid she wouldn't stay with him because he couldn't love her. He couldn't admit he loved her because he feared love more than anything. But he couldn't lose her like this.

Now was time to face his fears. All of them.

Garrett had searched everywhere for her, pulling all the strings he had, but she'd disconnected her cell phone, wasn't using any of her credit cards, and there were no flight records. When he hit dead end after dead end, Garrett had hired a private investigator. The idea of a stranger tailing his wife and daughter, observing them unseen and unheard, was distasteful, but they'd been gone for two months and he'd run out of options.

Garrett ran his hand down his face and slammed his laptop closed. The board of directors was convening in a few hours to vote on his appointment as CEO. If he hadn't been a shoo-in as the company's heir apparent, then closing the biggest deal in Hansol's history should secure him the position.

Becoming the head of Hansol had been Garrett's lifelong goal, but it had paled and wilted when Natalie left. He couldn't muster up much concern for his professional future. He had to win back his wife.

Imprisoned in his beautiful and terrifying hope, Garrett arrived close to half an hour late to the board meeting. He was out of his mind with desperation to see his wife, but he wiped his face clean of all emotions as he entered the boardroom.

"Gentlemen. Ladies." Garrett bowed from his waist

to the board members and sat opposite his grandmother. *"Hal-muh-nee."*

She acknowledged him with a nod and studied his face. Her expression betrayed nothing but her eyes clouded with concern. Garrett wanted to place his head on her knees and weep—something he'd never allowed himself to do, even as a child.

The board members continued to go down a list of items on the special agenda. As Garrett waited, the board reached the main agenda, and his grandmother straightened her spine imperceptibly.

"Dear ladies and gentlemen of the board…"

Garrett's cell vibrated in his pocket and his heart picked up speed. Without taking his eyes off the speaker, he took out his phone and unlocked it with his thumb. When it was ready, he lowered his gaze to his lap with the barest shift of his head.

I've located her current residence and workplace.

His private investigator had come through. He stood up so abruptly his chair tipped over and all eyes snapped to him. Garrett had no doubt leaving the meeting at a crucial moment like this could cause a scandal or convince his grandmother to block his CEO appointment. But every minute apart from Natalie was time lost. He made the only choice he could.

"Hal-muh-nee, I found Natalie."

His grandmother's lips trembled for just a second before she nodded with authority. "Go."

Garrett sprinted out of the conference room and the meeting erupted into chaos. He didn't care. All that mattered was finding his wife and fighting for forever.

Eighteen

"**S**ophie Harper Sobol!"

The eleven-month-old laughed and waddled around the living room buck naked. The rascal had, of course, skipped crawling and gone straight into walking. Natalie just prayed she'd outgrow the streaking phase.

"Look, missy," Natalie said after body tackling her. "Mommy has to go to work and you need to finish getting dressed." If she didn't drop Sophie off with her grandparents soon, she'd be late.

All Natalie got was another evil giggle in response. Raising a natural-born troublemaker was exhausting work, but she was grateful for the all-consuming distraction. Sophie had saved her. Had kept her alive. She shook away the bleak memory of her first days apart from Garrett.

Blowing out a calming breath, she ran to the closet and pulled on her work clothes. She was working as the office manager of a booming chain of diners around Queens and Brooklyn while she looked for a permanent job in New

York. She'd just about given up hope of getting a position in her field after leaving Hansol. If her latest interview didn't pan out, she would start applying for managerial or even entry-level positions and prove herself all over again.

For the time being, she enjoyed her job. There were two employees at the "corporate office." Herself and Debbie, the one-woman accounting department. Debbie was easygoing and kind, but more importantly, she never read tabloids or watched gossip shows, so she didn't know Natalie was Mrs. Garrett Song. Or rather, the soon-to-be ex-wife of Garrett Song.

They'd gotten into a little habit where Natalie brought in pastries and coffee in the morning, and Debbie shared her homemade lunch. Today was supposed to be blueberry-scone day, but after getting Sophie ready and dropping her off at Lily and Steve's, Natalie decided to stop by the nearby doughnut shop so she could make it to work on time.

She started pleading her case as soon as she reached the office. "I know this isn't your favorite, but Sophie was being extra rascally this morning and I was running late." Debbie was standing at the small reception desk with a strange expression on her face. "I'm so sorry. I got us the buttermilk ones that aren't drenched in sugar glaze…"

Natalie trailed off when a tall, dark figure stepped out from her office. His face was impassive, but his eyes were molten onyx, churning with unfathomable emotions.

Garrett.

Debbie took the bag of doughnuts and coffee from her slack hands. "Whoever he is, I'd keep him." With a sly wink, her coworker trotted off to unload their breakfast in the kitchen.

Natalie debated whether to run for it but she wasn't sure which way she would go. She'd missed him so much, and ached to wrap herself around his body. He had to leave before she gave in to her heart.

"How did you find me?" She turned her back because it hurt to look at him.

"You'd disappeared without a trace so I hired a PI to find you for me."

"You did what?" She hugged her arms around her midriff as a shudder ran through her. Her eyes darted around the office, imagining someone watching her.

"I'm so sorry, but I needed to find you." Garrett held out his hand as though to touch her but quickly withdrew it. "I promise you the investigator is discreet and thoroughly professional."

"It doesn't matter," she sighed, waving aside his apology. "I was going to contact you once we were settled in. We need to file our divorce papers. It's uncontested and we have no shared property, so it should be relatively simple."

"Natalie, we aren't finished."

She frowned at the odd tone of his voice. Whatever he'd meant by that, they couldn't talk about it out here. Natalie walked past him into her office and indicated for him to close the door. She sat behind her desk to create some distance between them.

"If you mean the divorce, then no, we aren't finished, but we soon will be. I want all the loose ends tied up, so Sophie and I can move on."

Garrett flinched, and Natalie's frown deepened. He acted as though her words were gutting him.

"How is she?" His voice was a rough whisper.

The suffocating pressure in her heart reached a breaking point and she nearly doubled over in pain. Gripping the arms of her chair, Natalie choked down the lump in her throat.

"She's doing great. She's getting bigger, stronger and faster, which means she can make more trouble in less time."

A sad but genuine smile tilted Garrett's mouth, and Natalie's eyes roamed hungrily over him. When he caught her gaze with fire in his own, yearning blanketed her mind like thick fog blinding a driver. He searched her face and something akin to hope swept across his features. Then, with a suddenness that startled her, he circled her desk and kneeled in front of her.

She pressed back into her seat, not trusting herself to be so close to him. Garrett caught her instinctive retreat and the brief spark that lit his eyes flickered and dimmed. He was quiet for a long moment before he spoke.

"We found the mole who passed the information on to Klapper. A woman in the media department…"

So that's what this is about. He found out she didn't betray him and the guilt was tearing him apart. She clenched her hands to fight her instinct to reach out for him. To hold his head on her lap. She hurt for him but she had nothing left in her to soothe his pain.

"If you're here to apologize, there's no need," she said, sounding as weary as she felt. "I'm sure you had your reasons for suspecting me in the first place."

"My reasons?" His laughter rang with bitter regret. "I had my damn reasons but none of them excuse what I did."

"I already told you. You don't need to apologize." He had to leave. She wouldn't be able to hold on much longer. "If it'll help you sleep better, then I forgive you. I really do, so please leave now. If you care even a little about me, please just leave."

"No." She thought she misheard him. It was a broken rasp. Then determination flared in his eyes and he said with finality, "No."

"How could you—"

"I care more than a little bit about you." He held her arms. "I love you, Natalie."

"Leave." She tugged her arms free and stumbled blindly away from him. "I want you to leave. Now."

"I can't." Garrett rose to his feet, but only his eyes—lost and frightened—followed her. "I'll do anything you want. Everything. Except leave you. I can't do that."

She shut her eyes to the naked need on his face. "Can't or won't?"

"Natalie…"

"How could you say you love me when you don't even trust me?"

"I never believed you betrayed me. I trust you with my life…with my heart." Garrett took a step toward her with his hand outstretched, but stopped short when she backed farther away. "*I* lied to myself because I needed an excuse to push you away. I saw what losing my mother did to my father. I swore never to love like that—to love someone so much that losing them meant losing myself. Then, I met you—beautiful, brave and so kind. I knew there wasn't a wall high enough to keep you out of my heart, and it scared me to death. I was so afraid of being hurt that I broke your heart instead."

"Yes. You did." She breathed in and out through her nose and spoke to a point above his shoulder. "But I understand. It doesn't make it hurt any less, but I think I understand. Maybe it's better this way. You ended whatever was between us. We should move past it and go on with our lives."

"No. I don't think you understand." Anguish drenched his eyes and his Adam's apple worked to swallow. "If you did, you wouldn't tell me to *move on* and *live*, because there is no life for me without you."

"But nothing has changed." Hurt, hope, anger and love screamed in her head and pulled her in opposite directions. "You broke my heart once, and I won't be able to survive a second time."

"Everything has changed." His face was a mask of pain, but his voice was deep and true. "With you gone, everything lost meaning. The company, my family's legacy, the

CEO spot. Those things are nothing more than duty and responsibility. Something I have to do for the benefit of others. Nothing gives me joy or satisfaction. Don't you see? I'm nothing more than a shadow without you."

He put one foot ahead of the other and cautiously approached her as though she was a bird ready to take flight. Natalie shook her head and retreated until she backed into a wall. But this time, Garrett didn't stop until he stood in front of her. He didn't touch her but his gaze roamed her face, desperate, naked and frantic.

No wall or barrier hid him from her, and she saw him. At last, he bared every part of himself, down to his very core. He was exposed and vulnerable, raw and true, and terrified and powerful—the only way a person in love could be.

"You…love me?" she said, body shaking so hard that her teeth were chattering.

"More than life." He lifted a trembling hand and brushed the pad of his thumb across her cheek. Only then did she realize she was crying, and so was he. "But I fought it. God, I fought it. Cancer took my mother, but I pushed you away from me. I know I hurt you and I don't have a right to ask this of you, but if you give me a chance, I'll spend the rest of my life making it up to you."

"The rest of your life?" She was dreaming. She had to be. He didn't want her, or her love, did he?

"The rest of our lives. Forever."

"You didn't want forever. You didn't want *me*." She looked away from him, biting her lip.

"Because I was a coward and a fool. Please, Natalie. Look at me." He cupped her cheek and turned her to face him. "I love you, Natalie. You are my heart."

"Do you…?" But she couldn't hold back the wrenching sobs any longer. Helpless in the face of her sorrow, Garrett gently ran his hands down her arms. "Do you really want to spend the rest of your life with me?"

"I can't live without you." He enveloped her in the warmth of his arms. "I was too afraid to admit to myself that I was in love with you, but I was desperate to hold on to you. I had the earrings made for you because I needed a way to ask you to stay with me. To tell you I didn't want our marriage to end."

"And I wouldn't take them." Her heart cracked and bled. "I didn't know."

"Of course not. How could you?"

"But then, why did you…?" She couldn't finish the sentence, their final encounter too painful to recall.

"When you refused the earrings, I was so terrified of losing you that I pushed you away. That way I could at least control *how* my heart was broken. But now I know. Even if my heart and soul shattered into a thousand pieces tomorrow, I would rather live one day to the fullest, knowing you are mine." Natalie watched in disbelief as Garrett went down on his knee and withdrew a small box from his blazer. He opened it to reveal the engagement ring she'd left behind. "Would you do me the honor of becoming my wife?"

A small sob tore from her and she gave him a watery smile. "I'm already your wife."

"But I need to know, will you be my wife now and forever? To love and to cherish?" His voice broke with the depth of his emotion. "Because I believe in love and marriage and forever. All of it. I believe in us."

Natalie smiled at him, not quite able to believe what was happening. To ensure it was all real—that he was real—she cradled his beautiful face in her hand, and with a shuddering sigh, he turned his head and kissed her palm with aching tenderness. Then, still holding her hand, he rose to his feet.

"I want you to have everything you've ever wanted. As promised, the VP of Human Resources position is yours.

You could transfer to New York at the end of the month as planned."

Confusion drew her eyebrows low and she searched his face. "But you'll be in Los Angeles."

"No, I need to be where you are. If you'd let me, I'd like to come with you."

"But your family, your life, the CEO appointment you worked so hard for... They're all in Los Angeles."

"My life is with you and our daughter," he said with a stubborn set to his jaw. "Besides, I don't even know if I'm the new CEO. I left in the middle of the board meeting when I found out where you were."

"You idiot."

She was angry he'd jeopardized his dream, but if she'd wanted proof of his love, she couldn't ask for anything stronger. Even so, he was an idiot. She grabbed his lapels to shake some sense into him, but changed her mind. Instead, she jerked him close and kissed him senseless until they needed to come up for air.

"That kiss." He sounded as breathless as she felt. "Does it mean what I think it means?"

"Only if you think it means I love you." Her voice shook with joy. She had held those words in check too many times. "I love you so much. I've loved you since you made me sit and watch you sign those damn HR documents. So, yes. I'll be your wife and we can be a real family...from now until forever."

Garrett seemed to stop breathing for a moment. Then a smile radiant with love spread across his face, and he captured her lips in a possessive, savoring kiss. When they at last drew apart, he held her face between his hands as though he couldn't stop touching her.

"I'm not sure if I could let you out of my sight right now, so don't mind me if I follow you around like a shadow," he said in a low, gravelly voice.

"Please do." Her heart filled with joy, and she burst out laughing. "I don't mind at all."

"Good." Garrett gathered her close and bent to kiss her again, but she put a hand on his chest to stop him.

"But if you lost the CEO seat, I'll kill you with my bare hands."

"That's not important right now."

"Like hell it isn't." Natalie crossed her arms over her chest and arched an eyebrow. "But I agree. For now, all that matters is that we'll be together. We'll figure out everything else."

"God, I love you."

"Say it again," she whispered, afraid she might wake up from this dream.

"I love you, Natalie."

"Again." *And again, and again.*

"I love you. More than life."

Smiling up at him with the brilliance of her glowing heart, Natalie kissed her husband, knowing she'd never grow tired of hearing those words.

* * * * *

COMING SOON!

We really hope you enjoyed reading this book. If you're looking for more romance, be sure to head to the shops when new books are available on

Thursday 6th March

To see which titles are coming soon, please visit

millsandboon.co.uk/nextmonth

LET'S TALK

Romance

For exclusive extracts, competitions
and special offers, find us online:

MILLS & BOON

THE HEART OF ROMANCE

A ROMANCE FOR EVERY KIND OF READER

MODERN

Prepare to be swept off your feet by sophisticated, sexy and seductive heroes, in some of the world's most glamourous and romantic locations, where power and passion collide.
8 stories per month.

HISTORICAL

Escape with historical heroes from time gone by. Whether your passion is for wicked Regency Rakes, muscled Vikings or rugged Highlanders, awaken the romance of the past.
6 stories per month.

MEDICAL

Set your pulse racing with dedicated, delectable doctors in the high-pressure world of medicine, where emotions run high and passion, comfort and love are the best medicine.
6 stories per month.

True Love

Celebrate true love with tender stories of heartfelt romance, from the rush of falling in love to the joy a new baby can bring, and a focus on the emotional heart of a relationship.
8 stories per month.

Desire

Indulge in secrets and scandal, intense drama and plenty of sizzling hot action with powerful and passionate heroes who have it all: wealth, status, good looks…everything but the right woman.
6 stories per month.

HEROES

Experience all the excitement of a gripping thriller, with an intense romance at its heart. Resourceful, true-to-life women and strong, fearless men face danger and desire - a killer combination!
8 stories per month.

DARE

Sensual love stories featuring smart, sassy heroines you'd want as a best friend, and compelling intense heroes who are worthy of them.
4 stories per month.

To see which titles are coming soon, please visit

millsandboon.co.uk/nextmonth

MILLS & BOON

HISTORICAL

Awaken the romance of the past

Escape with historical heroes from time gone by. Whether your passion is for wicked Regency Rakes, muscled Viking warriors or rugged Highlanders, indulge your fantasies and awaken the romance of the past.